THE ATTACK

A MAX AUSTIN THRILLER - BOOK THREE OF
THE RUSSIAN ASSASSIN SERIES

JACK ARBOR

HIGH CALIBER BOOKS

THE ATTACK
(A MAX AUSTIN THRILLER - BOOK THREE)

This book is a work of fiction. The characters, incidents, and dialogue are drawn from the author's imagination and are not to be construed as real. Any resemblance to actual events or persons, living or dead, is fictionalized or coincidental.

ISBN-13: 978-1-947696-03-7
ISBN-10: 1-947696-03-3

Requests to publish work from this book should be sent to:
jack@jackarbor.com

Edition 2

Published by High Caliber Books

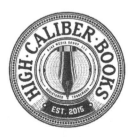

Cover art by: www.damonza.com
Bio photo credit: John Lilley Photography

For my father, who always told me to follow my heart. I never did until now.

"The man who chases two rabbits, catches neither."

- Confucius

ONE

Somewhere in Eastern Ukraine

The bullet-riddled pickup sped east at a high rate of speed. In the distance came the constant pounding of artillery shelling. The *thump, thump, thump* of ordnance followed by bright flashes cast an eerie apprehension over the truck's occupants.

Except for the bright red-and-white signs in the front and rear windows identifying the truck as a media vehicle, the clunker resembled many of those used by the ethnic Russian rebels in their fight against the Ukrainian army. The truck itself was dusty white with dents along its side quarter panels. The bumper was adorned with a rusty metal cattle guard, and a long crack ran the length of the front windshield. The rear bed was filled with duffle bags and black watertight cases held down with straps.

Max gripped the wheel with his right hand while his left cradled a lit cigarette so it was protected from the open window. A camouflaged bucket hat was pulled tight on his head, and he wore a flak jacket, cinched tight, with the words MEDIA in both English and Russian across the chest and back. A set of fake media credentials and passport were in a travel wallet around his neck. He was armed only with a combat knife secreted in his boot, which made him uncomfortable given the conflict zone they were in. He kept the speedometer pegged at 150 KPH, ignoring the shimmy from the poorly maintained chassis.

Riding the bench seat next to him was Kate Shaw, one time CIA assistant director. She was dressed like Max save for a ball cap taming her curly hair. An earbud cord was attached to a boxy satellite phone she clutched in her right hand. Kate's former CIA technical operations analyst, Kaamil Marafi, was on the other end of the line. Kaamil, safely nestled in his basement bunker on the outskirts of Abu Dhabi, was illicitly patched into the CIA's satellite surveillance system to get real-time updates on troop movements, roadblocks, and CIA activity in the area.

She touched her finger to the earbud in her ear. "Kaamil says there's a Ukrainian military checkpoint ten klicks ahead."

Max kept the pedal down. "Is there an alternative route?"

Kate spoke into her mic and waited for the response. "Negative. Not without going an hour out of our way."

"Christ on a cracker." Max made rapid calculations in his head. They were on a timeline and couldn't spare the time to go around.

Kate looked over. "Christ on a cracker?"

"I'm trying to Americanize my cussing."

Kate snorted. "No one says that."

Max touched the brakes when he saw red lights appearing through the dusty gloom. A line of vehicles was stopped in the middle of the highway in front of a concrete barrier running across the blacktop. Three tanks flying the Ukrainian flag lined the side of the road and Max counted at least eight soldiers carrying automatic weapons. "First test of our cover coming up."

Kate rolled down her window. "Pfft. No big deal."

Max chuckled. "You sure you can handle this?"

"If you ask me that again, I'll tell the roadblock soldiers you're a rebel sympathizer and take care of Volkov myself."

Max flicked his cigarette butt out the window and watched the shower of sparks disappear while his mind drifted to their job. Their target's name was Victor Volkov, one of Russia's most powerful mob bosses, who just happened to hold the ninth position on the list of twelve consortium members. Coincidentally, Volkov was also a high-value target of the CIA. Weeks earlier, Kate's asset team at the CIA was disbanded in favor of the director's new drone program, and Kate went AWOL from her job at the CIA and was now on the run along with Max. The drone team subsequently botched an assassination attempt on Volkov and instead killed fifteen civilians, including members of Volkov's extended family.

Now Max and Kate were teaming up to take out Volkov. For Max, it was a step toward his plan to eliminate each member of the consortium as retribution for killing his parents. For Kate, it was the perfect *fuck you* to Piper Montgomery, the CIA director who had eviscerated Kate's long and distinguished CIA career.

Ahead, several Ukrainian police cars with flashing lights left a narrow gap to allow civilian vehicles to pass single file through the concrete barricade. Four beefy men in blue-and-gray camouflage uniforms toting automatic rifles used high-powered flashlights to peer into vehicles and examine papers.

Max drummed his thumb on the wheel. "Scare tactics to prevent Ukrainian citizens from joining the rebels. Stay calm. Our cover is solid."

Kate tucked a strand of curly hair under her cap. "It's not my first rodeo, you know." She informed Kaamil of the upcoming checkpoint before shutting down the phone and stowing it in the glove box. She fussed with the wallet strapped across her chest and withdrew a French passport.

Max inched the truck forward. "First rodeo?"

"Forget it. It's just a dumb American saying."

"I get it. Like you go through military checkpoints every day using fake credentials on your way to Starbucks before heading to your plush office at Langley." He winked at her.

"Exactly like that. Except I don't have an office at Langley anymore." Kate's smile disappeared.

Max shielded his eyes from the strong lights blazing through the front windshield as a gorilla-sized Ukrainian soldier appeared next to the truck.

"Papers," the man demanded. The soldier held a flashlight pointed at Max's eyes while another stood off to the side with his hand on his weapon. Max handed over their passports along with a pair of laminated media credentials.

"News?" The soldier spoke in Ukrainian.

"*Tak*," Max said, jerking his thumb toward the back of the truck, speaking in halting Ukrainian. "Want to see the camera gear?"

The guard waved Max out of the truck with the flashlight while holding his paperwork. Max left the door open as he stepped out and made for the rear. He lowered the tailgate and pulled several hard-sided cases to the edge. The guard's grip tightened on the flashlight as Max unlatched the first one. He proceeded to open the rest of the cases and watched as the soldier rifled through camera bodies and lenses, in the process dropping one on the tailgate with a sickening crunch.

"Easy," Max said. He grabbed at the lens as it rolled to the edge.

The soldier's hands were on his gun in a flash, pointing the barrel of the rifle at Max and shouting in Ukrainian. Max put his hands in the air as the lens rolled off the tailgate and shattered on the pavement.

"We'll send you a bill," Max muttered under his breath.

Another soldier barked an order while motioning with his gun.

"They want me to pull over," Kate said in French. "Out of the line of traffic."

Max groaned. Tucked in the undercarriage of the truck were two handguns, a H&K G28 compact sniper rifle, two pair of night-vision scopes, a packet of C-4 with associated bomb-making parts, several boxes of ammunition, and various other tools and weapons. Max had soldered the steel himself to fashion the hiding spot. He felt confident the weapons were well hidden, but there was always the chance a dimwitted soldier might get lucky. Depending on how thorough they were, Max and Kate might face an extended stretch in one of Ukraine's prisons, known for its brutality and stark conditions.

Max shrugged. "Do it."

Kate slid over to the driver's seat, put the truck in gear, and eased over to the median of the blacktop. The man with the rifle walked alongside, keeping his gun trained on Max. Kate exited the vehicle as four soldiers converged on the truck. A hulking trooper, wearing a beret and four chevrons on his shoulder indicating the rank of senior sergeant, confronted Kate. He held her passport close to her face and studied the picture. After a few long moments, he grunted in satisfaction.

Kate moved off to the side, her hands in her pockets, while two soldiers pawed through their gear. The sergeant set a laptop on the hood of a military vehicle and started typing, periodically peering at their credentials. A third soldier walked around their truck with a handheld mirror equipped with a flashlight to examine the undercarriage.

Max stood with his arms crossed, tapping his foot, feigning irritation. He sensed Kate's nervousness and hoped she had not lost her operational edge after years of riding a desk at Langley.

As if to assuage his concern, she winked at him and smirked. Her jaw muscles were clenched, but her green eyes flashed with mischief. For a second, Max admired the curve of her jaw before pushing the emotion away as a Ukrainian soldier bent at the waist to rifle through the truck's cab.

After the sergeant spent several agonizing minutes peering into the laptop's screen, he shut it with a *thunk* and turned back to Max and Kate. Max forced himself to breathe as the soldier walked up and put his face a foot from Max's. "You know Ukrainian."

"A little," Max said, using Ukrainian, but with a French accent, thankful for the years he lived in Paris. If any hint of a Russian accent slipped through, they were dead.

The solider was at least as tall as Max, with a neck thicker than his head. "Destination?"

"Donetsk." As always, the best lies were shades of the truth. Max eyed the soldier circling the truck with the mirror. A trickle of sweat ran down Max's back despite the evening chill. His heart skipped a beat as the man paused to examine something, but he relaxed as the man continued his slow walk around the truck.

"What's the purpose of your visit?"

Max smiled, pointing his thumb at the sign on his flak jacket. "Reporting on the war for Le Monde."

The soldier's eyes narrowed. "Topic?"

"We have a source who claims to have evidence the Malaysian airliner was shot down by the rebels using Russian weaponry." Max wanted to avoid giving the solider the impression their reporting might be pro-Russian.

The sergeant pursed his lips. In his periphery, Max saw the soldier with the mirror stop again. After a gut-wrenching pause, the man removed the mirror and proclaimed the truck's undercarriage clean.

The sergeant grunted and slapped their credentials against Max's chest. "You're free to go. Stay safe."

Max and Kate jumped into the cab while a soldier held up traffic to allow them back onto the road. The sounds of artillery thudded in the distance and flashes of light flickered on the horizon as they wove through the concrete barricade and accelerated away from the checkpoint.

Max nudged a cigarette from the pack he kept wedged in his flak jacket. "That was just the first test of what's coming."

TWO

Donetsk, Ukraine

"No change in status."

Kate squatted behind a concrete buttress on the top floor of the crumbling parking garage and tried not to shiver in the midnight air. She whispered the update to Kaamil through her earpiece while watching for movement on the street below.

The building they were using for surveillance had at one time been bombed by the Ukrainian military. One end of the structure was destroyed by the shelling, leaving chunks of jagged concrete and exposed rebar. Their truck was hidden on the ground level behind a pile of rubble, and two duffle bags of gear rested on the dirty concrete behind them. She and Max had been watching the three black SUVs on the street below for the past two hours.

Tracking their target hadn't been easy. For over a week, they monitored Volkov's movements by triangulating one of his bodyguard's mobile phones. Prior to the CIA's bungled attack on Volkov, the agency had succeeded in planting malware on the bodyguard's phone, giving the agency unfettered access to his location. The bodyguard, a man named Ivanov, rarely left his boss's side. Kaamil had hacked into the CIA's systems, allowing him to track Ivanov's movements and, by extension, follow Volkov's whereabouts.

Intelligence uncovered by Kaamil indicated Volkov made the three-hour drive from Rostov, Russia every other week in a caravan of SUVs across the rebel-controlled border to check on his supply routes. Although they knew Volkov's schedule, they didn't know his destination in the city. Max and Kate had cooled their heels in the Ukrainian-held town of Bahatyr by smoking and drinking gas station coffee until Kaamil notified them that the blinking red dot that signified Ivanov's location had come to a stop. Fortunately, their target didn't move in the hour it took Max and Kate to speed east to rebel-held city of Donetsk.

Their vantage point afforded them a clear view of the row of Volkov's SUV's parked along the street in front of a building that Kaamil had identified as a former school. A long awning led from the building's front door and ended at the middle SUV. The mob boss had a reputation for impeccable dress, no matter the time or circumstances, and was famous for wearing bright red ties. While the red tie allowed for an easy identification, the awning prevented a clear shot.

A curfew and blackout were in effect to stem the shelling from Ukrainian troops, so the streets were empty. Here in Donetsk, the thunder of artillery fire to the north made the ground shake. Although a cease-fire was supposed to be in effect, Kaamil reported that a small group of rebels holding the Donetsk airport were under heavy attack from the Ukrainians and many of Donetsk's citizens had fled the city, leaving it to crumble under the constant bombardment.

Kaamil's voice sounded in her ear. "I dug into the Ukrainian military's computers. From the intelligence I found, the school you're looking at is thought to be the resistance's headquarters and the home of separatist leader Alexander Zakharchenko. They believe he has a bunker under the school. The intelligence confirms the CIA's information that Volkov runs the primary supply routes for small arms and other supplies between Russia and the rebels in Donetsk."

"Can't we just call in an air strike?" Max muttered. He was squatting next to Kate, peering through the darkness with a pair of night-vision binoculars and listening on a separate earpiece.

Silver moonlight illuminated Max's face and Kate found herself admiring his profile. He was even more handsome than when they first met several months ago outside Minsk. Back then, he was recovering from a two-foot piece of rebar that had impaled his side. Despite the constant strain of trying to keep his family alive, she noticed he was thriving under the pressure. A simmering fire burned behind the deep blackness of his eyes. He was bred for this sort of thing. Kate almost felt sorry for the consortium members, knowing Max wouldn't rest until they were all dead and buried.

Max's eyes flashed when he looked over at her, reminding her of the strength he possessed. When he held her gaze, she saw a powerful conviction, the confidence he had gained after surviving in the face of overwhelming danger, a resolve emanating from the depths of his soul, an aura she couldn't help but be attracted to. The moment lingered even as his eyes moved back to the binoculars and he went back into the dark recesses of his mind.

She fought back the attraction, willing it to a place somewhere out of reach. She was bad at love. She had a habit of falling fast and hard before paying the price as things fell apart. As she got older, she found she didn't want to bother with it anymore. It was too much work, too much of a distraction from what drove her. Besides, she couldn't imagine there was room in his heart while he fought for his family's survival.

She touched his bicep. "If you're from Belarus, and your given name was Mikhail, how did you end up with the nickname Max?"

He kept his eyes glued to the field glasses. "It's short for Maxim, a common name in Belarus. My mother started calling me Max when I was young. She said—"

"Your surrogate mother?"

"Right. The mother who raised me. She told me that she lost an argument with my father. She wanted to name me after Maxim Gorky, a Soviet Marxist writer and comrade of Lenin's. My father wouldn't hear of it. I think it was her way of getting back at him for bringing home a bastard son." He let out chuckle.

"Why did you pick Austin as your new last name?"

Max fidgeted with the focus dial on the binoculars. "I liked the town."

"In Texas? You've been there?"

"Yup. Something about the cold beer and the live music. The freedom of the American west."

"Texas is about as far from Russia as you can get."

"Right."

Kate pulled her gaze away from Max's face and watched as a guard paced along the sidewalk several blocks away. A rifle hung on his shoulder, and he held a glowing cigarette in his hand. The school remained dark and silent.

Kate shifted to stretch her legs. "What the fuck are they doing in there?"

Max handed her the night-vision binoculars and raised the H&K sniper rifle to his shoulder to peer through the scope. Kate lifted the binoculars to her eyes. They both panned right, following the guard until he disappeared around a corner.

As Kate moved her binoculars in the other direction, headlights from a van appeared, moving toward them. Max swung the rifle to track the approaching vehicle. The head-lights grew stronger until the van pulled into a parking spot in front of the line of black SUVs. When the van's side door opened, a stream of young women emerged, teetering on heels and shivering in revealing outfits before disappearing through the front door of the building.

Max removed his eye from the scope. "At least we know what they're doing."

Kate lowered the binoculars. "For fuck sake. What's the plan?"

Max checked his watch. "I like the C-4. Under a manhole cover. Radio controlled."

Kate shook her head. "Can't predict which way the cars will go. I like the rifle."

"Same problem, plus the issue of the partial awning cover makes it hard to see the target." Max lowered the rifle to the ground and rose to stretch his legs, staying bent at the waist to remain hidden. "We'll go with both."

————

Max pulled down a black balaclava, ensured his combat

knife was secure against his leg, touched the silenced 9mm Makarov pistol at his side, and grabbed a heavy waterproof duffle bag. For the first time since the bombing of his parents' house and the subsequent flight from Minsk, he felt in control. He was on the offensive, no longer back on his heels or running. He had a list of twelve people. Twelve people who ran the consortium. Twelve people who sanctioned the killing of his family. It was only a matter of time before Max picked them off one by one, doing what he was trained to do. The energy he felt was almost addictive. He held up his fist in Kate's direction.

Kate smirked as she touched her own fist to his. "Not sure why you're hell-bent on becoming Americanized."

"Everything I do is for Alex." Max slung the duffle across his back and took the concrete steps down two at a time to the street below. He entered the street at the rear of the parking garage, hidden from the view of the school, and found a manhole cover. He pried it open, ignoring the smell of sewage and mildew wafting out. He flicked on a headlamp and disappeared down the ladder with the agility of a cat.

"I'm in." A tiny mic was form-fitted to his jaw and hooked into an earpiece. He walked north, in the direction of the SUVs, gauging his distance by counting his steps, hunched over as he kicked through fetid water. A flurry of movement and the sound of splashing water coming from the shadows caused him to stop short. He grimaced but started moving again when he realized he had startled a pack of rats.

"Roger that," came Kate's hushed voice. "Joe Camel is on the street in front of the school, moving south." During their surveillance, they counted two visible guards on patrol around the building. They named the one with the cigarette

Joe Camel. The second was Charlie, for no good reason. "No sign of Charlie."

"Got it." Max increased his speed as he walked north along the tunnel. The pipe's slimy interior walls were crumbling in many places from the constant bombing of the city above.

When he reached an access point that he calculated was just north of the school, he gripped the rusty ladder and scampered up, pausing at the top. "Status?"

A burst of static filled his ear before Kate's voice came through. "You're clear."

He teased the round cover until it lifted, allowing him to peer through the narrow slit. Seeing that he was about three meters behind the last SUV, he climbed back down the ladder, dropped the duffel in the shallow water, and removed the items he needed.

"Exiting." He climbed back up the ladder and eased the cover up before snaking his body out and inching the cover back into place. He spider-crawled along the pavement until he was under the third SUV. As the smell of the driver's cigarette smoke wafted in his nose, he looked for a suitable place for the bomb in the SUV's undercarriage. The explosive consisted of four blocks of plastique held together with black tape, along with a radio transmitter.

Kate's voice sounded in his ear. "Charlie approaching from behind. Walking normally."

Max moved his hand to the gun at his waist and visualized his body sinking into the blacktop, willing the man to keep walking.

"Passing you," Kate said.

Through the cigarette smoke, Max smelled the sweet odor of cheap cologne as booted feet passed by a meter away. He heard a few words in Russian and a grunt as the guard acknowledged the driver before the gritty footsteps faded.

Max removed the backing from a length of double-sided tape. Moving with care, he secured the bomb behind the SUV's gas tank.

He rolled back onto his stomach and considered his options. The plan was to detonate the bomb as soon as Volkov's men stepped into the middle SUV. A second charge placed under the manhole cover in the SUV's most obvious path would be detonated next, taking out the middle SUV as it roared away. If the middle SUV escaped the blast, they'd take out that SUV's driver with the sniper rifle and kill Volkov if they had the shot.

But as he lay under the third vehicle, he contemplated placing the second charge in the middle vehicle's chassis instead.

Kate's voice came through loud in his ear. "Joe."

Max froze before realizing one of the adhesive backing strips had drifted onto the pavement so it stuck out from under the vehicle. He reached for it, but stopped when he heard crunching steps on the pavement. He eased his pistol out of its holster and waited, finger tight on the trigger.

A pair of scuffed combat boots appeared next to the truck and stopped, causing Max to hold his breath. He heard a few words of guttural Russian and the flare of a match. A second later, Max resumed breathing as the boots moved off. Figuring he had pushed his luck far enough, Max snagged the adhesive backing and wormed a semicircle to crawl back to the manhole. He lifted the heavy lid and disappeared into the tunnel, easing the lid closed over his head. "Back down. Package one in place."

"Roger Dodger," Kate whispered. "No other movement."

Ten minutes later, the second package of C-4 was secured to the underside of a manhole located ten meters in front of the line of SUVs. While their plan wasn't foolproof, it offered them more than an even chance of getting their man. Max had succeeded under worse odds plenty of times before.

He tossed the duffel into the rear of the truck before running up the stairs to join Kate behind the concrete buttress. She handed him the rifle and accepted two radio control transmitters in return.

He gave Kate a wry grin. "Now we wait."

THREE

Donetsk, Ukraine

"Would you ever go back to work for the CIA?"

Kate stirred, but didn't answer. Max checked his watch. It was over an hour since he had placed the C-4, and there was still no movement in the school. The sentries maintained their beat—first Joe strolled by, a cigarette held in curled fingers, and later Charlie ambled by. The SUV drivers sat and smoked, their faces lit up by the glow from their mobile phones. Soon the morning light would make their hiding place more precarious.

Max sensed she was ignoring the question. It was probably tough for her to think about since most of her adult life had been spent in the clandestine service of her country. It was in her blood. Replacing that sense of purpose with something else must be difficult. Although they had only known each other for three months, they had built an easy bond born from the shared trials they had endured. He decided not to push, and they descended into a comfortable silence.

As Kate swatted at a swarm of tiny bugs, the drivers stirred. On cue, all three tossed their cigarettes into the street and made their phones disappear. Headlights flicked on as engines roared to life.

"Go time." Max adjusted the rifle so the stock was secure against his shoulder. "See if you can tell which vehicle Volkov gets into. Watch for the red tie."

Kate put the night-vision binoculars up to her eyes.

In all the surveillance videos and imagery Max and Kate had studied, Victor Volkov appeared as an imposing man. Tall and broad-shouldered, with the body of an NFL cornerback, he towered over his entourage. The pictures Kaamil provided in their pre-op briefing showed the don in a gym, working out and flexing his large biceps, while being fawned over by subordinates. Short cropped hair covered his anvil-sized head, and his nose was crooked, like it had been broken multiple times. Perpetually wet lips and a constant sneer completed a look that instilled fear in those who incurred his violent wrath.

The son of a poor Western Siberian coal miner, Volkov was a self-made man. Now in his fifties, he started as a rough and tumble enforcer and moved to the violent and bloody executions of his rivals before learning business skills that would put a Harvard MBA to shame. During the massive privatization of industry as the Soviet Union fell apart, Volkov positioned himself to gobble up a large share of the available companies. Now his empire included one of the largest private holdings of natural gas and oil pipelines in Asia, along with hundreds of millions of dollars' worth of industrial manufacturing that complemented a vast network of prostitution, drugs, and gambling extending across Asia and west into Europe.

These sins were not enough to seal the man's fate. Volkov's crime in the CIA's eyes was his role as the largest distributor of weapons from Russia across the Ukrainian border and into the hands of pro-Russian rebels. To maintain plausible deniability, the Russian president had empowered the mob boss to use his pre-existing supply routes through the border to provide small arms, clothing, food, and medical supplies to the rebels. By taking out Volkov, so the American thinking went, they were sending a message to the Russian president while also disrupting the supply lines long enough for the Ukrainian military to surge and occupy Donetsk. None of this was relevant to Max. Volkov's only crime in his mind was his position as the ninth member of the consortium.

Max double-checked the G28 sniper rifle. This one was kitted out in matte black with short bi-pod legs, a telescoping stock, a suppressor screwed onto the barrel, and it was chambered for a 7.62x51mm NATO round. Max had a short ten-round magazine in the weapon with two more magazines in a pocket. The top rail was fitted with a Schmidt & Bender PMII 3-20x50 scope. At a 600-meter range, the rifle was more than enough weapon for the job at hand.

He bent to the scope's eyepiece and concentrated on a spot to the left of the center SUV. His view was partially blocked by the first SUV and the awning, so the most he might see were people's legs. Unless Volkov got into the lead vehicle, Max wouldn't know which of the last two SUVs he entered.

When Max saw movement under the awning, he moved a gloved finger to the trigger. "Here we go."

A short-legged man in a suit moved fast down the covered walkway, closely followed by a set of bare, lithe legs strutting on platform heels. Next came another pair of male legs strolling between the building and the SUV, his torso and head hidden by the awning. Max's instinct told him it was Volkov, and he tightened his finger on the trigger. One shot through the awning might do the trick, but he hesitated. When a second set of long male legs sauntered to the middle vehicle, Max eased his finger off the trigger. All three SUVs were full a few seconds later.

"Fire one."

Kate depressed a trigger on one remote control.

As the three SUVs pulled away from the curb in unison, the nighttime sky lit up with a ball of flame, launching the third SUV two meters off the ground and dumping it onto its side in a fiery shower of sparks. Max felt the heat from the shockwave on his cheeks.

"Hold."

As he expected, the first two SUVs reacted to the explosion behind them by accelerating away from the curb straight toward the parking garage where Max and Kate were hidden. Max sighted the rifle on the driver's side of the lead SUV and pulled the trigger. A single hole appeared in the windshield, followed by a spatter of blood on the interior. The figure in the driver's seat slumped as the vehicle careened to the right.

Max swung the rifle and focused on the second SUV before pulling the trigger. A hole appeared in the center of the windshield, but the vehicle continued accelerating.

"Fire two."

As the middle SUV executed an evasive maneuver by turning left into a side street, the bomb attached to the underside of the manhole cover exploded and took the car with it. The vehicle jumped into the air and came down on its wheels, engulfed in fire, flames licking out of its broken windows, screams ringing out from the inferno.

Max trained his scope on the burning wreckage and waited.

A door swung open.

Max breathed as time slowed.

A tall figure staggered from the hulk of burning metal, immersed in fire, his wails echoing through the buildings.

Max positioned the scope's crosshairs on the man's chest and waited.

A flash of bright red appeared through the smoke pouring from the man's body.

Max let out his breath and pulled the trigger. The bullet found the target's head, cutting off his screams and sending him face-first to the pavement. The target didn't move.

"Got him," Kate said as she stowed the binoculars.

Bullets ricocheted off the concrete buttress and gunfire cracked from the street below, causing Max to pull back.

Kate ducked as shards of stone and mortar flew through the air. "Time to go."

Holding the gun by its stock, Max followed Kate down the stairs. They climbed into the truck, and a minute later they were hurtling south through darkened streets. Max craned his head to look behind them and saw no one in pursuit.

When he was satisfied they had gotten away undetected, Max removed a piece of paper encased in clear plastic from his pocket and grabbed a felt-tip pen off the dashboard. On the paper were inscribed twelve names. After removing the paper from its protective cover, he used the pen to draw a heavy line through the name *Victor Volkov*.

"Eleven to go."

FOUR

Donetsk, Ukraine

Kate worked the accelerator, the brake, and the steering wheel like a rally car driver, moving the truck through the damaged streets as fast as she dared. Max had his pistol out and held the sniper rifle between his legs. Once they cleared the city limits, they would ditch the weapons and resume their cover as experienced Le Monde journalists, famed for their willingness to venture deep into conflict zones to capture a story.

Max glanced behind them. "Don't put a tire out on exposed rebar."

Kate's face was set with determination, intent on their escape. They followed a preplanned route through the city's northern neighborhoods and stuck to side roads to avoid checkpoints and roadblocks.

"Any chatter?" Max was connected to Kaamil via the satellite phone, and there were only a few minutes of battery life left. If it quit on them, they would be in the dark until they got to Ukrainian-held territory, where cellular services were still intact and he could use his secure mobile phone.

Kaamil's voice came through the static. "Lots. You guys are popular. Road blocks are set up at all major arteries out of Donetsk. Your route still looks good."

Max winced as the battery light switched from yellow to blinking red. "Out of battery. Hope for our sake your update doesn't change."

"See you on the other side," Kaamil said.

As Max thumbed off the phone, saving the battery for emergencies, he wondered if he was experiencing the same feeling of dread the Apollo 8 astronauts had when they crossed behind the moon for the first time and were cut off from Houston command.

Max gritted his teeth. "We're on our own."

———

Kaamil Marafi sat back in his chair and surveyed the workstation in front of him. Two forty-eight-inch television screens were mounted to the wall while three large computer monitors sat in a semi-circle on the desk. At his feet were six high-powered CPUs and a small laptop sat to his left. One of the monitors displayed a series of Twitter hashtag feeds specific to the rebel's war against the Ukrainians. Another screen showed results from a special bot Kaamil had coded and let loose on the internet to search for news, social media posts, and other data related to the conflict in Donetsk. The bot's user interface displayed a continuous scrolling list of results. The television screens above his head were tuned into world news media stations, including the BBC, the state-influenced Russian news channel RT, and a channel out of Kiev.

Despite all the distractions, his eyes were focused on the computer monitor directly in front of him. Twenty-four hours ago, he hacked through the CIA's firewall defenses by using credentials from his former position with the CIA, that were oddly still in place, and utilizing hacking techniques he taught himself during the downtime he had since being fired. The screen contained four green command line windows. Each window showed a stream of output that would look like gibberish to most people, but the stream made complete sense to Kaamil, a former CIA technical operative.

One of his jobs while on Kate's team at the CIA was to provide support to black-ops teams in the field, and he was often one of several tech ops in the Langley operations room providing intel and managing communications between the field agents and operations command. The windows in front of him provided a continuous update of CIA activity—chatter between ops teams, commands issued by various CIA operations leaders—just like the communications he used to monitor. To those who knew the code, it was the same as watching the CIA's activities and movements playing out in real time.

As Max and Kate carried out their operation, Kaamil monitored the feed for the CIA's reaction to Volkov's death. The communication chatter increased in intensity as soon as Volkov's SUV exploded. Kaamil grew more alarmed as he watched the volume of activity rise. Until that moment, there was nothing in the feed he deemed relevant to Max and Kate's escape. But now, several messages made Kaamil sit up in his seat.

How was it possible?

The unthinkable was playing out before his eyes, as if a CIA team was waiting for Max and Kate to complete their operation before springing into action. As the messages flew by, Kaamil's eyes widened.

He frantically typed on the laptop while initiating a voice-over IP call to Kate's satellite phone, knowing full well that they were preserving their battery. He gave up and grabbed his iPhone, scrolled, and found a number for Max that went to an emergency voicemail service. He dialed it, knowing it was hopeless since much of the cellular service in Donetsk had been shut down by the Ukrainians.

In desperation, he dashed off an encrypted email to one of Max's servers, figuring it was futile. Neither Max nor Kate would have service for at least another fifteen minutes. A dread settled into his gut, born from knowing there was nothing he could do.

He set the computer to autodial the satellite phone every fifteen seconds before standing and grabbing a baseball bat from the corner of the room. In frustration, he pounded the bat against a leather sofa until his muscles ached from the exertion.

"Get out of the truck," he screamed, knowing no one could hear him. "Get out of the truck, Kate! Get out of the fucking truck!"

———

Max breathed easier as they cleared the main downtown area of Donetsk and sped through a residential section spared from the brunt of the bombing. Soon they would cross into Maryinka, a city to the west of Donetsk that was recently retaken by the Ukrainian army. The Ukrainian's called it "liberating" the city, even though its citizens, most of whom spoke Russian, preferred the rebels over the Ukrainians. Among the Russian diaspora, loyalty to the motherland ran deep.

Before they reached the relative safety of Maryinka, they needed to cross acres of fields with sunflowers in full bloom. They planned to ditch the weapons in the middle of one of the fields and resume their personas as journalists. Max calculated that they would be in cellular service again when they arrived at the far eastern edge of the field, just before crossing into Maryinka.

He consulted a military-grade handheld GPS unit. The device had plenty of battery and didn't rely on cellular service to connect to the global positioning service. He pinched and scrolled until he found their location on the map.

"In one klick, you'll turn left down a dirt road. There's a clearing with a hut that's used for irrigation maintenance where we can ditch the weapons."

"Roger Dodger." A few minutes later, Kate wrenched the wheel, sending the truck jouncing over the rutted dirt track, Max holding on as the truck threatened to teeter over. In the split second before the truck's momentum sent it pitching onto its side, Kate hit the gas and the truck righted itself before surging ahead. The sunflower plants, in full bloom, towered over their truck's cab and whizzed by in a blur of yellows and greens.

Max felt something buzzing in his pocket. Surprised, he pulled his Blackphone from his pocket.

Kate wrestled with the steering wheel as a tire got stuck in a rut. "Got bars?"

Max frowned at his phone. "Shouldn't have." A text message was on his screen. As he read it, the hairs on the back of his neck stood up.

Get out of the truck.

––––––

Deep in a bunker under the Nevada desert, forty-five minutes northwest of the blinking lights of the Las Vegas Strip, a pilot and a sensor operator from the United States Air Force Command sat in leather chairs, working joy sticks while peering at several monitors.

The pilot, an Air Force Academy graduate, was distracted by that night's planned trip to Sheri's Ranch Brothel. The sensor operator, a former standout cornerback for the Nebraska Cornhuskers, sipped coffee from a mug with the words: *Terrorist, noun: 1. Someone my government tells me is a terrorist; 2. Someone my president decides to kill.*

The two men were in command of one of the US Military's most lethal weapons—a tan-colored MQ-9 Reaper drone. Manufactured by General Atomics Aeronautical Systems, the Reaper was thirty-six feet in length, almost thirteen feet tall, with a wingspan of sixty-six feet. At a top speed of 260 knots and a ceiling of 50,000 feet, it could fly for fourteen hours without refueling. Costing fifteen million dollars apiece, both airmen knew the drones represented one of the American military's latest and greatest weapons systems, and both were proud to operate her.

A large screen at eye level displayed a grainy black-and-white video feed of a speeding pickup truck. As the vehicle bounced over rough terrain, the sensor operator deftly maneuvered a joystick to manipulate a camera high above the truck's position. The vehicle was making fast progress down a two-lane road which was bordered on both sides by fields of sunflowers. With his other hand, he toyed with a toggle switch that controlled two semi-active laser homing

AGM-114A Hellfire missiles attached to the undercarriage of the Reaper. The Reaper's multi-spectral targeting system was locked on the speeding truck. Each Hellfire missile came equipped with an 8-kilogram high-explosive anti-tank warhead which would be overkill for the fleeing pickup truck. The pilot was in control of the drone's flight path—a series of wide, lazy circles at 10,000 feet. Just another day hunting terrorists at USAF Command and Control.

A static-filled voice came over their headsets. "Stand by."

The sensor operator took a sip of coffee. "Roger."

Both airmen watched as the truck careened off the road onto a narrow dirt track that was barely visible through the Reaper's STARLite radar system. The truck was moving fast, despite bouncing wildly on the rough terrain.

"Hold," said the voice. "Let's see what they do."

"Ten-four."

When the truck suddenly weaved again, the sensor operator leaned closer to the monitor. It looked like they left the dirt track and were now plowing through the field. All at once, the truck came to a halt, crowded by tall sunflowers.

Crackling in their ears. "Hold. But if the doors open, waste it."

"Holding," said the airman manning the weapons systems.

Seconds ticked by.

"What the fuck are they doing?" the static voice asked.

Movement appeared in the truck bed, although the sensor operator couldn't discern the details. "We got action, sir."

"I see it. Hold."

Confused, the pilot's finger fidgeted with the trigger, but orders were orders. "Copy."

A few seconds ticked off the clock before the response came back. "Waste 'em."

The pilot toggled the fire-switch. "Weapon away."

One of the Hellfire missiles detached from the drone and the single stage Thiokol TX-657 solid-fuel rocket motor fired, propelling the missile to a speed of Mach 1.3. Six seconds later, the rocket hit the hood of the truck and the twenty-pound anti-armor metal-augmented charge detonated.

The explosion engulfed the vehicle and blew a shallow crater of four meters in diameter in the sunflower field. When the cloud of smoke dissipated, the truck carcass lay in smoldering hunks of metal around the crater.

"Kill confirmed. Truck is destroyed."

"Roger that," said the voice. "Stand by with the second weapon."

"Standing by."

As seconds ticked off the clock, the avionics from the drone remained homed in on the scene. The pilots saw no movement. The coffee mug was forgotten, its contents cold. After three minutes, the voice returned. "We're done. One more threat to the United States eliminated. Nice job, gentlemen."

FIVE

London, England

Their exodus from Ukraine was long and uneventful. After breaking the truck's rear window with the butt of his pistol and climbing into the bed, Max and Kate split up and ran. When the Hellfire missile hit, the ground shook and Max was pushed forward by the concussion, forcing him face-first into the muddy ground between two rows of sunflowers. He shook off the shock, got up, and walked west, relying on the tall crops to hide his movements from the eye in the sky, knowing Kate would do the same. It took three hours to walk the remaining distance to Maryinka, where they met at a prearranged rendezvous point and secured train berths to Kiev. In the Kiev train station, they picked up gear bags they had previously stowed in lockers, and as the sun disappeared over the western horizon, they settled into first-class seats on a British Airways flight to Heathrow.

Max had booked a two-bedroom suite at the Mandarin Oriental in Hyde Park. The luxury hotel was off London's beaten path and afforded them a quiet respite from the tension of the operation. Max tossed his bag on the floor, yanked the curtains closed, stripped, and fell into the fluffy bed for an hour-long nap. He woke up and showered in scalding hot water for as long as he could before switching to an ice-cold spray for thirty seconds. He toweled off, put on jeans, a black T-shirt, his leather jacket, and met Kate in the lobby. Over bangers, mash, and cold beers at The Swan, a tiny pub just off Kensington Gardens, they went over the operation in hushed voices among the din of the crowded bar.

"Did Kaamil have any luck tracing the text message?" Max gulped half his glass of beer.

Kate set her pint down. "None. He was surprised it wasn't one of his. He tried everything to warn us."

Max forked a piece of sausage and ate it, chewing thoughtfully. The person who warned them must be someone with inside knowledge of the CIA's operations. "Your former boss has stepped up the attack on us. Each one of those Hellfire missiles is a hundred grand, not to mention the resources spent to track us and the cost of operating the drone. She must be desperate to get rid of us. Wonder what prompted the escalation."

Kate pushed her plate back, the food barely touched. "I don't know, but a hundred G's is nothing to the CIA. I find it interesting that she waited until after we took out Volkov."

Max toyed with his mashed potatoes. "The biggest question is how they tracked us." He could guess, but didn't want to tell Kate that he suspected Kaamil was the leak. It wasn't that Max didn't trust the Emirati—the youngster had shown his loyalty through their efforts to chase down and kill Wilbur Lynch—but he was inexperienced, and Max figured he had unwittingly left a trail for the CIA to follow.

Kate left the table and returned with the evening edition of The Telegraph. As Max sipped a fresh beer, she flipped through the newspaper and stopped when she found what she was searching for.

"Viktor Volkov, one of Russia's wealthiest and most ruthless mob oligarchs, was killed late Friday night in what the Ukrainian military is calling a major victory in their fight against Russian-backed insurgents. Sources said Volkov was linked to major supply routes between Moscow and Donetsk, and it was discovered he was responsible for funneling weapons, ammunition, and supplies to the area's Russian-speaking Ukrainian rebels. A Ukrainian military commander, who asked not to be identified, said that Volkov's death will put a serious dent in the rebel's supply routes and allow a Ukrainian surge which might end the conflict. Volkov was killed in what Kiev officials describe as a daring midnight raid on a rebel stronghold by Ukrainian Special Operations soldiers."

Max set his empty glass down on the table with a *thunk*. "Total crap."

Kate kept reading. "Four weeks ago, members of Volkov's family were killed by an errant air-to-surface missile. His wife, daughter, and twelve members of his entourage were instantly killed while riding in a caravan in a remote region of Ukraine between Donetsk and the Russian border. The rebels issued a statement claiming they had evidence the missile was launched from a US Predator drone. The US denied the accusations, and Kiev has supported the American's claims, saying evidence points to a Russian-manufactured surface-to-surface anti-tank missile, likely fired from a handheld launcher."

Max tossed his napkin onto his plate. "Absolute bullshit. Misdirection by your friends at Langley to prevent public outcry over the civilians killed in the blast. Any press outlet that has the true story will be discredited by the mainstream American media."

Kate wrinkled her nose. "Not my friends. Get a load of this." She kept reading. "Speculation is rampant that the CIA was behind the 2014 Euromaidan coup in Kiev that ousted the authoritarian regime and replaced it with a pro-western president. An unnamed source at the Pentagon said, 'The US unequivocally denies any involvement in anything the Ukrainian people have accomplished to rid themselves of the previous dictatorship.' When pressed, the source admitted to providing important intel that may have led to Volkov's death."

Kate threw the paper onto the table and sat back. "This article has the CIA's fingerprints all over it. Standard operating procedure. Deny the allegations, but plant the specter of the agency's involvement, causing people to believe the CIA was involved anyway."

Max downed the rest of his beer, stood, and tossed down a few pound notes. "Taking credit for something even as they deny it to the world. And the public never knows the real story."

————

They retreated to the suite, where Max produced a bottle of Jameson Irish whiskey along with two glasses. Kate sprawled on a chair, leg over the arm, and stared through the window at the London skyline.

Max sloshed a measure of the booze into a glass and handed it to Kate. "Troubling when your own agency wants you dead, no?"

Kate accepted it, swirled the light brown liquid, and took a sip.

Max grinned. "Good stuff, right? The Irish are better at whiskey than the Americans." He took a sip, savoring the subtle smoky flavor.

Kate made a face. "This is like a brown crayon dipped in water. You need to work on your palate." Kate tossed back the remainder of the whiskey and held out her glass. "I think it's time Bill and I had a little talk."

Max splashed an inch in her glass. William Blackwood was Kate's former boss at the CIA. "Do you trust him?"

"I thought I did. But after he left me to the wolves with Montgomery, I'm not sure."

Max poured another round before setting up a laptop and starting a secure video chat with Kaamil. He wanted to interrogate the former CIA tech op, but knew now was not the time. Maybe Kate would learn something from Bill. If not, Max would make a trip to the UAE and have a conversation with the young man. Until then, he would step cautiously. Kaamil might not even know he was compromised.

Max pulled the laminated list of twelve names from his pocket and set it on the table. The consortium, first exposed by Max's father, was a secret society of twelve men with an unknown set of objectives. Inexplicably, the group had taken out a contract on Max's family, resulting in the bombing death of his father and surrogate mother. In the wake of their killing, Max fled their homeland of Belarus with his sister Arina and her ten-year-old son Alex in tow, and both were now hiding in the United States, protected by Max's new friend and former CIA operative, Spencer White.

Four weeks prior, Max had acquired the list of consortium members by tracking down and killing one of the group's lieutenants, a man named Wilbur Lynch. Lynch, a shadowy arms dealer and trader in stolen art works, had hoped to use the list as blackmail to ensure his own ascension to consortium membership. Now, Max wouldn't stop until he eliminated each member of the consortium and he felt comfortable his sister's and nephew's lives were safe.

Unfortunately, Max was prevented from producing dossiers on each consortium member due to the disappearance of his main computer hacker and on-again, off-again lover, Goshawk. She vanished after a prolonged attack on her computer defenses by unknown assailants, and Max didn't know if she was holed up in a safe flat somewhere, in prison, or dead.

When planning an operation, his standard procedure was to hire Goshawk to compile a detailed file on the target. In addition to ordinary information like the target's finances, employment record, daily routine, travel preferences, and family status, she dug into the target's underbelly. What kind of fetishes and vices does the target have? Does he prefer gambling? Dark-haired women or blonds? Or does he like men? What is his drug of choice? Who does he owe money to?

This kind of information usually took her a few weeks to compile. Once a sufficient file was prepared Max looked for weaknesses—chinks in the target's armor that he might exploit. A properly planned hit could take months of planning and weeks of setup.

With Volkov, Kaamil had fast-tracked the process by hacking the CIA's database and producing an electronic version of the agency's dossier on the mob boss. Now that the first name on the list was eliminated, it was time to research the backgrounds of the remaining members of the consortium so he could pick his next target. Kaamil was his only resource, and he intended to constrain Kaamil's activities to eastern information sources like the FSB's databases and away from anything in the west that might trigger CIA surveillance.

Kaamil's head and shoulders appeared on the screen, and as usual, the young man was immaculately dressed in a baby blue oxford shirt with a wide collar and a pink silk tie worn in a thick Windsor knot. The walls behind him were covered in soundproofing materials. The connection was jumpy and wavy as the signal bounced through several proxy servers and was encrypted on both ends.

Kaamil's hands flew over the keyboard as he talked. "You guys really gave me a scare back there."

They could not have taken down Volkov without the Emirati's help, so Max kept his tone light. "We were just seeing if you were paying attention. Can you get into the FSB's database? They keep files on more people than the Germans did during World War Two."

Kaamil's typing slowed, and his hand moved to a mouse. "I was paying attention all right. My heart almost blew up. Give me a few minutes on the FSB thing. I need to establish a VPN between here and a remote server in Australia, then I need to bounce around through some proxies in Eastern Europe and install a few false flags to distract them before I can dig up a list of whitelisted IPs for their firewalls."

Max rolled his eyes. "I have no idea what you just said."

Kaamil winked and resumed typing. "Talk among yourselves for a few minutes."

For the thousandth time, Max wondered where Goshawk was. "Just make sure no one can trace you." He took a slug of the whiskey and looked over at Kate. Her glass was empty, and she stared out the window with unfocused eyes. She gave him a weak smile as he poured her another shot.

Until that point, Max had been coy with the information he found on the thumb drive hidden in Wilbur Lynch's wheelchair. Kate and Spencer had seen enough of the list to know that Victor Volkov's name occupied the ninth spot on the list.

One file on the thumb drive contained the list of twelve names, ordered by number, and the second file was a set of detailed financial statements. For now, Max put the financial statements aside to focus on the names. He had committed the names to memory and researched what he could about each one. He'd looked for a pattern, a common thread, but found nothing that linked the list of twelve people other than they were all wealthy heads of business or held senior positions in the Russian or Chinese governments. He needed the help of a researcher. With Goshawk's disappearance, Kaamil would have to do.

Kaamil's face lit up. "I'm in. Do you want to send me the list?"

Max had no intention of sending the list to Kaamil. He read the name in the number one position. "Nikita Ivanov." Max spelled it for him.

Kaamil typed and sat back. "I got hundreds of results in the FSB database."

"Fuck."

"Let me see something." Kaamil typed again. "According to Google, Nikita Ivanov is the most popular name in Russia. It's like Joe Smith in the US."

Max let that sink in. "It's probably a pseudonym. Let's try another one."

Kate stood and filled her glass to the rim with the Jameson. "The names are probably all fake."

"Volkov's wasn't." Max read the second name on the list and spelled it. "Ruslan Stepanov."

The sound of clacking on the keyboard came over the video feed before Kaamil looked up with a confused look on his face. "Nothing. Not a single hit in the FSB's database. Hold on." More typing. "According to Wikipedia, Ruslan Stepanov is the head of Russia's Main Intelligence Directorate, known as GRU."

Max turned from the camera and paced. "That explains why there's no file on him. The GRU is a Russian military intelligence group that fields more operatives than the FSB. It also controls about 25,000 Spetsnaz troops, some of the world's toughest commandos. I've trained with those guys. You don't want to tangle with them in a dark alley."

First, a mystery man with pseudonym, and then one of Russia's most powerful intelligence officers. So far, assassinating each one didn't look like an easy task.

Max turned back to the video camera and recited the third name from memory. "Andrey Pavlova."

Kaamil's eyes lit up. "This one's easier. Large file. Let's see. Part owner of Gazprom, the second largest oil and gas company in Russia. Majority-owned by the Russian government. Pavlova is the second largest shareholder. One of the top five richest men in Russia. Under investigation for tax fraud. Residences in Moscow, St. Petersburg, Monaco, and Mykonos. Married with three kids, all in college in Europe. Mistresses in Moscow and Monaco."

Kate stood, touched the chair's arm to steady herself, grabbed the bottle, and sloshed more whiskey in her glass. "Where do they find the time?"

Max snatched his glass away before Kate could pour him more. "Other than the tax issue, no evidence of criminal behavior?"

Kaamil's eyes moved back and forth as he read the screen. "None."

Max took a sip, barely tasting the smoky alcohol. "The tax investigation is probably harassment by the Russian government, which means the Russian president wants him out of Gazprom. Interesting. The next one on the list is Lik Wang."

Kate snorted, almost spitting out a mouthful of whiskey.

Max reached over and set the bottle out of her reach. Kate sat back in the chair with a pout.

Kaamil studied his computer screen. "Lik Wang. Chairman of Sinopec, China's largest oil company. Net worth of over five billion US."

Max drained the whiskey from his glass. "So far, we've got two oil guys and the head of Russia's largest intelligence agency."

"And a mystery man," Kaamil said.

A chirping and buzzing sound came from a nearby table, causing Max to look up in alarm. The combined sound and vibration was a preset notification on his specially designed Blackphone that meant the message could only be from one person. He grabbed the mobile phone from the table, swiped at the screen, and entered a ten-digit pin before the message appeared on the screen. The secure text was from Spencer White. A cold chill went down Max's spine as he read the message.

Call me. ASAP.

SIX

White Family Ranch, Somewhere in Colorado

The sun was low as long shadows crept across the open field in front of the log cabin when they pulled up the gravel drive. The small lake on the north edge of the property shimmered with late day sunshine, and a clear blue sky overhead promised a chilly evening. Golden aspen leaves fluttered in the breeze, signaling an early fall that was common at this elevation. A wide front porch held four bright green Adirondack chairs that stood out in contrast to the home's brown siding. The chairs made Max think fondly of the time he and Kate spent drinking bourbon with Spencer while watching the sun set over the mountains in the distance.

Max stepped from the SUV, taut with worry. Spencer was cryptic on the phone, saying only that Max needed to get back to Colorado as soon as possible. He refused to elaborate, citing the insecure connection on his end. Max and Kate caught a direct flight from Heathrow to Denver and rented a four-by-four for the three-hour drive into the mountains. Max drove the rental as fast as he dared while chain smoking and drinking coffee, trying not to be angry at Spencer for refusing to tell him the problem on the phone.

The home and yard were devoid of signs of life as Max surveyed the clearing. Every other time he had arrived home since they had been on the run, his ten-year-old nephew Alex had shot into his arms, followed by the bounding golden puppy they called Spike. Even Arina, his quiet and troubled sister, had always come out and stood on the porch in silent greeting. But now the cabin and the clearing were eerily quiet.

Max's boots ground in the gravel as he took a tentative step toward the house, wondering if he should have a weapon. As Kate paused by the four-by-four's hood, he sensed she was thinking the same thing. He took another step before he saw the cabin's front door swing open.

The entryway was partially hidden in dark shadows. Heavy steps sounded on wooden planking, and a tall, lanky figure emerged from the gloom. He wore jeans and cowboy boots, and his leathered face was drawn in worry. He pointed the barrel of a shotgun at the ground as he emerged into the soft twilight, walking with a slight limp. Spencer's face was drawn and dark circles were under his eyes. "Took you long enough."

Alarm rose in Max's chest, for the look on Spencer's face could only mean one thing. "What happened, Spencer? Where are Alex and Arina?"

The former operative's eyes were cast at the ground. "Not sure how to even say this."

Max fought to control his frustration. "Just spit it out."

Spencer shrugged. "They left."

Max gritted his teeth. "What do you mean, they left?"

"They just left." Spencer sat on the wooden stairs leading to the porch and leaned the shotgun between his legs.

Max's brow furrowed. "They just up and left? How—"

Kate moved to the front of the stairs and waved off Max's question. "You mean they were taken."

Spencer shook his head. "Their rooms are empty. Spike is gone. No sign of a struggle. They just..."

Max turned away and looked up, not seeing the thick white clouds piling up in preparation for their usual afternoon squall.

Kate knelt in front of her longtime friend and operative and put a hand on his knee. "Tell us the story from the beginning."

Spencer's voice was thick and quiet, and Max had to move closer to hear. "Yesterday, I drove to town for supplies. We needed food and paper goods. Arina gave me a long list. She said she wanted to do some baking."

Max shifted his weight. "Arina hates baking."

Kate shushed him. "Don't you normally take Alex with you?"

"No. It's too dangerous for them to be seen in town."

Max pushed back his rage, reminding himself to be thankful for Spencer's efforts. The operative didn't have to volunteer to stay and watch his family. That was Max's job. Now it looked as if Arina and Alex had left on their own accord, and it was his own fault they were gone.

Spencer hung his head and spoke at the ground. "I was gone maybe four hours. It's a long drive over rough roads, as you know, and I had to go to two stores to find everything she wanted. After gassing up the Jeep, I got back here as fast as I could. When I returned, the place was empty. No sign of a struggle. Closets cleaned out, all their stuff gone. Even Spike's dog bed is missing."

Max's anger was replaced by a gnawing fear. "Was there any kind of vehicle here for them to use?"

Spencer lifted his chin. "Just the quads. That was the first thing I checked. They're both still in the barn, untouched."

Max walked up the porch stairs, sidestepping Spencer and putting a reassuring hand on the old operative's shoulder. "It's not your fault." He didn't want to punish Spencer —the former CIA man would do enough of that himself.

The house was anything but rustic. Inside, a cathedral ceiling rose majestically overhead and a wall of thick-paned windows looked out over the mountain lake. He bypassed the modern kitchen and took the stairs up two at a time. At the top, he stepped into Alex's room. The plaid flannel bedsheets were tussled, and a half-full glass of water sat on the oaken nightstand. The closet stood open, empty save for three empty wire hangers. Even the floor at the foot of the bed where Alex had laid Spike's dog bed sat barren.

He performed a quick search but found nothing. It was just as Spencer had described. Arina's room was also empty, as was the Jack and Jill bathroom between their two bedrooms. Max found no sign of a struggle and instead got the impression the departure had been neatly planned. Not a shred of either Arina's or Alex's belongings remained.

The deep dread Max felt upon hearing the news was now replaced by a perplexed sense of mystery and anger. His instinct pointed to Arina orchestrating their own disappearance. But how was that possible? Did she get fed up with being cooped up in this cabin in the woods, always being on the run, and decide to take matters into her own hands? Did Arina think she could somehow care for their safety better than he and Spencer could?

As a thought struck him, he turned from Arina's room and walked down the hall to the tiny office where Max bunked when he stayed at the cabin. On a small table, next to the foldout couch, stood a framed picture of their family taken long before Alex was born. It was yellowed and faded with age, but showed Arina with Max when he was twelve years old. Behind them stood their parents, his late father's hulking figure taking up most of the left side of the frame. Max grabbed the picture off the table.

In it, his sister hammed for the camera, and her goofy smile showed a full set of braces, a luxury afforded by their father's senior position in the Belarusian branch of the KGB. Their mother, a tall dark-haired beauty with an aloof, blank stare stood behind Arina, hands on her daughter's shoulders. The picture was the last keepsake remaining after their childhood home was destroyed by a massive truck bomb several months prior. A thumb drive belonging to their father had been hidden in the backing and had provided clues to the location of the list of twelve consortium members that were after the Azimov family.

When Max flipped the picture over and removed the frame's backing, he saw a folded piece of white-lined paper. Max pried it out with a fingernail and put the picture frame back together before he set it back on the table.

He unfolded the paper with his heart thumping in his ears. At once he recognized his sister's handwriting. In Cyrillic script were the words:

I'm sorry, Mikhail. I just can't live this way any longer. Do not come looking for us.

Please know that Alex and I are protected. We're safer than we could be with you.

Perhaps someday you'll find it in your heart to forgive me.

Love, Arina.

With a heavy heart, Max took the letter downstairs. In the kitchen, he grabbed a bottle of bourbon from the pantry and found three glasses before going out onto the porch. Wordlessly, he handed the letter to Kate and poured a finger of the brown liquid into a glass and handed it to Spencer.

He sat in one of the Adirondack chairs and poured a second glass for Kate. "Nothing you could have done, Spencer. It's not your fault."

Kate, former CIA station chief in Moscow and fluent in Russian, read the note and handed it to Spencer, who was also well-versed in Cyrillic languages. "She must have planned and executed this whole thing herself."

Max poured himself a glass of bourbon and took a healthy gulp, feeling the burn of the alcohol in his throat. He looked out over the placid water of the lake, noticing the dark clouds for the first time. A few heavy drops of rain pattered on the four-by-four's hood.

Kate rose and sat in one of the chairs, putting her feet up on a stool. "She must have had help. Without a vehicle here..."

Max drained his glass before nodding. "I reached the same conclusion."

His mind went back to the time just before he and Kate left for Ukraine. In hindsight, his sister had been more quiet than normal, which Max had chalked up to sadness at the death of their parents and her husband, and perhaps pressure from the constant danger. He poured another round of the strong liquor.

Spencer came to sit in a chair next to Max, gingerly lowering his body into the wooden seat. The old operator had aged since he last saw him. New gray was laced through his beard, and the lines clustered around his eyes looked deeper. It was the look of a man under tremendous strain.

Spencer held out his empty glass, and Max poured him another shot. Something else seemed off to Max, but he couldn't place it. When he and Kate left the cabin to travel to Kiev, they had left a house full of life and energy. Alex was an endless bundle of energy and was usually out exploring the woods, Spike bounding behind him with the kind of enthusiasm reserved for puppies. Something occurred to him. He sat up and grabbed Spencer's arm. "Where's Charlie?"

Charlie was the gray-faced golden retriever they rescued from Max's grandfather's cabin in Eastern Pennsylvania. The dog grew attached to Spencer and didn't like to leave his side.

Spencer grinned. "I took him over to my daughter's place up north by Meeker. She and her husband have a ranch with a couple dozen head of cattle. They breed working horses, and they have two other dogs—a Border collie and an Aussie. Figured as soon as you got here we'd be traveling again. He's in a good place."

Max gave him a sideways look. "How was the visit?"

Spencer looked down at his drink. "Not great. But she agreed to take Charlie."

The ex-CIA agent was estranged from his two daughters for reasons he kept to himself. Max figured Spencer compensated by taking on the caretaker role for Arina and Alex. Except now he had failed at that too. Max poured him another finger, regretting the anger he'd directed at his friend. "Any theories on where they went?"

Spencer took a gulp of the bourbon and gazed out at the lake. The bourbon in his glass was gone by the time he spoke. "Arina kept to herself. When she wasn't on her laptop, she was taking Charlie and Spike on long walks. She spent a lot of time on the firing range, putting a ton of rounds through the Glock you got her. I had to tell her to ease off because I didn't want any suspicions raised from all the ammunition I was buying." Spencer looked at him. "She's an excellent shot, you know."

Max grunted. "Probably in her blood." Growing up, Max had received long hours of pistol training and spy tradecraft from their father, who groomed Max to follow in his footsteps. Max was a natural with a pistol, so he wasn't shocked to hear his sister was also a skilled shot.

Max removed a crumpled pack of Marlboros from his jacket pocket and lit one using a Zippo lighter with the tarnished image of the Belarusian flag on its side. The lighter had once been his grandfather's. As he rubbed a thumb over the etching of the flag, the image of his grandfather's face rose in his mind. He took a drag on the cigarette and blew smoke toward the porch ceiling. "What was she doing on her laptop?"

Spencer shook his head. "That's the thing. I don't know. In hindsight, I'm kicking myself for not finding out."

Max took another pull. "Don't beat yourself up. Everything's clearer in hindsight. She was probably communicating with whoever came and got her. Making her plans."

With an effort, Spencer crossed one leg over the other. "Once, while she was sleeping and left the machine on the counter, I tried accessing it to see what she was doing."

Max looked at him. "And?"

Spencer shook his head. "Couldn't get in. She had it password protected and locked with fingerprint security."

Max's eyebrows went up. "Fingerprint security?"

Spencer nodded. "I thought it odd too."

Kate made a come-hither gesture with two fingers, and Max handed her the lit cigarette. She took a drag and handed it back. "Does anyone know where she got the computer?"

They all looked at each other. Max's mind went back over the past few months through their escape from Minsk and their time at the compound in upstate New York. He realized the laptop didn't appear until after they arrived in Colorado. Either she had hidden it when fleeing Minsk, which seemed unlikely, or someone had slipped it to her. They all sipped in silence at the implications.

As quiet settled over the group, a ripple appeared on the placid pond. Shadows from the trees along the drive moved slowly across the gravel track, and a thick purple glow appeared on the mountains as the sun slowly disappeared. A gentle ticking emanated from the trees, rising and falling as male crickets marked their territory.

Kate finished her whiskey and cleared her throat. "What are you going to do? Let them go? Or chase after them?"

Max's fist tightened around the glass as he peered into the gloom. "I'll give you one guess."

SEVEN

Barcelona, Spain

It took Max three hours to run an elaborate surveillance detection route in Barcelona, a city he hadn't visited in over ten years. He started by using a taxi from the airport and spent thirty minutes reacquainting himself with the city's well-organized bus and metro system as he toured through El Ravel and the Gothic Quarter. Max strolled through the large crowds in Plaça Espanya, dodging throngs of tourists wearing Barça T-shirts and avoiding packs of the ubiquitous red bicycles, their riders gazing up at the city's backyard mountain of Montjuïc. By the time he exited the metro at the Diagonal, his black T-shirt was stuck to his skin from the humidity, but he was confident he didn't have a tail.

After catching a few hours of sleep at the cabin in Colorado, they had locked the house before jumping into the four-by-four for the trip to Denver International. There, they split up, with Kate and Spencer jumping a flight to the east coast, where Kate planned to talk with William Blackwood and investigate how they were targeted by the drone. Max caught a connection through Dulles to Barcelona, hoping to locate the one person who could help him find Arina and Alex.

He tried to sleep on the trip over the pond, but his mind cycled through the emotions of shock, anger, helplessness, and fear stemming from not knowing where his family was. Arina and Alex, after all, were the sole reasons Max was on the quest to eliminate the threat from the consortium. What had become a quest to preserve the Asimov family name had turned into genuine love and affection for the ten-year-old. Alex became fatherless in the same tragedy that killed Max's own father. Now, after more than forty years as a self-absorbed bachelor, Max wanted nothing more than to settle down and raise Alex as his own son. The eleven remaining men in the consortium were all that stood between him and his dream.

He made his way to a motorcycle shop he remembered from his last visit to Barcelona. After stumbling through a few words of Catalan to win over the proprietor, he paid cash for a Yamaha two-banger and talked the owner into throwing in a used helmet. Max flipped the visor down and disappeared into Barcelona's legendary traffic to run another surveillance detection route.

An hour later, satisfied he was alone, he backed into a row of motorbikes and entered the front terrace of Bar Lobo. He was guided to a small table by a smiling, freckled brown-haired hostess and sat with his back to the wall so he could survey the crowded patio. He ordered an iced café con leche from the white-smocked waiter and lit a cigarette.

As he sipped the cold drink, he let his mind drift to Julia Meier. Only months ago, she was revealed to him as his birth mother, a shocking but not altogether unpleasant discovery that shed light on his recently deceased surrogate mother's treatment of him as a child. Despite Julia's secrecy and unwillingness to reveal much of her background, he felt some comfort in knowing she was in the same business as his father and him. While in Zurich and Prague, Julia had proven herself a capable operator, even if her true employer and motives remained a secret. Now they operated as on-again, off-again partners in Max's quest for freedom and safety.

He was halfway through his coffee when the freckle-faced hostess placed a small white envelope next to his cup and disappeared. He ripped off the end of the envelop and fished out a tiny slip of paper. The writing was in flowing French cursive and the paper smelled of jasmine.

Get on your motorbike and follow the rider in the white helmet.

Max left a five euro note on the table and exited the café. At the end of the row of motorcycles was a leather-clad rider wearing a white full-faced helmet and sitting astride a gleaming green and red Italian sport bike. Despite the protective gear, he noted the rider had a distinct feminine shape to her hips and chest. He fired up his own bike, jammed the helmet on his head, and pulled behind her into traffic.

He soon fell behind as the rider roared through traffic, ducking and weaving between cars and racing around buses and lorries at a dangerous pace. Max bore down and urged the under-powered bike faster, barely managing to keep her in his sights. A puff of exhaust escaped her pipes as she downshifted and leaned onto an entrance ramp to the B-20. A moment later, all he saw was the glint of sun off her helmet in the distance. Cursing his choice of motorbikes, he kept the throttle cranked open and hunched over the handle bars as the wind buffeted his body, threatening to tear him off the old bike.

Somehow he managed to keep her in his sights as she turned onto the B-23, and Barcelona receded into the distance while they fought their way into the foothills of the Muntanyes d'Ordal. When they turned west onto the B-24, the road became windier. Here Max kept up, leaning low into the curves and working the throttle and the clutch without touching the brakes. Muscle memory from his days as a motorcycle racer returned unbidden, and several times he drove his front wheel perilously close to the lead motorcycle's thick rear tire.

After turning off the highway, they bounced along a dirt road through an open space, moving in the direction of a tree grove in the distance. To his left, a manicured vineyard rolled into a lavender sunset. To his right, scraggly trees and dark shadows covered a steep hillside. After another ten kilometers, Max pulled up next to her in front of a small but well-landscaped cottage. He removed his helmet, breathing in a lungful of cool air tinged with loam, pine needles, sage, and motor oil.

The woman vaulted off her bike and turned to him while pulling off her own helmet. A wave of static-filled platinum hair cascaded from the helmet, and Max groaned.

Julia Meier winked at him. "I didn't think you'd be able to keep up on that old thing."

———

A tall man in a white oxford shirt stood on the cabin's porch directly over Julia's shoulder, wearing a pistol in a leather shoulder holster along with a compact assault rifle slung over one shoulder. Max saw movement to his right and caught a glimpse of another man, this one in fatigues. The solider disappeared into the brambles before Max saw his face.

Julia smoothed her hair with a few well-placed strokes. "Bodyguards. Some you'll see, others you won't. We're safe here."

Max got off the bike, set his helmet on the ground, and followed Julia into the cabin. The guard on the porch glared at him, and Max wondered what had occurred to force Julia to assemble a team of guards, a departure from her previous living arrangements. Perhaps he was about to find out.

Julia placed her helmet on a table beside the door and led Max into a rustic but remodeled kitchen. A long center island dominated the room, and broad windows along the length of the wall afforded them an expansive view of the vineyard. She fished a bottle of white wine from a small refrigerator under the counter and poured them both a glass before leading him to a set of chairs on the deck. They sat and sipped as the sun retreated beyond a row of vine-covered foothills, leaving a cascade of purples and oranges as it receded.

Max leaned forward, elbows on his knees. "What is this place?"

Julia, who had applied glossy red lipstick after their frantic motorcycle ride, smiled at him. "Safe house."

"I gathered. Whose?"

"Been in my family for generations. When I die, it'll pass to you."

Max looked at her while the implications of her statement sank in. Her face was pleasantly tanned, and she wore diamond studded earrings. Her silver hair was held back with a barrette, and the only hint of trouble were the dark shadows in her blue eyes.

"I don't suppose this is the point where you unload all your secrets to me?" In all their previous encounters, Julia had withheld almost everything about her background.

Julia placed a warm hand on his arm before addressing him with his given name. "Mikhail, you have to trust me when I tell you that my actions are carefully orchestrated for your safety and the safety of your nephew and your sister. The less you know, the better. When the time is right, all will be revealed. Until then, please have faith. We're on the same side, you and me. In blood and in objective."

Her statement was meant to make him feel better, yet he wondered about her goals. He had spent enough time working for clandestine agencies to know that mission objectives and personal objectives rarely aligned. He pulled his arm away to take a sip of wine. "Don't you think the more I know, the better equipped I am to keep them, and myself, alive?"

Her eyes returned to focus on a point on the horizon. "I can tell you one thing. I know where your sister is, which I assume is why you're here."

Max stood, almost spilling his wine. "Where is she? And how do you know where they are?"

Julia gave him a wry smile. "Sources and methods."

It was tradecraft lingo, meaning it was a secret, and she wasn't about to tell him. It also added to Max's growing list of evidence that Julia worked for an intelligence agency. He just wished he knew which one. After he was failed by both the FSB and the CIA, he had no intention of partnering with another agency any time soon.

Max folded his arms across his chest and leaned against the railing. "Did you help her?"

Julia's eyes moved to the right, following a small animal darting through the underbrush. "I didn't. Regardless, it's

what she wants. She's a single mother, using her best judgment, trying to do the right thing for her son.

"Even if that judgment is flawed?"

"Do you know it's flawed? Maybe she's safer now than
in a remote cabin in the Colorado woods guarded by a crippled, washed-up ex-CIA agent."

Max frowned. "That crippled, washed-up ex-CIA agent
saved my life. I'd take him over any of your agents any day."

Julia gave no reaction. The sun had gone down, leaving
the perfectly trimmed rows of gnarled vines in deep
shadows.

Max accepted that he altered his plans, flew across the
ocean on a red eye, traipsed all over Barcelona, and was led
on a harrowing motorcycle ride to meet up with Julia. But
now he was tired and losing patience with this mysterious
woman who was his mother. Realizing his hands were
clenched, he forced them to relax. "Are you going to tell me
where she is?"

Her gaze focused on him, her blue eyes flashing. "On
one condition."

Max held her gaze. He wasn't in the mood for
conditions.

Julia's eyes softened. "It wouldn't do me any good to
prohibit you from going to see her."

Max shifted his weight but remained silent.

"Go to her and listen. Spend time with Alex and reserve
judgment, then leave her alone until this thing is over."

"Where is she?"

Julia sighed. "You can't control everything, Mikhail."

"God dammit, Julia. She's my sister for—"

Julia held up a manicured hand. "Half sister. I know
you love that little boy, and it makes a mother's heart melt to
see her son finally care for someone other than himself. I

know you're frustrated, but you can't take care of them and go after the consortium at the same time. You're getting closer, and it's sending shock waves through the delicate fabric that makes up the intelligence community. We're seeing new activity in Moscow, activity we knew was coming but we didn't expect for quite some time. You're making them nervous. You're getting under their skin, forcing them to make mistakes. We expect things to pick up speed now—"

"Who is we?" Max asked, feeling like he was looking at a sliver of a massive iceberg, the vast portion of which was hidden from him. He didn't like the sensation.

Julia avoided his eyes. "I'm not at liberty to say."

He turned away and gripped the railing, his knuckles turning white. He spoke into the blackness. "You're holding back information that could help me."

Julia shrugged.

Max turned back to face her. "I don't believe that any more. You obviously work for some kind of intelligence service. Whatever service it is will gladly put its own interests above those of individuals. My father realized that, and at the end it became about family for him. Well now it's about family for me."

Julia sat up and set her wine glass on the table with a thump. "The Western intelligence community is all that stands between ordinary citizens and a world overrun by militant extremists. Every organization will have its politics and dysfunction, but the majority of intelligence teams are hardworking people who are motivated to keep their country and their citizens safe. I know why you have a jaded view of spy organizations, but you're seeing the exception, not the rule. There will always be situations where the good of the group supersedes the good of the individual. Would you kill one person to save twenty? We have to make those decisions every day."

Max leaned back against the railing and crossed his arms.

The corners of Julia's eyes softened, and her eyes glazed over for a moment, as if she was reliving a memory. "You're just like your father, you know that? Passionate, impulsive, dedicated. You're also stubborn and headstrong. He would do exactly what you're doing."

Max guessed this argument was also a source of division between his father and Julia. "Where are they, Julia?"

"Promise me?"

"No promises."

She looked out into the darkness, and for a moment, he thought she wasn't going to tell him. When she caught his gaze, he saw moisture in her eyes.

"They're in Switzerland."

EIGHT

Alexandria, Virginia

A homeless drunk stumbled down the dark street, pausing every few steps to regain his bearings. He wore a green mackintosh open at the front, and his soiled oxford shirt hung untucked. One shoe was untied, and Kate watched from the front seat of her rental car as the man almost tripped over the laces and caught himself on a lamppost before bending at the waist to vomit. Most of the liquid splashed on his shoes and over the front of his shirt. The drunk wiped off his mouth with the back of his hand and took a tentative step, followed by another. Kate studied him and thought she discerned a slight limp hidden by his drunken shuffle. After he rounded a corner and disappeared, the street was silent.

A block away, her renovated warehouse-turned-apartment building rose four stories over South King Street, its wide windows and narrow balconies looking out over the gentrifying warehouse district near the Potomac River. A pang of sadness came over her as she realized she might never return to the idyllic, peaceful home she used as a respite from the chaos of her job. She loved Old Town Alexandria, with its brick sidewalks, the potted conifers, and the mixture of Georgian, Greek Revival, and Victorian architectures. She loved the brightly painted reds, blues, and greens of the store facades along King Street and the leafy green canopies covering the narrow side roads in the spring and summer. The families strolling safely and blissfully in this storybook setting always served as a reminder of why she chose her job. Even if she never pushed a baby carriage with a doting husband nearby, she wanted to preserve that dream for those who chose that life.

While she watched and waited, she toyed with a matte-black super-compact Glock 43 9mm. Attached to the barrel was a short black suppressor. The gun only carried six rounds in the single-stack magazine and one in the chamber, but she didn't anticipate getting into an all-out gun battle, and she wanted something concealable with the suppressor attached.

The street in front and behind her was empty and quiet. She did three drive-bys and noticed no one sitting in a vehicle watching her apartment. The windows in her unit, number six on the third floor, were dark. No shadows moved, no cigarette lighter flared. Of course, that didn't mean someone wasn't in there waiting for her, and it didn't mean someone wasn't crouched in the apartment building across the street with a high-powered rifle. Despite the risk of returning to her apartment, there were a few things she needed. The only question was how to get in and out without alerting anyone she was there.

She had two goals while in Alexandria. One was to retrieve a couple of items from her apartment, and the other was to call on an old friend, a man she thought was her friend and confidant but who had recently betrayed her. Kate slipped on a pair of snug-fitting black leather gloves and stuck the silenced Glock in a holster under her leather jacket before stepping out of the car. She kept to the shadows, careful with her footing on the pavement slick with moisture from that day's rain shower. After entering the building through the backdoor, she used the concrete stairs to ascend to the third floor. She darted to her door, drawing her gun before stepping into the darkened apartment and closing the door behind her.

The apartment was just as she and Max left it. A bottle of vodka sat open on the granite counter, the leather chairs were askew, and the blanket from the couch was wadded on the floor.

She smelled the intruder before she heard him, but when she turned with the gun, she saw only darkness.

"Hello, Kate."

The deep voice rang out from the darkness, familiar and disarming. A voice from the dark abyss of her past. She spun to her left, gun clenched in both hands, searching for the source of the voice. Her mind screamed out to shoot, to pull the trigger, but something in the voice made her hesitate.

A man's form materialized out of the shadows, moving closer, hands up and palms out, as if in surrender. He was tall and narrow-shouldered with rangy arms. A hawk-like nose dominated a strong face, and his shoulder length hair was pushed behind his ears. A broad smile covered his face. "Don't shoot. It's just me, Liam."

Her pistol drooped. Was the man standing in front of her really Liam Rousseau? Lines creased his weathered face, but his smile was unmistakable.

"What the fuck are you doing here?" Kate sputtered, her mind spinning. It had been at least twenty years.

Liam pushed his hair behind an ear, despite no strands having escaped the appendage. It was a mannerism she used to find endearing, and despite the time gap, she knew it was a gesture he used to convey sincerity.

When he smiled, full lips revealed a row of white teeth that glowed in the dim light. His eyes danced with mischief, and even with how things had ended, Kate felt a twinge deep in her belly. The gun fell to her side as he approached and took her in his arms.

She gave herself up to the hug, recognizing the familiar scents of leather and vanilla, smells she'd long associated with her first love and her first lust. Her belly twitched again, stirring a part of her that had remained dead and dormant since she left him in the final fiery argument that ended their relationship.

Liam let go and held her at arm's length. "You look as ravishing as ever, my dear." His baritone voice was thick with a French accent, the same voice that had so easily seduced her on that warm, stormy night in Paris two decades ago. The voice that would forever change the trajectory of her life.

Kate felt the smartphone in her back pocket buzz, but she ignored it. "Why are you here?" Despite the over-whelming power of her attraction to the man she had first fallen in love with, alarm bells sounded in the back of her mind. Something about coincidences.

As Liam placed a hand on her wrist before moving it to the gun in her hand, the touch of his strong fingers on her skin was electric. Even with the clash of ringing alarms in her mind, she was powerless to stop him from sliding the gun from her hand.

He placed the gun on the granite slab countertop and stepped into the kitchen, searching for glasses. "A drink?" He poured a dash of the vodka into a tumbler and handed it to her. After pouring himself a finger, he raised his glass. "To old times."

When he clinked his glass to hers, the memories came at her fast and furious. The tiny café where they'd met, him reading a dog-eared paperback of French poetry, her scribbling in a diary over a glass of red wine. The long strolls along the river Seine while they discussed the state of the world. Back then the news of the day was the violence in Ireland and the emergence of al-Qaeda, long before the scourge of ISIS wormed its icy tentacles of radicalism and fear throughout Europe. The long nights of marijuana and red wine-fueled love making, both furious and languid, were a perfect mirror of the French lifestyle she'd come to cherish. She shook it off as the niggle in the back of her mind forced her thoughts to the present.

She stepped back from him. "Answer my question."

He held up his hands again, his left clenching the glass, in a contrite show of surrender. "I'm a messenger. Nothing more."

She took another step back. "How did you know I'd be here?" The niggle turned to apprehension as some of the pieces fell together. Liam Rousseau was one of the CIA's master recruiters. He was an agent who lived in the field, preying on young, impressionable minds, brainwashing them until he convinced them to spy on foreign governments on behalf of the CIA. There could only be one reason Liam Rousseau was in her apartment. She glanced at the gun on the counter.

"We picked you up at Dulles," Rousseau explained. "Security camera facial recognition."

Kate let that sink in. "And you figured I was headed here."

Liam took a sip and let a smirk cross his face. "The most likely scenario, don't you think? Just playing the odds."

She edged to the counter, nearer to where he was leaning and closer to her gun. "What's the message, Liam?" Now that her wits had returned, the memories of her love affair with Liam Rousseau were overshadowed by remembrances of how it had ended and the implications of his sudden appearance twenty years later. Silently, she chastised herself for letting him disarm her so easily.

"They want you to come in." Liam's eyes tracked her movements. The same dark brown eyes she'd fallen for. Eyes she had peered into during their frequent and urgent lovemaking. Eyes that had seduced her physically and emotionally, convincing her that becoming a spy was her life's calling. He set his glass on the counter and reached into his leather jacket.

Her eyes were riveted to his hand, her mind screamed for her gun, but she couldn't move. "I'm sure they do."

Liam's hand emerged from his jacket holding a package of cigarettes. "Smoke?"

"No. Are you here to bring me in?"

He busied himself with the cigarettes, pounding one end of the box on his palm to pack the tobacco. The cellophane on the red box of Pall Mall's flashed in the soft light from the window. "They want you back, Kate."

She crossed her arms. "Bullshit. They just tried to kill me." She hoped her calculated statement would elicit a tell indicating how much Liam knew.

Liam lit a cigarette using a Zippo lighter, reminding her of Max. When he looked at her, she saw nothing in his eyes. "It's true. Why do you think they sent me?"

She remained silent, wishing Max were here.

"Your actions in Eastern Ukraine made them realize there's still a place for human asset teams. Congress is reviewing the use of drones. Montgomery wants you back, and they want you to rebuild your team."

She pursed her lips. *It's possible. Still, it doesn't sound right. It's too easy.*

She set her glass down on the counter, using the opportunity to step closer to the gun. "Answer one question."

He blew smoke at the ceiling. "Anything."

"Why did you leave me?"

Liam paused with a cigarette halfway to his mouth, his eyes narrowing and his mouth curling into a smirk. "After all these years, and your rise in the CIA, you still don't know?"

"I just want to hear you say it. It might have been nothing to you, but I was in love with you, Liam."

He snorted. She recognized it as his condescending laugh, the one he used when she argued with him against socialist ideals or when she expounded the benefits of capitalism. The snort meant she was wrong, and her naive little mind would never understand. It was the laugh of a man consumed by idealism who would never be content to live in the world of pragmatism. Of course, he left her when his job was done, after the CIA had its hooks in her deep enough so she would never leave. He never loved her, he just seduced her into joining. He was doing his job. The disgust rose into her mouth, and she felt like she was sucking on a penny.

From the corner of her eye, she saw the apartment door swing open and a black form move into the room in a blur. She reached for the gun on the counter, but Liam reacted a split- second faster, pulling a pistol from under his jacket.

She heard the *pfft, pfft* of a silenced gun, and Liam staggered back against the counter, the cigarette falling from his hand, his pistol clattering to the wood floor.

Kate grabbed the gun off the counter, finger searching for the trigger, trying in vain to aim for the intruder, her mind in a panic, knowing she was about to die. Bracing herself for the impact of the bullets, she dropped to a knee while looking for the target.

"Don't shoot," a voice said from the hallway. "I'm coming in."

Her body sagged, adrenaline coursing, fatigue and relief washing over her as she recognized the voice of Spencer White. He materialized out of the shadows, still wearing the green mackintosh and oxford shirt stained with vomit, holding a silenced pistol, his jaw set.

Kate wrinkled her nose. "Jesus, Spencer. You stink."

NINE

Undisclosed Location

In the history of the consortium, an emergency meeting had only been called five times. Today was the sixth. It wasn't often that ten wealthy, prominent men were in one room and didn't talk, and you could hear a pin drop. No one murmured to their neighbor at the massive oaken conference table, partly because no one liked each other enough to inquire about one's family. No one barked orders into a cell phone, and no one used a laptop because electronics were not allowed in the building. This was only one of a dozen security procedures required of each of them, so they waited in silence, casting uncomfortable glances at the two empty chairs.

Some men were irritated, a couple were angry, but most were pensive from the news that hit the wire just twenty-four hours prior. One of their own was killed in a brazen attack in the Eastern Ukrainian war zone of Donetsk. All the news reports credited the Ukrainians with the attack, but each man around the table knew the truth. The man they had been chasing, the man they had pledged to kill, had turned the tables and was now after them. Victor Volkov, also known as Number Nine, the ninth most senior member of the twelve-man consortium, had been assassinated by Mikhail Asimov.

Erich Stasko, Number Twelve, shivered as he eyed the other men around the table, even though he was used to the cold. Above them, a domed ceiling disappeared into darkness, and an immense Persian rug in reds and blues was underfoot. The rough-hewn conference table was bare, except for the water carafes evenly spaced around the table and the cups of tea in front of several members, steam rising from each in the chilly air. Note-taking was forbidden, and minutes were not kept, at least as far as Erich could tell. The room was probably bugged, and he assumed the sessions were recorded on hidden video cameras. He was always careful to say as little as possible. Erich sat at the massive table while drumming his fingers on the dark wood.

Across the table from him were four men. Four others sat on his side of the table, while a ninth man was at the foot. They all wore well-tailored suits and dark-colored ties, and their pale faces stuck out like beacons against the somber tones of the room. One chair on the side of the table opposite Erich was empty. It was Victor Volkov's chair. Occasionally a member of the group would glance at the empty chair.

The chair at the head of the table was also empty, but for a different reason. That chair belonged to the chancellor. Each member of the consortium was assigned a number, one through twelve, that corresponded to that person's seniority. The chancellor was Number One, and he chaired the monthly meetings. The man at the foot of the table was Number Two, direct in line to ascend to the number one position if Number One became incapacitated, died, or was otherwise incapable of performing his duties. Like the US Supreme Court, the position of chancellor was appointed for life, much to the irritation of Number Two and the several members at the table who supported him.

Erich was the youngest and the least wealthy of the group, so he kept his mouth shut unless called upon. He had one role in the group, he knew what it was, and he focused all his attention on playing that role as best he could. Continued success meant vast riches to come and eventual accession up the ladder of seniority, while one misstep would forfeit his life. He glanced at the empty chair again and rubbed his clammy palms on his pant leg under the table, where no one could see. It gave him little solace to realize he was now Number Eleven—seniority was meaningless if he was dead.

Over the past twenty-four hours, Erich had become obsessed with his own mortality. He was a banker, a man who appreciated routine, hard work, and the value of interest accumulated over time. He was on the council for one reason only—to launder money for the consortium and its members. Unlike many of the men around the table, Erich didn't have the stomach for violence. He appreciated the comforts that wealth provided, but money was simply a way to keep score. And at his young age, he was well on his way to winning. Until recently, he hadn't taken the physical threat to his life seriously, but yesterday's news prompted him to upgrade the security systems and increase the number of guards in all his houses and offices.

Because electronic devices of all kinds, including wrist watches, were forbidden in the room, Erich had no idea of the time. He guessed they had sat in the room for the better part of an hour, which was a lot of time to waste for men of this stature. The chancellor was militant about starting meetings on time, and his tardiness contributed to the discomfort in the room. It occurred to Erich that the chancellor might be dead, but he quickly realized the thought was stupid. The consortium had strict rules and protocols in place in the event of a death, and in that circumstance, Number Two would be in charge.

The massive doors behind the head of the table banged open, startling the group around the table. An unnaturally tall, broad-shouldered man strode into the room and took the seat at the head of the table. Some said his gigantic size was due to a tumor on his pituitary gland that caused a growth spurt during childhood. He resembled a boxer who had seen his fair share of fights. Several scars marred his cheeks and neck, and his nose was crooked, as if it had been broken several times. His features had a weathered look, as though rawhide was stretched over his face. Each man around the table tried to deduce the chancellor's emotions, but his face was blank. If he was worried about the sudden death of one of their members, he didn't show it.

The chancellor brought the meeting to order before launching into several pieces of ordinary business. Erich glanced around the room, seeing some men with openly incredulous looks on their faces. After a discussion on the latest report on oil production from OPEC, the man directly across the table from Erich, a stout man with a stone block for a head and a ridged forehead like a Cro-Magnon, interrupted. "With all due respect, shouldn't we address the elephant in the room?"

Erich held his breath as the room went silent. The chancellor was not a man who suffered insolence, so Erich was surprised when he said in his gravel-like voice, "Spartak, you're right." The chancellor steepled his long fingers. "It seems as if someone is targeting each member of this council for assassination."

Spartak almost came out of his seat. "It seems? Isn't it obvious that Asimov has a list with our names on it?"

There were several murmurs of assent around the room, and Erich forced himself to breathe. This was the closest the room had come to mutiny since he joined three years ago. In a physical confrontation between Spartak and the chancellor, Erich might put his money on Spartak. A Russian military commander, Spartak was a former member of Russia's elite special forces group known as Spetsnaz. The man at the foot of the table, Ruslan Stepanov, was head of Russia's military intelligence, oversaw the Spetsnaz, and it was common knowledge Ruslan and Spartak were aligned against the chancellor. These days, Spartak spent his time trading in illicit weapons sourced from former Soviet republics, some said with the help of Stepanov, and held the rank of number five in the consortium.

The chancellor was unfazed. He let Spartak finish speaking before standing from his chair and leaning forward with his hands on the table.

"It's crucial we don't lose our heads." The chancellor's voice washed over the group like a tenor in an a cappella group. The chatter stopped. The chancellor had never before stood when addressing them. "It appears Mikhail Asimov, despite our best efforts, has acquired a list with each of our names on it."

The room erupted. Cries of 'I don't believe it!' and 'What do you mean?' were heard around the table.

The chancellor banged his fist on the table. "Silence! I'll not allow this body to descend into chaos. That's exactly what Asimov and his handlers want."

Spartak slapped the table. "Handlers? You told us he was a lone wolf."

The chancellor glared at Spartak, who lost some of his fire under the withering gaze. "The situation has changed. My sources indicate that Asimov is being run by an intelligence agency. He's being provided with intel and weapons, and he's receiving operational support. How else would he have been able to get to Number Nine? We're unsure of which agency, but we'll know in twenty-four hours."

"My God," said Number Eight, a bookish man whose color had drained from his face.

The chancellor held up his hands. "The lengths to which our enemies will go to defeat us has exceeded even my own precognition."

Ruslan Stepanov stood. As tall as the chancellor, Stepanov's physique strained the seams of his suit. "The question is, what are we going to do about it?"

If Erich didn't fear for his life, he would think this was good drama. It was no secret that the chancellor and Ruslan Stepanov had no love for each other. As the only member of the consortium who held a post in the Russian government, Stepanov held enormous power outside the group. Impeccably groomed but rugged and hard as a rock under his wool suit, as the head of Russia's military intelligence, he was inside the Russian president's inner circle. Many in the consortium assumed he was the president's direct representative and provided the president with inside information on the body's actions. Stepanov's posture and his question were a direct challenge to the chancellor.

Number One gave no indication he was put off by Stepanov's question. "That is exactly the question. We didn't get this far by running at the first sign of trouble, and I don't intend to start now." He spread his arms wide. "I'm open to suggestions."

Erich looked around the room while some men studied their fingernails or sipped their tea. "We could buy him off." Instantly he regretted the outburst.

The chancellor smiled at him like a knowing grandfather. "I've considered that idea. But at this point, we have to assume it's personal. We did, after all, kill his parents and destroy his childhood home. We chased him out of his country and forced him to take up with the Americans. We helped make him an outcast from the CIA. I'm not sure there's any sum of money that would erase all that from his memory. He's a killer, and that's how he deals with problems. He kills."

Number Four cleared his throat. "There must be another assassin we can send after him." His voice was soft, and his words were spoken in precise English with an Asian accent. Number Four ran China's largest petroleum conglomerate, the state-owned Sinopec, and was known for his use of American idioms. "If we send enough killers after him, or take out a large contract on him, every two-bit assassin with a peashooter will come after him. He'll be dead within twenty-four hours."

A murmur of agreement went around the table, with several members nodding their heads.

The chancellor bowed his head. "I've considered this option. We've thrown capable men at him, yet he survives. We've attempted to kidnap his family to use them as bait. Now they've disappeared, presumably with the help of our enemies. No, I believe we need a stronger strategy, something he won't be able to recover from. A plan that will bury him, a situation he can't get out of by simply killing more people."

As the men around the table ran out of ideas, the room grew quiet. Abruptly, the chancellor snapped his fingers and the massive doors behind him creaked open. A steward, dressed in black and white, pushed a cart with a large screen TV into the room. The steward handed the chancellor a tablet computer and performed a shallow bow before exiting.

Erich felt the tension in the room escalate. The chancellor had just violated one of his own cardinal rules, a fact that would not be forgotten by Number Two.

The chancellor tapped on the tablet and the television screen came to life, showing a grainy black-and-white wide-angle view of a quaint city street. Erich got the impression the perspective was from a security camera mounted on a building. Leafy green trees moved in a light breeze as people strolled and window-shopped. Two blocks away from the camera was an outdoor café teeming with people. Waiters in white aprons bustled around the tables as well-dressed patrons sipped from coffee mugs and nibbled on pastries. Traffic on the street was light, consisting mostly of black hackney cabs with the yellow signs that were common in London.

When Spartak opened his mouth to speak, the chancellor hushed him with a wave of his hand.

The rear of a sprinter van appeared on the screen as it trundled down the street, moving away from the camera and toward the outdoor café. A basket of vegetables was stenciled on the side of the van. The chancellor violated protocol again by checking his wristwatch.

The idyllic scene was abruptly interrupted when the van accelerated and turned, smashing into the crowded café. As the screen turned dark for a moment, someone in the room muttered, "What the—"

When visibility returned, Erich blanched in horror at the scene before him.

TEN

Biasca, Switzerland

Max crouched behind a rock outcropping on a ledge and balanced his elbows on a chunk of granite, peering through a pair of high-powered binoculars. The jagged edges of the Alps towered behind him, casting a deep shadow over his position. Below him sprawled a lush green valley sprinkled with red-roofed farmhouses. A lazy blue stream meandered down the fall line of the valley while fluffy white clouds floated harmlessly overhead, occasionally blocking the warm morning sun.

The trek to get to this point took him two days, and sweat dripped down his back from the exertion. He had walked nonstop over three mountain passes, sticking to a seldom used game trail, finding his way by a dim headlamp while carrying a heavy pack. He enjoyed the time without cellular service, a temporary respite from the troubles in the world. Even though he knew there might be cellular service this close to the village below, he resisted the urge to check his messages—there would be plenty of time for that later. He drank from a jug of water, letting his face bask in the morning sun, contemplating his next move.

Julia warned him that the valley was heavily guarded, both with uniformed soldiers and disguised agents who were all on the lookout for intruders. The soldiers were a small private army whose sole mandate was to protect three of the valley's inhabitants—four if you included Spike the dog. The amount of security gave Max some comfort. On the other hand, it made it challenging for him to approach without triggering an alarm.

Through the heavily magnified glasses, Max watched a transport brimming with soldiers speeding along a dirt road and throwing up plumes of dust. The truck was headed up the valley in the direction of a massive compound that looked like a converted castle. He had to admit that he couldn't think of a better place for Alex and Arina to stay than in a castle guarded by a hundred well-trained men. Still, he knew if he could find them, their enemies could as well.

After watching the valley for several hours, he had the guard's rotation figured out. Every thirty minutes, a truck with three or four soldiers emerged from the south end of the compound and made a loop, using the valley's dirt roads. Max saw them wave to residents, hand out cigarettes to laborers, and toss candy to groups of children.

Glancing at his watch, he removed the holster and pistol from his belt and stowed them both in his pack. He took his Blackphone from his pocket and secured it in a small compartment in the pack. After he was satisfied it was all well hidden, he swung the heavy load onto his back before picking his way down the tight rocky switchbacks.

He kept his head down and followed the trail as it grad-

ually leveled out into lush green pastures. To his left was a
jagged mountain ridge towering overhead, and to his right
was a farmhouse surrounded by manicured fields and
stands of conifers.

Ahead, the castle rose majestically, its chipped and
faded ramparts perched on crumbling walls. Yellow paint
flecked off the building, and despite the enormous structure's disheveled appearance, Max noticed a regular parade
of heavily armed sentries along the upper walls. Several
satellite dishes pointed skyward, and rows of security
cameras lined the walls. A twelve-foot fence topped by
barbed wire surrounded the property. He wondered if Alex
liked living in what was effectively a prison compared to the
vast tracts of untamed wilderness he had access to in
Colorado.

As he walked, he ruminated on what Julia told him.
Arina indeed had help escaping Colorado, and the source
was both a surprise and alarming. The revelation had cast a
new light on his sister and gave Max another reason to seek
her out so she could explain herself. Arina owed him an
explanation, and he meant to get it. He also wanted to see
Alex's surroundings for himself. Was he getting an education? Was he safe? Was he happy?

From the corner of his eye Max saw a group of five
soldiers approaching on foot. He strolled down the rocky
trail with his head bent, as if he were a casual hiker intent
on the natural beauty of the surroundings and unconcerned
by the approaching soldiers.

The lead soldier stopped in the trail and shouted an
order in German when Max approached. "Halt!"

The soldiers were all dressed in fatigues and carried
rifles and sidearms. No one had yet pulled a weapon, but
Max sensed tension among the group and knew they were

ready to draw if Max made a wrong move. Two of the men fanned out on either side of the trail, standing at attention. Max was pleased to see they were a well-trained squad. He stopped and brought his hands up.

"Identify yourself," the squad commander demanded.

Max cleared his throat and spoke in German. "I seek an audience with the inhabitants of the château." Max gestured down the valley at the castle.

The lead man's brow furrowed. "Tell me your name."

As Max swung the pack off his back, he found himself looking down the barrels of two HK416 A5 assault rifles. Dropping the bag, he raised his hands again.

He pointed at the pack. "I need to show you something."

The squad commander barked an order, and two men sprung forward. Both were young, pale skinned, and blue eyed, looking like they were itching for a fight. One stepped in front of Max while the other grabbed his backpack. The two soldiers on his flanks moved in closer, holding their rifles steady.

"Search him."

Max raised his arms over his head and winked at the young man. The rosy cheeked young guard hesitated at first but did an adequate job of frisking Max, finding nothing.

A shout went up as the second guard tossed Max's pistol at the feet of the squad leader.

It took only seconds for them to bind Max with a pair of flexi-cuffs, and the sharp plastic dug into his wrists as the guard cinched them tight. The young soldier emptied the contents of Max's pack onto the ground and performed a thorough search of the contents. The guard looked up at his leader and shrugged. "No identification."

The squad leader glared at Max. "For the last time, tell

me who you are and why you're in this valley with an illegal firearm and no identification."

"You'll find a folded note from my sister hidden in the paperback you tossed onto the ground. She's currently residing in that castle. She'll vouch for me if you show her the note."

The squad leader folded his arms. "Tell me your name."

Max smiled at the young soldier. "You can either take that note to her, or you can take me to her. Your choice."

The squad leader, a tall, thin man with the narrow hips and shoulders of a cross-country runner, nodded at the guard to Max's left. Pain shot through Max's side as the man punched him in the kidney. Max stumbled forward, coughing and gagging, but managed to stay on his feet.

"Name."

"Donald." Max gasped for breath. "Donald Duck."

The leader nodded again, but this time Max was ready. He twisted with the blow, allowing it to glance off his side, using his momentum to sweep with his feet. When the guard behind him went down, Max fell onto the man's face with his knee, using all his weight. The soldier's nose burst, spattering blood onto the green grass and Max's shoes. The young man cried out in surprise and pain.

When Max stood, he found the muzzle of a pistol stuck in his face. The squad leader held it steady with an angry look in his eyes. "Name?"

"Bugs—"

The blow came fast. The squad leader stunned him with the butt of his pistol before a strike from behind caused a blinding pain to blossom at the back of his neck. Max crumpled to the ground, out cold.

———

As the world swam into a blurry view, Max felt like he was on a ship in stormy seas, with amorphous shapes tilting and sliding around him. When a wave of nausea hit, he thought he might vomit, but the feeling soon passed. The back of his head hurt, like it was in a vice with someone tightening the screw. As his vision cleared, he saw a small man in front of him leaning on a table with a coffee mug in hand. The man's widow's peak glistened with oil, and he wore a well-tailored linen shirt and linen pants with leather sandals.

Max sat in a comfortable upholstered chair against a wall in what looked like a study. Tall narrow windows over the table let in the morning light, luxurious carpets were laid on a tiled floor, and several large candles burned in sconces along the stone walls. It wasn't hard to imagine a medieval-era lord sitting at the table, drinking wine from a copper cup and scribbling on a scroll of vellum with a quill pen. Instead, an aluminum-colored laptop computer sat on the table next to an elaborate telephone console, and a large screen television was affixed to the wall, showing a muted BBC news station. The scent of vanilla from the candles mingled with the smell of strong coffee. Max flexed his arms and found them free from restraint. His eyes came to rest on the diminutive figure staring at him. No one else was in the room.

"Hello, Mikhail."

Max rubbed his wrists where the plastic cuffs had cut into his skin. "They didn't have to knock me out, Victor."

The man standing in front of Max, the man who had come to the rescue of Arina, was Victor Dedov, former Director of the Belarusian branch of the KGB, their father's former direct superior. Why he'd come to Arina's aide was something Julia had demurred from telling Max, insisting Arina tell him herself.

Victor sipped his coffee. "You're lucky you only sustained a bump on the head. Why didn't you tell them your name and save yourself all this trouble?"

Max shrugged. "Can I get some of that coffee?"

Victor toggled an intercom and issued a command in German.

Max stood, willing his woozy head to clear. The last time Max saw Victor Dedov, they were both being chased by Wilbur Lynch, and Victor had sustained life-threatening injuries. Prior to that, Dedov had tried to swindle Max out of ten million dollars. "I thought you were dead."

Victor smiled. "Turns out, I'm not so easy to kill."

They were interrupted by a steward in a uniform pushing a coffee service. The man, who looked ex-Russian military, handed Max a cup of black coffee in an ornate coffee cup etched with the seal of Belarus.

Victor waited for the steward to leave the room. "I must congratulate you for killing Wilbur Lynch. That certainly made my life easier."

Max smelled the coffee, appreciating the burned sugar and toasted nut aroma of the dark roast. "What makes you think it was me?"

"Because a second man is now dead. Victor Volkov, former Russian mobster, a man I've suspected of being a member of the consortium. I can only surmise that you recovered the list from Lynch and started eliminating the names."

Max shrugged and sipped his coffee. The hot liquid helped the pain in his head. "Good coffee."

"The Swiss know how to do it."

"Retirement suits you, Victor. You look rested, relaxed. What do old deposed spymasters do with their free time? Write books?"

Max saw a fire in the man's eyes that was replaced by the former spy's trademark glint. "Oh, this and that." Victor set his coffee cup on the desk. "I suppose you'd like to see your sister."

"And nephew."

Victor nodded. "She wants to stay here, you know."

"So I was told."

As Victor stared at him, Max was reminded of the man who ruled the Belarusian KGB with an iron fist. His father's boss, a man who instilled fear in those who worked for him. The Little General, they called him behind his back. Without a word, Victor strode from the room, leaving Max with a cup of hot coffee and a gargantuan headache.

ELEVEN

London, England

The schoolgirl had no way of knowing that today was her last day on planet earth. Had it not been for the arrival of the Very Important Person in the long black limousine, Sophia may have survived. Sadly, when she and her nanny stopped to see what all the commotion was about, the little girl's fate was sealed.

Like the rest of her schoolmates, the blond ten-year-old wore a khaki skirt, white leggings, and a blue jacket. The only personality afforded her by the school dress code was a bright hair ribbon, which her mother had tied onto her head before kissing her goodbye.

Sophia gripped her nanny's hand, pulling the young Spanish woman along, wanting to see whether anyone famous might exit the sleek black car that had just parked along the street, only a few meters from her mother's favorite neighborhood café.

Sophia yanked hard. "Come on."

Camila resisted, torn between the trouble she would be in if the little girl were late and satisfying her own curiosity about the occupant of the limousine. "You'll be late for school."

Sophia preyed on what she knew was Camila's curiosity. The young nanny was a voracious tabloid reader and soap opera watcher. "Don't you want to know who it is?" She uttered the final nail in Camila's coffin with a smirk. "I'll bet we can get an autograph."

The nanny glanced at her watch. "Okay, but only for a minute."

Sophia shrieked with joy and pulled a willing Camila along until they neared the car, hesitating only when they noticed several black-suited men taking up positions around the vehicle. The presence of the capable-looking men with the curly things in their ears made Sophia slow her pace and stirred her curiosity. *Whoever it was must be very important.* As she pulled Camila closer to the limousine, a light breeze ruffled the canopy of leafy green trees.

One of the dark-suited men held up his hand to block her path. "Now just hold on there, young lady." His face wore a smile, but his posture and eyes were all business. She stopped and put her free hand to her mouth.

"Who's in the car?" she asked in a brave but soft voice.

"Well now, young lady. I can't tell you that. That's classified information." He smiled down at her with a twinkle in his eye.

The sound of clattering glassware and the chattering of earnest conversations drifted over the sidewalk. Papers rustled as businessmen caught up on the world's news before making their way to their offices. The café was a busy place, popular with the posh neighborhood's residents, the smell of bitter espresso and charred mocha wafting over them during their morning ritual.

Sophia heard a *snick* when the limousine's rear door opened, and a man's foot stepped out onto the concrete sidewalk. Camila tugged on her arm, urging her to come along. The security man's arms were out as if to herd the two girls away from the car. The little girl, fascinated, resisted both, bouncing up and down to catch a glimpse. She saw an oxblood tasseled loafer, a bright blue sock, and a charcoal pant leg underneath the vehicle's door before the tall form of a well-bred man emerged, pausing to button his suit jacket.

Sophia's eyes widened in recognition and delight. He was one of the most handsome men she had ever seen, and she remembered hearing her mother exclaiming about the man's beauty when she saw his photo in the Daily Mail. Broad-shouldered, square jawed, and famous for his sparkling brown eyes, the former military commander was now England's most eligible bachelor. That much she knew, even if she didn't understand what the man's actual job was. Squealing, she turned to see if Camila was watching.

Instead of looking in the Very Important Man's direction, Camila was distracted, looking at the road with a curious expression on her face. Sophia followed her gaze, wondering what could possibly divert the young nanny's attention from England's most handsome man. As she turned, Sophia saw the security man staring in the same direction as Camila.

She heard a shout and the screech of tires on pavement, and a sprinter van, painted green, with an enormous picture of a basket of vegetables on its side, screamed by the limousine. From the corner of her eye, she saw the security man lunge back at the bachelor, wrapping him in his enormous arms while trying to open the door to the limousine.

Despite the commotion around her, Sophia's eyes were glued to the green sprinter van with the healthy-looking vegetables painted on the side. The vehicle's driver's side window was open, and she glimpsed a young man, clean-shaven, wide-eyed, his dark face covered in perspiration. Both his hands were on the wheel, and he was concentrating hard. When the van flashed passed them, she thought she saw the man's lips moving.

Sophia's last moment on earth moved in slow motion. She thought she heard someone yelling from the van's open window with a sing-song and melodic voice, but the language was foreign to her.

To her shock, the van made a hard right turn around the front of the black car and bumped up onto the sidewalk before plowing into the outdoor café. It hit a plump waitress and thumped over several patrons before coming to a rest among overturned tables and sprawled bodies. As screams erupted from the café, the dark-suited men were already in motion.

When the bomb erupted from the delivery van, the most eligible bachelor in England and his security man were attempting to crawl into the relative safety of the armored limousine. The fireball engulfed them and dozens of café patrons and bystanders, followed by a shock wave that shattered windows a block away.

Sophia, partially protected by the open door of the black car, might have survived the initial explosion if it hadn't been for the lethal blast of ball bearing shrapnel soaked in rat poison. Later, workers from the morgue would have to use a shovel and a large plastic bag to recover enough of the little girl's remains so her parents had something to bury.

———

As the smoke on the screen cleared, Erich Stasko leaned on the table, eyes squinting, both intrigued and sickened by the carnage. He'd never been a firsthand witness to a terrorist event carried out in broad daylight.

The first thing he saw was that both the van and the outdoor patio had disappeared, and in their place was an enormous crater. Nothing moved, save wafting smoke, fluttering leaves, and a smattering of papers drifting in the breeze. The large Mercedes limousine now rested at an angle in the middle of the street, a smoldering hulk. Erich saw no people. He peered closer and recoiled when he saw what looked like a severed leg on the pavement in the foreground. He saw another body part, and another, until he had to look away.

The chancellor tapped a button on the tablet and the screen went dark. Erich, still stunned, looked around. Several men had smiles on their faces while a few had gone pale.

It was Number Two who spoke first. "Do you want to explain what we just saw?"

Instead of answering, the chancellor tapped a few more times on the tablet to bring the television to life with a BBC news program, where a blond anchorwoman in a blue dress held a hand up to one ear, concentrating. A video feed overlay in the upper right corner showed the carnage from the bomb blast. A British policeman pushed at the cameraman, urging him to make way for first responders and rescue workers. The chancellor tapped another button, and the woman's voice came through the television's speakers.

"—told just a few minutes ago that a truck bomb exploded in the middle of Café Centrál in West Brompton. Details are sketchy. But as you can see from the video feed, there is an enormous crater where the café's outdoor seating once stood."

The anchorwoman paused, hand to her ear, as if receiving new information through her earpiece. "What?" Her face looked pale. "Please repeat that." She paused again, her eyes searching.

She addressed the camera. "Ladies and gentlemen, we're getting reports that Zachery Brent, England's controversial Labour candidate for MP in this year's election, was killed in the blast."

The chancellor muted the television's sound, and they watched in stunned silence as the BBC reporter struggled to keep up with the barrage of incoming information. The video feed jumped from images of the scene to still shots of Zachery Brent. Brent giving a speech, Brent shaking hands and kissing a baby's forehead, Brent on a night out on the town, caught by paparazzi on a date.

Number Two, Ruslan Stepanov, sat with his arms crossed, eyes narrowed. Spartak sat back in his chair nodding his head. The rest of the men around the table were silent, looking confused.

Spartak pointed at the chancellor. "You did this."

The chancellor smiled. "We did this."

The room grew quiet again as they watched the news report.

Stepanov drummed his fingers on the table. "Why?"

The chancellor waved a hand at Number Five. "Spartak can answer that question."

Spartak shot a glance at Stepanov. "Brent is—was Britain's leading candidate to unseat an incumbent conservative MP. Brent was also anti-big oil, pro-environment, pro-alternative fuel, preferring regulations on the exploration, processing, and shipments of oil and natural gas. He would have tied up our takeover of Groupe PetrolTech for years. With only weeks to the election, Britain will now most likely reelect the incumbent, a man who's proven friendly to our cause in the past."

The chancellor nodded. "Very good."

Stepanov placed his hands on the table. "That's all fine and good, but how does this help us with Asimov?"

The chancellor smirked. "Just watch."

Erich Stasko fidgeted in his seat, his emotions roiling. The foremost question on his mind was whether there was a better way to assassinate an MP candidate than explode a bomb in the middle of a crowded café. The BBC coverage continued unabated on the screen, showing scenes from the disaster while first responders and officials spoke to the cameras. After twenty minutes, there were audible sighs around the table. One man tapped his pen against the wooden table top.

"Patience," the chancellor ordered.

As if on cue, the blond BBC anchorwoman came back on as the teleprompter flashed at the bottom of the screen. *BREAKING – suspect identified in the West Brompton bombing.* The chancellor thumbed a button and the volume returned.

"—we have new information in the West Brompton bombing. The London Police are reporting that they have identified the mastermind of the attack."

A picture appeared on the screen showing a tanned and handsome middle-aged man with a shaved head, strong jawline, and piercing eyes the color of obsidian. Erich sucked in his breath while excited murmurs were heard around the table.

The picture was of none other than Mikhail Asimov.

TWELVE

Biasca, Switzerland

The wooden door banged open and Arina swept into the room, anger and irritation evident on her face. Her blond hair was up in a ponytail, and she wore a flannel shirt, untucked. Max was surprised to see a firearm on her hip.

She crossed her arms and stood by the door. "I thought I told you not to follow us."

Max had never been particularly close with his sister, a fact that hadn't bothered him until he started to grow fond of her son, Alex. Alex's father was killed in the same bomb attack that killed Max and Arina's parents. There was a part of Max that wished he could be a full-time father to the boy, both to compensate for his own estranged relationship with his late father and partly to assuage Max's guilt over his decision not to raise children. Max wondered if his strained relationship with his sister was because, as he recently found out, they were half brother and sister. Max's real mother was Julia Meier, their father's longtime lover.

Maybe on some level, they both sensed they were born of different mothers.

Max took a shaky step toward his sister, careful to keep his balance from the headache-induced dizziness. "Nice to see you too, Arina."

"Why the fuck are you here?"

It pained him that their family crisis wasn't bringing him closer to his sister. "It may come as a surprise to you, Arina, but I actually care about you and Alex. I want to make sure you are okay."

Arina waved a hand at the room. "Well, now you've seen it for yourself. We're holed up in a castle with an army of soldiers, but it's better than being locked in a cabin in the middle of nowhere with a washed-up CIA agent standing guard."

Max frowned. "That washed-up CIA agent saved your life, Arina. And mine."

Arina recrossed her arms. "Well, now he doesn't have to."

"Why are you so angry? All I've done for the past four months is fight to save your life and Alex's life."

She rolled her eyes. "So typical. Just like Father."

"What's just like Father?"

Arina sneered. "Always thinking about yourself."

Max's eyes went wide. "You can't be serious."

"Don't try to pretend you don't like running all over the world hunting down this so-called consortium. You get off on the thrill, but you're blind to the fact that it will get you killed."

There it was. She cared for him. Max walked over to her and gently gripped her shoulders. "Arina, believe me, that's ridiculous. All I care about is saving our lives."

She looked him in the eye. "What I don't understand is why you suddenly care."

He let go of her shoulders. "I know I wasn't there through Mother's cancer, but I've explained that. She wasn't good to me when we were growing up, and now we know why. That's all in the past. We're all we have—the three of us. I'm here now, and I'm doing what I can to free us from whatever Father did to cause all this."

Arina looked down as a tear ran down her cheek.

"Whatever is eating at you, whatever you're angry at me for, you can tell me. If you and Alex want to stay here, that's okay with me."

She walked to the windows and looked out. "That's not it."

He followed a few steps behind but kept his distance.

She stared out the window for a long time, fidgeting with the hem of her flannel shirt, before turning back to him. "I have to tell you something."

"Okay. You can tell me anything."

"I saw Father doing something." She pulled a thread from the hem of her shirt. "I walked in on him in his study. He was reading a file. He tried to cover it up, but I saw part of the cover. It wasn't a KGB file from his office in Belarus. It wasn't a Russian file, either. It was marked confidential and had a stamp on it I didn't recognize."

"He was a spy. He used confidential files regularly. I'm sure there were many things he hid from us."

"That's what I thought, too, but I've seen my share of confidential files. My husband brought them home sometimes. This one looked different."

"Maybe it was some kind of interagency—"

"I considered that too. I'm not sure what possessed me,

but that night, after everyone was asleep, I snuck into his office. Remember he gave me the combination to the door lock? I looked for the file."

Max's eyebrows went up.

Arina waved it off. "I know, Max. I know. But he was behaving oddly. You couldn't have known. You weren't around."

"Oddly how? He was a spy. All spies behave oddly."

"You're right, of course. I don't know how to explain it. He was just more removed. Aloof. Quiet. Nervous, if that's possible to say about Father."

"I've never seen him nervous in my life."

"Me neither. That's what made it odd. Anyway, I didn't find anything. I couldn't find the file, so I opened his safe."

Max's mouth fell open. "Arina!"

"I know."

"Wait a minute. How did you open the safe?"

She turned away, but not before Max saw her face turn a light shade of pink. "I know how to open safes." She yanked another thread out of the hem of her shirt. "Max, there are some things you don't know about me."

"So I gather." Max crossed his arms. "How on earth do you know how to open a safe? I don't even know how to do that without a chunk of explosives."

She shook her head. "That's not important right now, but what I found in the safe is significant."

Max shoved his hands in his pockets and waited, wondering what on earth could be so earth-shattering.

Arina spoke in hushed tones so Max leaned in to hear her voice. "The file was in the safe. I opened the file. It was written in German."

"German?"

"Yes, but that's not all." Arina glanced at the closed door. "I also found a German code book."

"What kind of code book?"

"Like someone would use to encode messages in German. Old-fashioned, like it was used during the war."

Max became lost in thought with the information. He knew she meant World War II. "After the bombing of our house, I went down and searched his office. The safe door was hanging open, and the safe was empty. There was no file. Did you go in and clear it out?"

Arina shook her head. "No, wasn't me."

"Okay, let's come back to that. Why were you so angry at me?"

"Obviously, it made me think Father was either a double agent for the Germans or maybe he had switched sides. I was stunned and angry to think he might betray his country. When you made the same decision to defect to the States, I felt the same way. And you did it without consulting me."

Max pinched his lips with his fingers. "I didn't exactly have a choice."

"I know, but it still made me angry. And there was that awful attack on the safe house in Minsk. We had to run from the ranch in New York. The cabin in Colorado was so remote. I was scared for Alex, and it made me angry. I focused my anger on you, Max, for putting us into a more precarious position. I know it was unfair, but that's how I felt."

He took her in his arms, and she put her head on his shoulder. "I'm sorry, Max. It wasn't fair."

"It's okay. No harm done. I understand why you felt that way. I'm not here to talk you into leaving. This looks like a safe place for you and Alex."

She pulled away and turned to the window to wipe her eyes.

Max's head was spinning with the information she shared about their father. "Can I ask you one question? Actually, two?"

She nodded. "Of course."

"Did you ever confront Father with what you found?"

"No. I didn't want to anger him. You know how he could get. I forgot about it until the bombing, and it made me wonder if the two things were connected."

Max nodded. He wanted to know why she had waited this long to tell him about the file, but it felt good to be talking to his sister again so he let it go.

"What's your second question?"

"Forgive me if this is too personal, but how long have you and Victor been seeing each other?"

Arina flushed and put her hand over her mouth. "How—"

Max smiled. "It's the only logical explanation for his behavior. And yours. You look happier than I've seen you look in years. If you're happy, I'm happy."

She turned back and hugged him again, but this time she held on tight. "Thank you."

———

Max found Alex in the compound's grassy courtyard, holding a remote controller in his hand. Above his head, a small drone buzzed as it rose and fell, darting back and forth. Spike, Alex's golden retriever puppy, bounded around the field trying in vain to catch the drone.

When Alex saw Max, he dropped the remote, and the drone crashed to the ground. Spike ran to the quadcopter and sniffed at it, unsure of what to do with it now that he caught it. Alex ran over and hugged Max's waist before rescuing the drone from Spike's mouth.

"Did you get the bad guys?"

Max tussled the youngster's blond hair and gave Spike's head a scratch. "Workin' on it, Sport."

Alex showed Max the drone. "It's cool. Victor got it for me." He retrieved the remote controller from the grass where it fell.

Max knelt to watch as Alex showed him how to work the tiny joysticks. The drone came to life, spinning into the air and hovering using its four rotors, causing Spike to go berserk. A small camera hung from the drone's center.

Max clapped and shot the boy a wide smile. "Bravo! Well done, Sport. Can I give it a try?"

Alex landed the drone like a seasoned pilot before handing over the remote controller, a device with two joysticks and a small tablet attached with the screen in landscape view. Alex held Spike's collar while Max practiced launching, hovering, and landing the drone. After he got the hang of it, Max launched the drone high into the air and directed it to his left.

The castle ward was a wide-open field that looked like it was once overgrown but was recently tamed. The grass was bright green in spots, dead in others, but well manicured, as if someone had recently spent a great deal of effort to revive it. In front of Max stood a small stone building with a cross at the apex of the roof. To his left was a large keep that now served as the main residence. Around the perimeter was a thick stone wall capped with a rampart. In the center of the field, surrounded by several outbuildings, was a large tower. Smaller towers rose from the corners of the walls.

Max directed the drone to the top of the main tower.

Through the tablet's viewfinder, he saw two men with long-range rifles stationed at the top. A scope was mounted on a tripod next to one of the men. A shout went up from the guards before they realized the buzzing drone was Alex's toy. Max guided the drone to his right, surveying each tower. Two men were stationed in each, all carrying long-range rifles. He flew the drone over to the keep and peered in the windows.

Alex grabbed at the remote controller. "Hey, Victor said I'm not to disturb anyone with the drone. If anyone complains—"

"I'll take the blame." Max grinned at him. "Sometimes in life you have to beg for forgiveness instead of asking for permission."

Alex huffed and crossed his arms. "I'm going to get in trouble."

As he surveyed the rooms through the keep's windows, Max decided the toy was a handy tool. If someone ever made a silent drone, they'd have a real weapon on their hands. In one room, he saw a vast dining table surrounded by a dozen upholstered chairs, dusty and unused. In another, he saw a bed covered in a bright duvet. He flew the drone close to a third window, aiming the camera inside, and saw Victor Dedov with his back to the window talking to another man. Victor stood ramrod straight, which Max recognized as a posture he took to assert his authority over someone more junior but taller than himself. The man he was speaking with faced the window and was a head taller than Victor. The middle-aged stranger's hair was red and thinning, and his face was freckled. He wore a Harris Tweed jacket, and when he yelled and pointed at the drone, Max noticed a set of uneven yellow teeth.

Victor whirled around and leaned out the window.

"Alex! How many times do I—" He broke off when he saw Max standing in the courtyard, holding the remote controller.

Max waved, a broad smile on his face. "Sorry, still learning how to fly this thing."

Dedov didn't wave back. "Keep it away from the buildings!" He disappeared back inside and cranked the window closed.

Alex smirked. "Busted."

Max winked at him as he landed the drone at their feet. "I assume this tablet records the video output from the drone?"

"Yup. Let me show you," Alex said, grabbing the remote controller and removing the tablet. He tapped a few times and held it up so Max could see a video of Victor and the second man.

"You got Bluetooth on that thing?"

"Yup."

Max fished his phone out of his pocket, activated the Bluetooth, and deactivated the security protocols that prevented Bluetooth pairings. "Can you beam that file to my smartphone?"

Alex rolled his eyes. "Of course." He tapped a few times, and a moment later the video file was on Max's phone.

Max reactivated the phone's security and shoved it in his pocket. "Thanks, Sport. Show me your room?"

Carrying the drone and the remote controller, Alex led him into the keep and up a massive set of curved stone stairs that culminated in a wide hallway lined with ancient portraits and hulking coats of arms. Spike padded behind them.

Alex's room was large with stone walls and an oak floor covered in rugs. One half was filled with toys, as if someone had gone to a department store and filled up a cart and brought it all home. Most of the toys were still in their packaging. A large bed dominated the other half of the room, its wadded sheets covered in Star Wars imagery. The puppy curled up in a doggie bed, snout on his paws, eyes following Alex's movements.

Max walked a few paces, taking it all in. "Do you like living here?"

Alex looked at the floor and shrugged. "Mom's happier. I have to stay in the castle. Spike is bored."

"Spike liked the ranch in Colorado, didn't he?"

Alex nodded and lowered his voice. "I did too."

Max picked up an unopened box of Legos still in its shrink-wrap. "Does Victor treat you okay?"

"Aw, he's okay. But we don't hang out like you and I do."

"He cares for your mother, and that's important right now. He's going to keep you both safe."

"I get it." Alex looked straight at him when he spoke, but Max got the sense he was putting on a brave face.

"How's your schooling?"

Alex put the drone down on a table and shrugged. "It's okay." His face lit up. "I'm learning about car engines from Victor's mechanic."

Max tussled his hair. "That's great, Sport. That's a handy skill to have. Don't forget to concentrate on your schoolwork though, okay?"

"Okay, Uncle Max."

"As soon as I can round up all the bad guys, you and I can hang out a lot more, okay? Maybe we can spend some time back in Colorado."

"Okay." Alex hugged him, and Max hugged him back, hard.

Without warning, the door to Alex's room banged open, startling them. Victor Dedov stood in the doorway, his lips drawn into a deep frown.

"Max, you need to leave right now."

THIRTEEN

London, England

The scene in West Brompton went from wild chaos to controlled pandemonium in the space of fifteen minutes. The first call to 9-9-9, the United Kingdom's emergency line, came from a pedestrian who had the misfortune of seeing the whole thing from a distance. The man, a retired constable from the Metropolitan Police Service, somehow managed to keep his wits about him while dialing his flip phone with trembling hands. After the call, he rushed headlong into the carnage and stumbled about, trying to find someone to help, despairing when he found no one alive.

The first official responders arrived at the scene in a car with blue-and-yellow markings, its lights flashing. Two uniformed constables jumped out and, with typical British efficiency, searched for survivors. Soon thereafter, yellow emergency ambulances and blue-and-yellow police vans appeared one after another. As a team of constables cordoned off the street, two black luxury sedans roared up from opposite directions and were immediately waved through.

From the black Jaguar with the tinted windows stepped two fit-looking men in dark suits. They might have been twins, save for Gordon's almost feminine cherubic face and Taylor's tanned complexion. The two men walked through the wreckage, taking care to give emergency workers wide berth, talking between themselves in hushed voices. No one bothered the men from MI5, the acronym that identified the United Kingdom's domestic counter-intelligence and security agency. Everyone knew it was just a matter of time before they asserted jurisdiction over the bombing scene.

The second vehicle, a long black BMW, pulled to a halt alongside a curb. The man who exited the vehicle's rear had either been fast asleep at the time of the call or had neglected to do laundry at any time in the past fortnight. If one looked close enough, they'd see a mustard splotch on his well-worn Harris Tweed jacket and dried egg in his tangled goatee.

Those who made the mistake of misjudging Callum Baxter the first time didn't make the same mistake twice. Those who worked closely with him poked fun at the absentminded professor behind his back, but often sought out his elephant-like memory, keen deductive powers, and python-like patience for help on their operations. Baxter, deputy head of MI6 Special Operations Division, was in his position for his effectiveness, not for his ability to fit in.

Ignoring the constables, paramedics, and rescue workers, Baxter ducked under the tape and approached the two blue-suited men, subconsciously adjusting his bow tie as he walked. The two men straightened when they saw him, and one grimaced when Baxter almost kicked over an evidence flag.

Unlike most countries, whose various agencies were hamstrung by intra-agency squabbles and turf battles, the Metropolitan Police Service, MI5, and MI6 worked well together. Baxter knew it was one of the reasons Great Britain had been somewhat successful in the war against terror, and he took great pains to maintain relationships with all the agencies. He also knew this was MI5's scene, so he would behave accordingly.

"Taylor. Gordon," Baxter said by way of greeting. He shook each man's hand, matching their firm grips.

"Baxter," Taylor said. John Taylor was the lead inspector under the investigations division of MI5. Despite his young-looking eyes, he was a veteran of dozens of terror investigations, and Baxter couldn't understand how the man wasn't wrinkled and gray by now from all he had witnessed.

Baxter's eyes roamed the scene, cataloging every detail in his mind. "What are we looking at?"

Taylor let out a sigh. "Still early, but the count is up to fifty-six dead. Only three survivors in the restaurant, and those were in the kitchen at the time of the explosion. Lucky blokes. Looks like the attacker used ball bearings in the explosive. There were only a few bystanders on the sidewalk, and all of them were killed by the ball bearings."

Taylor led Baxter to the street and pointed out the attack van's route as it had approached the café. "We have footage of the van from CCTV. Still too early to tell, but we're guessing the bomb was made from ammonium nitrate and nitromethane."

Baxter pointed at the burned-out hulk of the limousine sitting in the middle of the road, where it had fallen like the husk of a dead beetle. "And this?"

John Taylor crossed his arms. "Still working on it."

Baxter walked to the scorched shell, avoiding a

uniformed technician setting small flags near the locations of human remains. He ignored the overpowering scent of burned flesh and scorched metal. The limousine's metal exoskeleton was largely intact, but the paint had been blistered off, all its windows had disintegrated, and the rubber tires had melted from their rims. The front, which had taken the brunt of the blast, was mangled like it had been hit by a runaway freight train. He noticed the rear door was missing, making him think it was open at the time of the blast.

Baxter stooped to look inside. A charred headless carcass he assumed was the driver lay at an awkward angle in the front seat, and the rear compartment was empty of human remains.

———

It was another twenty minutes before the alert went out that the limousine occupant was none other than Zachary Brent, the Labour party's leading candidate for a parliamentary post and the man who was labeled by the British tabloids as Great Britain's most eligible bachelor. Brent, heir to the de Walden real estate fortune, former captain in Britain's Royal Navy, and a self-made man himself after the successful public offering of his technology company, had decided to leave corporate life at the young age of thirty-six to enter politics. As an outsider, and a handsome one at that, Brent quickly ascended on a liberal platform of reform and anti-corruption. His wide smile of bright-white teeth dazzled women everywhere as his muscular hands smoothed errant hairs on baby's heads. With men, he talked football over pints of the local lager and promised to fight for the working class. The tabloids were, of course, rife with gossip about his bachelorhood and eligibility, speculating on suitable brides for such a man on the rise.

Baxter got the news as he squatted near the front passenger side of the burned-out limousine, examining a chunk of leather that looked like it might have been a brief-case or shoulder bag. He snapped a few pictures of the item on his mobile phone while Taylor gave him the update.

Baxter's eyes roamed the carcass of the limousine. "Anyone claim responsibility yet?"

Taylor hunched over next to Baxter. "Just the usual crackpots. Nothing official. What are you thinking? Just a coincidence Brent was in the wrong place at the wrong time?"

Baxter hated to speculate, especially out loud. He listened to facts, but he followed his gut. "Too early to tell, but you know what they say about coincidences."

Taylor stood and surveyed the scene of the massacre. "Right."

———

Baxter remained at the scene for several hours. He was stepping through the interior of the café alongside John Taylor when the story broke that the bomber had been identified. Their pockets buzzed simultaneously, and each man reached for their phone with fear in their throats that another bombing had occurred. Instead, they were informed that the BBC was reporting that an ex-KGB man from Belarus was the mastermind behind the bombing.

Taylor snapped his phone shut and tossed it from hand to hand while he pursed his lips. Baxter shot Taylor a glance, his eyebrows knit together, before using the browser on his Blackberry to search for the BBC article. Instead of finding a BBC exclusive, he found dozens of news reports claiming the mastermind of the attack was a former KGB agent named Mikhail Asimov.

He stopped on a Telegraph article and read it three times. The news report stated that details were sparse, pending confirmation from authorities. Next to a headline that screamed TERRORIST IDENTIFIED was the faded picture of the perpetrator. He was handsome, with angular features, high cheekbones, proportioned nose, and full lips. But his eyes startled Baxter. They appeared frozen, ice-black, like the eyes of a demon. Baxter showed the article to John Taylor.

Taylor punched digits into his phone. "Last I checked, I was the lead on this investigation. As far as I know, I'm not being asked to confirm anything. What the bugger is going on?"

Baxter zoomed in on the photo until the man's eyes were as large as the phone's tiny screen could show. Despite the apparent age of the photograph, Baxter recognized the man in the picture. The realization sent an ice-cold chill down his spine and caused his hand to tremble.

———

TERRORIST IDENTIFIED, The Telegraph

LONDON – The Monarchy can rest a little easier tonight after the man responsible for killing MP Labour candidate Zachary Brent, along with fifty-six other men, women, and children in West Brompton just hours ago has been identified. A spokesman from MI5 has confirmed the name of the killer is one Mikhail Asimov. Asimov, a Belarusian national and a former KGB hit man, is thought to have recently gone into business for himself, selling himself to the highest bidder.

Asimov, confirmed as the mastermind of the attack, has a checkered past. The son of Belarus's famous spymaster Andrei Asimov, records show he was enrolled at Suvorov Military school in Minsk and graduated at the age of seventeen. Asimov then entered the Russian military as a junior lieutenant, performing tours in Afghanistan, Georgia, and the Caucasus Mountains and earned the rank of major before his induction into the KGB's Yuri Andropov Red Banner Institute. Asimov excelled there as a student, winning awards in marksmanship, receiving high praise from his instructors, and graduated at the top of his class. After the institute, Asimov was provided extensive 'westernization training' and subsequently stationed in Paris as a so-called sleeper agent.

Here Asimov's history turns blurry, although investigators believe this was when he went into private practice for himself, performing assassinations for cash payments. Using skills taught to him by the KGB, Asimov penetrated his target's defenses with ease and killed for the highest bidder. The deaths of media mogul Phillip Montfort, prominent Brussels attorney Arne Lambert, and even Konstantin Koskov, a colonel in the Russian army, have all been linked to Asimov. In all, over twenty deaths across both Western and Eastern Europe are attributed to Asimov's hand, making him one of the most prolific assassins of the twenty-first century.

Scotland Yard, MI5, and MI6 are jointly operating one of the modern world's largest manhunts to apprehend Asimov. Not since the search for Osama bin Laden has there been such a coordinated effort across dozens of Western intelligence agencies. According to an MI5 spokesman who wished to remain anonymous, sightings of the attacker are pouring in across the UK. "It's only a matter of time before we bring him in," he told this reporter in confidence. Authorities are offering a reward of one million pounds for information leading to the fugitive's capture.

Meanwhile, Central London can sleep more soundly knowing a deadly assassin is unmasked and will soon be brought to justice.

FOURTEEN

London, England

Callum Baxter enjoyed few vices and even fewer habits. Most women regarded him as a man with no redeeming qualities. He refused to exercise, ate what he wanted, and enjoyed a pint or three every evening, but somehow managed to stay a lean seventy-two kilograms. He hated wasting time on doctors and dentists, so he seldom went. Time spent on personal care was time away from his job.

Baxter's one indulgence, a holdover from when his mother spent her last years under his roof, was the employment of a young housekeeper named Eve. She did the shopping, the cooking, the cleaning, and paid the bills. He grudgingly admitted he would be lost without her. Still, there was one area of his home she was forbidden to enter.

A gentle drizzle fell as Baxter pushed through the door from the garage into the mudroom. He hastened through the kitchen in a beeline for the backdoor, trying to make the exit before Eve caught wind of his arrival.

"Callum!" a melodic voice rang out. "I just mopped the floors. Please remove your—"

He pushed the back door open and disappeared into the tiny yard without a backward glance. Baxter's house, a centuries-old brick Tudor covered in vines, had been in his family for generations. He spent no time thinking about what would become of it upon his death. The backyard was fenced and somehow manicured—Baxter had caught wind of Eve hiring a gardener of some sort—with flowering shrubbery, a patch of rose bushes, a towering red oak, and a few plum trees, the fruits from which Baxter nibbled on as he wandered the back yard, lost in thought about one operation or another.

Nestled among the rose bushes and thick cherry trees full of fruit was a tiny outbuilding that Baxter built when his late mother moved in with him years ago. It was only twenty meters square, but the cozy room had a desk, a chair, and most important, a worn leather couch that was perfect for naps. He used a key to unlock the door, tromped in, hung his duckbill on a hook, and tossed his mackintosh on a coat tree before heading for the desk. After pounding on the space bar to wake his laptop, he used Google to find the picture of the terrorist from The Telegraph news article. Another tap and the color printer came to life.

While the printer whirred and chunked, he turned to a bank of filing cabinets along one wall. Callum Baxter had no hobbies, aside for his famous long ramblings through the English countryside. He had no interest in bird watching, gardening, shooting, or any of the other distinctly British pastimes. He called them "wasted times." The one exception was his fascination with collecting materials and assembling files on assassinations.

His obsession began with the killing of the American

President John F. Kennedy, the assassination that had shocked the world. Baxter was six years old at the time, but the event shaped his life. One entire four-drawer filing cabinet was devoted to that case. Had he written a book on the topic, Callum Baxter would be regarded as one of the world's foremost experts on the event and the succession of conspiracy theories that followed. Baxter thought the idea was ludicrous that a US Marine radar operator with an old bolt-action Carcano rifle could make the shot that killed the US President. But like the rest of the researchers focused on the case, he couldn't produce a viable alternative theory. The other three cabinets were devoted to other assassination cases, some solved, many not. A bookcase to his left held rows of volumes dedicated to famous assassins in history: John Wilkes Booth, the Jackal, Gavrilo Princip, and, perhaps the most famous assassin in history, Marcus Julius Brutus.

He yanked out a drawer to rifle through a mess of manila folders before slamming the drawer shut. After yanking another drawer open, he pawed through more files and let out a grunt of satisfaction as he withdrew a large dossier. He shoved aside stacks of files and piles of books and dumped the contents out on the desk. After leafing through them, he yanked out a large glossy photograph. It was black and white, grainy, and yellowed with age. The photo was taken from afar, and the subject was walking along an unidentified street. Paper-clipped to the photo was an enlarged and cropped copy of a picture centered on the man's face. Baxter stuck the close-up to the wall with a pin.

For years, Baxter had collected evidence of a mysterious assassin who operated across Europe. He spent much of his free time combing through police and agency files of unsolved killings going back a decade or more. The evidence he found was thin, and if pressed, he admitted it was all theory and conjecture. Many at MI6 chuckled and teased him for his hobby. "Chasing ghosts," they said. "Reading too many spy novels," they chided.

But Baxter knew someone, or some group, was killing with impunity throughout the European Union. That much was indisputable. The list of unsolved assassinations was as long as his arm. Baxter maintained a painstaking list of unsolved murder and assassination cases on his computer and regularly printed it to stick on his wall. A corrupt Italian politician back in 1998. A mob boss on the island of Capri in 2001. A billionaire businessman in Athens in 2002. A terrorist recruiter in Rome in 2013, quickly followed by a disgraced and ruined media mogul in Paris. The methods of killing varied, but most consisted of two shots from a .22—one to the head, one to the heart. The bullets were all 124 grain and Federal HST jackets, one of the most common munitions available on the world market.

He pinned the picture from The Telegraph article next to the one from his file and stared, focusing on the cheek bones, the distance between the eye sockets, and the shape of the chin. Both men had clean faces with shaved heads. The picture from the file was black and white, so the man's eye color couldn't be determined. Baxter rummaged in the pile again and emerged with a third picture. This was a color headshot of a handsome young man in a Russian military uniform, looking directly at the camera. Baxter pinned it to the wall next to the others and compared the three. In all of them, the same piercing eyes stared back at him. They were eyes that always made him shiver.

After staring at the three images for a spell, he found his pipe, filled it with McClelland Blue Mountain, and lit the leaves with a wooden match. He blew a plume of the sweet smoke into the air and resumed his examination of the three pictures as an unrelenting rain pattered against the shingles overhead.

By the time he finished the pipe, he was convinced. A tiny smile crept across his face as he refilled the bowl.

He turned to the computer and printed all the articles he could find accusing Mikhail Asimov of the West Brompton bombing. By the time he quit, hundreds of printed pages sat on his desk, and those barely scratched the surface of the articles populating the internet.

As he paged through the stack of articles, a gentle tap sounded at the door. Baxter jumped up and opened it to find a wet and disheveled Eve holding a tea service. She entered, set the tray down on the desk, and turned to exit.

"Bless your heart, my dear," Baxter said, closing the door behind her. He balanced a tea cup brimming with steaming Earl Grey in his hand while munching a digestive biscuit and staring at the pictures of the ruthless assassin pinned to his wall.

"Hello, Mikhail Asimov."

FIFTEEN

Zürich, Switzerland

The sprinter van rolled through the outskirts of Zürich, driven by a taciturn and nervous young man with both hands clenched on the wheel. Despite the cars roaring by, some blasting their horns, he stayed under the speed limit, scared they might be hit by a careless driver. Another young man set next to him in the passenger seat hunched over with his eyes glued to the road and ignoring the glittering blue lake to his right. Whenever he saw an orange-and-white Swiss police car, he muttered "Polizei" loud enough for the driver to hear.

A third young man sat in the rear seat. His eyes darted out the rear, on the lookout for more police. The three men wore identical uniforms of black T-shirts and black tactical pants with black ball caps. Each wore a sidearm, fully licensed and approved by the Swiss government.

The three men were elite members of Victor Dedov's personal security team, and each had received extensive training during Victor's stint as head of the Belarusian KGB. Despite their field experience, all three security men's nerves were frayed to the point of panic after the two-hour drive to Zürich.

Their passenger sat statue-like on the rear bench seat, neither talking nor looking around. He wore a black leather jacket, blue jeans, and motorcycle boots.

The driver bore down, taking comfort in the fact that they were almost rid of their passenger. Transporting the most wanted man in the world was not something he cared to repeat, even if his boss had reassured them countless times the man was falsely accused.

If their passenger felt any hint of discomfort due to the worldwide manhunt of which he was the sole query, he didn't show it. He steepled his hands in front of him and maintained a passive expression, his eyes narrowed to slits. Occasionally he removed an expensive-looking smartphone from his pocket, looked at the screen as if expecting a message, and pocketed the device again. Never once did his icy-black eyes look upon one of the other men in the van.

The guard in the back seat wondered why a man who was wanted by half the world's police, a man with a price on his head of one million British pounds, would take the chance of having his mobile phone tracked. The guard's mind wandered to how he might spend one third of a million British pounds if he could somehow convince the two men in front to join him in turning their charge over to the police. Someone was going to collect the money, and it might as well be them. Let the police sort out whether the man is innocent or guilty.

The van turned into a subterranean parking garage and came to a halt in a section empty of cars. The tall man with the eyes of black ice pulled on a baseball cap and donned a pair of wraparound shades. Without a word, he opened the side door and disappeared into the darkness of the garage. As the door slammed shut, all three men gave an audible sigh of relief. The team leader typed a text message.

The package has been delivered.

————

Max read through a stack of newspapers, his anger building until he had to shove the pile aside. Most of his life had been spent living in the shadows, maintaining a fake public persona to obfuscate his true identity. His jazz club, the taxes he paid on the income generated by the club, the mortgage on his flat in Paris. All those things were a front to keep his real name hidden, a secret. Now his name and face were plastered on every newspaper and social media website on the planet. Every Joe Public was reading the paper with their morning breakfast, looking at his face with hatred and fear.

The worst part wasn't that he was framed or that his identity was outed. The worst part was that the world was looking at his picture and associating him with a dreadful atrocity that had killed fifty-six people along with one of Great Britain's promising new MPs.

Julia sat down across the table and sipped hot coffee. "You have to admit it was well played. Now every security camera, every immigration official—heck, every citizen—will be on the lookout for your face. Intelligence teams everywhere have programmed that picture into their systems. The minute a security camera focuses on you, its facial recognition technology will kick in and you'll be flagged. Maybe you should lay low for a while."

They were sitting in the kitchen of Julia's Barcelona

safe house, a half-eaten continental breakfast on the table. Max had to admit she was right.

She tore off a piece of a croissant. "How did you get here without triggering alarms, anyway?"

Max winked at her. "Sources and methods."

Julia rolled her eyes. "As long as you weren't followed. This house holds a special place in my heart."

"No way I was followed. Besides, Spain's CCTV system is horrible. What do you think about plastic surgery?"

Julia stuck the flaky pastry in her mouth, chewed, and swallowed. "That's an option." Outside the window, a pale morning sun warmed the tangled branches in the vineyard. "Problem is facial recognition technology focuses on things like the structure of your face, the distance between your eyes, the proportions of your features. The algorithm assigns a likelihood and alerts a human when that threshold is reached. Plastic surgery might not help."

"I can't lay low," Max said. "I've got shit to do."

"What if we finish off your list by proxy?"

"You mean hire someone to carry out the rest of the hits?"

Julia stirred sugar into her coffee. "Exactly."

"You know anyone?"

She shrugged. "No one as good as you. But if we provide the intel and the plans, I'm sure we could find someone to pull off the hits—for the right price."

Max stood and helped himself to an apple. "I'd still be a wanted man. Even if we kill them all, we may never be able to prove that I wasn't the bomber. I'll be in hiding the rest of my life."

Julia rose from the table and examined her fingernails as she paced. "Right. So, what's your plan?"

Max used a tactical knife to cut a chunk from the apple. "I need to find out who was really behind the attack. People will quickly forget about me once the truth comes out."

Julia wrinkled her nose. "That could take a while, and it has no guarantee of working."

"Better than laying low while every intelligence service in the world looks for me." He munched on an apple slice.

Julia set her coffee down and walked out of the kitchen. Max spooned instant coffee into a mug and added hot water from the kettle. A film of oil rose to the surface as he stirred the drink. He sipped and grimaced. Bitter and weak. He spooned another mound of crystals into the mug and stirred before sipping again. Now it was just bitter. As he sat back down at the table, Julia reappeared and tossed a thick folder onto the table.

The file was held together with three rubber bands and marked with the German words *streng geheim.* Top secret. Seeing the cover of the file made him think of his conversation with Arina. *Was he picking up where his father left off?* He didn't touch the file. "What's this?"

Julia picked up her coffee mug. "Your next target on the consortium list."

Max's eyes narrowed. "I think it's time you told me who you work for. You obviously have a team somewhere, maybe Germany, maybe Austria. Maybe Switzerland. You've provided them the list, and they are assembling case files for you. Maybe with the intent that you'll pass them along to me. I'd like to know who I'm working for."

Julia sat and tore another piece of the croissant. "Consider it your first lead. You want to find out who planted that bomb and who is framing you. I agree. Start with the consortium, the ones most likely to have framed you."

Max glanced at the dossier. It was over an inch thick,

with dog-eared pages and a tattered cover. This case file hadn't been assembled recently—it had been around for a while. He removed the rubber bands and flipped open the cover. Sitting on top of the stack was an 8x10 glossy of a man in his late thirties, maybe early forties, pale skinned, straw-colored hair, blue eyes, wearing a suit with a European cut. Max didn't recognize him.

Julia leaned over to look at the photo. "Meet Erich Stasko."

Erich Stasko was the twelfth man on the consortium list.

Julia leaned back. "Stasko is the richest man in Latvia. He owns the largest bank syndicate in Europe outside Switzerland. Latvia joined the EU back in 2013 and has one bank for every hundred citizens. They're on a path to becoming a northern version of Switzerland. Stasko's job is to launder the consortium's money, funneling it between Russia and the European Union. Find him. Interrogate him. Follow the money. It'll lead you to the man who planned the attack in London."

Max pulled the file closer and leafed through the thick stack of papers. It took several more cups of the bad coffee and half a pack of cigarettes before he made it through a first scan. After he read through the material a second time, he closed the file and leaned back in his chair.

"If I didn't know better, I might think you've had the list of consortium members for a while. This file is very thorough. How many more files of this depth do you have on these guys?"

Julia examined her nails.

"It's not going to work, keeping me in the dark like this." Max tapped the top of the file. "I know you and my father were working together. Either he was running you or maybe you were running him."

By running, Max meant controlling. The other phrase for it was source handling. An agent of an intelligent service, known as the source handler, worked to recruit foreign agents who he or she then ran, or handled. If Julia was working for a foreign agency, she could have seduced his father and convinced him to spy for her service. It happens all the time. Max just didn't think it could happen to his father.

Julia retrieved a packet of cigarettes from a handbag on the counter. She tapped one out and waved it at Max. He dug into his pocket and retrieved his grandfather's lighter with the Belarusian flag, snapped it open, and held a flame to the end. She inhaled deep before slowly letting it out.

Max tapped the dossier on the table again. "I know my father had a file in his possession at our house, written in German—probably identical to this one. By the time the house was bombed, the file was gone."

Julia took another drag, her face stoic.

Max flicked open the lighter and snapped it shut with a clang. "I'm guessing you work for the BND, given the scope of the consortium's influence. The Swiss tend to stay at home, and the Austrians are so secretive they're unlikely to utilize an outsider like me or my father, especially a former KGB agent. Is that it, Julia? You work for the Germans?" BND was the acronym for the German Federal Intelligence Service.

Julia used a coffee mug as an ashtray and let out a deep sigh. "You are, of course, correct. And you do deserve the truth. Unfortunately, as with most things in our business, I can only give you part of it."

Max reached for his pack of cigarettes.

Julia dropped the butt of her cigarette into the coffee mug. "I work for the BND. I used to be the assistant director on the Soviet desk. When the Soviet Union fell apart, I was diverted to a special task force under the auspices of the Directorate GU—the group that runs human intelligence. The task force is off the books."

Max used his grandfather's Zippo to light the end of a cigarette which he handed to Julia, who took it between two manicured fingers. "What's the mandate of the task force?"

Julia took a pull. "That's a good question, and it requires a much longer conversation."

Max lit his own cigarette. "Give me the short version."

Julia cleared her throat. "The consortium."

Max avoided her eyes. He wasn't sure which emotion would dominate—anger stemming from the fact she'd held out all this time or relief at hearing he might have an ally.

Julia crossed her free arm across her chest and flicked ashes into the mug. "I know what you're thinking. I had my reasons for keeping you in the dark."

Max studied the ceiling. "Someone recently told me that blood is thicker than water."

"Your appearance in Zurich was a shock, to say the least. You were never supposed to find out about me. That was the deal your father and I had."

Max tossed the stale cigarette into the mug where it fizzled out in the cold coffee. "Sorry to intrude on your plans."

Julia took another long draw on her cigarette. "You should know that your father came to us, Max. We didn't recruit him. He did what he did because he felt it was the right thing for Belarus and the Soviet Union. He firmly believed the consortium was bad for Russia, and by extension, Belarus."

Max's eyebrows went up. "The consortium has been around that long?"

Julia nodded and caught his eye. "Until the collapse of the Soviet Union, it was only a marginal threat. Your father and I met back in the early seventies after he uncovered the group and recognized the threat it posed. He thought, and we agreed, that sharing information about the consortium would be helpful. At the time, we put them on a watch list and did little else. We leveraged your father for the collection of intel, which he willingly provided. In a sense, I ran him, but it was more like a partnership. There was little threat to either side since he wasn't providing us with Soviet state secrets. Not that we didn't try, and not that he wouldn't have been drawn and quartered had the Kremlin found out."

She dropped her cigarette into the coffee mug and stood. Before she turned to the stove, he saw moisture in her eyes. "We had electricity between us from the beginning, and then you happened." She let out a throaty chuckle. As she fussed with the coffee pot on the stove, Max saw her brush at something on her cheek.

Max rose and stood beside her at the stove. "I have a lot of questions, Julia."

Julia turned away from him, walked to the other end of the kitchen, and leaned on the counter. "I'm sure you do. But before you start firing away, there's a story about your father you need to hear."

SIXTEEN

London, England

Callum Baxter sat with his feet up on a table in the corner of a makeshift operations room at Vauxhall Cross, MI6's hulking headquarters. The modernist structure overlooked the River Thames, spitting distance from the Vauxhall bridge and only ten minutes from Baxter's house. He didn't understand how people sat in traffic for hours or crammed themselves in the tube just to get to their homes in the suburbs. While he hated the pomp of being driven around in a garish luxury sedan, he admitted it afforded him more time to work.

The former spill-over cafeteria was jammed with folding tables and filled with every junior analyst, secretary, and mail room clerk available. Each manned a telephone and a laptop computer, fielding calls, emails, and surveying social media, culling through massive amounts of information, searching for a needle in a haystack. It seemed as if everyone and their mother had either seen the accused bombing mastermind or knew someone who had. The junior staffers' main job was to perform the first filter of the information and pass anything promising along to a senior agent, who would then follow up on the lead. Anything local was passed along to MI5, and anything international was handled by MI6. So far, sightings were coming in as near as Soho and as far as Okinawa, Japan. Several people in New York City reported sightings in and around Central Park, and John Taylor was working with his friends at the FBI to chase down those leads. In all, Great Britain had assembled the largest team of investigators since the central London bombings in July of 2006 that killed fifty-six and injured 700. Unless Asimov had gone deep underground, Baxter was confident they would find him. It was just a matter of time.

"Sir!" A young woman craned her neck to look at Baxter. She was one of the agency's most junior analysts, and Callum had no idea of her name. "I think I've got something."

With resignation, Callum let his feet hit the floor and shuffled over to her table. A cup of tea sat next to the woman's laptop. She pushed her horn-rimmed glasses up on her small nose.

Baxter hunched over her shoulder and tried to avoid looking down her sweater. "What's your name, hun?"

"Cindy, sir."

"Cindy what?"

Cindy Wallace, sir."

Baxter nodded in approval. "Okay, Cindy. What have you got?"

Her voice quivered. "I was going through the calls to the hotline. Callers can dial a number and leave a recording—"

"I'm familiar," Callum said, using his best grandfatherly voice.

"Oh, of course, sir. Sorry."

He longed to walk outside and take a few puffs on his pipe. The day they restricted smoking inside Vauxhall Cross was a dark day. "Go on."

Cindy pointed to her screen. "I've been listening to the voice files. I can just click them in the folder structure like this—"

Callum cleared his throat. His reputation among staffers for struggling with technology was self-inflicted and exaggerated.

Cindy flushed, but powered on. "Anyway, there was a caller who left a message in French, which I'm fluent in. I took it in school and spent a few semesters studying in Paris. Such an amazing city." She smiled at Callum, causing him to lose his train of thought.

He plunked himself into a chair and tried to pay attention. "Keep going."

"The caller claims to have seen a man resembling Asimov climb aboard a boat."

Callum looked around the room, hoping someone else might need his attention. "Indeed. Where?"

"Genoa, Italy."

Finding no one else in need of his help, Callum let out a sigh. "Did the caller leave the name of the boat?"

"Well, yes. But that's not the interesting part."

Callum raised his bushy eyebrows. "Well, go on, young lady. What is the interesting part?"

Cindy shifted, crossing her legs and smoothing down her skirt. "The man boarded the ship at around 2:00 am the night before the boat was due to leave port. The caller couldn't sleep and was up roaming the deck. After boarding, the man disappeared. The caller, who identified himself as the ship's first mate, never saw the stranger again."

Callum leaned forward, forearms on his knees. "What is the name of the boat?"

"It's the Renée, out of Marseille."

"Kind?"

Cindy cocked her head. "Pardon me?"

Callum's sixth sense had started buzzing. "What kind of boat was she? Freighter? Pleasure craft?"

Cindy's face brightened. "The caller didn't say, but I looked it up. She's a sixty-meter rear trawler."

Callum nodded. "Decent-sized boat. What was her destination?"

"Barcelona. The caller, who said he knew one of the bombing victims and seemed quite upset, described the mystery man as well over six feet tall, a shaved head, muscular. The boat docked in Barcelona, took on supplies, and returned to Marseille. I cross-checked the boat's manifest with the ports of call and confirmed the boat's route."

Baxter leaned back in the chair, his fingers probing and tugging his unkempt goatee. The man in question either departed the ship in Barcelona, or perhaps the trawler was met by another boat before reaching dock.

He stood and patted Cindy on the shoulder. "Great work." Remembering that touching a female associate was now frowned upon in the modern MI6, he pulled his hand away and reached for his mobile phone. He got John Taylor on the first ring. "We got a live one. Who do you have in Barcelona?"

Out of the side of his mouth, Baxter said to Cindy, "Pack up. You're coming with me."

It took Baxter and Cindy twenty-five minutes to navigate the heavy traffic along the five-kilometer route from Vauxhall Cross to the elegant neoclassical building that housed Thames House, the headquarters of MI5. Baxter was on his mobile phone the entire time, barking orders and listening intently while ignoring Cindy. She sat with her hands primly holding her computer on her lap while the driver stopped and started in the traffic and muttered curses under his breath.

The large security service operations room assigned to the case was teeming with people. Andrew Phillips, the Director General of MI5, the man on whose narrow shoulders rested the security of the constitutional monarchy, paced on a raised dais at the rear of the room. Phillips, a man who commanded deep respect among his staff, looked stooped, tired, and embattled. He wore a wireless headset and barked orders like a rabid dog, constantly pushing up his rimless spectacles. There was no doubt who was in charge of this operation, and no doubt on whose neck the ax would fall if the crime went unpunished. Phillips would not sleep until the perpetrator of this vile and heinous crime against the British people was put away for life.

Baxter parked Cindy at a table in the back and scanned the room for John Taylor. The octagonal room's walls were covered floor to ceiling with monitors. Along the left wall were images of the burned-out limousine and the crater where the café had once stood, smoke still swirling from the ashes. Another screen showed a newsfeed from the BBC. A group of men were huddled around yet another screen showing a picture of a green van with vegetables printed on the side. Baxter knew it wouldn't be long before they traced the truck and they had leads on the identity of the driver.

On the large screen at the front of the room was an enormous picture of Mikhail Asimov. In red text across the bottom were the words £1M *Reward for information leading to the capture of one Mikhail Asimov*. On another wall were various pictures of the Renée taken while underway and docked that Taylor's team had printed while Baxter and Cindy were in transit. Another monitor showed headshots of the boat's roster: the captain, first mate, and three crewmen. All attention was focused on the ship's captain, the one man who could enable a mystery guest to stow away on his ship and arrange for that man to disembark at an uncharted location.

Taylor's voice rang out over the din. "We've got the captain." Spotting Baxter, the MI5 agent walked over as he yelled, "DGSI has him in an interview room in Marseille." The DGSI was one of France's intelligence agencies. A video feed blinked on another large monitor showing an overweight man with a shaggy beard and soiled white T-shirt sitting on a chair in a tiny room.

Baxter introduced Cindy to John Taylor. "This is the gal who broke the lead on the ship. Figured she should at least see how all this goes down."

Taylor shook her hand enthusiastically, apologized for the chaos, and offered tea, which she declined, before guiding Baxter away from the girl.

Taylor put a hand on Baxter's shoulder, drawing him close. "Talked with Anne Bishop, deputy director general of the BBC a few minutes ago. She said one of their senior UK editors received a packet by courier fifteen minutes after the bomb went off. The packet contained an extensive dossier on Asimov as well as information specific to the attack, including the time, configuration of the bomb, and other details."

Baxter tugged at his goatee. "Don't they require confirmation of a second source before they run a story?"

"She said by the time they consumed the information, multiple news sources were already running the story. The internet was saturated, so they had no choice but to feed on the chum."

"Did they get confirmation later?"

Taylor let go of Baxter's shoulder and shoved his hands into his suit pant pockets. "She said they've been inundated with details from multiple sources. We've tried to the trace the sources but have turned up empty. Something stinks about this, Callum."

Baxter tugged at his goatee. "It's too easy. News travels fast these days, but not this fast." He yanked harder on his beard until a thought popped into his head. "You know what bots are, John?"

Taylor shook his head.

"It's internet technology that can automatically spread news or other content through email, social media, blogs, and other outlets."

Taylor pinched his lips with a thumb and forefinger. "Like a search spider, like Google uses to index web pages?"

"Exactly, only these bots can multiply and spread content. The bots can even apply thousands of likes to a post, causing the social media algorithms to think it's a popular post, duping them into replicating the content even more. It's a vicious circle, and it's all automatic."

Taylor shot him a sideways glance. "I thought you didn't know anything about technology?"

Baxter winked. "That's what I want people to think."

Taylor laughed. "I'll get the tech boys to jump on that

idea. Maybe they can trace the source and figure out who's behind the mass proliferation of this story."

Baxter grinned. "I believe the Americans call it fake news."

It only took fifteen minutes for the Renée's captain to break under interrogation, and soon the Spanish CNI were swarming the beaches along the coast south of Barcelona in search of the ship's mystery passenger. It took another hour for them to uncover a Zodiac hidden under a tarp five kilometers north of the beach resort town of Sitges, Spain. Despite the prolonged and stressful interrogation, the captain was steadfast in his assertion that he didn't know the man's name. All he knew was the time and date of the pickup and the time and date of the departure. Money was wired to him at a numbered account. The captain was unable to provide any other useful information.

In another hour, MI5 had a short list of stolen vehicles and soon thereafter, a grainy image of a tall man astride a motorcycle on the C-32 highway was found on a CCTV camera server. The image was blown up and put on a monitor next to the image of Asimov's face.

After that, mysteriously, the trail vanished. Phillips was heard barking on the phone to his Spanish counterpart, spewing a long string of expletives before hurling the headset to the ground. "Fucking Spaniards. Can't even implement a camera system that functions."

Baxter couldn't help but smile. It was common knowledge in the intelligence and law enforcement communities that various government and civilian factions in Spain, citing privacy concerns, resisted the implementation of a networked security camera system similar to other European countries. They were years behind even the Swiss.

Gradually, the din in the operations room died down and activity slowed as lead after lead grew cold. The grocery delivery van was stolen from a fenced lot two weeks before the bombing and wasn't seen until it was flying along Cranley Gardens in West Brompton on the morning of the bombing. There were no leads on the identity of the van's driver. Asimov had disappeared into the Spanish countryside.

As the investigation slowed to a snail's pace, investigators continued to work the phones and constables walked the streets. The Spanish CNI scoured the countryside around Barcelona. Known radical extremist cells were shaken down, informants were rousted and interrogated, neighborhoods were canvased. MI5 and MI6 computer forensics teams attempted to follow the trail of the fake news stories through the murky depths of the darknet. Mobile phone databases were searched, mugshots were examined by the few witnesses, and the machinery of police activity plodded ahead.

Baxter knew it was only a matter of time before another lead surfaced. Investigations were long hours of drudgery punctuated by moments of minor epiphany. He reached out to pat Cindy's hand, but withdrew and gave her a wink instead. She gave him a winning smile in return, before going to find them both some tea.

SEVENTEEN

Muntanyes d'Ordal, Spain

"Let's go for a walk."

Julia led Max out to the wooden deck that encircled the tiny cabin and down the steps to the vineyard. The fresh air felt good after the long hours of bad coffee and cigarettes. Two of Julia's bodyguards followed at a safe distance, both wearing fatigues and carrying automatic weapons. Their heads, eyes covered by wraparound shades, swiveled like robots while looking for any sign of danger. The sun was up and burning off the morning haze. As they started down a row of vines, their feet sank into soft earth.

Julia threaded her arm into the crook of Max's elbow. "If your father were here, he would tell the story much better. What I'm about to relate is from memory and is all secondhand from him. He was there, but it was before I met him."

"What year was this?"

"It started in the late sixties. The cold war was in full

force. Many people don't realize it, but the cold war officially started not long after World War II. The Russians resented that the Americans delayed getting into the war, which they believed caused the deaths of tens of millions of Russians. The Americans didn't trust communism and didn't like Stalin's violent tyranny over his own people."

Max nodded. "Can't say I blame them."

"By the time this story starts, the Russians had already put Gagarin in space. I think that was in '61. The race for nukes was underway. The Bay of Pigs had happened. The Vietnam war had started, with the Americans fighting desperately to curtail the advance of communism in Asia. Kennedy was shot, some would say through a Russian or Russian-Cuban conspiracy. It was a tense time for everyone."

She paused to stoop and pick up a handful of dirt, letting it sift through her fingers.

"As you know, Russia played a crucial support role for North Vietnam in the war. They sent medical supplies and a lot of weaponry. They provided training and strategic support to the National Liberation Front, and by some estimates, there were over twenty thousand Russians in Vietnam during the conflict."

Max wondered where she was going with all of this.

She took his arm again as they continued along the row of vines. "You probably don't know this, but your father was in Vietnam during the war."

Max's eyebrows went up, but he remained silent.

"The KGB spent a lot of time interrogating American POWs. The GRU did as well." She was referring to Russia's military intelligence directorate. "But the GRU was interested in troop movements, weapons stocks, procedures, that kind of thing, whereas the KGB was interested in converting American POWs to be spies. Your father spent over a year in Vietnam in the late '60's attempting to do just that. After the Russians realized it was a futile endeavor, he and the others were sent home."

Max let a hand trail along the vines, feeling the silky texture of the leaves. "Let me guess. The program wasn't entirely a failure."

Julia nodded. "Right, except not as you might expect. What most people forget is that the French occupied Indochina prior to the Vietnam war. Indochina was a region that now consists of Cambodia, Laos, and Vietnam. Sometime around 1954, the French were defeated by a group of communist-backed revolutionaries called the Viet Minh. This was the final straw for the French. They pulled out, leaving the Americans holding the bag. Incidentally, this was effectively the beginning of the Vietnam War for the Americans."

Max stayed silent.

"As you might expect, the French left behind several hundred POWs in the north. Your father, who was fluent in French, was assigned to interrogate the prisoners. He was quite a linguist, your father. Probably where you got it from."

Max grunted, waiting for her to connect the dots.

"One of the men your father interrogated was a young French soldier by the name of Fabron. Name ring a bell?"

Max shot her a sideways glance. "Last name?"

"Last name."

Max shook his head. "Nope."

"I'm surprised. Your father recruited only one spy during his time in Vietnam. To the KGB's annoyance, it was a Frenchman, not an American. Later, it turns out, they were not so annoyed."

"Go on."

"Jules Fabron was the son of Raymond Fabron. How about that name?"

Max shook his head again. "Sorry."

"Raymond Fabron started an oil company after World War I together with the French government, who thought, rightly so, that controlling oil would be crucial if they found themselves in a war with Germany."

A few things clicked into place for Max. The names and business interests of most of the consortium members revolved around oil and gas. A pattern was emerging.

Julia stared at him. "I can see by the look on your face that you're starting to put some of it together."

Max stopped next to a gnarled vine and took a stab in the dark. "The consortium exists to control oil prices?"

They reached the end of a row of vines. The cottage was far behind them and the security guards were right where they were supposed to be—close enough to keep watch but far enough away where they couldn't overhear. "You're partially right, but you jumped way ahead."

As Julia guided him along a row of alder trees, Max heard the gurgle of a stream through the leaves.

"Jules Fabron was a young and impressionable soldier. Impacted by what he perceived to be evil imperialist governments in France and the US, he reacted positively to the communist propaganda your father sprinkled throughout much of his interrogations. Fabron fell for the ideal of the absence of social classes and the common ownership of the means of production."

Max blew a puff of air through his lips. "Lots of us fell for that."

"This is a bit of a tangent, but try to imagine yourself living in Russia at the end of World War I. Famine, poverty, little food to eat. Millions killed during what was widely perceived to be an imperialist war. You might overlook Lenin's and Stalin's crimes and come to believe in ownership of the means of production by commoners, the proletariat."

Max snorted. "You're right, but the reality was very different. The means of production were still controlled by a few powerful men in the Kremlin. Still are."

Julia let go of his arm and stooped again to grab a handful of soil and hold it up to Max's face. "Here. Smell."

Max took a sniff, taking the rich scents of loam, mulch, and the fresh scent of water.

"Does it smell pleasant to you?"

Max nodded. "Smells like rain."

Julia let the brown granules fall to the ground. "That means the soil is healthy. If it smells rotten or swampy, it means the soil is unhealthy. Bad for growing grapes."

She started walking again, eyes on the horizon. "It's perception versus reality. I'm saying for millions of Russians, and apparently for Jules Fabron, the timing was ripe to believe in something like communism."

Max nodded. "When times are hard, humans naturally look for something to believe in. Communism and organized religion have that in common."

By now, they were walking along the outer edge of the vineyard. To their right sprawled the rolling ordered chaos of the grape vines. To the left, a lush forest carpeted the hills as far as the eye could see.

Julia glanced at him with piercing blue eyes. "When Jules Fabron got out of the POW camp, orchestrated by your father of course, he returned to Paris and started working for his father's company, which was already well on its way to becoming one of the world's largest oil companies. Today it's considered part of Big Oil.

"Big Oil?"

"I'll get to that in a second. The short version of the story is that Jules rose quickly in his father's business and, by the mid-70s, had taken over as chairman of the board. For decades, starting when he began at the company, Jules funneled information to your father. Not once did he ask for payment."

Max squinted his eyes. "Because the Fabron's oil company was part-owned by the French government, he presumably had access to inside information as to how the French ran its businesses?"

Julia nodded. "Correct. But it turns out it was much more than that. How much do you know about the oil business?"

"OPEC sets prices. That's about it."

Julia shook her head. "That's the public's perception, because OPEC is the only visible oil consortium, but it's not true. Since you brought it up, I'll start there. OPEC started in 1960 with five nations and now includes fourteen. Members of OPEC, dominated by the Saudis, also include niche players like Angola and Ecuador, and they control about seventy-three percent of the world's known oil reserves but only about forty-three percent of oil production. They have influence, but not direct control. Do you know what countries are the three largest oil producers?"

"Saudi Arabia, Russia and—" Max broke off in thought. "Iraq or Iran?"

"Right on the first two. The Saudis and the Russians are neck and neck. The third, however, are the Americans."

"Interesting."

"Right. However, three of the five largest oil and gas companies, measured by revenue, are Chinese."

Max thought of the two Chinese names on the consortium list. "Even more interesting."

Julia stopped and faced Max, putting her hand on his arm. "It's hard to understate the importance of oil on the world stage. Oil powers economic growth, and it directly affects budgets. You can't run a military or an economy without oil. You can't move freight faster than about twenty-five miles per hour without oil. Modern civilization would collapse without it. Wars have been fought over oil, policy has been set based on it, alliances formed around it, and atrocities have been overlooked because of it."

"The Americans build a relationship with the Saudis, even as Saudi Arabia sponsors terrorists."

Julia nodded her head emphatically. "Exactly. Same with the Russians and Syrians, for that matter. Failure to secure energy supplies dooms nations to collapse. The Mayans found this out too late. You can bet the Chinese, the Americans, and the Russians will not make the same mistake. The public doesn't realize it, but a huge amount of time and energy is spent by the world's economies securing sources of oil. It's why drilling in the Arctic National Wildlife Refuge in Alaska has become such a polarizing topic. There is no more important natural resource, including pristine wildlife, than oil."

"I'm starting to get the picture."

Julia's eyes twinkled in the soft light. "Let me paint it in more detail for you. There are three oil cartels in the world. OPEC, you know. They are, in effect, a public cartel. They don't set prices per se, but instead set production quotas. A reduction in production can dramatically impact the world economy, as it did in the seventies when production was low. This drove prices up and generated wealth for OPEC countries, but depressed the rest of the world economy."

Max crossed his arms over his chest. "But don't OPEC countries have incentive to cheat, by producing more than their quota, to drive profits up for themselves?"

Julia nodded. "Yes, exactly, which is one reason OPEC's influence has been limited in recent years. Cheating by member countries is rampant."

"You said there are three oil cartels. Who are the other two?"

"The second is a group of seven oil companies that used to be called the Seven Sisters before a couple of them merged to form five —British Petroleum, Gulf Oil, Chevron, Royal Dutch Shell, Exxon Mobile. Back in the fifties, they dominated oil production. OPEC was created in part to counterbalance this group."

Now it was Max's turn to smile. "Let me guess. Fabron's company was a member of the Seven Sisters."

Julia smiled, the corners of her eyes crinkling. "Your father always said you were smart. Keep in mind that while OPEC operates in plain sight, the Seven Sisters colluded together behind closed doors—illegally."

"And Jules Fabron funneled information about the Seven Sister's pricing and quota strategies to my father."

"Correct again. For many years, Jules Fabron was the secretary general of the Seven Sisters. He provided Andrei with the meeting minutes each month, as well as Jules's own strategies. Your father knew what the Seven Sisters would do before the member companies knew."

Max's eyes widened. "Wow."

Julia crossed her arms, the index finger of one hand touching her lip. "Wow is right. Now the Seven Sisters are the least powerful of the three oil cartels, partly because

Jules funneled information to your father. The other reason is that those seven now control a much smaller share of the world's reserves."

Max snapped his finger. "The third cartel is the consortium."

Julia's eyes lit up. "Bingo. Your father fed Fabron's information to the KGB who, unbeknownst to Andrei, in turn sent that information to the consortium."

Max rubbed his neck. "You're telling me that a group of oil company owners, all colluding to control oil reserves and pricing, is the group that's out to kill my family?"

Julia spread her arms. "I know it sounds implausible, but it goes to show how important oil is, doesn't it?"

Max shook his head. "There's still a piece missing. What did my father do to make them so angry? He was the one responsible for providing most of their intel."

Julia took Max's hand in hers. "That, my son, is as much a mystery to me as it is to you."

Max looked at her with wide eyes. "You're serious? You're not holding out on me?"

Julia shook her head. "Ever since your father was killed, my group has tried to answer the same question. We need to work together on it, Max, you and me."

She let go of his hands and threaded her arm through his again, guiding him back in the direction of the cottage. "But now, you need to get going. There's a jet waiting at a private airfield near here. It'll get you into Latvia unseen, where you can interrogate Erich Stasko. The rest of the operational details, including your local contact, are in a file waiting for you on the plane."

EIGHTEEN

Riga, Latvia

The Lear touched down at just after 9:00 pm Latvian time and taxied directly into a private hangar on the outskirts of Riga International Airport. Max came off the flight feeling tired and groggy. He spent the three hours reading through the thick file on Erich Stasko again. It was comprehensive and provided a detailed background of the banker, including his education, family life, and business dealings. A thick sheaf of paper outlined the vast banking network he had established by taking advantage of limited regulatory oversights to build one of the world's most secretive financial systems. He was suspected of hiding and laundering funds from most of Russia's corrupt mafia syndicates, monies from illegal groups in Mexico, the US, and Italy, as well as massive amounts of funds from shadowy sources in China. The file also contained blueprints and security schematics to Stasko's multiple homes and offices. Extensive log files detailed his daily habits for twelve months. Mobile phone records were included along with records of his travel to and from a dozen major European cities. Organizational charts of his operations named many of his lieutenants, including two sons who held senior positions in his banking syndicate. Someone from Julia's service had shadowed Stasko for a while to accumulate such a large dossier on the man. The fact that Stasko's file started before Max even became involved with the consortium was not lost on him. Once again, he got the familiar feeling at the back of his neck that he was being manipulated like a puppet on a string.

Waiting inside the hangar was a white Mercedes G-Class SUV with tinted windows. *The German's sure know how to travel in style,* Max thought as he tossed his small overnight bag and a steel briefcase into the backseat before slipping into the cool leather back seat. He caught a glimpse of his driver and was surprised to see a young woman with shoulder length blond hair pulled tight into a ponytail.

She turned, revealing a tanned face with a petite nose and flashing blue eyes. "Where to?"

He smiled at her. "I need coffee. Preferably espresso."

She frowned. "We make great espresso in Riga."

The driver, satisfied with Max's prearranged answer to the challenge phrase, squealed the SUV's wheels as they roared out of the hanger. She studiously ignored his attempts at small talk and focused on driving fast as they exited the airport and entered Riga proper.

It had been over twenty years since Max had operated in Riga, so his memory of the city was limited, making him appreciate the local contact and driver. Max wondered if the blond woman worked for Julia's service or if she was a contractor. All his attempts at conversation, including asking her name, were met with a stony stare through the rearview mirror.

The plan called for the driver to drop him at the Dome Hotel and Spa, a luxury hotel downtown Riga. But first, they had a stop to make. Max needed to shop for a few items.

Julia had discouraged him from bringing weapons and tactical gear into Latvia, indicating that the country was known to make surprise inspections of private planes, and her network didn't extend to the bribery of Latvian immigration and customs officials. Instead, she insisted upon a local weapons procurement plan prearranged by her local team. Max deferred to her expertise and entered Latvia weaponless, leaving himself at the mercy of Julia's team. She assured him that they had used this supplier before and found him trustworthy.

The white SUV left the busier section of the city behind and entered a warehouse district. As they raced through damp and dark streets, the driver intent on her task, Max's senses were on high alert while he attempted to trace their route on his smartphone and watch for tails. The driver turned a corner and bounced through the dark open door of a warehouse. The door closed behind them as the vehicle came to a halt, tires screeching on clean cement. His driver stared wordlessly ahead, drumming her fingers on the steering wheel.

Through the windshield, illuminated by the SUV's headlights, Max saw a folding table standing about ten meters away. To his left were neat rows of pallets containing tall stacks of shrink-wrapped boxes. Three forklifts, all dark and silent, sat to his right. A heavyset man in a suit stood to the side of the table and waved his hand across his throat in a cutting gesture. His driver shut off the SUV's lights, bathing them in darkness.

Max shifted in his seat. "You've worked with these guys before?"

The driver turned to reply, keeping her hands on the wheel. "Yes, many times. They won't do anything to jeopardize their position with us. They'll want to know you're unarmed. Remove your jacket. When you get out, keep your hands up and let them see your waist. Don't approach the table until instructed."

"Got it." Max waited a beat to let his eyes adjust to the darkness before getting out of the SUV, briefcase in hand. He did as he was instructed, and as he turned, an intense light hit him and played over his body.

"Approach," a male voice said in English tinged with a Russian accent.

The light rested on his face, blinding him as he walked. As he shielded his eyes with a hand, he caught a glimpse of two men standing among the rows of pallets, one holding a pistol, the other an assault rifle. Despite his driver's assurances, and the fact this was set up by Julia, he got an uncomfortable feeling in his gut. Nothing about this seemed like a friendly buy. It felt more like a drug deal between two groups that hadn't worked together before. An arrangement where the odds were stacked in favor of the seller. Despite the knot in his gut, Max kept walking. If he couldn't trust his own mother, who could he trust?

When he got to the table, the light was directed away from his face. After a second, the spots in his eyes disappeared and his eyesight returned.

Standing in front of him was a large man in a suit with a

wide pale face and blood-red lips. His nose was crooked, like it had been broken once or twice and never fixed, a diamond stud was in one ear, and when he reached out to shake Max's hand, a thick gold chain slipped from his coat sleeve. A black tooth showed when he grinned.

Max shook the man's hand. The gun merchant looked like a low-level Russian mafia enforcer. Behind him was a handful of weapons stacked on the table, including several pistols, dozens of magazines, boxes of ammunition, and a pile of suppressors.

The man in the suit gave Max a crooked grin. "Sorry for the security measures, Max." Max's name came out like a sneer. "Can't be too careful. Let's see the money."

Max set the briefcase on the table, careful to avoid putting his back to the man or the two thugs standing among the pallets. The use of his name sent another pang through his gut. "No problem. You know my name. What do I call you?"

The big man with the crooked nose looked surprised before sneering. Loud enough so the other men in the room could hear he said, "Mr. Max here wants to get friendly. Okay, pretty boy. You can call me Jānis."

Max turned the case so it would open toward Jānis before he moved to undo the latches.

Jānis stopped him with an outstretched hand. "Point the case back at you. Open it slowly."

Max spun the case around, undid the latches, opened the lid, and turned it back around so Jānis could see inside. Rows of strapped one hundred dollar bills were visible. Jānis leaned over and thumbed through the stacks and smiled before slamming the case shut and snapping his fingers.

Bright flashes of light and the sound of automatic gun fire erupted, filling the confined space with an ear-splitting chatter of bullets impacting metal and brass hitting the cement.

NINETEEN

Riga, Latvia

Muzzle bursts from an assault rifle winked like fire crackers in the darkness as a barrage of gunfire filled the cavernous warehouse. The sound of bullets plinking into metal was intermingled with the tinkle of shattering glass and the pings of bullet casings hitting the concrete.

Max reacted by flipping the table up between him and Jānis and flinging himself in the direction of the weapons clattering to the concrete floor. With a practiced effort honed from years in battle zones, he ignored the fear caused by the chattering weapons and acted on instinct, his body propelled by adrenaline and conditioned muscle memory. He didn't have the luxury of time to wonder whether Julia had set him up. He would sort that out later. Now it was all about survival.

Max landed hard on the concrete and slid forward, coming to rest among the scattered weapons. His hand found a pistol, and he felt for a magazine in the handle, but found none. He searched the floor with his hand until he came up with a magazine. He slammed it home and flipped over onto his back with the gun held out, looking for a target. There was no sign of Jānis, and he had no line of sight to the two gunmen.

The automatic fire stopped, leaving a foreboding silence in the darkness. His ears rang, and he smelled gunpowder and something else, something thick, organic, and metallic. Blood.

The overhead lights snapped on. Max, still on his back, held the gun in both hands and searched for a target. The SUV was torn to shreds, its windows blown out and bullet holes riddled the side panels. The four tires were flat, and Max saw the bloody and lifeless form of the blond in the driver's seat. The cabin inside was covered with blood spatter. He swung the gun in an arc, but still found no marks.

Jānis stepped out from behind a stack of pallets, his arms held wide as if offering himself as a target. Max snapped his gun toward him and pulled the trigger. The firing pin caused a loud bang, but no bullet flew from the gun's barrel.

Jānis smiled and walked to Max. Another man appeared next to Jānis, arms rippling with muscles, holding an assault rifle pointed at Max. A third man appeared in the shadows created by the stacks of pallets and held a pistol trained on Max.

Max pulled the trigger again. Same effect—loud bang, no bullet.

Jānis laughed and snatched the pistol from Max's hand. "Do you think we'd give you live ammunition?" He pointed the gun at Max's leg and pulled the trigger.

Bang!

Pain shot through Max's shin. He looked down and saw a ragged hole in his pant leg, but no blood.

"Blanks." Jānis laughed again. "You'd be surprised how much damage a wad of paper can do when fired from a gun. You wouldn't want to hold this up to your head." He dropped the magazine from the gun and let it clatter to the floor before racking the slide to eject the blank in the chamber. Jānis pulled another magazine from his suit coat pocket and banged it into the butt of the gun and racked the slide. "There. Now we have a live gun." He pointed it at Max. "Why don't you go sit in that chair."

Max did as he was instructed. The thug with bulging muscles approached and secured Max's arms behind him using a roll of silver tape. As the muscle-bound man moved off to a dark corner of the warehouse, Max flexed his arm muscles, working to stretch the pliable tape. Jānis, who had shoved his pistol into the waistband of his trousers, was focused on his mobile phone and didn't see Max's movements. The third man was too far away to notice.

Jānis came up close to Max while typing on his phone with two hands before shoving the device into his pocket. "Well, well. If it isn't the most wanted man in the world come to visit our little town. Andris, can you believe our luck?"

The man holding the pistol grunted. "Awesome luck, Boss."

Jānis fished in his suit jacket pocket and withdrew a folded piece of paper. He unfolded it and held it in front of Max's face. It was the picture of Max from The Telegraph article. The caption read, £1M *Reward for Information Leading to the Capture of Mikhail Asimov.*

"If you're not Mikhail Asimov, I'm Donald Duck," he

said with a laugh. "Andris, how often does one million pounds drop into your lap like this?"

"Never, Boss."

Jānis leaned down to look at Max, hands on his knees. "Too bad it doesn't say *Alive or Dead* or this would be a whole lot easier."

Andris took a step out of the shadows. "Yeah, too bad, Boss." The man Jānis called Andris was tall and wiry, wearing a tight white tank, wife beater undershirt and baggy jeans.

Max kept flexing and relaxing his muscles. "Good job. You got me."

Jānis folded up the mugshot and slipped it into a jacket pocket, his black-toothed smile unwavering.

Max smiled at him. "The only problem is now you have to figure out how to turn me over to law enforcement without getting captured or killed yourself. The moment you contact them, this place is going to be swarming with MIDD, MI6, and the Latvian Security Police. You sure you want that kind of heat coming down on your little operation here? You think they're going to pay the reward money to a couple of amateur thugs like you guys? You think they care if you live or die? You're going to end up dead or in a prison cell."

Jānis's eyes flashed for an instant.

Max chuckled. "You really thought this through, didn't you? Who did you send that message to? The Latvian Security Police? You should probably get as far away from here as possible. You have about fifteen minutes before they trace your phone, triangulate this warehouse, and surround this place with a hoard of commandos. An OMEGA team is probably already on its way."

Jānis's face became red with anger. He lunged, putting

all his weight behind a punch that crushed into Max's solar plexus. Max doubled over as the wind went out of him. While he fought for breath, he moved his wrists back and forth, stretching the tape.

Jānis stepped back and adjusted his coat, shooting his cuffs. The man with the bulging arms appeared with a newspaper and held it to the side of Max's head. Jānis chuckled while snapping a photo with his smartphone. He typed on the tiny screen before putting the phone in his pocket.

Max caught his breath. "They'll think it's fake. I need to hold it. This is your first kidnapping, isn't it?"

Jānis scowled but hesitated, as if weighing Max's point, before smiling. He addressed the thug with the muscles. "Ivars, set the newspaper on his lap, and lean it up against his stomach."

Max laughed. "You really are an idiot, aren't you? If I'm not holding it, the picture will look fake."

Andris took another step, emerging fully into the light. His face was craggy and leathered from the elements. "He's right, Boss. I remember one time back in Chechnya—"

"Su'ds!" Jānis said, cursing in Latvian. "Ivars, undo his arms. Andris, he makes one false move, put a bullet in his chest."

Max eyed the thin gangster. "Andris, think twice about pulling the trigger. Kill me and the reward money disappears." Max continued tensing his muscles behind his back to loosen the tape.

Andris's eyes, alive with adrenaline, shifted between Jānis and Max. His finger was tight on the trigger, with the gun pointed at Max.

Ivars went around behind Max's back, holding a Glock. 45 in one hand and a switchblade in the other.

Max heard the *snick* of the knife opening.

Big mistake, thought Max.

———

Ivars flicked the blade across the tape, and Max's arms came free.

As his wrists snapped free, Max planted his feet and pushed himself up and back while reaching behind him for Ivars' gun arm. He gripped the man's wrist, wrenched his arm, and used his momentum to force the man to lose his balance.

Like many overly muscled men, Ivars was overconfident in his strength and poorly coordinated. Relying on his muscles, he tried to wrench his wrist free while also regaining his balance.

Max held tight, levered his body under the thug and shifted his weight, flipping the heavier man over his shoulder. Ivars landed on the ground with a grunt. In the process, Max came away with the .45 in a two-handed grip.

Jānis fumbled for his own gun, dropping his mobile phone to the warehouse floor with a crunch. "Shoot him!"

Andris recovered faster than Max anticipated, but Max was partially hidden from his view by Jānis' large body, preventing a direct shot. As Andris stepped to the side to find a lane around his boss, Max pulled the trigger again and again and two holes appeared in Andris's chest. Andris staggered back, red blossoming on his white wife beater, a surprised look on his face, before he stumbled to the ground.

Max shifted and brought the gun around to Jānis, who was in the process of drawing a pistol from his waistband. Max fired twice, hitting Jānis in the torso and thigh.

Jānis grunted as he was spun to the side by the force of

the bullets. He dropped the pistol, which clattered to the floor, and felt for his chest and his leg, as if confused by which injury to tend to.

Max felt a sharp, wet pain in his thigh as Ivars swiped at his leg with the switchblade from a kneeling position. Before Ivars could pull back for another strike, Max stepped back and simultaneously fired down at the man, pulling the trigger twice. One bullet found the target's throat while the other plunked into his chest. Ivars fell face-first to the ground, the knife falling from his grasp.

Max turned to see Jānis fumbling on the floor, searching for his gun with a wide-eyed expression on his face. Max aimed a vicious kick at his leg. Jānis screamed as Max's booted foot connected with the bloody wound. Max toed Jānis's pistol away, knelt, and grabbed Jānis by the neck while jamming his gun into Jānis's cheek.

Max smelled stale cigarettes on the gangster's breath. He smelled something else from closer to the ground. Something acetic. He noticed a wet stain had spread over Jānis's crotch. "Aw. You ruined your suit."

Jānis struggled to speak through Max's grip. "Fuck off, Asimov."

Max tightened his hold. "Who told you that I was coming to buy the guns? Someone tipped you off. I want to know who."

"I don't—"

Max increased the pressure on the thug's neck. "Wrong answer. Who tipped you off?"

Jānis gulped for breath as Max eased off. "I don't know the name. I got an email."

Max's adrenaline surged, his anger at the tipping point because of his driver's senseless death. She was just doing her job, and now she was dead because of him. He increased the pressure on the man's throat.

Jānis's face turned red and his eyes bulged out. Realizing he would pass out in a few seconds, he let go of the thug's neck and took a step back. "Show me."

Jānis rubbed his neck and took his time retrieving his phone from where it had fallen. The glass screen had spiderwebbed from its impact with the warehouse floor, but it was still operable. Jānis's hands shook as he tried to access the email program. After an agonizing minute, he handed it over.

Max took it with his free hand and saw a short email displayed on the broken screen. As he looked at the phone, momentarily distracted, Jānis made his move by reaching up and grasping Max's gun with a two-handed grip, attempting to wrest the weapon from his hand.

Holding the phone in his fist, Max punched Jānis in the face, causing Jānis's grasp to weaken. Max pulled his gun hand away and shot Jānis in the forehead. The thug jerked backward as the bullet blew out brain matter, blood, and bone fragments onto the warehouse floor.

Knowing the authorities were likely locked onto the signal from Jānis's phone, Max used his Blackphone to snap a picture of the screen, capturing an image of the email text, before using the butt of his gun to pound Jānis's cell phone into pieces. He didn't want the contents of the phone falling into the hands of the authorities.

With his adrenaline pumping, Max frisked Jānis and found a key fob to a BMW, a wallet, and the folded picture of himself. He pocketed all three before searching the other two dead men, finding nothing of value. Max stepped to the white SUV to check on his driver, hesitating to reach in and feel for a pulse. The young woman had been hit by at least a dozen slugs, and blood was everywhere. He searched her, pocketing a mobile phone and grabbing a purse.

The warehouse was a mess. Four dead bodies lay strewn on the cement, blood covered everything, and the bullet-riddled SUV sat on four flat tires. Max grabbed his bag from the back of the SUV, wiped his prints from the door handle, and moved to the overturned table, where he shoved the cash back into the silver case and snapped it closed.

He found a BMW parked in the dark shadows in the back of the warehouse. The car chirped as he used the clicker to unlock it before tossing his bag and briefcase on the front passenger seat. He returned to the overturned table and rummaged through the weapons on the ground, selecting a new-looking Beretta pistol with a threaded barrel. He grabbed several boxes of 9mm ammunition, three magazines for the Beretta, and a suppressor that fit the Beretta's threads. After ripping a chunk of material from Jānis's suit coat and wrapping it around his injured thigh, he wiped down everything he had touched before climbing into the BMW and speeding out of the warehouse into the darkness of Riga.

He spun the wheel and took a route through the dark warehouses away from the city center. After taking a zigzag path through the darkened streets to ensure he was not followed, he turned the car toward downtown Riga. As he passed over the Daugava River, he rolled the window down and tossed out the Glock before lighting a cigarette and holding his hand up to the light of the city. It remained just as steady as the first day his father had taught him to shoot.

TWENTY

Themes House, London, England

A shout went up from one of the analysts on the far side of the room. "I've got something!"

Baxter's feet hit the floor. He tossed aside the transcript from the ship captain's interrogation that he had read for the umpteenth time in the hopes he might unearth some new detail.

A picture flickered on the large screen in the center of the operations room. The image was underexposed, but the subject was clear. A man sat in a chair, arms behind him, a newspaper held next to his head by someone off-camera. The photo was taken in what looked like a cavernous warehouse, but the image was too dark to see the man's features.

Baxter approached the screen and stood next to John Taylor. The senior MI5 investigator's shirt was rumpled, and his tie was loose. Dark crescents hung under his normally bright eyes. An analyst at a nearby workstation clicked a few times with a mouse, and the image lightened as he adjusted the brightness of the photo.

Baxter sucked in his breath as he realized the image was Mikhail Asimov. "Where did this come from?"

Taylor studied the picture before answering. "It was attached to an email that just came in." Turning to the analyst, he said, "Call Phillips. And give me a close-up on that newspaper."

A second later, a blurry newspaper appeared on the screen.

"Get that into focus," Taylor ordered. The room was silent except for the rapid-fire clicking of a mouse. When the image cleared, Baxter saw a newspaper with a header showing a colorful globe of blues and greens with wispy white clouds next to the word *Diena* in a large font.

Taylor stepped closer to the screen. "Zoom in on the dateline."

The image blurred before a string of characters appeared. The number was clear, showing today's date, but the rest of the date was in a language foreign to Baxter.

Taylor cursed. "What bloody language is that?"

The room was silent before a voice piped up from the rear of the room. "That's Latvian."

Everyone in the room looked back at the tiny blond with her hair in a ponytail at the rear table who wore a cardigan over a smart dress. Cindy flushed bright crimson with embarrassment.

An analyst looked up from his computer screen. "She's right. The *Diena* is one of Latvia's largest circulation newspapers."

Taylor cursed again. "Anyone speak Latvian?"

No one spoke until Cindy's voice came again from the back of the room. "I do."

Baxter could have sworn he saw John Taylor's jaw drop a fraction of an inch, but the agent recovered nicely. "Well, don't just sit there, young lady. Front and center. Pronto."

The entire room of seasoned intelligence agents and law enforcement professionals watched as the young blond analyst from MI6, barely six months on the job, scampered to the front of the room.

Baxter moved to put his arm around her shoulders but thought better of it. "What does the dateline on the newspaper say, Cindy?"

Cindy's voice was soft. "September 19, 2016."

Baxter whispered in her ear. "Say it again, this time with force."

"September 19, 2016!" she shouted.

The room descended into organized chaos and didn't skip a beat when Director Phillips strode into the room to take his place on the rear dais.

Taylor hastened to brief Phillips, yelling as he ran. "Trace that email."

"Already on it, sir," came the response.

Baxter accompanied Cindy back to the rear table where she took her seat with a coy smile on her face.

Baxter's bushy eyebrows were still up. "Latvian?"

She smiled, showing an even row of white teeth. "My father's Latvian. We still have family there."

Baxter nodded. Of course, she did. He put his Blackberry to his ear and dialed the MI6 switchboard. Officially, the investigation had just switched over to MI6, but Baxter would continue to let Taylor take the lead. MI5 didn't have any jets, a fact that Baxter chided Taylor about at every possible opportunity.

While he waited for the switchboard to answer, Baxter wondered what Asimov was doing in Latvia. It might make for a good place to hide. The country's intelligence apparatus was not well developed. Latvia's history as a former Soviet Republic might mean Asimov has contacts there that would help him stay hidden. Maybe those contacts decided to collect on the reward money.

When the switchboard at Vauxhall Cross answered, Baxter told the operator to patch him through to the director on a priority. Minutes later, the MI6 team was in full swing. Files were pulled, databases cross referenced, and operatives and friendlies local to Latvia were rousted. The director himself placed a call to the director of MIDD, Latvia's Secret Service Agency. A MI6 Lear was mobilized, its on-call pilots yanked from their bunks and the Pratt & Whitney turbofans warmed.

While the vast MI6 apparatus cranked into gear, Baxter feverishly tugged on his goatee. How did Asimov get to Latvia so quickly? They had one confirmed sighting in Spain, followed only twenty-four hours later by a confirmed sighting in Riga, Latvia. The only conclusion he could draw was that Asimov had help. High-powered help. He was so lost in thought he almost missed the call on his mobile phone. It was in his back pocket, where it always sat, and now it buzzed incessantly.

Baxter dragged it out of his pocket and glanced at the screen. The caller ID read *Unknown*. This was a routine occurrence for him, as he knew many law enforcement types who blocked their caller ID, himself included. He fingered the green answer button and held the device to his ear.

"Baxter."

There was a series of clicks, followed by static and more clicks. He was just about to thumb the disconnect button in irritation when he heard a metallic voice say, "Callum Baxter?"

His interest piqued, he paused. "Yes, that's me. Who's—"

"Mr. Baxter, please recite your national insurance number for me."

"What the devil?"

"Sir, please. We're running out of time to capture Mikhail Asimov. Please recite your national insurance number for me. I need to confirm your identity."

Baxter recited the nine digits from memory. "Now identify yourself," he growled, while frantically gesturing for John Taylor.

"Mr. Baxter, you may call me Bluefish."

———

Callum Baxter had seen and experienced a lot in his life. As a youngster, he did poorly in school. Instead of studying, he spent his free time exploring the rainy moors outside his hometown of Liverpool. At the ripe age of eighteen, after fully squandering his education and with nothing better to do, he enlisted in the Royal Navy. He floundered for years as a low-level seaman on various destroyers and patrol boats, mostly swabbing decks and cleaning heads.

Despite struggling early in the military, Callum saw the world and along with it, every nuance of human nature imaginable. He battled pirates in the Gulf of Guinea, Russians in the Norwegian Sea, and terrorists in the Mediterranean. After five years of passive and unintentional insubordination, a fed-up admiral looking to get rid of the youngster suggested Baxter join Defense Intelligence, a department in the Britain's Ministry of Defense. There

Baxter found his true calling. He excelled as an analyst before making the switch to MI6 where he quickly rose on the backs of several high profile and successful operations.

Despite his years in the intelligence game, Callum had yet to receive a voice-disguised phone call from a person identifying themselves with a code word from a children's book. This wasn't the first time, however, he had to deal with a crackpot calling in a fake witness sighting, and it wouldn't be the last. He rapidly recovered and addressed the strange caller.

He smiled into the phone. "How may I help you, Mr. Bluefish?" He was ready to hang up the minute the caller went off the deep end. Meanwhile, he hastily wrote on a slip of paper which he handed to John Taylor. *Trace this call!*

"It seems, Mr. Baxter, that we may be able to help each other."

Baxter rolled his eyes. "Is that right? I'm listening, for about a minute."

"It sounds as if I need to get your attention." Static blared from the phone forcing Baxter to hold the phone away from his ear. "See, Mr. Baxter, I know things. Things that might come in handy in your search for London's most wanted terrorist. Information that will take you a long time to unearth are things I already know."

Callum frowned. "Give me an example."

"Ah, yes. A freebie, as it were."

"More like proof."

More static filled the line. "I know Mikhail Asimov was spotted aboard a fishing trawler named the Renée. I know the French authorities have the ship captain under interrogation. I know a group of Latvian thugs has captured Asimov, and they're offering him up for the ransom."

Baxter looked around the operations room, sure he was being pranked by someone. "So you're in law enforcement somewhere. Anyone that can hack into our systems could get that information."

John Taylor flashed him a thumbs-up.

More static. "I also know that at this instant your friend John Taylor of MI5 is attempting to trace this call."

Callum's eyebrows went up.

"I can also tell you that in about five seconds, he will indicate failure as his attempt at a trace runs into a wall even his considerable resources cannot breach."

Baxter looked back at Taylor, who dragged a finger across his throat.

Baxter strolled to the back of the room. "Impressive, Mr. Bluefish. You now have my attention."

"Excellent. As I was saying, I believe you and I have a common quarry. You and your government want Mikhail Asimov apprehended and put through a trial so the public might be assured you have some chance of preventing terrorism on British soil. I also want Asimov off the street."

"Why?"

"That's irrelevant."

"I'm guessing you're in law enforcement?"

"Do not waste your time trying to discern my identity. Spend your precious efforts and vast teams of personnel locating and apprehending Mr. Asimov. My capabilities so vastly outweigh your own that it would be hopeless to attempt to trace me. Spare yourself the embarrassment."

"Okay, Mr. Bluefish. The ground rules have been established. Why don't we cut to the chase? What information can you provide me?"

"Now we're getting somewhere. When the time comes, our little arrangement will provide you with an advantage."

Baxter rolled his eyes again. "So you have nothing."

"Go to Latvia. On the off chance the thugs still have him, our work is done. I suspect when you arrive you'll find the abductors dead and Asimov gone. I assure you if that is the case, Asimov will still be in Riga."

"Very well. How do I contact you, Mr. Bluefish?"

"You don't. I'll contact you. Oh, and one other thing. Let's keep these little conversations just between us, shall we? It would do neither of us any good for your director to know you're receiving information from an outside source."

Baxter winked at Cindy, who was staring at him. "Of course."

"Goodbye for now, Mr. Baxter."

The line went dead.

TWENTY-ONE

Riga, Latvia

"Everyone and their brother wants my head on a platter."

Max sat in a stolen Volkswagen sedan on a side street lined by leafy green trees. He had originated the call on his secure Blackphone and threaded it through a half dozen servers before it was answered at the tiny cottage among the vineyards outside Barcelona.

Julia's voice sounded strained. "A million pounds is a strong motivator." There was silence on the line for a few beats before Julia spoke again. "She was a good agent, you know."

"I'm sure. I sent you a screenshot of the email from Jānis's phone. It shows the email address, although I'm sure it's untraceable. It's signed by someone calling themselves Bluefish. Does that ring a bell?"

"No, but we'll research it."

Did Julia answer too quickly, or was it his imagination? The only people who knew he was in Latvia were Julia and a handful of her staff. He purposefully didn't inform Kaamil of his whereabouts, still not trusting the young computer hacker's security systems. Someone obviously had compromised the security on Julia's team. Someone with powerful computer systems and tracking capabilities. It occurred to him that perhaps there was never a mole in Kate's organization, but she had been compromised from outside the agency. Perhaps the consortium had employed this Bluefish person or group to take him down. The thought unsettled him—he much preferred his enemies to stay in the physical realm.

Max watched a retiree amble down the sidewalk with a puppy straining on its leash. The dog made him think of Alex and Spike. "Can you get the scene cleaned before that warehouse is lit up like a Christmas tree with law enforcement?

"We're resource-constrained up there, as you can imagine, but we'll do what we can. You should come back in. It's too hot up there. We'll find another way."

The man and the puppy disappeared around a corner. "No way. I'm too close."

"Max, every agency with an acronym is scouring the country for you. You're too exposed. Come in. While you're on your way back, I'll have my team look for another angle."

Max smiled into the phone. "Luckily, you're not paying my salary. I'll check in again in twenty-four hours."

"Max—"

He ended the transmission.

———

Max sat low in the driver's seat of the stolen car, Beretta on his lap, going over in his head the information from the file on Erich Stasko. He sipped tepid coffee from a Styrofoam cup and flicked cigarette ash out a crack in the window. The car's ashtray was filled with butts, and empty coffee cups littered the back seat.

He was at a cross street near the bottom of a hill leading up to Stasko's compound. Information in the file indicated the man took his security seriously. The entire residence was surrounded by a tall stone wall. A wrought iron gate was reinforced by steel plating and a hulking yellow Hummer blocked the drive inside the entrance. Security cameras were mounted every dozen meters along the perimeter, and although he couldn't see them, the file indicated guards with dogs patrolled the inside of the fence.

Like most Soviet Bloc oligarchs, Erich Stasko utilized contingents of bodyguards who hovered around him in public and were seconds away in private. Julia's surveillance established that he never traveled without at least two hulking men in suits, earpieces connected to a central security command and armpits bulging with pistols.

Stasko was married to a former Russian model, and their two daughters were in European universities. This left the former model to idle away her time and her husband's money by shopping in Europe's most expensive boutiques and dining with like-minded girlfriends in Europe's finest restaurants. Stasko, by all accounts a workaholic, remained in the Riga compound while his wife spent most of her time in the couple's posh London flat.

The file was stuffed with intimate pictures of his wife's affair with one of her bodyguards, a cliché that made Max chuckle. The file was silent, however, about any extracurricular activities by the husband. As far as the BND could tell, if Erich Stasko was cheating on his wife, it was only with his business.

The oligarch's behavior patterns were remarkably consistent. Up before dawn each morning, he was led through a brief, but intense, workout in his home gym by a trainer who also served as a bodyguard. A shower, a quick breakfast of a protein shake and eggs, and he was out the door riding in the back of an armored luxury sedan flanked by two massive black SUVs for the short ride to his office. When not taking the vehicle caravan, he flew in a Bell 525 Relentless helicopter from a landing pad on his estate grounds to a pad atop his office building. Stasko's office was in the penthouse suite of Riga's tallest office building, which Stasko also owned. Most days the banker returned home by 11:00 pm and enjoyed a single chilled vodka before retiring at midnight.

Stasko looked like a man of few interests and no vices other than work. How a man who married a former Russian model turned himself into a lonely workaholic was a mystery. The path to a successful assassination often led through a man's vices. Women, drugs, gambling, or even a weakness for fast cars could be turned into an advantage. Stasko, it appeared, didn't have any weaknesses.

Max saw one thing in the file that might afford an opportunity. It was a detail most operatives would miss, but Max knew it was the key to gaining some alone time with the wealthy oligarch. And alone time was all the advantage Max needed.

The one aberration in Erich Stasko's surveillance log was a night over a month ago when he left work early, giving the surveillance team a thrill as they scrambled to prepare their telephoto lenses and remote listening mics. A team of six in three cars took turns following Stasko's caravan, peeling off and rejoining, a silent cavalcade of vehicles parading through Riga's nighttime streets. Eventually their quarry stopped at the rear entrance of a massive white-washed building of Roman architecture fronted by vast gardens. Erich Stasko had stepped out, flanked by two large men, and immediately disappeared through the back door of the Latvian National Opera and Ballet.

The file indicated Stasko attended Bolero that night, a ballet composed by a Frenchman named Maurice Ravel and commissioned by the Russian actress and dancer Ida Rubinstein. Subsequent research by Julia's computer team indicated Stasko was one of the largest, albeit anonymous, benefactors of the Latvian National Opera and Ballet and maintained a private box.

Evidence of Stasko's appearance at various operas and ballets went back years. Attendance records indicated he preferred the operatic combination of drama, music, and song over the classical form of dance. Stasko had a pattern of attending various ballets, but he always made a point to attend every Russian opera that visited the Latvian National Opera and Ballet. Max looked up the schedule. Two nights hence was a performance of Eugene Onegin, a Russian opera by the famous Russian composer, Tchaikovsky, and Max bet Stasko wouldn't miss such a performance.

When his phone buzzed, he saw a text message from Kaamil. Max tapped on the link included in the text message, and after a moment, he heard Kaamil's voice come over a secure voice-over-IP connection. Max spoke slowly to accommodate the two-second delay between transmissions as the call was routed through various firewalls and six servers.

Despite his discomfort with the young man's skills, Max was forced to rely on the former CIA operative for operational tech support. "What do you have?"

"I got you a private box three doors down from Stasko's for Wednesday night's performance of Eugene Onegin."

Max flicked cigarette ash out a crack in the window. "Perfect. Now all I need is a tux."

"Can't help you there, but I can give you some insight into Stasko's role in the consortium."

Max stubbed the butt out in the overflowing ashtray. "Tell me."

"As you know, Stasko owns the largest network of private and public banking institutions in Latvia. Turns out, Latvia's banking laws and regulations are friendly to private banks that wish to obscure the details of their customer's holdings and transactions. Apparently, the country believes banking is its ticket to economic growth."

Max fished out another cigarette, wondering if Kaamil had any new information for him. "Go on."

"Well, with their admittance to the EU back in 2014, and the country's connection to Russia and the former Soviet Union, Latvia has become the prime conduit for Russian oligarchs to launder their money into the EU."

Max clicked his grandfather's lighter open and held a flame to the end of the cigarette. "Makes sense."

"My guess is most of the consortium's bank accounts and financial transactions go through Stasko's system. If we can trace the consortium's flow of money, we'll get insight into what they're doing."

Max sat up. "Is that something you can do?"

"I'll let you know."

Max thought of Goshawk. Whatever security the consortium and the Latvian banks had in place would be child's play for his old friend. He hoped she was still alive, wherever she was. "Do that, but be careful. Someone is either inadvertently leaking information to the consortium or doing it on purpose. We can't have this getting out."

"I'm on it. I also sent you the blueprints for the Latvian National Opera and Ballet building."

Max thanked him and ended the call, his mind still with his former computer resource. Despite Goshawk's appetite for recreational drugs and her obsessive paranoia, Max missed her. Goshawk's raw intellect was a turn-on, as was her lithe tattoo-covered body and her voracious sexual appetite. Max shook off his daydream and forced himself to focus on the operation at hand. He stubbed out his cigarette in the ashtray and tossed back the dregs of his cold coffee before starting up the Volkswagen. He steered the car out into the street in search of a hot meal, a long sleep, and an upscale men's shop where he could purchase a tailor-made tux and a few other props he needed for the operation.

TWENTY-TWO

Riga, Latvia

By the time the MI5 Lear touched down at Riga International, the computer jockeys at Vauxhall Crossing had traced the email with the attachment of Mikhail Asimov's image, pinpointing its origin at a location just outside Riga in a sprawling complex of warehouses and trucking businesses.

Baxter, Taylor, Gordon, and Cindy clambered into a SUV and were whisked into the darkness of Riga. At first, Taylor refused to bring Cindy on the trip, but Baxter convinced him by pointing out they could use her native knowledge of the country and her fluency in Latvian. Taylor looked pained, but acquiesced before admonishing the young woman to stay out from underfoot. She mouthed the words *Thank You* to Baxter and busied herself with a text message.

By the time they roared up to the warehouse, a cacophony of cars, flashing lights, law enforcement, and press had taken over the industrial area. Yellow tape, the ubiquitous international sign for a crime scene, was used to cordon off a wide radius around the warehouse. Baxter recognized the insignia of various Latvian law enforcement agencies: the Drošības policija, or Security Police; the Satversmes aizsardzības birojs, or SAB; and the Militārās izlūkošanas un drošības dienests, or MIDD. The Security Police acted as the local police force and controlled the perimeter and interviewed civilians. The MIDD, also known as the Defense Intelligence and Security Service, equivalent to Britain's MI6, was in charge.

Taylor made the necessary introductions. After the usual turf battles were fought, Taylor agreed the team from Great Britain would play the role of observer if they got unfettered access to the scene and the ongoing investigation reports. The Latvians, mildly impressed the Brits brought a Latvian interpreter with them, agreed. By that time, Baxter was already poking around the interior of the warehouse.

A medical examination team was in the process of removing the bodies so Baxter had to rely on photographs to piece together the scene. Blood spatter was everywhere, and pools of the drying dark red liquid were surrounded by taped outlines of the corpses in several spots where bodies had lain. Baxter was puzzled by the weapons scattered on the concrete floor. He snapped on a pair of black latex gloves and examined each gun.

There was an assault rifle fitted with a long black suppressor. There were several pistols of various makes and models and a long gun that Baxter identified as a Russian-made sniper rifle. He removed the magazines from each weapon. Both rifles' magazines were empty, as were their chambers. He moved his attention to the pistols. When he examined the bullets, he was startled to find that all the magazines were loaded with bullets with crimped ends. Baxter knew that meant the bullets were blanks. He snapped a few photos with his phone.

Next he went over the bullet-riddled SUV inch by inch, noting how clean it was. The glove box was empty, and there weren't any water bottles or other trash on the floor. The forensics team had gone through it before proclaiming it devoid of fingerprints.

Baxter waved over a forensics technician. "Was there a body in the car?"

The woman shook her head. "No, sir."

"But there were three bodies on the floor of the warehouse?"

The technician nodded and pointed. In halting English, she said, "One here, one there, and one there. Official autopsy is tomorrow, but cause of death looks like bullet wounds."

Baxter went back outside and ran into Taylor and Cindy. He held up an arm, suggesting Cindy not enter the warehouse. "Graphic violence in there."

Blood drained from her face, and she remained put.

Baxter relayed what he found in the warehouse. "I think we're missing a body. Either that or someone was severely wounded in the driver's seat of the SUV and managed to escape. I think it was a gun buy gone wrong. The sellers figured they'd cash in on the reward instead of making a few measly bucks by selling a couple guns."

Taylor nodded. "Any sign of cash?"

"None. Asimov shows up in the SUV with an accomplice. Gets out, accomplice stays in the car. The trap is sprung. Asimov is captured, his accomplice killed. Asimov somehow kills the attackers, takes the guns he needs, the cash, grabs the accomplice out of the SUV, and makes off in the gun seller's car."

Taylor pinched his lower lip. "So we have a pissed-off assassin roaming the streets of Riga with his choice of weapons."

"And maybe a dead body." Baxter's rear pocket buzzed with an incoming call. He removed his Blackberry and looked at the screen. *Unknown caller.*

He walked away from Taylor and Cindy. "Baxter."

There were a series of clicks and a hiss before the metallic voice of the man who called himself Bluefish came on the line.

"Hello, Callum."

The gravely, machine-generated voice sounded ominous and caused his stomach to drop out from under him like he was on a merry-go-round. He waved a hand at Cindy, who came running over. "Hello, Mr. Bluefish."

"I see you made it to Latvia. I assume you arrived to find three dead men and Asimov missing."

"Correct. Three dead guys and no sign of Asimov." As he talked, he went through his logic for establishing a relationship with Bluefish. During the flight over to Latvia, he mulled over the ethics of developing the source. On the one hand, he didn't trust Bluefish's intentions. Obviously the man, and Baxter assumed it was a man, was using Baxter as a puppet to carry out actions he didn't want to do himself. Bluefish also wanted Asimov out of the way, *making Baxter wonder what his true motives were.* On the positive side, an intelligence officer's primary weapon was information. If he could glean information from Bluefish, he might stand a better chance of catching Asimov.

The electronics squawked, making Baxter jump. "Details, please."

Baxter gave Bluefish the details of the scene, sticking to the facts. He looked over at Cindy, who was watching him.

"I'd like to remind you that our little relationship should be kept just between ourselves. I trust that your young protégé there, the precocious Ms. Cindy Walsh, knows nothing of our conversations."

A chill went down Baxter's spine. How did Bluefish know Cindy was standing right next to him? He slowly turned to scan the area. A small set of onlookers stood just outside the crime scene boundary. The rest of the scene was organized chaos as investigators, various Latvian officials, and other law enforcement bustled about. No one was on their phone.

Baxter called his bluff. "Of course not."

There was a hesitation on the line while Baxter held his breath.

"Excellent. Now, where were we? Ah, yes. The where-abouts of Mr. Mikhail Asimov. Have you determined his target yet, Mr. Baxter? There must be a reason he's in Latvia, don't you think? He didn't go there just to purchase a weapon."

Baxter chided himself. He assumed Asimov was on the run. It didn't occur to him that the assassin might be targeting someone. "You think he's after a target so soon after the bombing? Logic would tell me that he would lay low. Maybe he was making a weapon purchase for self-defense? Maybe he's here in Latvia to cross the border into Russia, where he plans to disappear."

Baxter held the phone away from his ear when the mechanical laughter turned into static.

"I can assure you that Mikhail Asimov has no intention of disappearing."

Baxter made a show of rolling his eyes at Cindy, who

stifled a laugh with her hand. "Okay, so let's assume for the moment he's not going to vanish into the woodwork. Why would he risk exposure by going after a target?"

Bluefish's metallic voice was devoid of humor. "Mikhail Asimov is a man on a mission. Not even your little investigation will stop him from carrying out his mission."

"Our investigation isn't so little. Is this where you impart to me some earth-shattering wisdom that unearths the great assassin's location?"

"The sarcasm is not appreciated, Mr. Baxter. Stay close to your phone. Whatever Asimov has planned in Latvia will become known soon. And when it does, you'll want me there by your side."

The connection went dead.

———

Baxter went to find Taylor. A few things weren't adding up, and he wanted to talk it through with his old friend. He found the MI5 man talking with the medical examiner. When Taylor was through, Baxter pulled him aside.

"Anything about all of this bothering you, John?"

John Taylor ran a hand through his thinning hair. "The whole bloody lot bothers me."

Baxter shoved his hands in his pockets. "A truck bomb driven by what looks like an Islamic extremist explodes in a busy London café killing fifty-six people, one of whom is a popular MP candidate. Immediately after the explosion, the media somehow miraculously receives buckets of information showing the mastermind is an ex-KGB hitman, which made us think the target was Zachary Brent. Anything odd in that?"

Taylor looked around like he'd rather be somewhere

else. "I ran your web bot idea by our head of cyber. He didn't dismiss the concept outright."

"Forget about that for a minute. How much do you know about Asimov?"

Taylor looked at his watch. "I was briefed on the way over. Not much. Seems to be some circumstantial evidence he's now an assassin for hire. Now Callum, I need to—"

Baxter touched John Taylor's tie. "Hear me out for a second. We have an extensive file on him. Our intel—"

Taylor's brow furrowed as he interjected. "You have a file on this guy you're not sharing?"

Baxter grimaced. "It's my personal hobby, actually. I'll have it bundled up and sent over."

Taylor crossed his arms and stared at him, looking like a man talking to a teenage girl late for her curfew.

Baxter ignored the look. "To begin with, the modus operandi was all wrong. Asimov is a sophisticated assassin who relies on surgical precision, stealth, and fastidiously planned operations. A bomb that takes out civilians is way outside his standard approach, as is working with others, like an unpredictable suicide driver."

Taylor glanced at the warehouse. "Money is a big motivator. What's a few civilian lives for a few million bucks?"

"All the targets I have attributed to Asimov were men who turned out to be criminals, shadowy men who operated above the law, men who were guilty of crimes like money laundering or large-scale illicit weapons sales. There are very few political figures on the list. And those that were, ended up corrupt."

"Maybe Brent will turn out to have some skeletons in his closet."

Baxter controlled his irritation. "Don't get blinded by—"

Taylor knitted his eyebrows together. "Do you know

what's on the line here? We're talking about our citizens being able to sleep tonight. We're talking about ensuring people feel comfortable enough to go out at night and spend their hard-earned money. We're talking about tourists coming over to spend their dollars. Great Britain's economy."

Baxter nodded. "I know, John. But catching the wrong man is a placebo. It only makes you feel better in the short term until the symptoms crop up again."

Taylor rolled his eyes before turning away and walking back into the warehouse. Over his shoulder he called, "Don't forget that not pursuing Asimov is a career-limiting decision."

Baxter let him go and went looking for Cindy. The last thing he cared about was his career.

TWENTY-THREE

Riga, Latvia

The loading dock area of the Latvian National Opera and Ballet building was quiet, clean, and trash-free. Even the dumpster was freshly painted and hidden behind an ivy-covered fence. Out front, among the manicured flower gardens of the building's Roman column-dominated entrance, limousines, foreign-made luxury sedans, and taxi-cabs jockeyed for position to drop off well-coifed men and women resplendent in elegant evening wear. On the rear loading dock, two stage hands puffed on cigarettes before disappearing through a narrow door.

When the door closed behind them, Max used an ornate cane to totter across the parking lot before ascending a set of concrete stairs to the loading platform. He leaned the cane against the wall and fished out his own cigarettes and lighter. Smoking was such a useful spy prop, he didn't understand, nor trust, an operative who didn't smoke. He

tapped the end of a cigarette on his palm and lit it with his
Zippo, the one with the Belarusian flag on its side.

His shoes were shiny patent leather Prada, and his
tuxedo was Hugo Boss off the rack, nipped and tucked to fit
Max's broad shoulders and muscular frame. In addition to
the cane, he wore a black fedora over a black wig, a fake
goatee, and a pair of smoked glasses. Nestled in a shoulder
holster was a Beretta M9, modified to take a .22 caliber
round and fitted with a threaded barrel. A long black
suppressor was in his pocket.

He finished the cigarette and stubbed it out with the
bottom of his shoe before putting the butt into his pocket.
Snapping on a pair of tight-fitting black leather gloves, he
pulled open the door and stepped into the darkened rear of
the building. The ceiling towered several stories above and
was filled with all manner of stage props, sound and lighting
gear, a ballast, and rigging. Everything needed to operate a
modern theater.

Max sauntered across the room and exited through a
door marked *Stage*, skirting the scaffolding that made up the
rear of the stage area, and found the door to the lobby. He
walked, using the cane to brace himself, and emphasized a
lame left leg, which wasn't difficult, considering the knife
wound in his left thigh.

Several stagehands shoved past, intent on their duties,
ignoring his presence. Max knew a man in a suit backstage
attracted little attention. Certain patrons had access to
backstage, the green room, and dressing rooms, either to
visit the cast or because of relationships with management.
You were seldom questioned if you walked with confidence
through a restricted area, and if you were challenged, it was
a simple matter to claim you were lost. He exited the back-

stage area into a plush hallway with bright red carpet and blended into the milling crowd.

He followed a group of men in black tuxedos and women in black gowns and fur wraps up several sets of stairs until he found the door marked *Private*. There he showed his ticket to an attendant in a black vest and was admitted to a wide hallway dimly lit with small floor sconces. Six doorways along the hall led to private boxes. Moving slowly with the cane, he passed by the door to Erich Stasko's suite and stopped to listen and heard nothing, so Max continued to his appointed suite, opened the door, and stepped inside.

Max knew from the plans provided by Kaamil that each box was outfitted the same. Six chairs, situated in two rows of three, faced the stage three stories above the cavernous room's main floor. Behind the chairs was room for a small wet bar and a tiny coat closet. Max took a seat in the second row of chairs, wishing he could smoke. While he waited, he screwed the suppressor into the threaded barrel of the Beretta, taking his time to ensure he made no noise.

Max didn't care for opera, despite the art form's long history in Russian culture. He preferred the improvisation and soul-moving art form of jazz. Soon the rustling and chatter in the cavernous hall grew still as the house lights flickered and darkness descended over the audience.

Max waited until the first song died away before leaving his box and moving into the darkened hallway. Carrying the gun next to his leg, he put a gloved hand on the doorknob to Stasko's suite. Max knew theaters of the caliber of the Latvian National Opera and Ballet took excruciating care of their suite's doors to prevent an offending squeal or click from reverberating through the auditorium. For that reason, the building also prohibited locks on the doors to private boxes.

Max tested the knob and waited until the tenor's voice reached a crescendo before opening it and slipping through. The room was pitch black, the sparse lighting from the stage barely penetrating the box three floors above the stage. In front of him were three silhouettes: One sitting in the front row, the other two flanking him in the second row. Across the open auditorium another row of private boxes was visible, but their openings and occupants were shrouded in shadows. Even if someone were to glance their way, Max knew no one would see into their box.

Max waited for the singer and the orchestra to work itself into a frenzy before taking two steps on the plush carpet and putting a bullet into one bodyguard's neck. Pivoting, he shot the second guard at the base of the skull. Both men slumped to the ground, the sound muffled by the orchestra's booming timpani and crashing cymbals.

Erich Stasko must have sensed movement behind him or perhaps felt a slight tremor in the floor from the guard's bodies. He turned just as Max took a seat behind him and shoved the gun muzzle in the man's side. Max placed a forefinger against his lips as Stasko's eyes widened.

Max waited for the opera singer to crank up her voice, the sopranos and tenors ringing off the ceiling while the bases boomed over the audience. He gripped Stasko by the collar and yanked him sideways, around the affixed chair, and shoved him into the coat closet. A quick frisk revealed no weapons. Max pocketed Stasko's smartphone and stuck the gun up under Stasko's chin. "Speak louder than a whisper and I'll put a bullet into your brain."

Erich Stasko's eyes flashed in the faint light from the

auditorium. "You're making a big mistake. Do you know who I am?"

Max leaned close, his nose inches from Stasko's. "The more important question is, Erich, do you know who I am?"

Stasko's eyes went wide with recognition. "How'd you—"

The pitch of his voice went up an octave, forcing Max to clamp his free hand over Stasko's mouth. "I assume you value your life?"

Stasko nodded, eyes bulging under Max's gloved grip.

"That's good. That means you and I might have a chance of getting along. I need some information. The more useful you are to me, the more likely I am to let you live. Do you understand?"

Stasko nodded his head.

"See, I know everything about you, Erich. I know where your wife and daughters live. You may not care about your wife, but I'm guessing you care about your girls. I'm guessing you'd prefer not to receive their carved-up body parts in the mail. Am I right?"

Stasko's eyebrows met his hairline, which Max took for agreement.

"When I ask a question, I'll remove my hand. If you answer in a whisper, you live. Anything louder than a whisper, you die. Lucky for me there are ten other members of the consortium who remain alive. Any one of them can get me the information I'm looking for. Do you read me?"

Stasko nodded.

"Let's start with an easy question. Are you a member of the consortium?" Max lifted his hand a fraction of a centimeter.

"Yes," came the whispered response.

"Good. What is your assigned number?"

Stasko looked surprised, and Max nudged him with the gun.

"Twelve."

"Respectable job so far. See, this is easy. Elizabeth Edgars is your daughter's pseudonym. She's nineteen, and a student at King's College in London. Studying pre-med, wants to be a pediatrician. I have her address and photos. Her bodyguards can be easily eliminated."

The blood drained from Stasko's cheeks, and his eyes welled up.

"Victoria Edgars, her older sister, is studying economics at Cambridge. Destined for greatness, she wants to work for the UN and do good things. It would be a shame to prevent the world from benefiting from such young and strong minds."

A tear rolled down one of Stasko's cheek.

"Who carried out the bombing in West Brompton?"

Erich Stasko shook his head.

"It wasn't me," Max said. "You know it, and I know it. And it wasn't the poor slob driving the grocery van. He was the patsy. Who planned and carried out the attack?"

Stasko continued shaking his head. "I don't know. Number One made us watch it as it happened."

"We all being who?"

Stasko squirmed. "The rest of the members."

"Nikita Ivanov did the whole thing by himself? Without help from the rest of the membership?"

Stasko nodded. "As far as I know. The rest of the group was as surprised as I was."

"What is Nikita Ivanov's real name?"

"I don't know. No one knows."

Max adjusted his grip and checked his watch. He wanted to time his departure with the first intermission and knew he needed to end the conversation quickly. "You control the consortium's cash flow, correct?"

Stasko hesitated, then nodded.

"You now work for me, Stasko, assuming you value your daughters' lives. If Ivanov carried out the attack or planned the bombing, there must be a trail of cash. Supplies had to be paid for, people bought off. The master planner was paid. The van driver's family was also paid."

Max let go of Stasko and produced a slip of paper. Written on one side was a ten-digit IP address. He shoved the paper into Stasko's mouth.

"You have forty-eight hours to get me that paper trail. When you do, put the details on this server. Your youngest daughter's college ID number is the user name and your wife's passport number is the password. I'll be alerted when the data is there. Assuming the information is what I need, your daughters will be safe. For every hour past the deadline, I'll remove one of Victoria's fingers. Then I'll move to her toes. Nod your head if you understand."

Stasko nodded, a tear rolling down one cheek.

"One other thing, Erich. Both your daughters are being watched right now. If one or the other deviates from their normal movements in the next forty-eight hours, they'll be snatched and you'll never see them again. The best thing you can do is let them go about their business, never the wiser about our little arrangement. Do you follow?"

Stasko gave a shaky nod.

Max clamped his hand over Erich's mouth. "Remember what I said. You're working for me now. If you produce useful information, you and your family will stay safe."

Max reversed his grip on the pistol and brought the butt down on Stasko's temple, knocking the man out cold. He wrenched the gold Cartier watch from his wrist and snatched the billfold from his pocket. The police would be on the lookout for an armed robber with a cane and goatee, and the media would have a field day with the brazen robbery of the country's wealthiest man. Max would be long gone from Latvia by then.

He grabbed the cane and holstered the pistol before exiting the suite and disappearing into the throng of patrons enjoying refreshments and talking in excited huddles about the quality of that night's performance.

TWENTY-FOUR

Riga, Latvia

The scene at the Latvian National Opera and Ballet was pandemonium. The entire building was surrounded by every make and model of law enforcement vehicle. Tall spotlights illuminated the area as low-level policemen cordoned off the scene with yellow tape.

No matter how many times Baxter visited a crime scene, he still wasn't used to the chaos. Once again, it wasn't clear who had jurisdiction. Men in suits spoke into mobile phones while uniformed officers listened on handheld radios. Along with their Latvian escort, Baxter, Taylor, Gordon, and Cindy were led under the tape, through the bright lights, and up the wide marble staircase of the National Opera's entrance.

The fact the call came through normal Latvian channels, and not through the seemingly ever-omniscient Mr. Bluefish, was not lost on Baxter. Perhaps the source was fallible after all, or perhaps Mr. Bluefish simply decided to allow the notification to come through normal channels. Either way, Asimov's target in Latvia was now clear. The question was why. And why had Asimov allowed him to live?

Erich Stasko sat in a chair in the National Opera's green room where he was whisked after a cleaning crew member had stumbled into the crime scene and reeled in horror from seeing two dead men. When one of them groaned and stirred, the old attendant almost fainted but managed to call his supervisor, who alerted management. The opera's director, a nervous man in his sixties, rushed to his most important benefactor's side and supplied him with a bottle of chilled vodka before alerting Stasko's people. Only after Erich Stasko's two attorneys and three other handlers arrived did the director alert the police. That decision would come to haunt the director for weeks.

Baxter knelt to examine the two dead guards, noting the small entry wounds at the base of their necks. "Twenty-two caliber, the bullet choice of first-time shooters and professionals and no one in between."

Cindy leaned over to get a better look. "Why professionals? I'd think pros would want more fire power."

Baxter stood and surveyed the room as he talked. "Pros want lightweight guns, the absence of recoil with precision accuracy, and as little sound as possible. Hence the twenty-two. Pros are confident of their ability to put the bullet exactly where they want it. They don't need more firepower."

Cindy nodded as if Baxter had communicated the meaning of life.

He guided her back down the stairs and into the green room, where a dour-faced Latvian in a rumpled suit was questioning Erich Stasko. Cindy translated for Baxter in a hushed voice.

"Mr. Stasko, I understand and commiserate with your situation. But the man must have wanted to talk to you about something. Otherwise, why would he go to all this trouble?"

"As I've said already, I can't answer that. All I know is I heard my bodyguards hit the floor. When I turned, the intruder hit me in the head and I blacked out. When I came to, the director was hunched over me, and my watch and wallet and phone were gone."

Stasko's lawyer, a big man in a well-tailored suit, intervened. "That's enough. Mr. Stasko has had a tough night, and it's time for him to go home. You can get in touch with him through me." The lawyer handed the official a card before taking Erich Stasko's arm and guiding him from the room. As they disappeared, the Latvian MIDD official sputtered and tossed his hands in the air.

Baxter didn't buy Stasko's story and knew the trail to Asimov hinged on what went down between Asimov and Stasko. He turned and left the green room, pacing through the cavernous backstage area, barely aware that Cindy followed along behind him. He found a coffee maker and coaxed the machine to life, propped up his feet on a folding table, and sipped the hot brew.

"Boss."

Baxter was so lost in thought, he failed to notice Cindy had set up her laptop on the folding table.

"What?"

She stopped typing and pointed to the screen. "I think you're going to want to see this."

Baxter forced himself to his feet and came around to her side of the table.

She clicked on her trackpad. "Hold on."

Baxter glanced at the screen and saw a command window with streams of green font, similar to an opening sequence to a movie he suffered through called *The Matrix*, except these were going from left to right at the same pace Cindy typed.

She jabbed a manicured fingernail at her screen. "There."

The green font vanished, and a video window appeared. In the video, Baxter saw throngs of operagoers, most of the men in tuxedos and many of the women dressed in long gowns and furs. "What am I looking at?"

"Wait—there." Her finger traced the screen, following a tall man wearing a black fedora. He walked with a limp, relying on a cane to balance his weight. A bushy goatee covered his upper lip and chin, and he wore a pair of glasses with smoke-colored lenses.

Baxter sucked in his breath. "Where did you get this?"

Cindy beamed. "I connected to their Wi-Fi and hacked into their system. Their firewall hasn't been updated in years."

Baxter groaned.

Cindy tapped a few times on the keyboard, changing the screen to another camera angle. "That was on the way in. This one shows the man disappearing through the door to the private boxes. No cameras in the boxes."

"Of course not."

Cindy's fingers flew over the keyboard in a blur. "But wait. I can fast-forward the feed. This is just after they broke for the first intermission."

After a few seconds of footage, the limping man exited the door from the private boxes and picked his way down a packed hallway, leaning on the cane and politely allowing women to pass in front of him. He did not look like someone who had just killed two men and robbed the richest man in Latvia.

Cindy tapped, and a new camera angle appeared. The man exited the lobby through a door leading to backstage. Another tap showed the man moving through bustling stagehands while removing a packet of cigarettes from his jacket. Another screen showed him exit onto the rear loading dock where he stopped to light the cigarette before hobbling away from the rest of the smokers.

Baxter saw the man's hand was steady as he held the cigarette. "He's got elephant-sized balls. I'll give him that."

Cindy smiled up at him. "You sound impressed."

Baxter ignored her comment and watched the screen as the other smokers reentered the building, leaving the man with the limp to finish his cigarette alone. After the last person disappeared back inside, Asimov dropped his cigarette, ground it under the ball of his foot, picked up the butt, and slipped it into his pocket. Taking his time and using the cane for balance, he descended the stairs before disappearing into the shrubbery that divided the rear loading area from the sidewalk.

Baxter realized his skin was covered in goosebumps. He had just watched one of the world's most famous assassins in action.

———

Baxter sat next to Cindy in the SUV's back seat as they thundered through the dark and empty streets of the Latvian capital, driven by a capable MIDD staffer. The MI5 team of Taylor and Grant planned to join them at the hanger after making a stop at the local police headquarters.

He held his Blackberry in his hand, expecting it to buzz at any second. While the colored lights of the city flashed by, he pondered the last forty-eight hours.

They were just behind the assassin every step of the way while tracing him across the channel into France and from Marseille to Barcelona via ship, where they lost the trail. Somehow, Asimov made it from Barcelona to Latvia only to turn up in the clutches of a Latvian gang before disappearing and leaving dead bodies behind, after which he mysteriously accosted the wealthiest man in Latvia. Now the assassin had vanished again. Baxter's head spun trying to put it all together.

The Latvians had eyes and ears at every port of call and border crossing. Their coast guard was on high alert, with every available man on patrol in the cold blue waters of the Gulf of Riga. The Lithuanians, Estonians, Belarusians, and the Russians had all been alerted, flooding the borders with foot and motorized patrols. It was an international effort to find the world's most wanted terrorist. Baxter knew the law enforcement agencies in any country would love to capture Asimov and garner the accolades and bask in the press coverage while thumbing their collective noses at the inept British secret services that couldn't even capture their own fugitive.

Baxter was transfixed, horrified, and to his own chagrin, thrilled that he witnessed the famous assassin at work. The sight of the killer slipping out of the opera house was not something he would soon forget.

What was Asimov up to? How did the Latvian fit into the scheme? If Asimov caused the car bombing in West Brompton, what was his ulterior motive? From Baxter's experience, assassins of Asimov's caliber and pedigree didn't commit acts of terror. Only one man had the answer to all the questions, but that man had vanished. Baxter's instinct told him none of the roadblocks, immigration flags, or border patrols would catch him. Asimov would turn up at a time and location of his own choosing.

The SUV bounced over speed bumps as it roared onto the tarmac of Riga International Airport. The MI6 Lear was in a private hanger, its engine's warmed, waiting to take the four of them back to British soil. The caravan screeched to a halt and the team exited. As Baxter climbed down from the car, his Blackberry buzzed. He froze when he saw *Unknown Caller* on the screen. Heart pounding, he touched the green answer key.

The metallic voice ground in his ear making him cringe. "Leave the MI5 team behind."

"What?"

"They need to find their own way home."

In the background, Baxter thought he heard a ding, like the sound of an email notification. "What the—"

"Asimov has already left Latvia. While you and your friends bumbled through the National Opera building, Asimov was already winging his way west. Take Cindy. You'll need her help."

Baxter pressed the phone harder to his ear and turned away from the group. "How do you know?"

"Don't worry about how I know. Trust me."

He covered the phone's mic and yelled, "Cindy!"

The blond, hair perfectly done in a ponytail held with a polka-dot ribbon and looking none the worse for wear after being awake for more than twenty-four hours, came running with her laptop bag bouncing on one hip.

Baxter pointed up the Lear's ramp. "Get on the plane."

Cindy did as she was told.

Baxter walked to the base of the Lear's stairs and

watched Cindy disappear into the plane's interior. "If you want me to trust you, you have to give me something I can use. I can't just jump on a plane to who knows where. Asimov crosses borders like you and I change underwear. He could be deep into Russia by now. I can't just gallivant into international jurisdictions without going through the proper channels. I'm not going to cause an international incident."

"He's not going into Russia. He's headed to England. And if you don't get moving, you'll lose him again."

Baxter leapt up the Lear's stairs. "Bugger me." Taylor would be hot, but he would explain his disappearance later. Baxter was on the hunt for an assassin, and some hunts were better executed alone.

TWENTY-FIVE

Cambridge, England

The German BND's Lear jet touched down at a private airstrip an hour west of London. Max stepped off the plane into the back seat of a waiting German luxury sedan. After Max and the driver exchanged the mutual passphrases, the car glided forward and soon they were humming north on the M3 at a rapid clip.

Max pulled out his Blackphone, punched in a long string of digits, and waited for the encrypted connection to take place. When Julia's voice came through, it was full of static.

"Ja?" came her greeting in German.

Max also spoke in German. "Any change in her status?"

"None. The bodyguards still don't accompany her on campus. I still don't like the idea of you kidnapping an innocent student while on British soil."

Max watched the lush green English countryside rush

by. "Who said anything about kidnapping? We're just going to have a little conversation."

"How are you going to do it without incapacitating her bodyguards and taking her somewhere against her will?"

Max smiled into the phone. "Tinder."

A pause. "What's Tinder?"

"It's a social media dating app."

"Max."

"I'm kidding. I'm going to use roofies."

"Max!"

Max rolled his eyes. "I'm kidding. Let me worry about that part. It'll be a simple five-minute conversation. That's it."

While holding his phone to his ear with his shoulder, he removed a file folder from his bag that had been waiting for him in the jet. The dossier contained a stack of papers showing the transcripts and class schedules of a student named Victoria Edgars. Stapled to the file folder was a headshot, Victoria's most recent yearbook photo. Under the class schedules were several dozen surveillance shots. Max had memorized the file on the flight over from Latvia, but wanted to take one last look before destroying the file.

"Better be," Julia said. "Call me when it's done, and get out of there as soon as possible. I still don't understand why we can't have someone from my team snap a few pictures of her and call it good."

Max paged through the photos of the college student. "As I said, I want the threat to be as real as possible. Anyone can snap pictures. Stasko has to believe his daughter's life is in imminent danger."

Silence on the other end indicated Julia didn't agree. Luckily, Max was a volunteer on her staff, so he called his own shots. He didn't want to take chances. Not with the entire world looking for him. Dozens of intelligence agencies were hunting him. One false step would land him in prison where he would waste away while the consortium hunted his sister and nephew. He was going to run this operation his way, the right way.

"Give me an hour to get into place before pulling the surveillance. The fewer people who know I'm here, the better."

Julia's voice sounded strained. "Will do."

Max hung up, still paging through the surveillance images. Victoria Edgars was a beautiful young lady—silky black hair, somber eyes rimmed by dark mascara, and skin the color of ivory. She was hardworking and intelligent, as evidenced by the marks on her transcripts. Comments from her professors indicated she would go far in the world of economics. Max didn't want to do any irreparable damage to the innocent young lady. He wouldn't force her to pay for her father's sins.

———

Max stood just off King's Parade, gazing like a tourist at the ivy-covered ramparts of Kings College, smack in the middle of Cambridge. With a digital SLR camera around his neck, he wore a floppy hat to ward off the sun and provide partial disguise. Completing his ensemble were oversized wraparound sunglasses covering his eyes and a backpack with the name of a French football team slung over one shoulder. A compact pistol, for emergencies only, was at the small of his back. His adopted cover was that of the father of a French high school girl who wished to attend Cambridge the

following year. He was in London on business and came to
Cambridge to take a tour and scout the place on behalf of
his daughter.

The manicured grass of the quadrangle was empty
while the students attended midmorning classes. A rare
English blue sky was overhead, but clouds on the horizon
threatened rain. Max hoped the moisture would stay at bay
long enough to complete his mission. He walked to a pair of
double doors set into tall Gothic yellow walls topped with
towering spires and confirmed the building was indeed the
economics department.

He took a few steps back to snap photos of the building
before following a gravel path to the gentle River Cam. He
turned right to stroll north toward St. Johns and stopped
when he saw the Bridge of Sighs. He checked his watch,
removed a guidebook from his pocket, and learned that the
Bridge of Sighs, built in the neo-gothic tradition with arched
windows and stone ramparts, was named after a covered
bridge in Venice where prisoners sighed as they were
escorted to their cells. Several skiffs containing tourists
floated on the river, piloted by drivers wearing green vests
over white shirts who guided the boats with long poles.

He captured a few pictures of the river before saun-
tering back in the direction of King's College. As he
approached the wide grassy field, bells tolled and a stream
of students exited the buildings, spreading out like
lemmings. Soon the quadrangle was filled with students in
small groups, talking, sharing cigarettes, and laughing at
jokes. In front of him, walking with a purpose and hunched
under a large rucksack, came a short but curvy student with
heavy mascara and her dark hair held back with a barrette.

Max pretended to ignore her, but watched her out of his
periphery. He knew she had twenty minutes to make it

from King's College to St. John's, where she had a class in romantic literature. Based on what Max read in her file, he guessed she would rather be anywhere than in a literature class, but her attendance proved she was also determined not to let the class bring down her average.

Despite the warm temperature, she wore a gray knee-length skirt over black leggings, sensible but expensive-looking shoes, and a jean jacket that looked worn but was probably purchased in a boutique on London's Oxford Street. As Max guessed, she took the gravel path along the river, the shortest route to St John's.

Max removed his sunglasses. "Excuse me, Miss." He used English and applied his best French accent. He had his guide book open and the pull-out maps were unfurled and flapping in the breeze.

The young woman slowed and glanced at Max, but she didn't stop.

"My daughter is considering attending Cambridge next year. I wonder if I might ask you a couple of questions? I'm afraid I'm all turned around here. See, she wants to study economics, which for the life of me I don't understand, but there's no telling that girl anything. And I can't seem to find—"

The young woman stopped and turned around. A brief look of annoyance was replaced by a warm smile. "Economics, did you say? Why, that's my course of study." Her accent was British.

Max stepped forward, fumbling with the guidebook. "You don't say. How far along are you?"

"Third year. Just getting into macro theory and looking into the supply side garbage invented by the bloody Americans. Is she good at math?"

Max smiled like a proud father. "She won't shut up

about it. She's into all these new schemes I don't understand. Have to look most of it up on the internet just to keep up with her, I'm afraid."

The student shifted her oversized backpack. "Well then, she's setting herself up right."

Max smiled. "Any other recommendations?"

"Study hard, and nail the exams."

Max nodded. "She's very focused. Much more than I was at her age." He held out the map. "Just one more quick question?"

She nodded and bent forward to follow the finger he traced along the map.

Max stabbed at a spot on the map. "We're here."

She nodded.

He tapped another spot. "The economics department is where? Here?"

She leaned over to study the map. "Not quite." She took the map from his hand and reoriented it. "The Economics department is here." Straightening, she pointed the way she'd come. "That building there."

Max's face lit up. "Splendid. Thank you."

She stole a glance at her watch. "No problem."

"I'm sure you're in a hurry, but one other thing?"

She glanced in the direction of St. John's.

"Does the economics department have anyone she can talk to before she applies? Someone who can answer her questions about what the curriculum is like? What it's like to be a student here?"

She looked up at the sky for a moment, deep in thought. "I don't know, but she can email me. I'd be happy to answer her questions."

"I couldn't impose—"

"It's nothing, really." She slung her bag to the ground, crouched, and unzipped it, digging until she found a pen. She ripped a piece of paper out of a notebook before scribbling something and handing it to him.

Max made a point of studying it. "Victoria Edgars."

She shot him a bright smile. "That's me."

"That is kind of you. She'll be thrilled."

Victoria hitched her bag up again and stuck out her hand. "Nice to meet you, um—"

"Louis. Louis Martin. My daughter's name is Clara. She'll be just, how do the British say it—gobsmacked?"

She pressed a hand to her mouth to quiet a gale of laughter.

Max did his best to look apologetic. "I don't suppose we could take a quick selfie together so I can send it to her? That way she'll know who she's writing to."

Victoria brushed a strand of brown hair from her eyes before glancing at her watch. "Sure. Why not?"

Max sidled up to her and held his phone at arm's reach to snap a few photos.

She moved away, her feet crunching on the gravel. "Cheerio."

Max waved. "Au revoir. Merci beaucoup."

As soon as she disappeared, he surveyed the photos on his phone and noted he had a couple that would work perfectly.

Max walked back in the direction of the economics department before veering off onto Kings Parade, moving as fast as he dared. As usual, his eyes and ears were attuned to everything around him. Students moved in groups of twos and threes, some smoking, many looking at their phones as they walked, while almost all were hunched over by thick backpacks. He found himself on Trumpington Street, passing the newer but still neo-gothic yellow-and-white-washed walls of Pembroke college.

Having accomplished his mission, he wanted nothing more than to distance himself from the island of Great Britain and hole up at the cottage outside Barcelona to wait out Erich Stasko. The German sedan with Julia's driver was supposed to be two blocks down and one block over. As he strolled down the sidewalk, admiring Pembroke's cloistered walkway running next to the bright green quadrangle, his thigh ached where the Latvian thug had cut him with the switchblade. He wanted to pick up his pace, but his training won out and he forced himself to slow and continue in his tourist disguise. He snapped a few photos of Pembroke and meandered another block before turning on Fitzwilliam street.

The first sign of trouble was the missing German sedan. Max examined the street signs to ensure he was in the right spot, but the car was not where it was supposed to be. Maybe it was the fact he was in England, the country where he was framed for a massive terrorist attack, or maybe it was the fact he was working with a new agency, an intelligence service who, until recently, was regarded as one of the world's worst, but a feeling of deep unease set over him. As a precaution, he typed on his Blackphone and sent several pictures of himself and Victoria to Julia using a secure and encrypted email that instructed her to send them anonymously to Erich Stasko. No warning messages from Julia were in his inbox.

He was about to make his way around the block, thinking perhaps the car was in the wrong location, when he heard tires screeching. He turned, his hand moving to the pistol at his lower back but froze when he saw three men leap from a black sprinter van with darkened windows.

One of the men approached with a silenced pistol held in a two-fisted grip pointed at Max. "On your stomach!" His red-and-blue rep tie stuck in Max's mind.

Max balanced himself on the balls of his feet. There was no one on the street but him and the three men. The students had all disappeared to class, leaving the grassy quad behind him eerily silent. The pistol at his back would take a full second or two to draw, time in which he might easily be shot. The men looked serious and capable—hard middle-aged men with field experience. They were men who wouldn't hesitate to drop the United Kingdom's most wanted man with a 9mm to the chest. He put his hands up.

A second man approached, also wearing a rep tie, and pointed a silenced pistol at Max's chest as the third man circled around behind him. They moved with the precision of operatives who'd trained and fought together. These men were used to firing their weapons, used to killing. These were not your garden variety constables of the MET.

It was over in a matter of seconds. A violent kick sent him to his knees, and a shove pushed him face-first into the concrete sidewalk. His arms were pulled behind him, and he felt metal cuffs ratcheted tight around his wrists. He was searched, and the gun was plucked from his back before two of the men picked him up by his shoulders. He was hurled into the van's interior and sprawled on the floor. As he struggled to sit up, he saw a fourth man—this one with a bushy goatee and a pink-and-white polka-dot bow tie. Behind him was a prim-looking young blond woman, whose eyes were as big as saucers.

Before he could say anything, he felt a prick in his neck and the polka dots began swimming in lazy circles like little round fish in a pink ocean. He thought he heard a man say something like, "At last, the famous Russian assassin."

Max tried to talk, but his mouth felt like it was full of peanut butter. He wanted to shout, *"Belarusian, you fuck,"* but all he could do was mumble incoherently before the polka dots disappeared, replaced with blackness.

TWENTY-SIX

Monaco

The tactical team's leader was named Jean. A former sergeant in France's Special Forces Brigade and a veteran of many so-called peace-keeping conflicts in Chad, Somalia, Libya, and Iraq, Jean figured his luck would eventually run out so he jumped at a chance to join Monaco's Corps des Sapeurs-Pompiers, or civil defense service. One of the smallest militaries in the world at 250 soldiers, Monaco's civil defense was largely ornamental. He figured he could slide into retirement with little chance of bodily injury.

Jean didn't count on the city-state taking advantage of his background and found himself in charge of a new, but well-trained, squad of tactical soldiers called the *force de frappe*, or the strike force. This was the third time his crew was mobilized for real operation. The first time was to help secure a go-fast boat laden with drugs and cash in Port Hercules, Monaco's deepwater harbor. The second time was to help the Compagnie des Carabiniers du Prince, the militarized bodyguard unit for Monaco's Prince Albert II, investigate a bomb threat that turned out to be a hoax.

So it was with excitement mixed with trepidation that Jean found himself sitting in a van with three of his men outside the rear loading dock of the Hotel Metropole Monte-Carlo, one of the city-state's finest and most exclusive properties. They were dressed in suits as their prime directive was to not disturb the hotel's well-heeled guests. Each man carried a silenced compact pistol strapped in an arm holster and a set of handcuffs at the back of their belts. The pistols were H&K SFP9's, and Jean was pleased his service spared no expense. Still, the operative felt naked without more powerful weaponry. They had strict orders not to discharge their firearms unless they were under attack.

"Nervous, Sarge?" one of his men asked. A distant relative of the prince, some said one of the prince's many bastard children, the young man had requested an assignment to Jean's team. Jean stared at him without answering, hoping to God the young man would not get shot. It would be bad for his career if a relative of the prince was killed on his watch.

That seemed a remote possibility on this operation. Jean's orders were to enter the hotel at the rear loading dock where he would receive a plastic key card from the night manager. They were to proceed to the third floor where he would leave one man at the elevator and one at the stairwell. He and the fourth man would move to room 320, where they would use the key to enter the room. In the event the door guard was enabled, the fourth man carried a thin foot-long metal strip they would use to deactivate the guard.

Once they were in the room, they were to apprehend a

single female, the room's sole occupant, and cuff and hood her before hustling her out through the hotel's rear door. At this moment, a private jet was en route to Monaco to pick the woman up.

One of his men took out a pack of cigarettes and shook one out. Jean caught the man's eye and shook his head. The man put the pack away.

Jean heard a command through his earbud. "It's a go."

He slid the van's door open. "Let's go, boys. Remember, do not discharge your weapon unless you're faced with mortal danger. We are to avoid an international incident here in our fair city at all costs. Out you go."

They filed out of the van and walked across the parking lot. As they approached the back of the hotel, a roll-top door above a loading dock opened and lone figure in a well-tailored suit stood with a look of disdain on his pale face. With a sniff, he handed Jean a plastic card before turning and disappearing without a word.

Jean and his team moved through the busy halls, forcing bellhops and housekeepers to step aside, and took the service stairs up to a gilded gold-and-cream hallway in a practiced formation. The prince's relative took a position outside the stairwell while a second man hustled down the hallway and took a similar position next to the elevator. Jean and his number two stopped in front of room 320.

Jean counted down from three with his fingers, his partner poised with the metal strip. When he got to one, he slid the keycard into the slot. The lock mechanism deactivated, and he pushed the handle down while opening the door but leaving a two-centimeter gap. His partner slid the metal strip against the outer part of the door guard, preventing the bar from slipping forward. As Jean pulled the door closed, the outer part of the door guard slipped off

the metal ball and he shoved the door open while simultaneously drawing his gun.

He stepped into the dark room.

———

Goshawk typed furiously on the keyboard of a tiny laptop,
her lacquered nails clicking on the plastic keys. She was
hunched over the table with her eyes a foot from the screen,
ignoring her aching shoulder muscles. She was so close to
the information she wanted, she could almost taste it. She
just needed a few more minutes and a lucky break.

She was oblivious to the baroque interior of the hotel
room, its opulence and finery the farthest thing from her
mind. She chose the hotel for one reason—the IT staffer
who sat in a basement office owed her a favor. Her fingers
flew over the keys, the command line instructions all but
gibberish to anyone who didn't understand her world.

There. The opening she needed. The final firewall fell
away, and she was in. She let herself stretch, bending her
arms back as far as they would go, a counterbalance to the
hunched shoulders she endured for the past three hours.

The last few days were a whirlwind, starting the
moment she knew she was compromised. The amount of
technical fire power that was thrown at her was stunning,
the patterns of attacks unique and more sophisticated than
anything she had seen before. Her firewalls crumbled one
by one until she knew she had to disappear. Having one's
identity and physical location exposed was a hacker's worst
nightmare. She would rather go dark and destroy everything
she'd built than suffer the indignity and danger of discovery.
It was with an urgent hand and a heavy heart that she activated the self-destruct sequence.

The rest was a blur. The scramble to find her go-bag, another self-destruct sequence to wipe her home network, and the mad bicycle ride through downtown Paris to the storage unit where she kept her escape vehicle. The sleek Ducati Panigale superbike was propelled by a 1198cc Superquadro engine that could generate 196 horses. Not even the French police on their Yamaha FJR1300s could keep pace with it. A few minutes later she had on her leathers and a black helmet with a smoked visor, and she was flying south on the A6, her legs locked around the vibrating chassis and her torso form-fitted to the gas tank. An hour-long ride brought her to the safety of a farmhouse on ten acres protected by a state-of-the-art security system. After laying low for four weeks and using the dial-up internet connection only to stay current on the news and track down her ride to her final destination, she hopped astride the Ducati for another midnight race from the farm to the hotel in Monaco where she now sat. It was here, using the hotel's internet while she waited for her ride, that Goshawk began her quest to find the one man she knew who might be able to help her.

The sophistication of last week's onslaught against her and many of the attack vectors and digital signatures confirmed her biggest fears. Based on the evidence she accumulated to this point, there could be only one institution that wielded the kind of digital firepower thrown at her —the US National Security Agency. Several years ago, two billion dollars were invested in building a one million square foot data center in the Utah desert capable of crunching through yottabytes of data collected through a surveillance program called PRISM. In addition to the analysis of email, social media, telephony, and other forms of digital communication it collected, the NSA's Utah data center contained several buildings dedicated to cryptography.

Unknown to the public, the facility also housed server blocks and human resources responsible for developing weaponized computer viruses. Unwilling to simply watch and defend, the NSA was also charged with building weaponized computer viruses and preparing the United States for the inevitable cyberwar. Most civilians think the cold war is over. Little do most people realize that the cold war has simply shifted from a nuclear arms race to a cyber arms race.

All evidence pointed to the fact that one of the NSA's cyber-attack teams was targeting her. There was only one thing she had done to warrant the attention of such a powerful force—helping her dear friend Max Austin. How he had come to be on their radar was a mystery. Before Goshawk could continue to help him, she needed to keep herself from being thrown into a dark hole she might never escape. To manage that, she needed to find a mysterious and elusive man who waged his own war against the NSA. A man who so far had lived to tell the tale.

After taking a long gulp from a can of Red Bull, she bent forward, intent on her task, oblivious again to the world around her. To find this man, Goshawk needed to navigate through a virtual gauntlet of traps, puzzles, mazes, and barriers. Her mind entered a virtual cyberworld made up of abstract constructs of bits and bytes. Some pathways she sought were blocked by complicated security while others were open to only those who knew where to look. Some of the blockades were deceptively simple, and she realized they were traps for the unwary. Other impediments to her progress were cryptographic challenges that stretched her mind almost to the breaking point. Some puzzles required decoding messages hidden among the pixels of images. Most hackers would turn back, while those who dared to proceed this far were foolhardy, backed by foreign governments, or desperate. She was the latter.

At her house in Paris, she had been shielded by layers of physical and virtual security that gave her comfort and allowed her to escape into the virtual world without fear of intrusion. Her home was a structure built within a warehouse with state-of-the-art locks, lead shielding, security cameras, motion sensors, and electronic fencing—all the best money could buy. Here in the hotel, she was forced to ignore her deepest fear—that she would be discovered and captured, or worse, killed. No risk, no reward.

That's it! Her fingers froze as she made another breakthrough, the console window on her screen lighting up with a long file structure. She scrolled through the documents, her mind trying to comprehend the enormity of what she saw. The breadth of the information contained in the files was stunning, a virtual treasure trove of data identifying the members of various hacker groups across the globe.

Now what? Was the man's name contained within this vast cache of data?

She drained the can of Red Bull, crumpled the can, and tossed it into her backpack. She had no intention of leaving any of her DNA behind. As the can disappeared into her backpack, she heard a *ding*, and a message window appeared on the computer's monitor.

You're compromised. You need to go.

Her heart rate quickened at the surprise message. *How had she been found? And who was the messenger?* It couldn't be the pimple-faced IT guy in the basement, he didn't have the sophistication to message her let alone know she was compromised.

She regained her composure and started typing again, issuing commands to the computer to copy the documents to a thumb drive she inserted into a USB port. She drummed the nail of her index finger against the lacquered desk as a progress window appeared, showing ten percent complete. She stood with impatience.

Come on!

As she shrugged on her backpack and tucked her hair up under a ball cap, she caught a glimpse of the lights of Monaco winking in the darkness through the window to the balcony. On the horizon, the dark sky met the black ocean where a sprinkle of lights bobbed on the calm sea. Goshawk moved to the hotel room door and crouched to listen but heard nothing. She avoided looking out the peephole, knowing a shadow crossing the lens was a dead giveaway.

She returned to the computer. The progress bar was at fifty-five percent. She drummed her fingers on the desk, wondering if she should go or let the download complete.

Move faster, damn you!

———

Jean slammed the door open and entered first, his pistol held out in front. He sensed his partner entering behind him, pistol also drawn. Jean peeled off to the left, taking in the empty room with a glance, and made for the closed bathroom door. The hotel room was dark, and he smelled and felt the salty humid outside air. And he smelled something else.

He kicked open the bathroom door, placing a well-practiced boot next to the gold door handle. With a crack, the old wood of the jamb gave way and the door popped open. Gun out, Jean moved into the bathroom, knowing with a sinking heart they were too late. The bathroom was empty, but the mystery smell was stronger. He sniffed again before placing it. It was the scent of vanilla. Masculine, but somehow stirring.

"Clear." He moved back into the bedroom. His number two stood next to an open set of French doors holding aside a set of heavy velour curtains and looking out onto the balcony. He stepped through the door and holstered his gun. Jean appreciated the professionalism, erring on the side of caution in case he was seen by a hotel patron. The last thing they needed was someone calling the front desk to complain about a gun-wielding man on a balcony.

"Clear," the soldier said as he came back into the room. "She's gone."

Knowing in his heart they missed their target, Jean directed his number two to spend a few more moments searching the room. The perfectly made king-sized bed sat on a pedestal base that left no room for a human to hide underneath. The closet was empty save for two terry cloth robes and the ubiquitous ironing board and iron.

Jean slammed the closet door closed and toggled his mic. "We just missed her."

The response crackled in his ear. "Roger. We've got roadblocks set up and patrol boats out. She won't get far."

Jean didn't reply, disheartened at his failure. How had she disappeared?

"Sarge, look at this."

Jean joined his number two by the room's narrow desk. When he saw what his man was pointing at, his disappointment turned to anger and chagrin. On the desk was a tiny laptop, its screen blank except for the bouncing image of a female figure in a tight-fitting superhero outfit, cape and all.

The superhero had both hands extended, each with its middle finger sticking up from a closed fist.

———

Goshawk braced herself with both hands on the handle in front of her as the go-fast boat pounded across a light surf. A peek behind and she saw the lights of Monaco receding in the distance, but she also saw the flashing blue-and-red lights of a city government patrol boat in fast pursuit. The officials were a few hundred meters behind, and it didn't look like they were falling back. She turned and tapped the bicep of the man standing next to her. Unable to make herself heard over the roar of the engines, she indicated behind them using her thumb.

Carlu, the swarthy broad-shouldered Corsican she'd known since childhood, glanced back. As his long wavy hair flew in the wind, his dark tanned face turned back to her with a wry grin. He stood at the helm, his six-foot muscled frame stretching the fabric of his T-shirt, while his biceps and shoulders rippled with every move. Carlu had one hand on the throttle and the other gripped the wheel. The long hull of the Fountain 47 Lightning stretched out in front of them, dipping and rising in a staccato rhythm from the light chop.

Goshawk returned the grin and faced ahead, turning her cap backwards and bracing herself for what she knew would come next. She tasted salt on her lips, and for a moment she let herself smile at the thrill of their flight, forgetting that she was running into the abyss, a darkness of unknown, where she feared for her own survival. She chanced a glance at Carlu and found him still looking at her with a crafty smile on his face, his brown eyes sparkling, clearly taking pleasure in the chase.

"What are you waiting for?" Her words were carried away by the wind and drone of the engines.

With a wink, Carlu goosed the throttle and the modified twin Mercuries roared to life. She held on as the craft jumped ahead, its V-hull easily hydroplaning on the jet-black surface of the water. The custom speedboat could do over 90 knots on calm waters. Carlu and his crew used the boat and others like it to run cash and drugs between Corsica and the mainland on behalf of the Gang de la Brise de Mer, Corsica's most powerful organized crime group. He assured her there were no patrol boats, military or otherwise, that could catch them. She held on as the boat picked up speed, forgetting her predicament and her pursuit of the only man she knew who could help her. She inhaled the salty air and let herself get lost in the heart-pounding speed of the boat.

A few minutes later, she risked another look back. All she could see of the patrol boat was the faint blinking red-and-blue lights on the horizon. After another fifteen minutes, Carlu eased back the throttle and they settled into the ride to Corsica. The ferry would take four hours, but the speedboat would take half that amount of time. Goshawk would find temporary safety nestled in the bosom of the organized family, where even the boldest police force could not get to her.

TWENTY-SEVEN

Undisclosed Location

In his drug-induced dream, Max was freezing. It was a bitter, mind-numbing cold, the kind where frostbite might easily appear on exposed extremities. The icy temperature pounded into his forehead, giving him a headache and numbing his skin. Ignoring extreme temperatures and the conditions around him came easy to Max. He had trained in the mountains around Mt. Elbrus in the dead of night in January. He had trekked through the Alps in March while carrying fifty kilos of gear. He'd spent endless days and nights camping in the tundra of Siberia, running drills with weapons, swimming in frozen lakes, and conditioning himself to operate in the cold. Still, for some reason, the cold always made him think about his father and the most pivotal moment in Max's life.

Max's father, Andrei Asimov, was six foot four inches of bear-like girth and leathered skin. He was impervious to heat, cold, water, or any other element that mother nature might throw at him. Max saw him plow through a freezing swamp with just a pair of woolen leggings and canvas boots, emerge on the other side, and put sniper rounds into the center of a target at a thousand meters. The elder Asimov viewed the ability to operate in all conditions a huge operational advantage. He would often say, *While lesser men cower in their tent, you'll be outside putting a bullet in their head.*

So it was with reverence and a lot of determination that a high school-aged Max accompanied his father on training mission after training mission. When he was a young boy, his father took him to a KGB training compound on the outskirts of Minsk to teach him self-defense, how to shoot, and the basics of spy tradecraft. As Max got older, the instruction moved into the field, where Max was subjected to what his father called ride-alongs. Sometimes they accompanied squads of grim-faced warriors with thousand-yard stares. Sometimes not all the men who went on the trips returned home.

It was on one of those missions where the cold sank in so deep that Max would never forget the feeling. Whenever the temperature dipped, Max suffered through fitful dreams of the first time he killed a man. Now the memories spun through his mind, and he was powerless to stop it.

Max sensed this mission was different the moment they arrived at the airbase. Before boarding the Antonov An-26, Max, who had just celebrated his eighteenth birthday, was provided a set of tactical clothing that matched the rest of the team. His father presented him with a Beretta pistol and an AK-47—weapons Max was intimately familiar with. Feeling nauseous with anticipation, he followed his father up the

ramp of the military transport and took a seat among the line
of soldiers strapped into the fold-down seats, holding his rifle
between his legs like the rest of the men. The platoon wore no
insignia on their fatigues, but Max's father had told him the
group was a unit of Spetsnaz, Russia's elite special forces.

His father sat on one side of him, dressed for battle. The
man to Max's right wore a hard look on his face. A jagged
scar ran down his cheek, distorting his nose, and wraparound
sunglasses hid his eyes. Max smelled garlic and onions as the
soldier's breath formed puffs of moisture in the cold air.
During the two-hour flight, the man didn't speak.

When the plane touched down on a snow-covered
runway somewhere in southern Russia, snow flurries flew
around Max's face as he followed the squad down the plane's
ramp and into a cold hangar erected of thin aluminum. Later
he learned they were slightly north of the Georgian border
where the Russian military was aiding the Georgians against
the Zviadist uprising. The Spetsnaz unit's objective was to
take out a rebel communication installation in the northern
Georgian mountains. The target was a rugged cave in the
side of a cliff, but the rebels had outfitted the cave with
enough surveillance gear to spot and track Russian bombers
approaching from the north, at which time they would call in
alerts to their teams to the south. Multiple bombing runs had
failed to take out the well-hidden installation, and thus the
Spetsnaz platoon was deployed. Max's role was to remain
back with his father and observe. Or so he thought.

After three hours of cold sleep under a moth-eaten
blanket on a cot in the hangar, Max was up with the team at
2:00 am. The squad piled into two MI-26 heavy transport
helicopters and took off south, the drone of the rotors making
talk impossible. Several men smoked against regulations,

while others ran through weapons checks. Most of the men simply sat and stared ahead.

As they approached the Russian border with Georgia, the men stirred and there was a palpable increase in tension. When the bird started its descent, Max felt his father slip something into his hand. It was several inches in length, cylindrical with a threaded end, and cold to the touch. He knew from the item's feel it was suppressor. Max spent enough time with his father to not question his intentions. Keeping his movements to a minimum, Max slipped the silencer into his pocket.

The helicopters touched down, and men humped down the rear ramps. The birds lifted off, while snow, dirt, and debris swirled under their rotors, as the group ran for the cover of the woods, hunched over against the back draft. Max felt a tap on his shoulder—his father was beckoning.

"We're not going with them. Follow me, and keep up."

Max took off after his father, who made a beeline for a stand of trees. His father moved fast, and Max got the distinct impression of the deceptive speed of a grizzly bear. Max ran after him, tactical boots gripping the crusty snow, an icy wind cutting into his skin.

When they got to the tree line, his father stopped. "Ditch the rifle. You won't need it." As Max gripped a tree, breathing hard, his father tossed him a set of night-vision goggles. He fastened the unit onto his head, like he was trained, using the straps to secure it over his wool cap.

Max propped his rifle against a tree and without being told, took a second to screw the silencer into the Beretta's barrel. He double-checked the magazine and replaced the gun in a shoulder holster under his thick wool tactical jacket. He wasn't sure what his father had in mind, but this opera-

tion was not to observe the Spetsnaz as they took out a rebel observation post.

"Keep up." Max's father took off again, this time on a vector that Max estimated would cause them to intercept the team of Spetsnaz soldiers. He was surprised to find himself struggling to keep up with his father, since Max held several individual and team records for high school cross-country.

His father stopped once to consult a handheld device and adjusted their trajectory. After what seemed like eternity, he held up a fist, bringing them to a halt.

In the distance, Max heard the chatter of small arms fire and explosions from rocket-propelled grenades indicating the observation post was under attack. His father stood hunched over, studying whatever device he was holding. Despite the cold and the sounds of battle, Max's heart pounded with excitement. He was used to his father's training methods, and he knew the only thing he could expect was the unexpected. He was ready for anything. In a few months, Max would graduate from high school and join the Red Army. He would miss the time spent under his father's tutelage, so he tried to savor every second.

His father motioned for him to draw his pistol before taking off again, this time on a different vector. Max removed the pistol with a gloved hand, pointing it down as he ran through the thick trees trying to catch up.

Max estimated they ran another kilometer before his father held up an open hand and pushed it down several times, the signal to move slow and quiet. Max followed several paces behind his father as they crept through the trees, his heart thumping in his ears.

As the wind picked up again, blowing icy cuts into Max's face, they came to the edge of a small clearing. Their breath formed little puffs in front of their faces, and Max's *fingers were numb inside his thin woolen gloves. His father crouched, finger on his lips. Max joined him, fighting to keep his breath even.*

Across the clearing, at the edge of the tree line, Max saw a man bending down, his back to them, fiddling with something. His outfit matched that of the Spetsnaz soldiers they rode in with.

His father gestured with his hand, fingers held like a gun.

Max stood and brought up the gun, just like he'd done thousands of times before, holding the pistol in a two-handed grip. The Beretta felt familiar, like a worn pair of gloves. The distance was about twenty meters, an easy shot for him even considering the wind, the temperature, and his surging adrenaline. In the distance came the sound of small arms fire.

Questioning his father never occurred to him. Andrei Asimov was a legend at the KGB, and at home he wielded the same kind of authority. Andrei had been training Max since the age of eight, modeling him into a younger version of himself. While other kids played stick hockey in the street, Max was plinking targets with a Makarov 9mm or learning how to use a set of lock picks. Before that night, Max had only killed a few animals—dogs and livestock that were too sick to keep alive—conditioning him to take a life. But this was the first time Max had ever pointed a loaded weapon at another human.

Max held the gun steady, willed his pulse to calm, and pulled the trigger. The bullet entered the target's neck at the base of his spine, and the soldier keeled over face-first into the snow.

His father took off across the clearing, Max on his heels. Before Max could catch up, his father had pushed the body aside and was fumbling in the snow. Max's training kicked in and he pulled off a glove to feel the man's neck for a pulse.

As he heaved the body over, he caught a glimpse of the man's face. A horrible scar ran down the side of his face, disfiguring his nose. It was the man Max sat next to in the transport.

His father snatched something out of the snow. "Grab his dog tags."

Max reached into the man's shirt and yanked the chain from around his neck, stuffing the tags into his pocket.

"Now put a second bullet into his heart."

Max stood, held the gun at arm's length with a steady hand, and fired a bullet into the soldier's chest.

"We call that insurance, my son."

A second later, they were humping through the forest on a direct line away from the battle. The sound of gun fire faded before a massive explosion sounded behind them. Max's father came to a stop, chuckling, barely breathing hard from their run through the snowy forest. "That's the sound of success, Mikhail."

Thirty minutes later, the two men piled into the MI-26 along with the squad of Spetsnaz. Max put his head back, avoiding the glances from the men who sat opposite him.

When they landed, his father pulled him aside. They stood out on the tarmac of the air force base, smoking. His father lit up one of his favored Turkish cigarettes while Max smoked a Belomorkanal, the filterless Russian cigarette famous for its extra-strong blend of tobacco.

The elder Asimov pulled something from his pocket and handed it to Max. "You became a man today, Mikhail."

It was a tiny GPS transceiver, used for covert tracking and surveillance.

His father took a pull on his cigarette. "That's how we tracked him. He had this hidden on him."

Max turned over the device in his hand. "You've been watching him for a while?"

His father nodded, his large head encased in smoke.

Max handed the transceiver back. "What was he doing?"

His father pulled another device out of his pocket and tossed it to Max. It was a mobile phone, something Max had only seen once or twice before.

Max looked at it in wonder. "Who was he calling?"

His father's eyes narrowed. "The rebels. Remember this day, Mikhail. This is how we take care of traitors in the Soviet Union."

TWENTY-EIGHT

Great Falls Park, Virginia

"He's on his way."

Spencer's voice came over her earpiece full of static, causing her to wince. "How much time do I have?"

"Twenty minutes."

Plenty of time to do what she had to do. She opened the drawers of an antique shaker-styled dresser and rifled through piles of neatly rolled silk boxer shorts, men's pajama bottoms, and stacks of white T-shirts, marveling at the neatness of the house's single male occupant. She ran her latex-gloved hands under each of the drawers before shining a flashlight down the back. Through the bedroom window of the partially restored farmhouse the cloudy rural sky fought off the distant glow from Washington DC, twenty miles to the east.

Truth be known, she didn't know what she was looking for. She had time to kill, so she did what every good operative did while waiting for their quarry—she searched.

Maybe something would turn up she could use for leverage. Maybe she'd discover a hidden weapon or a cloaked video camera. In her business, one could never be careful enough.

She shoved the last drawer closed and moved to the single night stand. On the surface, a Tom Clancy paperback sat next to an empty water glass. The top drawer contained a set of moisturizing gloves and a blackout mask that smelled of chamomile.

Between the box spring and mattress, the grip sticking out for easy access, she found a 9mm Beretta M9 pistol. Kate released the magazine to see if it was loaded and ejected the round from the chamber. She shoved the bullet into the top of the magazine before slamming it back in and racking the slide to chamber the round again. She stuck the gun in her waistband at the small of her back.

Spencer's voice crackled in her ear. "He's five minutes out."

"Got it."

"I'll be right outside if you need me."

"Thank you, my dear."

She went downstairs to the study, a large room designed with leather furniture, lush carpets over mahogany floors, and the standard stuffed animal head mounted on the wall above a stout cherry desk. She picked through everything on the desk, finding nothing of interest.

On a shelf behind the desk stood a row of photos showing the home's owner in a variety of poses. Most were of him as a younger man dressed in desert battle fatigues, standing alongside fellow soldiers, rifle held in the traditional grip. Kate knew the photos were from Desert Storm.

One photo of two men caught her eye. The man on the left was the home's occupant, the other was Kate's father. The men's hands were clasped together, and there were proud looks on their faces. Seeing the image of her father put a lump in Kate's throat. She turned away and left the study.

She found a half bottle of Grey Goose in the kitchen freezer and poured an inch of the vodka into a tumbler. She hid herself in the shadows of the dining room, sipped, and waited.

———

Kate heard the garage door opening and closing, followed by the sound of the side door opening into the kitchen nook. Heavy footsteps banged on the oak floor and keys hit the granite counter, followed by the slap of papers or maybe a briefcase. She risked a glimpse into the kitchen, relying on the shadows in the dining room to keep her hidden.

The man who entered the house was big—tall and solid, but with a slight bulge in his waistline, like an Olympic weight lifter. His dark suit was well tailored, but his rumpled blue tie hung askew. He reached for a bottle of brown liquid Kate knew was expensive Scotch, and she saw the flash of a leather gun holster under his jacket. His thinning reddish-blond hair was shot with gray and cut short. She waited until he poured a finger of the Scotch before stepping into the kitchen, the Beretta 9mm hanging loosely in one hand and the drink glass in the other.

"Hello, Bill."

A veteran of years in the field as a covert CIA operative and a distinguished career as an officer in the Marines before that, William Blackwood wasn't easily startled. He dropped the whiskey tumbler, letting it shatter on the floor, and reached under his jacket. He froze when he saw the pistol pointed at him.

Kate waved the gun. "Take it out slow. Drop it to the floor, and kick it over. Nice and easy."

Bill smiled, and his eyebrows went up. "Fuck, Kate. You almost gave me a heart attack."

She didn't return the smile. "The gun, Bill. Don't make me shoot you with your own gun."

Bill's eyes narrowed. He retrieved the weapon from under his jacket, holding it by the butt between thumb and index finger, and dropped it to the floor, where it landed with a *thunk*. He kicked it at her, hard.

Kate trapped it with her foot. "Pour yourself another drink. We need to chat."

"How'd you get in here, anyway?" His voice was a deep baritone, wary, and he moved with a slow assuredness as if he was used to a gun being pointed at him and knew not to make any sudden moves.

"You never changed the alarm code."

"Christ." He shot her a rueful look while he poured himself another Scotch. "I didn't even remember to check it when I walked in."

Kate waved her pistol at the far side of the room. "Kitchen table, all slow like."

Kate stooped and grabbed the pistol on the floor, stowing it in her waistband before following him around the center island and stepping over the broken glass. She leaned against the counter while Bill shrugged out of his suit jacket and fell into a chair.

They looked at each other while they sipped their drinks. Until Kate's unceremonious dismissal from the agency, she reported to Bill. For much of her career, he was her confidant, her mentor. A longtime friend of her father's, she had known Bill since she was a small child. On her father's deathbed, Bill pledged to watch over Kate, becoming her unofficial godfather.

For years, the two were a powerful team. Kate operated one of the agency's most effective human asset teams while Bill handled the politics and secured the funding. Between them, they accounted for thirty high-value targets and a host of other successful missions. On a summer day several weeks ago in the new CIA director's office, it all unraveled when Director Piper Montgomery summarily demoted Kate and dismantled her team, replacing it with a drone program. Through it all, Bill had treated Kate as an outcast, refusing even to look her in the eye while Montgomery took her apart piece by piece.

Kate broke the silence. "Someone's trying to kill me, Bill."

Bill sighed. "I know."

"You know?"

Bill's eyes narrowed. "Don't convict me without hearing me out. Who do you think warned you to get out of the truck in Ukraine? How do you think Spencer knew to take out Liam?"

Kate pondered that a moment. Spencer had shown her a text message from an anonymous sender that simply read, *Kate's in danger.*

Bill took a big gulp of his Scotch, setting the glass down on the table with a grin. "You really went off the reservation when you took out Volkov. You should have seen how pissed Montgomery was." He chuckled like a father proud of his daughter for beating the boys at their own game.

Kate tried to hide her grin. "I had ulterior motives, but it would have been fun to see that."

Bill sighed. "Listen, I'm sorry about how that whole thing went down."

"Save it. If nothing else, you're a master at the politics."

"All of a sudden, someone way over my pay grade pulled a switch and turned you into a persona non grata. You were like poison."

Kate's eyes flashed. "You could have at least warned me. You owed me at least that."

Bill hung his head over his Scotch glass. "It happened so suddenly, I couldn't react fast enough. Then you disappeared."

Kate thought he was lying, but she didn't know why. Whatever was eating him was strong enough for Bill to betray their father-daughter-like relationship. "I don't believe you."

Bill's face remained passive, but his eyes stared at something far away. He drained his Scotch and banged the glass on the wood table. With her free hand, she grabbed the bottle from the center island and tossed it to him. He caught it and splashed a couple fingers into his glass. When he held the bottle, his hand trembled.

He took a gulp before looking over at her. "Why are you here?"

Kate noticed his eyes were dead and devoid of the fire that was once there. "I need information."

Bill swirled the light brown liquid in his glass. "You didn't have to react the way you did, you know. You didn't have to disappear, raid the black-ops site, and taunt her by taking out Volkov. You could have stuck around and played by the rules. Weathered the storm. We could have turned things around. Now you're on the outside. That's on you, Kate."

Kate clenched her fist around her glass as the frustration welled up. "Ever since we brought Asimov in, things have gone to shit. Somewhere there is a leak in the team. I couldn't make a move without Asimov's enemies finding out about it. Then we uncovered a connection between the leak and the NSA—"

Bill's head snapped up from his drink. "What are you talking about?"

Kate told him about the connection Kaamil found between Wilbur Lynch and the NSA. As she talked, his eyes turned into slits as if he was deep in thought. The fire reappeared, but vanished again.

"What is it?"

He shook his head.

"Come on, Bill. You owe me."

"I don't owe you shit, Kate." His voice was laced with acid. "Do you know how many times I went to bat for you? How many times I put my career on the line for you?"

"You wouldn't even have a career if it weren't for my father." She regretted it as soon as she said it.

His pained expression told her that he was torn between two poor choices. As he gazed through the window, his eyes became glassy. It startled her to realize he looked scared. As long as she'd known him, he'd been her rock, a man who showed no fear, a man who never backed down from a fight. She had never seen fear on his face. And then it came to her.

"What do they have on you, Bill?"

He turned and grimaced at her, and suddenly she understood. "Are you fucking serious?"

He looked back out the window and nodded.

Kate gripped her glass so hard she thought she might break it. "I can't believe it matters in this day and age."

"It fucking matters."

"I thought the CIA changed its policy?"

"For the rank and file. At my level, it matters. Besides, that's not all."

Kate set the pistol on the counter. "What exactly do they have? Pictures?"

"More. They set me up."

A tear welled in her eye. "Christ, Bill. Tell me it's not a video of you with a prostitute."

Bill avoided her gaze and nodded. He wiped his cheek. "A week later, they found his body in the Potomac."

She crossed her arms and shifted her weight to her other foot. "Holy shit."

Bill tapped his glass on the table. "For now, the case remains unsolved. If I step out of line, they'll release DNA evidence tying me to the crime."

Her cheeks burned. All the anger she had directed at Bill drained away, replaced by a simmering outrage. "What do they want you to do?"

Bill stared out the window.

Kate took a step in the direction of the table. "You're running the hit on me."

He swiped at his cheek again and stayed silent.

She set her glass on the table with a crack. "It was you who ran the drone strike operation."

He nodded.

She ran both hands through her hair. "Jesus Christ, Bill."

He nodded again. "That's putting it mildly."

The picture was now clear. Why he had acted the way he did. The back channel messages that had helped them while he had outwardly overseen her termination. Despite the anger at his betrayal, she couldn't help but feel empathy for the man she loved like a father. Kate poured another splash of the vodka into her glass and walked to the table.

She wanted to comfort him, but she was unsure of how to approach him. She poured another shot of Scotch into his glass before sitting in a chair and putting her hand on his leg. "We can fix this."

Bill took a gulp of the whiskey and looked at her with red-rimmed eyes. "Your father is rolling over in his grave."

Kate studied Bill for a moment, a memory of her father appearing in her mind as clear as a movie. The late Bernard Shaw was one of the longest reigning US attorneys for the Southern District of New York and earned himself the reputation as a crime fighter beyond reproach by busting several prominent state and federal politicians for corruption. He was killed in broad daylight by a sniper as he exited the New York City Supreme Court building. Despite finding a bolt-action Remington 700 configured in a .300 Winchester Magnum caliber on the fourth floor of the construction site two blocks away, the killer was never found. To this day, Bernard Shaw's murder remained unsolved.

Kate put her hand on his forearm. "We have to take these fuckers down. It's what my father would do. He was a fighter, and he taught me to fight. It was his legacy that drove me to be the best agent I could, and it was his compassion that gave you a second chance. We'll do it for him. We'll do it for the country we love."

Bill nodded, tears filling his eyes. She clinked her glass against his and felt him squeeze her hand.

TWENTY-NINE

Undisclosed Location

It took some time for Max to fully regain consciousness. While the world in front of him swam in a gauzy blur, his mind played back the memory of his first kill over and over again like a broken movie reel. He felt the pull of the trigger, the buck of the gun, and heard the *pfft* of the gasses escaping from the silencer. He saw the bullet's trajectory through the cold air and its impact in the man's neck before it extinguished his life in a blink. A man who was born into the world from the warmth of his mother's womb just like every other. A man who, for some reason known only to him, decided to betray his country by providing tactical intel to the Zviadist rebels. For that sin, his life ended abruptly in a bitter cold field on the Russian border with Georgia, his hopes and dreams and fears snuffed out by a piece of lead weighing 124 grains, or about a quarter of an ounce.

Max remembered firing a second bullet into the man's

heart as he lay on the ground, a trickle of crimson staining the pristine white snow, but mostly Max remembered the look of pride on his father's face as the older man's plan for his only son came to fruition. Despite the long run through the cold snowy forest, his heart rate remained near resting levels, he acted without hesitation, and the bullet was fired on an accurate trajectory. Max executed the task with effortless precision, joining his mind and body into a single fluid action that culminated in the perfect kill.

As Max's surroundings lightened and crystallized, the visions faded. The first thing he noticed was a man leaning against the wall in front of him. He was painfully thin, like he'd been on a starvation diet for months. He wore a pink-and-white polka-dot bow tie, its vivid brightness standing out against the dull beige of the rest of his attire. The butt of a pistol peeked out from a well-worn leather shoulder holster. He stroked a ragged gray goatee, the traditional kind where the upper lip remained shaved.

Max sat on a wooden chair in the living room of a run-down house. The only other furniture in the room was a scuffed wooden table to his right and a second chair near the man with the bow tie. The house reminded him of the cinder block dwellings built in the Soviet era that permeated the neighborhoods surrounding Minsk. The paint was olive drabs and peeling yellows, and the wood floor was covered with dark splotches from dried unidentifiable liquids. The only thing new about the place was the eggcrate-styled soundproofing that covered the walls, perhaps to prevent screams from startling the neighbors.

His wrists were secured behind him, his arms were pressed awkwardly into the back slats of the chair, and his legs were attached to the chair with zip ties. After a brief wiggle failed to move the chair, he deduced it was bolted to the floor. He was happy to see he still had his clothes on, but his phone, watch, and his grandfather's lighter were missing. Flexing his muscles, he felt stiffness in his joints, and besides a slight headache, he was injury free.

The man with the bow tie stirred. "Welcome back." His voice was gravely and heavy with a northern English accent, reminding Max of an American singer he liked named Joe Cocker.

Max turned his head to see if they were alone. Behind him was an arched opening to a kitchen-dining area with cracked linoleum floors and old appliances the color of pea soup. Several of the cabinet doors were missing. He saw no one else, but assumed a closed-circuit video feed was recording them. Maybe the rep tie-wearing goons were in a back room watching on a monitor. He turned back to see the man with the bow tie spinning a Blackberry phone in his hand.

"It's just you and me. No video."

Max tried to talk, but found his tongue was as dry as sandpaper. Noticing his difficulty, the man with the bow tie took a cup off the floor and directed a straw at Max's mouth, reaching with his arm to keep his distance. Max leaned over and drank mouthfuls before the man pulled the straw away. The cool liquid sank into the arid crevices of his mouth, helping him speak. "Somehow, I doubt that."

The man set the cup on the floor. "It's the truth. There are men outside, but they can't hear us."

"Where's the blond?"

"She's knackered from chasing you all over Europe. I left her at a hotel, which I don't think she's happy about. I dare say without her, we would still be casting about like a green broke."

It took Max a moment to understand his thick accent. "Green broke?"

"It means a rookie hunting dog."

Max inspected the man's disheveled clothes and worn loafers. "You're not Scotland Yard. Otherwise, I'd be in a jail cell instead of a safe house living room."

The man spun the Blackberry. "Perceptive."

"Also, you're not MI5 because I'd be having the shit beat out of me right now."

The man said nothing, but Max read conflict in his eyes.

"You didn't capture me for the reward money or again, I'd be getting the snot beaten out of me by MI5."

The Blackberry spun faster. "True."

"You're obviously British. It's possible you're Defense Intelligence or National Crime, but I don't think so. Ordinarily I might think you're an independent contractor, but you're definitely government."

"What makes you think that?"

Max smiled. "No one other than a government employee would use a Blackberry."

The man rolled his eyes but slipped his phone into his back pocket. "It's very secure."

Max chuckled. Despite being in handcuffs, he found himself drawn to the old eccentric. "Not as secure as my Blackphone, which you've probably discovered by now."

The man grunted. "We'll see."

Max straightened his shoulders. "I'm going to guess you're MI6, although it makes no sense why the world's most wanted terrorist is holed up in a safe house somewhere and not being paraded in front of the media to make a jittery public feel more at ease."

The man shifted his weight onto his opposite foot. "I've been asking myself that same question for the past twenty-four hours." He pushed himself from the wall and, giving Max wide berth, went into the kitchen, where Max heard him banging around. After a few minutes, he returned with a steaming mug of tea. "Sorry, old man. I'd offer you some, but given your reputation, I like your hands right where they are."

Max shifted in an attempt to relieve the pressure on his wrists. "I don't blame you. Since you know who I am, how about we start with a proper introduction?"

The man took a sip of tea and grimaced. "Bloody awful stuff." He went back into the kitchen. Max heard a cupboard slam before he returned and took a seat on the second wooden chair and set the steaming mug on the table. "You can call me Baxter."

Max marveled at the politeness of the Brits. Baxter looked genuinely rattled not to be able to offer Max a cup of tea. "Nice to meet you, Baxter. If I'm not going to jail, and I'm not going to get the snot beat out of me, why am I here?"

Baxter stood and put one foot on the chair's seat. "My back can't handle this kind of chair." He picked up the cup of tea and blew on its surface. "Your assertion remains to be seen."

Max cocked his head. "Fair enough. What can I do for you, Mr. Baxter? I assume you want something from me. Everyone seems to these days."

"It's just Baxter." He balanced his tea in one hand while he ran the fingers of his other hand through his long goatee. "Let's start with you telling me what your business was with Victoria Edgars."

If Max avoided his questions, he knew Baxter would simply threaten to turn him over to MI5. While MI5 was similar to the American FBI, MI6 was akin to their CIA or Russia's KGB. Spy agencies usually had divergent agendas from their domestic law enforcement counterparts. It didn't at all strike him as odd that Baxter wanted something before turning him over to MI5. "How much did you see?"

"Enough to guess your business is with her father. After putting together some of the pieces, I think you want something from Erich Stasko, so you're using the daughter as bait. Given the size of the manhunt for you, you're either desperate or stupid to come to England, and I know you're not stupid."

Max raised his eyebrows.

Baxter took his foot off the chair, set his mug on the table, and paced while stroking his goatee. "I understand your reluctance to talk. I really do. I'm not going to torture you. I have neither the means nor the stomach for it. The only thing I can threaten is if we can't have a meaningful conversation, my only recourse will be to turn you over to MI5. As you yourself have indicated, life gets more complicated for you if that happens."

"And you become the hero."

Baxter stopped pacing and jammed his hands into his pockets. "If I cared about that, you'd already be down a dark hole."

"I was joking. You obviously have some other game in mind."

"Joking, huh?" Baxter paced to his chair, retrieved the tea mug and took a hesitant sip. "What's your business with Erich Stasko?"

Max tried to read him. Baxter's outward appearance resembled that of a tired detective inspector: Stained oxford shirt of some indeterminate color, pleated khakis held up with a braided leather belt, and ragged leather loafers off the discount rack. The bow tie and the goatee made him look like the mascot of a certain fried chicken fast-food chain. But Max also saw a fire in his eyes, an intellect and passion that somehow garnered his respect and reminded Max to stay on his guard. Plus, somehow Baxter had caught him, which meant he was no slouch. Max knew he was on thin ice and vowed not to underestimate him. "Stasko has information I need."

"What kind of information?"

"If you turn me in to MI5, I'll walk eventually. I didn't do that bombing, and you know it. It's not my MO, which is why you haven't turned me in yet."

Baxter's eyes flashed with what Max interpreted as cunning, and he tugged harder on his goatee. "I assume you have an alibi?"

Max was hiking in pristine mountain wilderness north of the Matterhorn at the time of the bombing, but he wasn't about to tell Baxter that. "Not one I would use."

Baxter paced like a professor in front of his class. "What you say may be true, but meanwhile, you would be in the system for months while you fight for your innocence. The entire world wants blood, and who knows what else might bubble up from your background? Mysterious assassin with many kills under his belt, and Bob's your uncle. You don't need that kind of publicity."

"Too late for that."

Baxter paced back and forth. "My guess is Stasko has information related to the identity of the real bomber. You want that information so you can apprehend him and clear your name. The only thing I can't figure out is what does the owner of a Latvian banking conglomerate have in common with someone who kills using terror?"

Baxter's face lit up, and he turned to face Max. "The money. I can't believe I didn't see it until now. Stasko's a banker. You want Stasko to provide a paper trail for the exchange of money."

Max shook his head. "You're giving me a lot of credit."

"Don't take the piss out of me. You're more than capable—"

"Let's assume for a minute you're right. You obviously want something from me. Can we get to that before my hands go numb?"

Baxter walked again, one arm crossed over his chest, the other tugging at his goatee. "What will you do with the actual perp if you catch him?"

Max flexed the fingers on his left hand to start the blood flowing. "When."

"Pardon?"

Max managed to slide forward in the chair a fraction of an inch to relieve the pressure on his left hand. "When I catch him."

Baxter gave a dismissive wave. "Of course. What will you do when you catch him?"

Max hadn't given that question much thought. He assumed he would just hand the bomber over to authorities, but the question posed obvious challenges.

Baxter leaned down so his face was level with Max's. "I'm guessing this kind of thing is a bit outside your wheelhouse. Normally, you track people down with the end goal of, um... eliminating them. In this case, you can't simply kill him and toss his body in the channel."

A slow grin spread on Max's face. "You want the arrest."

Baxter straightened up and leaned back on the wall. "I want the real perp. We bring you in, there's plenty of fanfare. Maybe you get strung up as the scapegoat. As you said, the public feels better for a time. People get promoted.

Until the next attack. At which point it becomes clear we got the wrong guy. Then heads roll."

Max's ignored the pain in his shoulders. "Worse yet, more innocent civilians are killed."

"Precisely." Baxter paced again and tugged hard enough at his goatee to make Max think he might rip it from his chin. "I wonder if you've thought about another line of inquiry?" Without waiting for an answer, Baxter kept talking. "How many people in the world are capable of making such a large, complicated bomb? Maybe a dozen? As you know, our little war on terror could be going better. If we put down one of these expert bomb makers, the world will be a little safer."

Max licked his lips with a dry tongue. "You've got some forensics evidence, don't you? You think you know who it is."

Baxter waved his arms as he paced, his face animated with the possibilities. "Yes, and no. We have evidence, but our forensics teams are in the process of putting it together. It's just a matter of time before the question becomes *how* we get to the bomber instead of *who* is the bomber."

Max realized he was looking at the rarest kind of man, someone who put his country and her citizens ahead of his own career. Either that or Baxter was a talented actor playing a game Max couldn't see. "You're going out on a limb, which isn't something the Brits are known for doing. Is the MI6 brass aware of your plan, or are you flying solo on this?"

Baxter stopped in the middle of the room and his eyes darkened. "Indeed. Let me worry about that."

Max wiggled his hands and shoulders in a futile attempt to stave off the numbness creeping up his arms. "I just want to know how fragile a possible alliance would be."

Baxter pulled hard at a fistful of goatee. "Eggshell-like."

Max smiled. "Raw?"

"Fresh out of the hen's vagina." Baxter laughed, but his eyes remained hard.

"I don't think eggs come out of a hen's vagina."

"I really don't give a dog's bollocks. Do we have a deal?"

"In principle. Just one question."

Baxter scowled. "Go ahead, but I can't guarantee an answer."

"How'd you find me?"

Baxter gave a knowing father's smile and took off on a pacing expedition around the room. He did three laps before stopping in front of Max. He nibbled on a thumbnail for a long moment before answering. "Do you know someone who calls themselves Bluefish?"

THIRTY

Undisclosed Location

Years of KGB counter-interrogation training came in handy, allowing Max to keep his face blank at the mention of the name. It was the second time in forty-eight hours the name Bluefish had come up. Bluefish had somehow notified Jānis, the Latvian gun-selling thug, of Max's true identity. And now Bluefish had provided Baxter, an MI6 agent, with enough information to capture Max as he walked through a college campus. He was starting to get a bad feeling about the power and reach of this person or group that called themselves Bluefish. "Is that some kind of code name?"

Baxter hitched up his trousers and adjusted the leather shoulder holster. "Apparently. He speaks through a machine that disguises his voice. He purports to know a great deal about many things, and he has access to a lot of surveillance information. He, or she, I suppose, is very interested in making sure you are apprehended."

Max pursed his lips while he ran through several possibilities. The most likely scenario was this Bluefish person either worked for, or was part of, the consortium. Max wasn't sure if Baxter knew about the consortium. If he didn't, Max wasn't going to volunteer the information. "What did he tell you?"

Baxter turned away and gnawed at a thumbnail. It occurred to Max that Baxter was playing both sides by collaborating with Bluefish to find Max so he could partner with Max to find the real bombers. It was a dangerous gambit. "Listen. We're contemplating a partnership here. I need some indication I can trust you. Besides, if this Bluefish person wants me dead and gets his wish, I can't very well help you take down the true perp, can I?"

Baxter mumbled at the ceiling. "Partners is too strong of a word."

"Fine. You pick the word. My point is still—"

"Bluefish said you would arrive in a Lear at an airport outside Cambridge."

Max frowned, his eyes searching. "That's it?"

"That's it."

"Why didn't you take me at the airport?"

Baxter shrugged. "Wanted to see what you were up to."

"How did he know where I'd be?"

"He didn't specify."

The only person who knew of his flight plan between Latvia and the UK was Julia and her team. Obviously, either the BND was hacked or Bluefish had someone on the inside of Julia's team. It smelled like the mole Kate had at the CIA. The mole they never uncovered.

Max's shoulders slumped as his thoughts went to his old partner Goshawk. "I know someone who can find this Bluefish person. Too bad she's run underground."

Baxter cocked his head. "Who's that?"

"Never mind. Say, do you mind undoing these cuffs? They're cutting into my wrists."

Baxter pawed at his goatee. "I gave you something. Now it's your turn. Tell me something that will make me trust you. What will stop you from wringing my neck with your bare hands if I let you go free?"

Max remembered the last time he agreed to a partnership with an enemy. He ended up falling hard for her before she was killed. That was only weeks ago, and it was a reminder to tread carefully. But he was no good to Alex and Arina if he was fighting the consortium from a prison cell deep under Vauxhall Cross in London. "What do you want to know?"

Baxter sat in the wooden chair and leaned back on two legs against the wall. "Why did someone go to such lengths to frame you for such a terrible bombing?"

Max sighed. "That's a long story. My hands will fall off from blood loss before I get halfway through."

"I'm not going anywhere. Neither are you."

Max wiggled to allow blood to get to his numb posterior. "The longer we fuck around, the colder the bomber's trail becomes. I promise I'll tell you, but let's get after this guy while we can."

Baxter pinched his lips together. "Fine. How did you convince Stasko's daughter to take a selfie with you?"

"Easy. I told her my daughter was considering attending Cambridge to study economics, which just so happens to be Veronica's field."

Baxter's eyebrows went up. "How do you get your intel?"

"We probably need some ground rules. First, don't ask about my methods and sources. Second—"

Clunk! The front legs of Baxter's chair hit the floor.

"Yes, let's get something clear. I'm the only thing standing between you and a long line of MI5 and MI6 officers who'd love to get a piece of you. If you think this is a partnership, you're mistaken."

Max's eyes narrowed, and he realized he had misjudged Baxter's absentminded professor act.

Baxter stood and regarded Max as though he was a child. "That's how things work in this business. We'll find the bomber. When we do, you're going to apprehend him. And if that's not possible, you'll take him out. Otherwise, you're on the first bus to Vauxhall Cross."

Max sat back, hunching his shoulders to create space between the wooden slats and his wrists. "Okay, Baxter, if that's even your name. For that kind of thing to work, you need leverage."

Baxter smiled. "You're right. Leverage with you isn't easy. There isn't much you care about—or at least that we know you care about. Except one thing." He turned and strode out of the room, his footsteps creaking on the old wooden floor as he disappeared down a hall.

Max threw his weight from side to side to move the chair or force something loose, but he only succeeded in increasing the pain from the zip ties at his ankles and the cuffs on his wrists. He stopped thrashing when he heard a set of footsteps approaching from behind.

Baxter reappeared with a silver laptop he set on the table and opened so Max could see the screen. The MI6 man's face was set in a grim scowl which made Max uneasy. What kind of leverage could the MI6 possibly have over him?

Baxter fussed with the machine before stalking off with a huff. "Bloody hell, this thing's a tosser." The laptop's screen was still dark.

Max called after him. "Dead battery?"

A few minutes later, Baxter reappeared with a white power cable and an extension cord. After plugging the laptop into the power source, the screen lit up with the push of a button. After a lengthy boot up process, a picture of rose bushes in full bloom appeared on the monitor.

Max smirked. "Pretty. Those yours?"

Baxter worked the keyboard and trackpad. The MI6 man kept his profile to Max, but his body hid the screen from Max's view. When Baxter straightened and stepped aside, a video chat window showed on the screen. The chat window was dark, but a green light was lit on the edge of the laptop window where a built-in video camera was located. After a second window appeared, Max saw his own image from the shoulders up, making him realize they were broadcasting. The other window was dark, indicating the second party had not yet joined the chat.

Baxter removed the Blackberry from his pocket, tapped a few buttons, and held the phone to his ear. "Put him on."

When the video chat window brightened, Max sucked in his breath.

———

The cottage was tiny, even by Corsican standards. A single bedroom with a water closet sat next to common room with cupboards, a sink, a two-burner stove, an icebox, and a brick fireplace. Wool rugs in reds and blues covered a terra-cotta floor and exposed wooden beams supported a roof made of planks made from locally grown chestnut trees. The gravity-fed shower was outside, sheltered from view by an ivy-covered trellis. There was no danger of being seen in the nude; the cottage was on three acres of land bordered on one side by the Mediterranean and three other sides by dense forest. Her only visitors were a brook salamander she named Sam and dozens of song birds that woke her up as the sun rose each morning. The only evidence of modernity was the laptop computer on the rickety kitchen table and a satellite dish on the roof hidden from view by more ivy-covered trellises.

The cottage and land were hers, a reward for a complicated and dangerous piece of computer forensics she performed for Don Paoli many years prior. The Corsican mafioso boss bestowed the gift as a token of his thanks and maintained the property on her behalf when she was away, which was most of the time. An added benefit of being under the don's protection was that nothing moved on the south side of the island without his permission, which afforded her an added layer of security.

When the songbirds sounded that morning, Carlu's scent on the crisp white sheets was the only trace left of their late-night tryst. He lived on the north side of the island and needed to get back to his family before daybreak. Goshawk put a kettle on for tea, brushed her teeth, and performed a short yoga routine before tapping the space bar of the computer. While the machine cycled on, she poured hot water over a green tea blend and blew on the water's surface to cool the beverage. When the desktop appeared, she inserted the thumb drive and sat down on an old wooden stool.

When not at the cottage, Goshawk kept the computer under lock and key and off the internet as a precaution, so she was startled when a lemon yellow color swept over the computer's screen. She tapped on several keys but found the computer unresponsive. Setting down her tea, she unplugged the power cable and moved to restart the computer. Her hand froze, hovering over the power button as the avatar of a clown appeared on the screen's yellow background. The clown wore white face paint, a large red nose, and a white jumpsuit with bright tassels where the buttons should be.

Goshawk's stomach flipped when the clown's mouth moved. She had been duped into thinking the data file she retrieved the previous evening was safe. Instead, she had introduced a Trojan horse onto her computer which had taken over the machine. She was so caught up in her success the previous night she was blinded to the trap.

The clown spoke with a mechanical voice. "Hello, Goshawk."

Goshawk put her hand to her mouth. Her mind screamed at her to turn off the machine but her hand was unwilling to comply.

"As you now realize, the data file you found and downloaded is fake. I'm sure you're disappointed, but I can assure you, what you managed to uncover is far better for you."

The clown animation started a little dance as it talked. "You passed a series of challenging tests I constructed to assess your skills and cover our tracks so we may converse in privacy. By passing these trials, you achieved what no other has done, earning you an audience with the man you seek. I assume you're watching this alone, but if you are not, I'll give you some time to get to a secluded location."

Goshawk glanced through the open door behind her and saw only the gentle waving of tree branches and heard only the rhythmic ebb and flow of the ocean. When she turned back, the clown's outfit shifted into a set of brown monk's robes, but its white face paint and red mouth were unchanged, as was the mechanical voice. "The man you seek goes by the name The Monk. He is willing to meet you but can only spare a short amount of time. To see him, you must go to the city of Prague. Ensure you're not followed and carry no electronic devices or The Monk will disappear and you'll never see nor hear from him again."

She leaned forward. "How will I—" She broke off when she realized she had no way to interact with the avatar.

The clown in the monk's robes produced a silver horn and gave the rubber bulb a squeeze, making her jump. "I'm told the St. Mary of the Angels has a decent soup line." The clown waggled his finger at her. "Don't dally, dearie."

Before she could react, the clown disappeared and the screen went black. She tapped on the keyboard until she realized the machine was dead. She performed a hard reboot, and when the machine came back on, a message appeared on the screen that read *Operating System Not Found*. The clown's malware had wiped her computer clean.

She picked up her mug with a shaking hand and walked barefoot out the door and down the sandy path to the beach. The celadon water lapping at her toes was almost still, and she let it warm her skin. Despite the jolt caused by the clown, she knew she had passed the first test.

How many more would there be?

After finishing her tea, she plucked her mobile phone from her robe pocket and dialed a number from memory.

Carlu answered in a sleepy voice. "Bonjour."

"Good morning, darling. I need a ride to Rome."

THIRTY-ONE

Undisclosed Location

"Hi, Uncle Max."

Alex, Max's tow-headed nephew, appeared in the video chat window. The youngster spoke in perfect German.

Max fought hard to control his surging anxiety and forced a smile. "Hey, Buddy. How are you doing?"

"Good. Except the drone broke. I crashed it, and Spike chewed one of the rotors. Victor said he would get another rotor, but it hasn't come yet."

Relief washed over Max as he realized his nephew thought this was an ordinary conversation. "I'm happy to hear he's getting you another one. Your German sounds good. Have you been practicing?"

Alex shot a look behind him as if to check to see who might be listening. In the background, Max recognized the boy's room with its stacks of toys and bed with the Star Wars sheets. "Yes. Victor hired a tutor who makes me practice." Alex made a face as if he had just eaten a lemon.

Max forced a smile. "It's a good language to know, Sport. You never know when you might need it. Keep at it. You're doing well."

"Okay, Uncle Max. If you say so. Where are you?"

Max grimaced. "Can't tell you that right now, Buddy. I'll come visit you and your mom real soon, okay?"

Alex's eyes flicked up as if he were distracted by something above the camera. "Okay. I know you can't tell me. Mom says I'm not allowed to ask."

Max smiled. "Mind your mother. She's a wise woman, and she loves you very much."

Alex fidgeted and looked around his room. "I know."

Max knew he only had a few minutes left before the youngster's attention went elsewhere. "Hey, Alex?"

Alex looked back into the camera. "Yeah?"

"Will you give Victor a message for me?"

"Sure."

Max did his best to smile. "Tell him I'm coming to talk with him real soon, okay?"

Alex's eyes lit up. "Sure will, Uncle Max. Maybe the new drone rotor will be here by then."

Max winked at him. "Yeah, maybe. Tell you what. I'll bring you a brand new drone when I come visit. The biggest drone you've ever seen, with big propellers and a super-long battery life. You'll be able to fly it all around the valley. Deal?"

A wide grin appeared as Alex pumped his fist in the air. "Okay, it's a deal!" A creaking sound came from somewhere off-camera, and Alex's smile vanished. "Gotta go, Uncle Max."

"Okay, Sport, me too. Just remember to tell Victor I'll be there real soon to talk to him."

Alex's eyes shifted left as more creaking came from off-camera. "I will. Bye, Uncle Max."

"Bye, Buddy."

The screen went blank.

———

"This is a dangerous game you're playing, Baxter. I hope you know what you're doing."

The assassin's voice was thick with anger, and his face was as hard as stone. Callum Baxter knew he was walking on thin ice. He had just performed the equivalent of caging a Bengal tiger, starving it for a week, and poking it repeatedly with a sharp stick. Now he was going to release the angry animal out into the wild.

Baxter walked around behind the famous assassin and checked his captive's bindings. The beefy wooden chair was holding fast, and the thin white zip ties were tight against his pant legs. The metal cuffs securing his wrists were scraping off skin, and when Baxter touched the cuff's chain to test its strength, the assassin thrashed and strained against the bindings making Baxter jump back and touch the grip of his pistol. He walked around to the front of his captive and leaned back against the wall.

Asimov was a machine who understood only one purpose: To kill. Baxter knew he was raised by his father to become one of the KGB's most dangerous assassins. He had reams of files on both Mikhail and his father back in his tiny wood-slatted backyard office. Though Baxter possessed no hard evidence linking Asimov to any kills, he had scores of theories, hypotheses, and anecdotal clues. Baxter knew where there was smoke there was fire.

Baxter had never met a true assassin in the flesh, and

the experience was unnerving. The man's eyes were now ice-cold black pools devoid of emotion. Whatever warmth had appeared there during the rapport-building phase was gone, replaced by an unreadable mask—a passive blank slate that Baxter guessed hid a roiling ocean of seething anger. The only evidence of emotion was the smoldering fire behind the obsidian eyes that stared at him unblinkingly.

Despite his fear, Baxter's adrenaline surged at the prospect of watching the assassin in action. He was fascinated by the methods, histories, and conspiracy theories surrounding assassins—men who roamed the earth as virtual ghosts, accepting contracts or orders to end another's life. Some assassins were the dregs of the earth, two-bit killers with nothing but money as their guidepost, unconstrained by a value system. Others were specialists, killers who gained access to protected targets and only accepted top dollar in exchange for their skills. These were men, and a few women, who anointed themselves judge and jury and operated outside the inconvenient constraints of the law. In Baxter's wildest dreams, he was one of those men, an avenging angel working tirelessly against the evils of the world. He was introspective enough to know that he lacked the constitution for such an adventure, so he studied the assassins from afar, researching and poking at the fringes of the dark underbelly of a life he could only imagine.

Now he had the opportunity to control such a man from a safe distance and live vicariously through him. Despite the danger he was unleashing, he couldn't help himself. The urge to make this leap was so compelling, he imagined it was like a heroin addiction. He was powerless to stop himself.

Baxter had participated in and led his share of MI6 sanctioned hits, but they were all against terrorist targets or what the director liked to call combatants. Most of these operations were in partnership with other agencies, usually the CIA, and all were executed through the partner agency's special forces teams or black-ops personnel. The legend of MI6 operating a team of special agents licensed to kill was just that—fiction. The official directive in MI6 is lethal force can only be used in circumstances that are emergencies or crises which causes danger to the UK or its citizens. Neither the MI6 brass nor the foreign secretary had approved an assassination in as long as Baxter could remember.

Baxter's own obsession with assassinations was a legend among his colleagues. His peers called such killers *unicorns*. Few believed they existed and instead portrayed them as figments of an impressionable public's imagination. Some men searched their entire lives for evidence of the Loch Ness Monster or Sasquatch. Baxter hunted assassins and didn't care what his coworkers thought.

Now one of them was sitting right in front of him. He had caught the proverbial unicorn. If he wanted the opportunity to observe Mikhail Asimov in action, he would have to take the next step. A small part of his brain called out in warning, but his addiction got the better of him.

Girding himself, he put on a mask of his own and addressed the assassin. "This is what you call leverage."

The assassin threw himself against his bindings like a starving dog might hurl itself against its leash when shown a piece of raw meat. His words came out like a snarl. "You son of a bitch. This is extortion."

Baxter narrowed his eyes and shook his head. "I call it insurance."

The assassin struggled, veins popping out of his neck and spittle flying from his mouth. Baxter held his breath as the chair creaked and groaned under the killer's strength, exhaling when he saw the bindings hold. He squatted and leaned against the wall while the assassin wore himself down. Eventually the outburst subsided and the killer calmed. Perspiration covered the man's shaved head and a permanent snarl was frozen on his face.

Baxter took a sip of his cold tea, praying his hand wouldn't shake. "You're looking at this all wrong, Mikhail. No one is going to hurt young Alex. That's the last thing anyone wants."

All the fight had gone out of the assassin. Instead of thrashing about, he sat hunched over in the chair, glaring at Baxter, his jaw muscles flexing. When he spoke, it was through clenched teeth. "This is my family you're fucking with. I've got a list, and I just added your name to it."

Baxter's skin broke out in goosebumps. To hide his fear, he stood and paced around behind the assassin. "Let me remind you of a few things. My position with MI6 should make you pause. Once you calm down and see things for what they really are, I believe you'll find your time and energy is better spent—"

"I have a long memory."

Baxter cleared his throat. "As I was saying, your time will be better spent finding the West Brompton terrorist and clearing your name, as it were."

Once again in control of his jitters, he walked around the killer and was surprised to see a smile on Asimov's face. *His smile is so cold*, Baxter thought. It was practiced, a smile reserved for the ladies at a bar or perhaps to win over a public servant or charm his way through a closed door. There was no warmth behind the ice-black eyes. He reminded himself that if Asimov thought for a moment that his nephew was safe, the assassin would kill him in an instant and walk away. Baxter had been in rooms with plenty of vicious men—cunning terrorists, gang leaders, and skin heads—but he had never been in a room with an assassin. He took no comfort from the smile.

"How much did you pay Victor Dedov to give up my nephew?"

Baxter stroked his goatee. His mother often got after him for the pervasive tic, and he figured his colleagues mocked him for it behind his back. "Let's not talk about the specifics. The leverage is this. If I turn up dead, or you fail to perform as instructed, little Alex's life will get more difficult."

The assassin's smile disappeared, and Baxter's stomach did a little flip as he gazed into the dark pools of bottomless ice. He powered on, fueled by his addiction. "You can be sure the British government would never physically hurt the little boy. That is not in our nature." Baxter took a deep breath just as he was about to enter uncharted territory. For him, anyway. "But we can certainly enable a transaction whereby little Alex is, how shall we say, more vulnerable to your enemies than he is currently."

Baxter expected his captive to unleash another physical assault on his bonds. Instead, Asimov sat in the chair like a Stoic, undergoing a transformation in front of his eyes. Instead of the expletive-laced anger and fiery ice-black eyes, a warmth crept over his features. The eyes softened, his posture relaxed, and a different smile came over his face.

Don't be lulled into vulnerability.

Baxter was on a tightrope. One false move would mean his own destruction. Baxter's pulse raced and the rush of adrenaline felt empowering, like something he'd never felt before.

"How about loosening these bonds?" The assassin's voice was calm, hypnotic.

The smile is a ploy. Don't get sucked in.

Baxter stood and fought off a wave of dizziness he attributed to the adrenaline coursing through his blood stream. "Not just yet. We're going to exchange some information first. Then we'll see about releasing you."

"Let's stop fucking around before my hands fall off. Tell me what you know about the bombing. I'm sure your forensic whiz kids have turned up a few things the media don't know."

Baxter walked to the kitchen and turned on the gas fire under the teapot with a shaking hand. He used the tea-making ritual to calm his frayed nerves. By the time he carried the cup into the living room, his hand was steady. He set the tea on the table to cool and picked up the water cup, holding the straw out to the assassin who drank the rest of the liquid in big gulps.

The warm smile reappeared. "Thanks."

Remarkable. He was all business now, as if there was no threat to his nephew.

Baxter sat on the chair with his elbows on his knees and sipped his tea.

"Okay, Mikhail—"

"Call me Max."

"Okay, Max. Here's what I know. The bomb was made of HMX—"

A slight uptick in the assassin's eyebrows. "Interesting. That explosive is rare. Terrorists don't typically use HMX. Where did it come from?"

"Exactly right. We don't know it's origin for certain, but our working hypothesis is it came from a cache of 377 tons of

HMX and RDX taken out of Iraq by the Baathist insurgents after the 2003 US invasion. This is classified, but we know for certain some of that material was retained by the resistance, but most of it was sold. About half the amount sold was recovered using intel discovered when they killed bin Laden. The other half has not been recovered." Baxter paused to sip his tea, thankful they had moved into more operational aspects.

Baxter set his cup down on the table and crossed one leg over the other. "So far, HMX has only turned up in two other bombings that we're aware of. The first was the 2006 car bombing in Paris that killed fifteen and injured over a hundred. The second was the 2009 car bombing in Rotterdam that killed seven and injured twelve. Despite what the public thinks, car bombings in Europe are fairly rare. Most terrorists use IEDs, improvised explosive devices—"

"I'm aware of what an IED is. Any similarities among the three bombings other than the HMX and the use of vehicles?"

"One big one."

The assassin's eyes became slits. "Let me guess. Each one was an assassination disguised as a terrorist act."

Baxter tried, but failed, to keep from yanking on his goatee. "Must take one to know one. The Paris bombing took out France's Minster of Ecology. The Rotterdam bombing killed Britain's Minister of Energy, who was there for a high-level conference on climate change."

"Isn't France's Minister of Ecology actually just another name for the Minister of Energy? He's more focused on energy issues than conservation issues?"

"I believe that's correct."

Max shifted in his chair. "Pretty crude to use a car

bomb as an assassination technique. My guess is the killer wanted to disguise it as a terrorist event."

"Seems obvious, but no terrorist group ever claimed credit for the first two. And so far, there haven't been any credible claims on the West Brompton bombing either."

"Eventually law enforcement will see the pattern. That means he's a good bomb maker but not a great tactician."

Baxter nodded. "As far as we can tell, he's a great bomb maker. Not sure how much you know about HMX, but it's not easy to use. You can't just stick a blasting cap in it and hit a button. It comes in a powder form, and to stabilize it so it can be used in a vehicle application, it must first either be combined with oil or compounded with mineral jelly to form a plastic explosive."

The handcuffs clanged as Max move in his seat. "RDX is plentiful in Russia. HMX, not so much."

Baxter adjusted the pleat on his trouser. "We're good at detecting nitrogen, which is used in a lot of bomb-making applications. HMX is made from nitrogen, which makes it suitable for environments where the detectors aren't in place."

"Like a car bomb detonated in a city where the vehicle can be hidden and driven into a crowd."

Baxter's face went grim. "Exactly."

"Do you have a line on this guy?"

Baxter's face fell. "Unfortunately, no. We have a file. A thin file."

Max furrowed his eyebrows. "Bombers can't just learn their technique on the internet. It's possible he studied with some of the bomb makers that come out of Libya and Syria."

"We've considered that. We've cross-referenced everything we know about this guy with the known bomb-making camps in Afghanistan, Iraq, Libya, and Syria. But so far, we're not getting much."

"What exactly do we know, other than he uses HMX he likely purchased on the black market and he's a crude assassin for hire?"

Baxter paused, unsure of how much to reveal. "There is one other thing."

The assassin's eyes widened. "Don't hold back on me, Baxter. If I'm going to help you—"

"All three bombs contained buckshot soaked in poison."

Baxter thought he saw a light bulb go off somewhere behind the assassin's stoic veneer, but the emotion vanished as quickly as it had appeared, making him second-guess himself.

The assassin cocked his head. "What about a motive for the three assassinations conducted by this guy? Two energy ministers and now an MP on the rise. Any link between the three?"

There was indeed a link between the three, but Baxter wasn't sure he wanted to share it. "Most of the agency's energy since the London bombing has been spent on finding you. But we did a rundown on the policies of the other two—" He stopped.

"Don't hold out on me, Baxter."

Baxter couldn't think of a reason not to share the information. "The French Minister of Ecology was on the take. He was on the payroll of several oil industry lobbyists and a couple of Russia's largest oil companies."

Max's eyes flickered again.

Baxter cocked his head. "What is it?"

The glimmer disappeared. "Nothing. Just triggered a memory of something someone recently told me. I need to think through whether there might be a connection."

Baxter removed his Blackberry from his pocket and spun it in his hand. "If you have something to share..."

The warm smile appeared again. "You've given me enough so I know where to start looking for this guy. You going to untie me now?"

Baxter stood. "Almost. First, we have some house-keeping to do." He walked away from the assassin on rubbery legs and took the hallway to the rear-most bedroom to retrieve Max's things from a table. There was a tarnished and dinged Zippo lighter with a faded etching of a flag he didn't recognize. A half-full pack of Russian cigarettes sat next to a travel wallet containing a stack of euros and several forms of identification in addition to a mobile phone, a heavy chunk of machined metal that looked like it could be dropped onto concrete from several floors up and still function. While he had waited for Max to return to consciousness, Baxter had flipped the phone on, at which point it prompted him for a ten-digit number. Baxter killed a few minutes by trying several combinations with no luck. He wished he could send the device to the lads at Q branch, the department responsible for all the fancy gear and digital forensics, but he was off the reservation on this deal. Besides, he needed a way to communicate with the assassin. He shoved everything into Asimov's backpack and walked back into the living room.

He set the bag on the table. "All your stuff is in there."

The assassin's face was passive. "How do we communicate?"

Baxter removed his Blackberry from his rear pocket and waved it.

The assassin rolled his eyes. "You haven't thought this all the way through, have you?"

Baxter flushed. "How do you mean?"

"You're in my world now. I'll set up a secure email site. You should get yourself another phone that's not monitored by MI6."

Baxter chastised himself for not thinking it through. "Right."

"How are you going to release me so I don't immediately kill you? Have you thought about that?"

Baxter smiled. This he had thought about. A lot. He walked around behind Max and dropped a pair of handcuff keys in the assassin's hand. Without a backward glance, Baxter walked to the front door, opened it, and left the building.

———

Max fumbled with the keys in his numb hands and almost dropped them twice before managing to undo one side of the cuffs. By the time he opened the other side, the keys and cuffs were smeared with blood from his raw wrists. He ignored the thin plastic zip ties cutting into his legs and lunged, managing to snag the edge of the wooden table. He dragged it to him, fumbled in the backpack and produced a knife. A few seconds later, his legs were free.

When he stood, his numb legs failed him and he tumbled to the floor. After massaging his calf muscles, Max crawled to the door and yanked it open. A fresh breeze tinged with honeysuckle and dogwood hit him in the face. Across the narrow road lined with Mini Coopers and flowering shrubs, a neighbor in a fishing hat knelt to work in a flowerbed. Nothing else moved. The MI6 man was gone.

He eased the door shut, crawled back to the table, and dug his phone out of his backpack. After powering it on and typing in the ten-digit passcode, he accessed his secure

email. It contained one unread email. The sender was Erich
Stasko.

———

"Where the fuck have you been?"

The boat hit a wave, spraying Max with frigid ocean
water. He sat with his back against the small metal building
that contained the bridge, and wore a gray rain slicker over a
wool coat to keep him warm against the early morning chill.
The roaring engines made it difficult to hear an angry Julia
on the other end and required him to yell into the phone.

"I had to take a detour."

There was silence on the other end of the line.

The custom forty-foot inflatable sped across the flat gray
water of the English Channel, it's eight 250-horsepower
outboard Mercuries making sixty knots. The boat's captain,
a grouchy pensioner who now earned his living smuggling
cargo, and sometimes people, between England and
Europe's mainland, built the craft so its low profile and
matte-gray color would keep it off the coast guard's radar.
Despite their long history of working together, the captain
demanded an extra-large sum of cash to ferry Europe's most
wanted man.

"Everything's fine. I got an email from Stasko."

More silence.

Stasko's message came from an anonymous email
address—a series of random characters and numbers—and
was sent to the secure email server Max had given Stasko.
The message was brief, but Max read it several times to
memorize the contents.

Max checked the strength of his cellular connection.
"You still there?"

Her voice was strained. "Go ahead."

Max grinned, enjoying the high-speed boat ride on the open water. "The money trail originated at a bank in Moscow. It was routed through several of Stasko's banks in Latvia before it was sent to a bank in Lebanon."

"Lebanon?"

"You heard right."

"How much?"

"Two payments of ten million US each."

"Forward me the message."

Max lied. "Already deleted it."

Julia's voice was laced with frustration. "We could have tried tracing it."

"You wouldn't have gotten far. It was anonymous."

Silence on the other end.

Max shielded his phone from another spray of ocean water. Despite the phone's rugged casing, salt water and electronics didn't mix. "I think I know who the bomber is."

"Who? And how do you know?"

Max smiled. "A man named Usam Islamov."

"Come again? Where are you anyway? There's a ton of background noise."

"I'm on a boat." He spelled the name out for her.

Julia didn't respond right away. "ISIS or al-Qaeda? Doesn't ring a bell."

"Chechen. I pieced it together with some information I uncovered in London combined with Stasko's email." Max had observed Russia's two wars with Chechnya from the sidelines of Paris where he was stationed and forgotten by the Belarusian KGB. He watched the conflicts with great interest, primarily because they were Russia's largest armed conflict since the 1979 invasion of Afghanistan. The two wars, the first in 1994 and the second in 1999, were brutal, with both sides committing atrocities and widespread killing of civilians. Mass graves of Chechen citizens were still being uncovered around Grozny, even decades later. His father played a role in both wars, running both Russian agents and double agents. Usam Islamov became known to the KGB during the first war and infamous during the second.

Silence on the other end. Max assumed Julia was accessing the BND's databases to see what the Germans had on Islamov.

He decided to preempt Julia's research. "In 1995, a year after the Russians first invaded Chechnya, a group of Chechen rebels attacked a town in southern Russia called Blagodarny. Over a period of ten days, the rebels imprisoned about three hundred civilians in a movie theater—men, women, and children. A standoff ensued. The Russians stormed the theater only to trigger an explosion that leveled almost the entire city block. Most of the Russians and a handful of Chechens perished. The KGB later discovered the bomb was built and placed by Usam Islamov."

Max paused to ward off another splash of water before continuing. "The event galvanized the Russians. Public support for the invasion soared. Islamov was later linked to several other bombings around Russia—including two in Moscow."

"I remember the movie theater incident. How do you know he's the same guy that did the West Brompton bombing?"

Max watched the foggy coast of Belgium appear on the horizon. "Can't tell you that now." What he wasn't telling Julia was the Blagodarny movie theater bomb was made from HMX, but the bomber used poison-soaked buckshot to maximize the carnage. "What I can tell you is the bank in Lebanon mentioned by Stasko was used by my father in a series of operations he ran during the first Chechen war."

More silence on the other end of the phone. "What now?"

"Heading to Grozny. I have to see a guy about a horse."

"Good lord, Max! You can't—"

Max smiled into the phone. "Sorry, you're breaking up. I think I'm losing you." He hit the button to end the call before tucking the phone away in his pocket.

His smile vanished as he contemplated a return to Russia, the very country that would execute him on sight for treason. As he jammed his hands in his pockets to keep them warm, he touched his grandfather's Zippo lighter. He ran his thumb over the pockmarked surface, the memory of old Yuri making him think of Alex. Max didn't know how Baxter and Victor arranged the video chat, but as soon as he chased down a bomber in the remote mountains of southern Russia, he meant to find out.

THIRTY-TWO

Alexandria, Virginia

Kate approached the bench with caution. She hated meeting in parks like this—it was such a clandestine cliché. She pictured park benches all over the greater Washington DC area populated with men and woman in trench coats having surreptitious conversations while talking in code. She had provided Bill with a burner phone so they could talk without fear of being tracked, but he insisted on meeting in person. He said he had a lead. While Kate loved the man, she still wasn't a hundred percent sure she trusted him. The blackmail file the CIA had on him would destroy his life which made him unpredictable. She approached the bench where he sat from behind and circled so she could see him from the front.

She pulled her rain hat down and tugged the belt on her Burberry trench coat tight against a light rain. In her right pocket, she carried a compact pistol. For the past hour, she watched the appointed rendezvous spot and the surrounding park, seeing nothing to cause her alarm. Fifteen minutes ago, a tall man in an olive green rain jacket walked by, nursing a slight limp. Otherwise, the rain kept the park empty. Bill was dressed in a dark overcoat and held an umbrella open over his head.

He gave her a wan smile as she sat down next to him. "Not sure how much longer I can do this. I'm under a microscope. I ran a surveillance detection route for an hour to get here and had to shake a tail. It's unnerving when my own agency has me under surveillance."

Kate looked ahead, her eyes roaming the park for movement. "You're the one that wanted to meet in person."

Bill moved the umbrella so it sheltered her from the rain. "They're demanding results, Kate."

"On me, you mean. They want me taken care of."

"Yeah."

Kate shot him a look. "How many do you have after me?"

Bill spoke as he turned to look the other way. "Only one contractor right now. We no longer have anyone in the human asset group, so I have to go outside the agency."

Kate crossed a leg and adjusted her raincoat. "What about Liam?"

"He was a special case, that prick. I'm glad Spencer iced him."

"You see the irony in all this, don't you?"

Bill's jacket rustled as he shifted in his seat. "It's fucking ridiculous. With Liam buried, my options are thankfully limited. The current guy is an ex-Delta who went off the reservation a decade ago and now works for despots and dictators as their errand boy and dirty little secret." Bill took out a mobile phone.

Kate took the umbrella while he worked the device. Her

father's best friend was running an op to eliminate her. "How close is he?"

Bill held up a smartphone and showed her a picture of the agent. Late forties, grizzled, deep tan, wrinkled face. Hard eyes, square jaw. Your basic washed-up tactical jock. "Not very. I fed him some fake intel that indicated you were in Berlin. Right now, he's staking out a small hotel on Ritterstrabe. You're supposed to turn up there sometime in the next seventy-two hours."

Kate couldn't help but smile. "Nice."

Bill put the phone away. "Sooner or later they're going to catch on, if they haven't already."

Kate handed him back the umbrella. "So you've said." At least Bill's admission made it less likely he was wearing a wire, unless everything he said was a lie. She had asked Kaamil to dig into Director Montgomery's background for anything they could use as leverage. He burrowed into her personal email account, breached the CIA's firewalls, and hacked into her work email. While he scoured her servers and compiled a dossier on her background, Kate followed Montgomery and noted a detailed log of her movements.

While in the director's contemporary duplex on Georgetown's west side, she placed a tiny device on Montgomery's home computer that monitored all internet traffic while routing a copy of every transmission to a secure server managed by Kaamil. So far, there was no evidence that suggested a clandestine relationship with someone in the NSA, the consortium, or anywhere else for that matter. And she never found evidence of the mole that had made her life at the CIA so difficult.

Bill picked at his thumb's cuticle with his index finger. "Maybe we should take her out."

Kate snorted. "What? And bring that kind of heat down

on us? If we do that, we'll lose any hope of finding out who the mole is. Besides, I want to pin it on her and see her squirm." She gave him a report of her activities over the past three days. "So far, we got nothing."

Bill grunted. "I'm not surprised. She didn't get to where she is by being sloppy. But I might have something."

Kate turned to look at him. His skin was pale, and he had dark circles under his eyes. "Tell me."

He grinned. "She's got a burner phone."

Kate's eyebrows went up. "How do you know?"

"You know how the agency issues everyone a Blackberry?"

Kate nodded. "They say the security is better—"

"Right. Well, I saw her using a different phone, which is a clear violation of policy."

Kate sniffed. "So is having a private email server, but that hasn't stopped her from doing that. Maybe she uses the mobile phone to communicate with her mother at the nursing home."

"Maybe. Maybe not."

Kate weighed the possibilities. "Since it's a burner, the only way to know for sure is to gain access to it and install malware on it—a program that will broadcast her calls and text messages to a server we monitor."

Bill shifted the umbrella to his other hand causing rain to start pattering on her hat. "Exactly."

Kate knew such a movement could be a signal to someone watching, and her heart rate quickened. She stood. "If I get you something on a micro-SD card, do you think you can somehow get it installed?"

Bill looked up at her from under the umbrella. "Unlikely. I doubt she'd leave it lying around."

Kate scanned the area, her eyes searching for movement. The rain stopped, and a few rays of sunshine broke through the thick clouds, leaving the gravel path glistening. "I think I know a way."

———————

Recruiting the operative was tougher than she thought. First, he was angry enough to make Kate afraid he might turn violent. After that, he was in denial before threatening to go directly to Montgomery and turn Kate in. In the end, the Agent Butterfield buried his head in his hands and begged for mercy. He had a family, for Christ sake. A wife pregnant with twin girls while raising a three-year-old daughter. His family must not find out. He would do anything.

Contrary to common belief, the director of the Central Intelligence Agency does not warrant Secret Service protection. Instead, the position maintains a special detail of rotating bodyguards provided by the CIA. Butterfield was one of those bodyguards assigned to Montgomery's detail. How Kate found his secret stash of cocaine was a mystery to him. He was happy to do whatever Kate asked to prevent him from washing out of the Agency because of his drug use. *Besides,* he thought, *she'd been unfairly treated anyway.* Agent Butterfield was now on Kate's team.

Kate sat in a rented Honda two blocks from Montgomery's Georgetown townhouse. The street grew quiet as the night progressed, and just after midnight, there was no traffic on the narrow residential street. On the seat next to her was a small laptop, its screen open. A small box was attached to the laptop via a USB cable. An earbud was in her ear, the other end plugged into the laptop. In the cup holder was an oversized Styrofoam cup of coffee.

Kaamil's voice sounded in her ear. "You sure he'll be able to pull this off?"

The computer expert was in his basement bunker at his parents' compound in the UAE. For him, it was just after 9:00 a.m. Their voice transmissions incurred a slight delay as they routed through several servers and encryption algorithms.

Kate tapped her fingernail against the steering wheel as she watched a tall figure in an olive-green overcoat walk down the sidewalk, doing an admirable job of hiding his limp. "Fear is a big motivator. As the lead on her security detail, he's got access to her home's security system. All he needs to do is shut off the system from the remote control in his SUV, enter the house and find the phone, which is probably plugged into a charger at her bedside, plug in the dongle containing the malware, wait a minute, and reverse the steps."

"All without her waking up."

Kate watched the limping figure tug on his hat before turning left at the corner, indicating the all-clear signal. "Right. All without her waking up."

―――――

Agent Butterfield's pits were soaked and perspiration rolled down his forehead as he sat in the front seat of his CIA-issued SUV. The cocaine habit had started innocently enough. He needed a pick-me-up to help him through a night shift after a sleepless forty-eight hours with a sick wife and daughter. He once tried a couple Red Bulls, but they made him ill. His partner that night, a chiseled Marine vet who took an early retirement from the military and landed the job with the CIA, tossed him a small vial of white powder. The coke worked wonders. Butterfield felt alert, on top of his game. That was two years ago. Eventually, the drug found its way into his recreational routine, and he was hooked. He kept telling himself he could quit, but he never did. It didn't help that the same Marine taught him how to get around the agency's so-called random drug testing.

Using a tiny spoon, he dug out a dose of the white powder from a vial he wore around his neck, put it up to a nostril, and snorted. He repeated the process with the second nostril before putting his head back as the drug surged into his bloodstream. The drug artificially prevented his dopamine from dissipating, which allowed the pooled dopamine to surge into his brain. He felt invincible.

He tapped a few times on the tablet computer attached to the dashboard, waited for the green light to signal the deactivation of the home's alarm system, and stepped out of the car while pulling on a pair of black latex gloves. He wore an agency-issued shoulder holster with a compact 9mm fitted with a short suppressor. If found, the gun would be traced to a local gangbanger. Butterfield purchased it a while back through a man who was connected to an underground black market network of law enforcement.

He jumped when a cat darted across his path and disappeared into the shrubbery. *Calm down. Breathe.*

As he approached the front door of Montgomery's townhouse, it didn't occur to him to question his actions. His defection began as a simple act of preservation. But now, with the stimulant coursing through his brain, he pictured himself as a CIA field agent, a job he was denied because of his inferior performance on the psych tests. Or so they said. The anger and resentment combined with the drug put him in a state of self-righteous confidence. He slipped the key into the lock, twisted, and stepped into the foyer.

Silence greeted him as he padded across the tile entryway. Piper Montgomery, divorced from a prominent Washington attorney, had no kids and no pets. Even her plants were plastic. *An operational necessity*, she often quipped. The modern townhouse was once featured in Architectural Digest, and the magazine had hauled in truckloads of real plants for the occasion and removed them shortly after the shoot.

The director was a woman of routine, married to her job, with no known vices, no dalliances, and the will and fortitude of an Olympic athlete. Her routine was well known by her security team. In bed by eleven pm, she was up every morning at four-thirty for a quick but ruthless workout and was in the office before six-thirty.

Butterfield took the plush carpeted stairs to the second floor and entered the master bedroom. He took comfort in the fact that his body temperature had regulated with the help of the drug, so he was no longer perspiring freely.

He paused in the open doorway of the master bedroom. The large room was dominated by a king-sized poster bed. In the center, sleeping on her back and shrouded by a white sheet, lay the director, her head supported by a single pillow. A black mask covered her eyes, and her chest was rising and falling. Under the covers, about a foot from her hand, Butterfield knew she kept a pistol.

After stepping into the room, he approached the bed. On either side were two oversized bedside tables. On one was a reading lamp, a glass of water, a bottle of pills, a box of tissues, and her CIA-issued Blackberry connected to a wall plug with a charging cord. Gently, he slid the drawer open. In it he found a stack of magazines, a spare blackout mask, and a jar of Vaseline. The burner phone was nowhere in sight.

He fought off panic with the help of the drugs and his surging adrenaline. He gave the bed a wide berth as he moved to the second bedside table. This one held a lamp and nothing else. The drawer contained a new box of tissues and something else, causing him to stifle a chuckle. The director kept an unopened box of condoms in her bedside table.

While keeping the sleeping director in sight, he moved to a large walk-in closet the size of his own bedroom. An island filled with drawers dominated the closet's center, and intricately ordered rows of clothing, boots, shoes, suits, and scarves covered the walls. In the center of the island, attached to a cord plugged into an outlet, was a tiny black Motorola flip phone. Butterfield smiled. Montgomery had a weakness after all, a single digression. He unplugged the burner phone from the charging cord and plugged in the dongle Kate gave him. A red light appeared on the tiny box connected to the dongle. Facing the door to the bedroom, his hand tight around the grip of his pistol, Butterfield waited. His toe tapped a fast rhythm on the wool carpet as he waited.

———

Kate's finger tapped against the steering wheel at an ever-increasing rate. Perhaps Butterfield had gotten cold feet. Maybe he was unable to locate the burner phone. God forbid he had gotten caught or shot by the director. Kate knew he would never hold up under questioning. It would take the interrogation experts at Langley less than five minutes to discover his drug habit and Kate's blackmail scheme, at which point she would lose any opportunity to penetrate Montgomery's veil of protection. Her security detail would increase to near-presidential levels, making it impossible to get close to her. Kate dug out a cigarette and fired it up before cracking a window. The hit of nicotine calmed her.

A faint *ding* sounded from her laptop. She glanced at the screen and saw a green bar, indicating the virus had activated, which meant Butterfield had successfully introduced the software to Montgomery's phone.

Kate breathed out a lungful of smoke before toggling her earbud mic. "We're in."

Kaamil was looking at an identical application on his side. "Got it. It's starting to download the phone's contents."

The virus Butterfield installed on the burner phone would perform two functions invisible to the user's eye. It would allow Kaamil to examine the phone's data logs, a list of phone numbers called and received, a readout of all text messages, all apps installed, and even photos taken. It would also route any text messages to Kaamil's workstation and allow him to listen in on all calls.

"Pretty light payload," Kaamil said. "Only one phone number, both in and out."

"Can you trace it?"

"Doubtful. Probably another burner, but I'll give it a shot."

Kate hung up, snapped the laptop shut, turned on the car, and pulled out into the street, typing a text message to Bill as she drove.

THIRTY-THREE

Prague, Czech Republic

The men in the soup line moved like prisoners in a chain gang. Each carried a metal plate and cup, the same kind used in the nation's prison system, a fitting accessory that reminded the homeless of their own personal hell. Some mumbled to themselves, but no one greeted the well-meaning volunteers who ladled steaming stew onto their plates. All of them avoided the volunteers' eyes, some in shame, some in indifference. Next door, a gleaming church stood erected to a God none of them knew, each person instead focused on survival or confusion borne from the highs and lows of addiction or mental illness.

The line wound out the door of the service hall and down the street, disappearing around a corner. Many of the men in line sucked on cigarette butts, hoping to glean a few milligrams of nicotine. A few lucky ones puffed on shorties they scrounged from ashtrays or the gutter, warding off their linemate's envious stares with glares and incoherent rants.

Most of the homeless were men in later stages of life, many with open sores on their skin that refused to heal from malnutrition or constant substance abuse.

During the evening mealtime at St. Mary of the Angels, when the city's poorest and homeless gathered for their nightly portions of the rich beef stew and soft bread the church was known for, the rest of the city's population stayed away. Most preferred to avoid looking the homeless problem in the eye while others were simply unwilling to subject themselves to the stench, filth, and erratic behaviors of the city's downtrodden.

This was one reason the willowy woman known to some as Goshawk frequented the food line each night. She could have hidden in a doorway with a clear view of the soup line or even sat in the nave of the church itself waiting to be contacted. The soup kitchen, however, was an anonymous and free way to get sustenance as well as information, so each night around 7:00 pm, she donned a pair of frayed and soiled jeans, combat boots with a hole in one toe, and a ratty army jacket, covered her shaved head with a black watch cap, and left her tenement to join the line. She'd been coming now for several days, and many of the regulars were starting to notice her. If The Monk didn't show soon, she would move on.

Nowadays, her appearance was a far cry from the sultry lounge-singing persona she used while living in France. Her normally clear porcelain skin was dirty and unwashed. Her head was shaved, revealing tattoos that showed a disturbing and bloody scene. Her fingernails were cut to the quick, and she had dragged them through the tenement's garden to sufficiently darken them. She rarely left her basement flat in Prague's southern town, but when she did, she donned a pair of wraparound shades and often wore a scarf like a hijab around her head.

Her main concern was being recorded by one of the hundreds of security cameras mounted around the city. Facial recognition software had improved to the point where cameras were easily configured to programmatically capture an individual's height, gait, and facial structure to calculate a probable match within a few degrees of confidence. She assumed that many of the modern western nations' camera systems were programmed to recognize her, which is why she presumed she was instructed to meet her contact here in Prague where the cameras were less advanced rather than in western Europe.

Once she made contact and got the information she needed, she would melt back to the island of Corsica where cameras were nonexistent. Goshawk removed a cigarette from a soft pack and used a match to light it, ignoring envious glances from the men around her.

"Bum a smoke, missy?" The scratchy voice came from right behind her.

On instinct, her right hand dipped into her jacket pocket and fingered a straight razor, slipping it open and nestling it in the palm of her hand. Her arm tensed, ready to strike. She turned and looked at the speaker from the corner of her eye.

He was a stooped old man, his grizzled face covered with a week's growth and shaggy white hair gathered behind his neck in a ragged ponytail. Like her, he wore an olive-green army jacket, but he wore a button on his breast that read *Viva la Stalin*. His breath reeked of wine, and he held out a pair of quivering curled fingers.

Upon her arrival in Prague, she had received an encrypted email indicating she should watch for someone wearing a button identical to the one this man wore. Her hand gripping the razor relaxed, and she removed her pack of cigarettes, shaking one out. The man managed to grasp it with a trembling hand. Goshawk lit a match and cupped her hands around the flame, helping him to light it. He pulled back and sucked the smoke in deep while his watery eyes roamed over her.

He blew smoke into the air. "Join me to light a prayer candle?" His voice was slurred, and his breath smelled of strong wine.

"I'm not religious, but I'll accompany you anyway," Goshawk said, completing the agreed-upon code sequence.

She followed as the old man left the line and shuffled across the vacant street to the main doors of the church. As he walked, his head swiveled side to side, and he muttered to himself as if he had lost his senses. Goshawk knew better. This shuffling drunk, who called himself The Monk, possessed one of the computer world's clearest and most knowledgeable minds.

Once in the nave of the cavernous church, The Monk strode to the front where he stopped in front of a long rack of prayer votives. Most of the candles were lit, sending flickering shadows over the alter and across the now dark stained glass windows of the transept. She went and stood next to him.

He stared into the candlelight, his posture straight. "The famous Goshawk. I assume you're clean?"

She snorted. "Of course." *Clean* in the cyberworld meant you weren't carrying any electronic devices like cell phones, tablets, or computers that might be compromised. The best way to ensure no one triangulated your location or listened to your conversation was to avoid carrying electronics.

He no longer slurred his words. "Listen, missy. Survival on this side requires many things. Take nothing for granted. Assume nothing."

She rolled her eyes. "It's not my first—"

"Until you've been fighting the NSA for a couple years and lived to tell about it, you're still a rookie in my book. Do you want my help, or should I disappear?"

She bit back her retort. The man who now called himself The Monk was a legend. He was one of the first to blow the whistle on the NSA's illegal behavior, and he now waged a personal battle against the institution. Rumor had it he was the leader of an anti-NSA hacker group called The Freedom Project who spent their time hacking into the organization's servers and releasing material to a variety of journalists and public watchdog groups. Little was known about The Freedom Project, but it was widely known in the hacker community that the mysterious man who led the group was among the NSA's most wanted. No one outside the NSA knew more about the NSA's capabilities than this man, and she would need his help if she were to survive.

"My apologies. I appreciate you meeting me in person."

"Still the safest way."

Goshawk assumed this man's moniker, The Monk, was among several he used interchangeably, depending on the situation.

The Monk slid two bank notes into the offering box and used a long match to light three votives while muttering under his breath. "One for each of my children."

"How long has it been since you've seen them?"

He finished lighting the candles before turning to address her in a hushed voice. "I have the information you want."

Her mouth dropped open a fraction of an inch, and it

took her a moment to recover. "I haven't even asked for it yet."

He held a finger to his lips. "Keep your voice down. You don't need to. There is only one reason you reached out to me."

Goshawk gasped. "How—" She cut off her own sentence when she realized she was still speaking in a loud voice.

The Monk smirked. "It's my business to know what's going on with the NSA. You, my dear, have been on their radar for a short but intense period of time."

His smirk was replaced by a scowl. "They will hunt you down using every resource at their disposal. Bank accounts, immigration, border crossings, ship manifests, airline rosters. Even train tickets, security camera footage, social media profiles. Nothing escapes their algorithms. They'll use artificial intelligence on massive server farms to crunch every piece of data they can find, looking for patterns that suggest your location. Every piece of digital information you spin off will be gathered and pieced together until one day you'll find yourself living in a cave in Canada's Yukon Territory hundreds of miles from the grid. Even then, you'd be well served to watch your back."

Goshawk felt her stomach turn. She knew the power of the NSA—every hacker knew they held enormous power over vast swaths of the internet—but hearing him say it made her jittery. She looked around before whispering, "How have you managed to stay out of their clutches?"

He smiled like he was trying to sell a child a piece of candy. "Before we go any further, I'll have you know my information comes with a price."

Goshawk's eyes narrowed. "What kind of price?"

The Monk snickered. "Nothing you can't afford, my darling."

Goshawk shook off a shudder and ignored the flirting. Money was of no use to The Monk, but her computer skills were. *Should she take the risk? Could she afford not to?* The Monk was her one hope, her life raft in the storm. He was the one person she knew who could help her. She was out of options.

The Monk noticed her hesitation. "Trusting me is your only hope. Otherwise, in a week, a month, maybe six months, you'll find yourself down a hole so deep the world will never see you again." His eyes roamed over her. "And that, luvvie, would be a shame."

Goshawk crossed her arms over her chest. "Fine. I'm in. Where do we start?"

When he smiled, she saw something in his eyes she hadn't seen before. It was a glint, a mischievous smirk, as if he was about to embark on something he relished with all his passion. "Like in any war, my dear, the best defense starts with a good offense."

THIRTY-FOUR

Grozny, Chechnya

Max stared up at the silver skyscrapers glinting in the morning sun, framed by a bright blue sky and surrounded by lush green trees. The Grozny-City Towers consisted of five buildings that soared over the downtown, a symbol of Russia's will to rebuild a city they annihilated with bombs in 1999. The five towers housed a hotel, a business complex, and upscale residential units.

The cab driver, a turbaned man with deeply wrinkled skin, spoke to Max in Russian while holding up a fist with the thumb pointed up. "Second tallest in all of Europe."

Max grunted, wondering where this man was during the two wars. At the height of the conflict, Grozny was leveled by the Russian army, leaving only twenty thousand civilians remaining in the city. The war created one of the largest immigration and humanitarian disasters in history. After the war, Russia invested millions of rubles to rebuild the city, and now several hundred thousand Russian-speaking Chechens were proud to call the city home.

At the end of the second Chechen war, Usam Islamov's last known hiding place was the vast mountainous region controlled by Islamist separatists in southern Chechnya. Even now, almost twenty years later, the region still simmered with anti-Russian and anti-imperialist sentiment. It was a place where the bomb maker could disappear into the protective veil of a people still angry at the Russians for preventing their independence and at the rest of the world for letting it happen. Islamov was also known to have extended family in the region, and there was no reason to think he had moved elsewhere. To be sure, Max asked Kaamil to hack into the FSB's databases, and the resulting intel confirmed Max's suspicions. The only trick was to root out the bomb maker without getting himself killed. He was in Grozny to meet with the one man he knew who could help him find Islamov.

Once again, Max was headed into the maw of the beast, even if the Northern Caucasus regions of southern Russia felt much different than Moscow. Here the jagged white-capped mountains and rolling green valleys reminded him of Colorado. While Moscow was cold, indifferent, and suspicious, Chechnya was warm, inviting, and passionate, and the people greeted visitors with warm smiles. Chechens were a gracious people, despite having been bombed into oblivion twice by their Russian overlords. They were also hot-blooded and willing to fight for their rights and their land, and Max respected their grit. As with everywhere in the Muslim world, it was unfortunate that a small group of extremists gave a bad name to such wonderful people.

Despite the welcoming nature of the Chechens, Max reminded himself that he needed to watch his back—not because the FSB was surveilling his every move, but because he was now on Usam Islamov's turf. Max assumed the bomb maker had people on every corner watching for suspicious-looking Caucasians. For that reason, he steered clear of the city's Muslim quarter. Instead, he had the cabbie drop him in the Russian city district of Leninsky, where he hitched up his backpack and disappeared into the crowds of civilians shopping in the central market.

Max marveled at how the neighborhood had been rebuilt. The gleaming skyscrapers rose behind him while the market stall owners displayed their modern merchandise for sale. Signs indicated that most known credit cards were accepted, and many of the patrons were well dressed. He wondered if they had all forgotten the ten hypersonic scud missiles the Russians launched in 1999 that killed 150 civilians and leveled the very market he now walked through. Perhaps prosperity erased old wounds. Perhaps not.

He wound his way through hordes of people, all shopping for food items, kitchen wares, and brightly colored articles of clothing. He stopped in front of a stall selling the traditional Middle Eastern scarves called the keffiyeh, bought one in a black-and-white checked pattern and wrapped it around his neck. Exiting the far side of the market, he found the storefront he was looking for along a dirty side street.

The sign over the door advertised *Electronics* in both Russian and Chechen. Where white letters had once been etched into the door's glass were now covered in graffiti. Two small but high-powered security cameras were mounted over the door, the shop's only clue that it might be more than it appeared.

He stopped himself from opening the door. Inside the

electronics shop was a man who knew firsthand the consequences of the two armed struggles against the Russian
oppressors. He was a man who once made the hard choice
to betray his own people to save their very lives. He figured
the man still harbored anger and resentment from that
period of his life, and unfortunately Max personified that
rage by simply carrying the Asimov surname.

Bracing himself for a fight, Max pushed the door open
and stepped into the dim interior.

———

"You have a lot of fucking nerve, Asimov."

The baritone voice came from behind a tall stack of
broken radios, televisions, and other home electronics. A
large man stood behind a display case, barrel chest encased
in a camouflaged army jacket that had seen better days. His
salt-and-pepper hair was cropped short, and his battle-
scarred face and eyes looked like he'd seen a lot in his fifty-
plus years. His hands were out of sight below the counter.

Max held up both hands with his palms forward. "Don't
shoot, Sultan. I'm unarmed."

Sultan Zakayev was once a respected high-level
Chechen resistance leader. During the first Chechen war,
he grew sick of the toll the fight took on the civilians and on
the city he loved. As Russian troops marched into
Chechnya in October of 1999, he recognized the futility of
the resistance and agreed to provide intelligence to the
Russians. Some said he was paid by the KGB, a rumor that
riled the former freedom fighter. For over a year, as the
Russians and Chechens fought one of the most brutal wars
of the twentieth century, he was one of Andrei Asimov's
greatest sources of intel. It was said around the KGB that

Sultan single-handedly turned the conflict in Russia's favor in early 2000, paving the way for the fall of Grozny.

Sultan's mouth was turned down in a wicked frown. "Turn the fuck around and walk out before I blow you away. I don't think anyone will mind if I kill the most wanted man in the world. Maybe I can even collect the reward."

Max approached the counter with his hands still in the air. He knew Sultan had survived two brutal wars, managed to spy for the opposite side while still commanding thousands of insurgents, and survived to tell his grandkids. He was a tough man, and Max didn't doubt Sultan would shoot first and ask questions later.

"Sultan, you know I didn't do that bombing in London."

"That's the only reason I haven't shot you yet."

"Five minutes, that's all."

"You have one minute." Sultan took a step to his right.

"Is there somewhere we can talk?" The depth of Sultan's anger took Max by surprise. He figured Sultan wouldn't want his past dredged up, fearing his role in the conflict might become known and put his life in jeopardy. But he didn't count on this level of animosity.

"Are you deaf? Now you have thirty seconds." The big man's hands shifted below the counter.

Max took two more tentative steps until he was standing in front of the counter. "Sultan, we can do this two ways. Either we have a civil conversation somewhere away from all the monitoring equipment I know you have, or I can take that shotgun from you and shove it so far up your ass the barrel comes out your mouth." Max was balanced on the balls of his feet, ready.

The corner of Sultan's mouth twitched and his eyes flashed. When a sawed-off double-barreled shotgun appeared over the glass countertop, Max batted it away with his left forearm. The gun roared as a shell full of steel and tungsten buckshot tore into a display of mobile phones, exploding plastic, glass, and metal beads in a burst of debris.

Max grabbed Sultan by the throat with his right hand, crushing his larynx with all his strength. As the former rebel commander tried to bring the gun around for another shot, Max grabbed the barrel with his left hand. He squeezed Sultan's neck, causing him to gasp for breath. While Sultan clawed at his throat, Max yanked the shotgun from his grasp, let go of his throat, and flipped the gun around. The former rebel commander gasped for air while staring into the side-by-side shotgun barrels.

"One barrel left, Sultan."

THIRTY-FIVE

Grozny, Chechnya

"Follow me." Sultan's voice was thick as he struggled to speak.

Max kept the shotgun trained on Sultan's back as he followed the bear of a man through stacks of electronics to a cluttered back room. After both men ducked to navigate a narrow set of stairs, Max found himself in a cramped, but comfortable, underground office. A piece of shag carpet sat on the concrete floor, a mismatched group of chairs were jumbled in a partial circle, and a desk with a dusty computer sat next to the wooden steps. Behind the chairs were storage shelves crammed with all manner of televisions, some new in the box, some used, and some in various states of repair.

He prodded Sultan with the shotgun barrel. "In a chair. Hands where I can see them."

Sultan dropped himself into the nearest chair, sending a cloud of dust into the air.

Max stood where he could see both Sultan and the stairs. "I thought you'd be more grateful. You made a lot of money from my father."

Sultan crossed his arms over his broad chest. "Fuck you, Mikhail. You don't know shit."

"Enlighten me."

"Even after I started handing over intel, the Russians kept murdering innocent Chechens."

"I heard it was a two-way street."

Sultan's eyes narrowed to slits before he reeled off a string of profanities in Chechen. "The Russian's started it. We were perfectly happy with our independence. The rest of the former soviet republics got theirs, why couldn't we stay independent?"

Max shrugged. "You tell me."

Sultan snorted. "Fucking oil. The Russian president had to have our oil. And...they're fucking racists. They killed two birds with one stone. Take out some Muslims and get the oil at the same time."

Max had heard similar theories about the conflict before. "So why did you flip? Why did you help your mortal enemy? Money?"

He waved his hands at their surroundings. "Fuck you, Asimov. Do I look like I did it for the money?"

"Then why?"

"Because they were going to win anyway. I did it to try to stop innocent civilians from becoming victims. On both sides. The faster the war ended, the less mothers and children would be killed. Are we better off as prosperous members of the Russian Federation or as poor but free and independent?"

Some said Sultan did it for altruism, but Max's father told him that they paid out over three million US dollars, delivered in suitcases of cash, over the nine-month period Sultan worked for them. He didn't think his father was lying, so where did the money go?

Sultan blew out a big sigh and massaged his throat. "What the fuck do you want?"

"I need your help. I need to find someone. Someone who is here in Chechnya. Someone who used to work for you."

Sultan's eyes narrowed to slits. "You must be kidding."

"I didn't do that bombing in London, Sultan. You know it as well as I do."

"What makes you think he did it?"

"Intel."

"What kind of intel?"

"The best kind. Financial and forensic."

Sultan's eyebrows went up. "Who are you working with?"

Max pointed the shotgun at the floor. "Doesn't matter. He's a bomber for hire now. He's disguising assassinations with bombs, killing innocent people."

Sultan stroked his chin. "I know, I know."

"Do you know how many civilians are getting killed because of what he's doing? Sixty-two in London just last week. How many will it be the next time?"

Sultan let out a big sigh.

"Help me take him down, Sultan. Before he kills again."

Sultan slouched in the chair. "Okay, okay. I get it. I can help."

———

They bounced along Grozny's potholed roads in Sultan's beat-up Toyota Land Cruiser. The leather seats were cracked, and the gear shift handle was an 8-ball from a billiards table. Dust and mud covered the exterior, and the inside was full of food wrappers and discarded coffee cups. Sultan drove while Max sat at an angle in the passenger seat so he could watch the old rebel leader.

Sultan had put the closed sign up in the electronics store, and they just left his decrepit tenement with a duffel of clothing and gear. Max borrowed an old army jacket, and they raided Sultan's private weapons cache. Max had a Glock .45 in his pocket, and under a blanket on the Toyota's back deck was a scarred AK-47 and a beat-to-hell tactical shotgun. Sultan assured him the weapons were in good working order. Two duffel bags of assorted gear, including a pair of ratty tactical vests, a set of high-powered binoculars, a dated night-vision scope, tactical knives, assorted survival gear, and first aid kits were on the back seat. A cardboard box, a gift for the man they were going to see, sat next to the AK-47.

Behind them followed a Toyota pickup truck that had seen better days. In the cab were three clean-cut former rebels, men who had given up the insurgent life to establish homes and families in the rebuilt city of Grozny. Three more men sat in the truck bed next to a pile of AK-47s and assorted other weapons.

Max glanced back at the men. "Changing more diapers now than rifle magazines?"

Sultan drove the SUV like a man on a mission—two meaty hands on the wheel, wrestling the car around curves, and dodging potholes like a Formula One driver while his eyes roamed the busy streets. "Believe me, you don't want to head into the South Caucasus as an army of two. These men have seen more action than a Moscow prostitute."

Sultan pointed the vehicle south, and they left downtown Grozny driving toward the rugged mountains on the horizon. This time of year the crags and hills were covered with lush green grass, giving the mountains a mossy look from the distance. Max knew the beautiful environment was misleading—the mountainous region along the border of Georgia and Russia hid a treacherous network of Georgian and Chechen rebels who didn't hide their hatred for their imperial oppressors. Even the Russian army rarely forayed into the region. It was into this warren of radical militants that they were headed.

They put together the foundation of a plan before leaving Sultan's shop. The ex-rebel didn't know exactly where Usam Islamov was hiding, but heard reports he was holed up in a Georgian rebel enclave just south of the border in a lawless area known as South Ossetia. Sultan knew a man named Gurgen, an old rebel who had lived in the mountains and canyons of southern Chechnya for most of his life, who might know of the bomb maker's whereabouts.

The rumor was that Gurgen was Islamov's front man. If you wanted to get in touch with Islamov for a job, you went through Gurgen. He lived in a tiny mountain village on the border with Georgia called Salgi. To get there, they needed to traverse fifty kilometers of mountains on a dirt road, passable only by a four-wheel drive vehicle. For much of the trip, they'd be under the watchful eye of the rebels, hidden in the rocky crags and thick forests of the mountains.

Unbeknownst to Sultan, the KGB had a file on Gurgen, and the man had a brief history with Max's father. Kaamil had dug up the file as part of Max's pre-operation research, giving Max an ace up his sleeve. For the time being, he decided to keep this information from Sultan.

Sultan sipped water from a dinged army canteen. "What's your intention with Islamov?"

Max double-checked the Glock by racking the slide to eject the bullet and dropping the magazine. "I need evidence he carried out the West Brompton bombing. I'm guessing he's the only one that can provide that evidence."

Sultan grunted. "I had to call ahead. Otherwise, we'd never make it within a hundred kilometers of the village. Your cover is you're a representative from a Russian oligarch looking to hire a bomber. This negotiation needs to be delicate. You need to be coy. Don't give up your employer's name. Gurgen's going to want to check you out. This is the first meeting of many. You need to build confidence with Gurgen. Hiring a bomber isn't like hiring a housekeeper."

Max chuckled. "Got it."

"This meeting will be all about whether or not he likes you. If he likes you, you get to move on to the next step. If he doesn't, he'll either kill you or you'll never be able to set foot in the southern Caucasus Mountains again."

Max gazed out the window, listening to Sultan, but letting his mind drift elsewhere. He wondered how Alex was getting along in the castle. He wondered why Victor Dedov had agreed to the deal with Baxter to offer Alex as leverage over Max. He wondered what Baxter would do to Alex if he felt threatened. Max noticed he was gripping the pistol so hard his knuckles were white, and he forced himself to calm. *Little drops of water wear down big stones*, his father often said.

Now that they were on the long straight road between Grozny and the foothills to the south, Sultan drove with one hand on the wheel and punctuated his sentences with his other fist. "No way this guy is going to give up Islamov without coercion. But if we coerce, he will alert Islamov, who will then disappear. If we kill Gurgen, Islamov will find out and disappear."

Max watched the green hills roll by as he wondered how much he could trust Sultan. If the former rebel commander wanted Max gone, or dead, the easiest way would be to lead him into a trap up here in the mountains, away from civilization. Since Max couldn't see another way, he would just have to proceed with caution. Julia had set him up with a fake background, one that should hold up under the scrutiny of a Chechen rebel. Max also had a few tricks up his sleeve. He wasn't heading up into the rebel-held mountains without a strategy.

He turned to look at Sultan, who had clear lines of worry etched on his craggy face, and smiled. "Don't worry. I have a plan."

———

As the Land Cruiser trundled into the small town of Salgi, five kilometers from the Georgian border, Sultan's eyes grew more restless. The village, if you could call it that, was a gathering of tiny stone huts jumbled on either side of the dirt track like bags of trash left by a roadside crew. They instructed the pickup truck of soldiers to wait at a stony crossroad three klicks to the west and entered the cluster of buildings alone.

Two men appeared on a rocky rise to their left as the SUV entered the village. Both men looked like they had survived scores of battles and had lived in hiding in the mountains for most of their lives. They wore ragged military clothing—green-and-black camouflage jackets, blue jeans, and scarves around their necks. Both carried AK-47s and wore sidearms on their hips. They glared at Sultan and Max as the SUV rolled by.

Max traced a thumb over the Glock's barrel and kept the gun hidden from sight. "How long has it been since you've been here?"

Sultan removed a pistol from a holster and laid it on his lap. "Ten years. Not much has changed." Sultan turned off the road and piloted the SUV over a berm and across a grassy open spot before parking in front of a stone hut with a moss-covered roof. A curl of smoke streamed from the chimney, and the smell of meat hung in the air. Sultan stuffed the pistol back in his holster before exiting the vehicle.

As they stepped out of the truck, a man appeared at the hut's door. He was short and wiry, with the same hard look on his face as the other men they saw along the way. Swarthy and tanned from the exposure to the elements, the man was easily in his fifties. He wore a ragged beard, and a scar ran down his neck from his ear, disappearing under his collar. A sidearm peeked out from under a camouflage jacket. He greeted Sultan with a wary handshake, but regarded Max with a glare.

"This him?"

Sultan introduced Max. "This is Eduard. Eduard, this is Gurgen."

Max reached to shake Gurgen's hand, but the old insurgent shot him an icy scowl and turned and entered the hut.

Max glanced at Sultan, who shrugged. "I warned you."

Max went around to the back of the SUV and removed a large cardboard box from the vehicle before following Sultan into the hut.

Inside, a fire in a stone hearth gave off the room's only light. Smoke from the blaze and cigarettes hung in the air.

Two men, both cut from the same grizzled cloth as Gurgen, smoked while eating out of crude bowls. Max dropped the box on the room's only table.

Sultan spoke first. "A gift for you and your men, Gurgen."

The rebel glanced at the box before withdrawing a long-bladed knife and carving a hunk from an apple. "What's in it?"

Max opened the flaps and dumped several dozen cartons of cigarettes onto the table. Gurgen squinted at the gift.

Gurgen set the apple down and wiped the knife on his shirt before using it to open a carton. He removed a pack of cigarettes, opened it, put one in his mouth, and lit it before turning to look at Sultan. "Been a long time."

Max stood by the fire, his eyes roaming the cottage, while the two men caught up. Gurgen stubbed the cigarette out on the table and flipped the butt into the fire as he came over and stood in front of Max. Max had six inches in height and twenty pounds on the old rebel, but he was on his own turf, and Max saw no fear in his eyes.

Gurgen looked Max up and down before staring into his eyes for a beat. He turned and addressed Sultan.

"From our initial checks, your man here seems legit. Obviously more work needs to be done before we're convinced."

There was a standard protocol for gaining the rebel's trust. The only reason Max was standing here was because Julia had set up an ironclad fake background and Sultan had vouched for him. Unfortunately for Gurgen, Max didn't have months to go through the delicate dance required to hire a shadowy bomber.

Max kept his voice even. "Let's talk, just you and me,

Gurgen."

The room went still. The men eating at the table put down their spoons. Gurgen stared at Sultan, who stared back at the rebel as if to say *Don't ask me*. Gurgen turned and cocked his head at Max. "Eduard. That's what you said your name was?"

Max stood still, arms at his sides.

"Eduard, why don't you get the fuck out of here and take these shitty cigarettes with you."

Max decided not to point out that the cigarettes were some of the best money could buy. "What you're about to hear, you're going to want to keep to yourself."

Gurgen took a step forward so he was an inch from Max's face. Out of the corner of his eye, Max saw Sultan take a step toward them, his hand moving to the butt of his pistol. Gurgen's men stood from the table, hands reaching for weapons.

The rebel jabbed Max in the chest. "You dare come in here, up here to my land, land I fought for with my own blood, and tell me how—"

Max whispered one word so only Gurgen could hear. "Lebanon."

Gurgen's eye's narrowed. He stared at Max for a moment before growling, "Clear the room."

His men didn't move. Sultan stood rooted in place.

Gurgen turned to them. "Clear the goddamn room."

The scraping of chairs was the only sound as the men filed out of the hut.

Gurgen glared at Sultan. "You too."

Max caught Sultan's eye and nodded once. Sultan scowled, but he stepped out of the hut.

After the door slammed shut, Gurgen turned back to Max. One hand combed through his hair while the other rested on the butt of his gun. His eyes searched Max's face. "Who the fuck are you?"

Knowing his pistol would be useless in a physical confrontation at close range, Max kept his hands free at his sides. "Doesn't matter. You only need to worry about one thing."

"I'm listening."

Max smiled. "You're going to take us to Usam Islamov."

Gurgen's face turned crimson underneath his rugged tan. "The fuck I am."

"If you don't, that little multi-million-dollar retirement fund you have hidden away in Crédit Libanais in Lebanon will disappear."

Gurgen's shoulders hunched, and he looked like he was going to spring at Max. His voice was a low growl. "You'll never get out of here alive—"

Max stood his ground. "Let me be clear. The three of us are going to ride out of this valley in Sultan's car. You're going to take us to Usam Islamov. I'm going to have a long conversation with him. If I end up dead, or we don't find Islamov, that money disappears." Max snapped his fingers in front of Gurgen's face. "Just like that."

Gurgen's shoulders slumped, and he didn't answer for what felt like a long time. "You're going to need more men than just the two of you."

"Let me worry about that part."

Gurgen took a step back. "You're FSB?"

Max shrugged. "Doesn't matter."

Gurgen studied the floor for a moment. "You're playing a dangerous game, Eduard. Or whatever the fuck your name is."

Max chuckled. "Funny. I recently told someone else that exact same thing."

THIRTY-SIX

Salgi, Chechen Republic of Russia

The three men departed the tiny hamlet of Salgi in the Land Cruiser. Sultan drove with Gurgen in the front passenger seat while Max rode in the backseat behind Gurgen with the Glock pointed at his back through the seat.

The ease with which Gurgen submitted made Max think he either had some ideas about how to get out of his predicament or he really cared about his money. Max also suspected the rebel didn't want his men to know he had squirreled away millions while they lived in poverty. Maybe it would undermine his authority. Still, Max knew he needed to keep a watchful eye out, hence the pistol pointed at the man's back.

Before they left, Gurgen told them that Usam Islamov was staying in a small village to the south, across the border in Georgia. The border between Georgia and Chechnya was a mountainous stretch of land controlled by various groups of loosely affiliated ethnic Chechen warlords, all of whom lived in an uneasy truce with the Russians to the north. Every so often, a splinter group ventured north and attacked a government installation or bombed a train of civilians, prompting the Russian army to make incursions into the region to, as they liked to say, hunt terrorists.

"How do you know that's where he is?"

Gurgen turned so he could see Max from the corner of his eye. "Because his mother lives there, and she's on her death bed."

The pickup fell in behind the SUV, its bed bristling with men hardened by years of conflict, each holding an AK-47, their barrels pointed at the sky. Max cyed a dozen men along the ridge to the south of town watching the vehicles as they left the last stone building behind. He made a mental note to avoid Salgi in the future. Something told him that he wouldn't be welcome back here.

The 200-kilometer drive from Gurgen's village south to Makarta, Georgia would take them over six hours. Along the way, they would pass over the border using a dirt road traveled only by what Gurgen called *The Chechen Resistance*. To pass the time, he filled them in on some of the history of the Caucasus region.

"You're probably Russian, so you already know much of this, but our fight goes back to Stalin. He executed thousands of Chechens and deported the rest of our people during World War II. He forced them into Siberia and Kazakstan. Over a hundred thousand died."

Max chuckled. "Because you sided with the Nazis."

There was ice in Gurgen's voice. "Lies. It was pure racism. Besides, Israilov hated the Germans."

Gurgen was referring to Khasan Israilov, the Chechen guerrilla fighter who led a four-year resistance against the Russians during World War II. At the same time, the

Germans attempted an invasion of the North Caucasus region, an invasion that ultimately failed.

Max shifted the gun to his left hand. "There's evidence a small number of Chechens aided the Germans at one point. But I'll concede that Israilov only agreed to aid the Germans if they guaranteed the Chechens their own independence. The Germans said no, so Israilov stayed independent."

Gurgen's eyebrows lifted a millimeter. "Russians don't like to admit that."

"I'm not Russian."

Gurgen turned and stared out the window at the rolling green mountains before turning back to Max. "Israilov always said we preferred the Russians as overlords over the Germans."

Sultan, intent on the road, muttered, "Fucking Germans."

Max smiled. "Then Khrushchev let you back into Russia, which I think most Russians regret."

Gurgen turned back to look out the window. Max knew he was seething on the inside, wanting to know who Max was and who he worked for.

The three men were quiet as the truck bounced over ruts and teetered on a rocky ledge with a long drop-off from the passenger side. Sultan drove as fast as he dared, his two ham-sized fists griping the steering wheel. Even with the truck full of fighters behind them, Max stayed alert, pistol held at the ready. He knew the chance of an ambush or attack increased as they traveled deeper into rebel territory. The Chechen people were made up of over a hundred different clans, each with their own agenda. One of the Chechens' great failures was uniting all the clans under a single leader, which made for dangerous traveling through the region.

Max leaned forward and put his free arm on the back of Gurgen's seat. "Clear something up for me, Gurgen. What is the Chechens' real relationship with al-Qaeda?"

Gurgen shifted in his seat. "More lies. We have none."

Max persisted. "But isn't the Taliban the only entity that recognizes Chechnya as independent?"

Gurgen's retort was laced with anger. "We can't help what the Taliban does. We didn't ask for that."

Max smiled. "Isn't it true that before 2002, most of the world supported the idea of Chechen independence? Before then, you fought only the Russian army, combatants versus combatants. But around 2002, you guys followed al-Qaeda's lead and started killing innocent Russian civilians. After that point, you were abandoned by the rest of the world."

"For someone who claims not to be Russian, you certainly think you know a lot."

"It's just history, Gurgen. It's a fact you targeted women and children. That's not Russian propaganda."

Gurgen mumbled out the window. "Stalin started it."

"Two wrongs don't make a right." Max raised the gun and tapped its barrel on the side of Gurgen's neck. "Isn't it also true that much of your funding comes through the Islamic International Peacekeeping Brigade, whose money comes in turn from al-Qaeda sources in Saudi Arabia? And didn't bin Laden give you guys weapons, fighters, and money? He especially liked giving money to families of suicide bombers to compensate them."

Gurgen shrugged. "I'm not part of that anymore."

Max laughed. "Sure you're not. You just route clients and money to a terrorist bomber." Max pressed the pistol's muzzle hard into Gurgen's neck. "If you're the one screening Islamov's clients, you must know who last hired him."

Gurgen pulled away from the gun. "I don't know all of them. I'm not his only agent."

Max tapped the gun barrel against Gurgen's ear. "Bull-shit. Who was his most recent client?"

Gurgen turned and swatted at the gun.

Max smiled as he pulled the gun away. "Come on, Gurgen. Who was his client for the West Brompton bombing?"

The rebel commander glowered at Max. "I swear, I don't know. I wasn't involved in that one."

Maybe he was telling the truth. The fact Gurgen didn't recognize Max might mean he wasn't part of the transaction. After they found Islamov, there would be time for Max to interrogate Gurgen to find out what he knew.

They drove in silence for a few kilometers before Sultan spoke. "What's the plan when we get there?"

Gurgen turned so he faced forward. "Ask your man back there."

The road smoothed out into a well-maintained dirt track, which allowed Sultan to drive one-handed, the other arm out the window. "How do you contact him?"

"I usually don't. He checks in with me from time to time."

Sultan looked over at Gurgen. "How? Get specific."

Gurgen glared at Sultan. "There's a special place in hell for traitors like you. You're turning your back on your people."

"My people don't use terrorism to kill innocent civilians. Now answer the fucking question."

Gurgen turned and spit out the window. "I get a text message. From a different phone every time."

"If you need to contact him, how do you do it?"

"Email to a blind email account. It can take several days for him to get back to me."

"How do you email from that tiny village? You don't even have running water, let alone electricity and internet."

"Same way you got in touch with me." Gurgen pointed through the window to a mountain range in the distance. "There's a town on the Georgian side of the border with an internet café. My cousin is the owner. I check every other day."

They ascended a steep switchback, and Sultan put both hands back on the wheel. Max took over the questioning. "Do you ever meet in person?"

Gurgen snorted. "Never."

Max knew Gurgen was lying about at least one part of his story. During the first and second Chechen wars, the rebels had established a robust network of human couriers patterned after the communication systems used by terrorist organizations. Max suspected Gurgen only communicated with Islamov via this means, never electronically.

Max pulled a picture of Usam Islamov out of his pocket and handed it to Gurgen. The image showed a man in his forties wearing a black skullcap with a full beard. In this picture, the bomber wore a black ankle-length shirt called a thwab and was walking with his hands clasped in front of him. It was a surveillance photo taken many years ago, plucked out of MI6's records. Gurgen looked at it for a long time, as if the image were of a long-lost distant relative.

"What if he's not in Makarta?" Sultan asked.

Gurgen handed the photo back. "Then I guess we're all fucked."

———

Max brought the procession to a halt five kilometers outside of Makarta, the village in northern Georgia where Gurgen claimed Islamov stayed. From their vantage point on top of a ridge, they looked down over a lush valley with a meandering creek winding through the trees. A tiny group of houses and town buildings sat at the confluence of the road and the river. As Max stepped down from the Land Cruiser, he marveled that some of the most dangerous conflict zones were in some of the most beautiful places in the world.

The men in the pickup dismounted and huddled in small groups, trading cigarettes and eating food while talking among themselves. Max told one of the fighters to watch Gurgen before removing a set of high-powered binoculars from the SUV and scanning the village and the surrounding ridges and valleys. The village sat in a box canyon with sheer craggy cliffs on two sides and a set of rolling hills to the north. Only one road led in and out of the canyon. Max figured the only way Islamov would hide in a place like this, with such little room to maneuver, is if he either had a large army of men standing guard or he had an escape route. Max saw no evidence of an army, so he figured the most likely escape route was on foot through the hills to the north.

"Okay, here's the plan." Max handed out copies of Usam Islamov's picture to the team. "I can't think of another way to flush him out except to go house by house. We'll station a two-man team in the Land Cruiser at the entrance to the town. Another two-man team will go north to scour the foothills for trails. They'll need to find a position—"

Max broke off when he heard a sound. A bush rustled as if an animal had darted through the underbrush. Max turned and brought up the Glock, scanning the ridge. As he did, he saw a flash of color in a row of scraggly underbrush to his left. He trained the gun at the bushes with a two-handed grip. The team behind him grew still, and several men raised their rifles.

"Come out of there," Max called out in Russian. "Nice and slow."

Max took a step toward the brush before darting his arm into the branches and yanking out a young boy struggling against his grip.

The boy looked to be ten or eleven years old and was dressed in a tattered military uniform shirt with jeans that were several sizes too large for him. He tried pulling away, but Max held tight and forced the boy to his knees. Defiance in the child's eyes gave Max the impression he was older than his years, hardened by a lifestyle of growing up with insurgents. Thinking about Alex, Max's heart went out to the boy, sad he was prohibited from getting an education by both his economic circumstances and his parents' choices.

Max directed one of their men, a muscle-bound man named Doku, to search the bushes where the boy was hidden. After a moment, Doku held up a battered AK-47, some food rations, and a radio. He tossed the radio to Max, who caught it in his free hand.

Max holstered his pistol and squatted in front of the boy. "What's your name?"

The boy stared straight ahead, his eyes welling with tears.

Max slapped him hard on the cheek. "I asked you a question."

The blow caused the boy to whimper. "Kh... Kha... Khassam."

Max smiled at the boy. "Okay, Khassam. What are you doing hiding in that bush with that rifle? Are you planning on shooting someone?"

The boy stuck his jaw out and glared at Max.

Max slapped him again, causing the boy to fall sideways. Max helped him back to his knees. "You're here to watch, right? Watch for strangers?"

The boy gave a tearful nod.

Max turned to Sultan. "I think we just found our way to Usam."

THIRTY-SEVEN

Outside Juta, Georgia

It took another slap across Khassam's face to prompt the boy to pour out everything he knew in a long jumble of words. He was born in the village, the youngest son of the town's elder. A strange man was staying in their village as a guest of Khassam's father. The boy's father had established a rotation of several townspeople to watch the road from the safety of the bushes and to report sightings of anyone they didn't recognize.

Max held up the picture of Usam Islamov. "Is this the man staying with your father?"

The boy glanced at it and nodded.

"Okay, Khassam. One more question. When you saw us approaching on the road, did you use your radio to report the sighting?"

A tear rolled down Khassam's cheek.

Max put his hand on the boy's shoulder. "It's okay if

you did. You didn't do anything wrong. You were just doing what you were told to do."

The boy nodded.

"Did you report back?"

Khassam nodded his head again.

Max withdrew a wad of lari, the bright-colored Georgian currency, and handed several notes to Khassam. After a moment's coaxing, he pointed down the valley to the building where Usam Islamov was staying. It was one of the smaller houses, painted blue with a bright-white roof and green shutters. It sat at an angle, next to the river, on the north side of town. At any other time, in any other village, it might be a pleasant place to call home.

Max left the boy in the custody of one of the fighters, admonishing the older man to treat the boy with care, and watched them walk back to the bushes where soon they were sharing a smoke.

Sultan stood beside Max, and they gazed together down the valley. "You think he's making a break for it?"

Max watched the little blue house with the white roof and the green shutters, seeing no movement.

"He's probably already gone. We need to move."

———

The Land Cruiser and the pickup truck approached the village at a high rate of speed, throwing up a rooster tail of dust. Sultan drove the big SUV while Max rode shotgun with an AK-47 clutched in his hands. His tactical vest was pulled snug, a half inch of armor plating snug within the sand-colored webbing. In the vest's pockets were two spare clips for the Glock and two spare banana clips for the AK.

The raid reminded him of his tour in Afghanistan—

relying on questionable intel, kicking in civilians' doors, looking for the enemy, anxious about what waited for you on the other side. The all too familiar knot of fear sat in his gut, a feeling he didn't like.

Sitting behind Max were two fighters, both equipped with AK-47s. The pickup trying to keep pace with Sultan's driving held four more fighters. The remaining men were back on the ridge, standing guard over Gurgen and Khassam, watching the road for the enemy and civilians. They kept in touch via old-fashioned walkie-talkies that were dinged and dented and caked with grime.

While they sped toward the village, Max's mind drifted to the ten-year-old boy. It was hard to separate enemy from civilian in this kind of conflict zone and difficult to discern allegiances. How much did a certain civilian hate the Russians for two hundred years of oppression? Was it enough to cause a housewife to want to pull a handmade bomb from under her robes and toss it at a procession of trucks? How much did the local population crave independence or the freedom to practice their religion? How much did a local cleric want to enforce Sharia law? Was it enough to take up arms against his overlords?

This region was a microcosm of the complexity of the Middle East. Here in the Caucasus Mountains, a small subgroup of a Muslim majority used terrorism as a means to an end. How many of the one million ethnic Chechens in the world supported the use of terrorism, and how many resented their own people for killing non-combatants? Where would Khassam's life lead him? Where were the boy's alliances? Was he being brainwashed into hating the Russians, his fate already set to lead a life of hate? Would he ever escape the village and get an education, or would he die by a bullet from a Russian soldier's gun? It was into this microcosm of unpredictable hostility that Max and his team were hurtling at top speed.

The dust plume dissipated as the two trucks slowed at the edge of town. They wound through a smattering of buildings until they came to the small blue house with the white roof. The tiny building was made of clapboard construction with an unkempt front yard. It looked remarkably more disheveled up close than it had from the vantage point on the ridge. No vehicles were in sight, and they didn't see any townspeople on the street. In fact, the village was dead quiet.

Two of Sultan's men leaped from the pickup's rear bed and moved around to the back of the house. Max jumped down from the Land Cruiser and joined Sultan at the vehicle's hood, studying the front door with their rifles held at the ready. It occurred to Max the boy could have lied, using a stall tactic to give Usam more time to make an escape. But he dismissed the idea, remembering how scared he looked. No ten-year-old could lie under that kind of duress—or could he?

Sultan took several steps in the direction of the blue house, boots grinding in the dirt. Max held back, holding his position near the Land Cruiser. Something nagged at the back of his mind, an unsettled feeling beyond the fact that he was in the middle of guerrilla-held territory in the Caucasus Mountains, holding a rifle, about to kick down the door of a terrorist bomber.

Two of their men rushed past, taking positions on either side of the front door. Max's father described Sultan as a man of action with more brawn than brains. As a brash, loud man of action, Sultan commanded the respect of his troops. After years of toiling in the electronics shop, Sultan looked happy to be out in the field once more, his hands around the stock of a rifle. With the stock of the AK-47 pressed to his cheek, Sultan moved to the door. It was obvious he was enjoying the moment, reliving his former glory.

Like a slow-motion video, Max glanced left but saw no one. He glanced right, but nothing moved. There were no children playing in the street. No housewives hanging their laundry. No groups of men sitting outside enjoying a smoke. No smoke curled from chimneys. The village was a ghost town.

Khassam's eyes appeared in his mind. The ten-year-old boy who was born in the village, the youngest son of the town's elder. In his vision, the boy's eyes flashed anger and hatred instead of the fear Max thought he saw when he interrogated him. *Just who was the town's elder?*

The answer dawned on him, and he saw Gurgen's treachery as vibrant as the sun. It was the boy's eyes. Clear wide pools of deep brown eyes welling with tears. But through the fear, there was an intense pride. It was the same pride Max saw in Gurgen's eyes back in the hut in Salgi. They were the same eyes—

"Wait—" Max yelled, reaching with his hand to stop Sultan.

It was too late. Sultan kicked hard, and the thin wooden door shattered under his booted foot. As if on cue, an immense fireball roared up and out, engulfing the former commander and his two men. The blast wave pushed Max off his feet and flung him onto his back. The hard, sharp rocks from the gravel road punctured the skin off his arms before his world went silent. It felt as if all the hair on his face had been singed away, and he smelled burning flesh and hair intermixed with an overpowering odor of chemicals.

Another vision flashed through his mind. This time it was his father's house in the gated neighborhood in Minsk before it was destroyed by an ammonium nitrate bomb hidden in a rental truck. A truck that had mysteriously gotten past his father's security detail.

Through the haze of the blast's concussion, he felt searing heat and the rocks in the road. Wood and metal debris rained down on him before hands clawed at him, patting him down, extinguishing his burning clothing. Strong arms pulled him back, and somehow, with assistance, he managed to stand.

The spot where the blue house with the white roof once sat was now a burning hulk with a large crater in the foreground, surrounded by scorched and burned walls. Debris littered the yard in a circle around the crater. One of Sultan's men stumbled around the corner of the building, coughing, face and body covered with soot. Max let himself sit back on the Land Cruiser's rear bumper, once again suffering the déjà vu feeling of the explosion at his parents' house. His gaze came to rest on a leather boot resting on the gravel in front of him, a bloody appendage sticking from the boot, missing the rest of its owner.

The boot was Sultan's.

THIRTY-EIGHT

Prague, Czech Republic

"CCTV can read lips."

The walk from St. Mary's took fifteen minutes, during which The Monk refused to speak. He led her down a flight of gritty stairs and through a long hallway before cupping his hand around a keypad and typing in a string of digits. The metal door popped open, and he ushered her inside.

The basement flat, if you could call it that, was industrial chic or shabby poverty, depending on your point of view. The concrete floors were covered with discarded swatches of stained carpet. Exposed plumbing and electrical in the ceiling was painted matte black. The furnishings were thirdhand, and included two leather couches, a coffee table, and a desk with three computer monitors. The space was devoid of any personal touches—no pictures, no candles, no keepsakes. There were no windows for natural light.

Goshawk wandered through the room, examining its contents. "Why Prague?"

The Monk shushed her with a finger to his lips. He removed a handheld device from his pocket and walked slowly around the room, watching the device's screen before flipping a wall switch. Three computers came to life, their monitors casting a blue light over the room. After he tapped several keys, six images of security camera feeds appeared in a grid on one of the screens.

The Monk studied the screens for a long time before declaring, "Now it's safe to talk."

She ran a finger through a layer of dust on a bookcase made from chipped particle board. "Is this where you live?"

The Monk sniffed. "You think I would bring you to where I live? This is one of our safe houses. Sit. Get comfortable. You can speak freely now. Want something to drink? I have red wine, and I have red wine."

She walked over to examine the computer setup. The monitors were standard issue, but the CPUs were black boxes with no markings. "I'll take a glass of red wine." She bent to get a closer look at the CPUs. "What kind of system are you running?"

There was no response from the darkened corner of the room where The Monk was pulling the cork from a wine bottle. He emerged with two stemmed goblets half full of the burgundy-colored liquid. "Hard to get good wine in this country, so you'll have to make do with a blend." He held up his glass and clinked it to hers. "To new friends."

Goshawk tipped her glass and sipped before sitting on the edge of one of the leather couches.

The Monk fell into a swivel desk chair, turning to face her while taking another big gulp. "You asked why Prague. Because my daughters are both in school in Berlin, and it's a four-hour drive. Of course, I can't be seen visiting them. I'm sure they're under surveillance. But I can go up there and at least look at them, like a fucking stalker."

Goshawk slipped one long leg over the other. "Wouldn't it be better to pick a country with no extradition treaty with the US? Or a hostile country like Bolivia or Venezuela?"

The Monk snorted. "Like Snowden? That guy is such an idiot. Persona non grata as far as we're concerned. Publicity junkie, and look where it got him. Now he's a shill for the Russians."

Goshawk sipped her wine. She hated haughty computer nerds, but she needed this man—for now. He held the key to finding out who was after her, and he might be able to help her stop the attacks. She swallowed her distaste and smiled.

He rubbed a finger along the rim of his wine glass. "Don't assume I'm a US citizen. Besides, in the world I live, extradition is irrelevant. I'm on a hit list. The NSA, the CIA, or any other acronym agency will shoot first, ask questions later. If I'm not outright assassinated, I'll be nabbed by a team in black suits and tossed into a secret prison. The kind of team that operates without regard for borders, laws, or basic human rights."

He took a sip of his wine. "And by the way, Snowden was stupid for going to Hong Kong, which has a history of extraditing people. But the most idiotic thing he did was go public. If he had any real cojones, he would have just released the information anonymously. Once his name was out there, his only recourse was to disappear to Russia. Now all he can do is live in the godforsaken tundra of Russia and make appearances via video conference. His days as a real activist are over."

The Monk's eyes drifted to the monitor showing the

surveillance feeds. "Snowden fucked things up for himself, but it turned out to be a nice distraction for us. Our rule is no publicity. We operate behind the scenes, with the mission to expose government wrongdoing. We're the watchdog without a podium."

"How do you expose your information? Wikileaks?"

The Monk sneered. "Wikileaks is a front for the Russians. Why do you think Assange has a show on RT, the Russian state-sponsored television network? And why do you think the leak of the Democratic National Convention documents that implicated Clinton all came from the Russian foreign intelligence service?"

Goshawk shrugged. She was too preoccupied lately to read the news. "Despite how he did it, do you think Snowden did the right thing by exposing the Americans' broad surveillance scheme of its own citizens?"

"Absolutely. Don't you? If the public doesn't keep an eye on the government, who's going to? Your elected representatives? Law enforcement? His only mistake was attaching his name to the information."

Goshawk sipped her wine and tried to look contrite. "So how do you get your information out there?"

The Monk gazed at the ceiling. "We have a list of journalists and bloggers we trust who work with us. We were the ones who exposed Britain's data collection system, similar to America's PRISM that Snowden exposed. But did we strut around like a peacock?" The Monk got up and refilled Goshawk's glass. She gave him a demure smile and thought she saw him blush.

He refilled his own glass. "Let's get down to business, shall we?"

"Please."

He got a faraway look in his eyes. "We've been watching

you for a while now. Or should I say, we've been watching your activity. We didn't know your identity, of course, but your activity online had a certain uniqueness to it. A crispness, a freshness. Brash, yet exacting. We knew whoever was behind your activity was wicked smart and a risk-taker, yet someone who was careful enough not to give away too much."

Goshawk fought to keep from rolling her eyes. The Monk's flattery was awkward, like a schoolboy on his first date. Still, being watched disturbed her.

He beamed at her. "When you were attacked like that, we were alerted. We recognized many of the attack signatures as those from our long-time enemy. You were no longer simply on our radar, you became a person of interest, so to speak. Initially, we wondered why you were a target, but after some digging, we figured it out. Or figured out part of it."

"Which part?"

"You tracked a man named Wilbur Lynch. Lynch had been on our list for a long time." The Monk cocked his eye at Goshawk. "Wilbur Lynch looks like he's recently deceased. You wouldn't know anything about that, would you?"

Goshawk raised her eyebrows. "That's a shame." Her mind spun with that information. She had to cut off all contact from Max, partly to protect him, and partly to protect herself. She was on the move for the past two weeks and missed the news of Wilbur Lynch's death.

The Monk smirked. "I see the wheels moving in your head. I interpret that to mean you didn't know."

Goshawk twirled her empty wine glass and stared at him.

The Monk laughed. "Okay, have it your way. Here's

what we know. Wilbur Lynch had a communication channel open to someone high up in the American government. We believe, but don't know for certain, that his contact was a high-ranking official at the National Security Agency. We believe that official is acting outside the auspices of the NSA. We don't know who he works for or what his agenda is, but this fits the patterns we've seen. Our information suggests he is the one after you."

Goshawk rested her chin in the cup of her hand. It made sense that her pursuer was the NSA or had access to NSA resources. "No way that the amount of fire power directed at me could have come from one person."

The Monk's eyes drifted again to the monitors showing the feed from the security cameras. "And we agree. What I mean is that we believe this individual is acting outside the normal bounds of the agency, but he has a team behind him, and he's somehow using agency resources. We believe it was your work to uncover Lynch's identity that exposed you to this person or group and landed your name on his hit list."

For the first time since the attacks started, Goshawk felt the specter of fear overcoming her. For years she operated as a clandestine computer hacker, selling her own services to the highest bidder. Never in a million years did she think she would run afoul of an agency as powerful as the NSA. The idea of hiding in caves the rest of her life was a depressing thought. She sat back into the leather cushions and studied her broken nails. There was another theory, of course. That this person or persons were chasing after her to get at Max. She wasn't about to share that with The Monk.

The Monk pursed his lips. "I can see the prospect of being hunted by the NSA for the rest of your life is weighing on you. Trust me, it's not something to take lightly.

I've chosen to wage a battle for something I believe in. You just happened to piss off the wrong guy." He stood and approached her with the bottle.

Goshawk put her hand over her wine glass.

The Monk hesitated before sitting back down in his chair and setting the bottle down. "It's a lonely life, but it's a calling. It's a necessary counterbalance to authoritarian power."

"Is it worth sacrificing your life for? Aren't there more important things in life? Like your daughters?"

The Monk swirled his wine. "No one expects you to take the kinds of risks I do. I chose this life for personal reasons. I don't expect people to understand." He turned his chair around with the toe of his foot and banged on the keyboard. Another monitor sprang to life.

She decided to let it go. "Does Lynch's contact have a name?"

The Monk used his index fingers to peck on the keyboard and answered without turning. "He calls himself Bluefish."

Goshawk let that name roll around in her head. *Bluefish.* Like the Dr. Seuss book. She pictured the oblong blue fish-like caricature with the long eyelashes on the book's cover. "I always thought the blue fish was a female."

The Monk shrugged while he pecked at the keyboard. "Maybe."

After an agonizing few minutes, when Goshawk wished she could type for him, he stopped typing and looked back at her. "We have a plan. We're going to expose this NSA official, and you're going to help us do it. When Bluefish is rotting in that supermax prison in Colorado, you'll get your life back."

"I like the sound of that."

"We'll also set you up with protection protocols so you can operate autonomously and safely within our network. I'll arrange for firewalls, proxies, and a series of vetted identities for you."

Goshawk sighed. "I can't thank you enough."

The Monk grinned at her. "You will. Remember when I said everything comes with a price?"

————

By the time Goshawk returned home to her tiny cottage on the southern end of Corsica, the sunset was casting a glow the color of burnt sienna and the tides were leaving the usual flotsam of ocean vegetation behind on the beach. Ten large boxes stacked on the terra-cotta floor greeted her when she stepped through the door. Despite the fatigue from the long day of travel, she ripped open the boxes of computer equipment the don's underlings had left in her sitting room and bent to the task of setting up a new workstation. She unpacked two Samsung thirty-four-inch 4K monitors along with two HP towers, a laptop, and a flat box the size of a case of beer with dozens of flashing red and green LEDs on the front.

It took four hours. But when she was done, three of The Monk's remote firewalls protected her from external attack, and her internet traffic was routed through two of his proxy servers and two of her own. The box with the flashing lights —a firewall appliance—was set up as her final level of protection. She reestablished connections with her servers that were stashed in remote corners of the internet and checked her messages, happy to see a few notes from Max. She typed him a brief message to let him know she was back in business before putting the computers to sleep. By midnight, she was in a deep slumber, dreaming about a piano lounge she used to sing in back in Paris called La Caravelle.

By the time the birds started chirping their morning greeting, Goshawk was already up, a steaming mug of Italian coffee in her hand, navigating to a dark web chat room called CyberGrape. *The Grape,* as it was referred to by the small but highly capable band of anonymous hackers who populated the chat room, was a virtual forum used by thousands of disaffected computer nerds and teens to rail against the world. Despite mainstream media reports to the contrary, forums were rarely used by hackers to exchange real information, although sometimes, buried among the paragraphs of innocuous sophomoric banter, encoded messages were hidden to all but those who knew where to look.

Knowing the forum was probably crawling with law enforcement posing as hackers, Goshawk logged in with one of her avatars, a female elfin image with the name *Caramel-Camel.* She left a few comments on random posts before clicking over to a string of messages comparing the US President to an alien supposedly found in the Nevada desert in 2003. Most of the posts were by someone going by the name *1eftw1ngnut49.*

When she left Prague, The Monk's final instructions to her were simple. Go home, implement the security protocols, and watch *The Grape* for further instructions.

How will I know what to look for?

We'll find you, don't worry.

Goshawk burned another twenty minutes on the forum. After draining the dregs of her coffee, she shut down the browser and rose from the table. As she walked into the bedroom, she untied her silk robe and let it drop to the floor before pulling the sheets down to reveal Carlu's golden-tan body. As she joined her groggy lover, her mind went to Max for a moment before it cleared and she let herself be taken away.

THIRTY-NINE

Juta, Georgia

One of Sultan's fighters had a hand on Max's arm, urging him to sit and rest. Max remembered his name was Doku. Max pushed Doku's hand away and made for the Land Cruiser's driver side door. "Get in the truck. We have to go."

No sooner had he yanked the door open when automatic rifle fire spit up dirt at his feet and plinked into the side of the vehicles. The soot-covered fighter who was spared from the bomb blast took a round in the chest, staggered, and fell to his knees. Two more rounds hit his torso, and he fell face-first into the dust. The gunfire came from multiple shooters positioned at the windows of three houses clustered around their location.

Max yelled at the men as he jumped into the SUV and cranked the engine. "Go, go, go!"

Of the eight men who came down with him into the valley, only Max, Doku, and a fighter named Ruman were alive. Doku jumped into the pickup's cab and fired the ignition. Ruman vaulted into the truck bed, landing on his stomach and ducking under the automatic rifle fire.

The Land Cruiser took a round in the windshield as Max tore up the gravel and spun the wheel, heading for the road leading out of town. The tires caught, and the big SUV lunged forward. Another round hit the front quarter panel and another spit through the driver's side window, showering Max with shards of glass while ricocheting into the leather passenger seat. Bullets pelted the rear of the SUV as he roared out of town.

Max snapped the radio off his tactical vest and toggled the mic. "Three coming up the road, hot. Hold your fire."

"Roger that."

Max clicked the mic again. "Sultan's dead. Don't let Gurgen out of your sight."

There was a moment of silence on the other end of the radio. "Ten-four."

Max drove as hard and as fast as he dared, the top-heavy SUV teetering on two wheels, its big tires carrying him over ruts and large rocks in the road. When he crested the ridge, he pulled hard on the wheel to turn in the direction of the group standing at the overlook. He stomped on the brakes and ground to a halt a few feet from where Gurgen and the boy stood next to each other. Looking at them standing together, the resemblance between the two was uncanny. He couldn't believe he missed it before.

Max stepped from the truck and stalked over to Gurgen. He launched a right fist into Gurgen's jaw with all his weight behind it, startling the fighters and causing Khassam to cry out.

Gurgen stumbled backward, stunned. One of Sultan's men caught him and helped him stay on his feet. Max hit him again, and a third time. Blood spattered from the rebel's mouth as Max kept swinging. When Gurgen fell to the ground, Max jumped on top of him and kept punching him, pelting his head with blow after blow.

By the time Doku managed to get Max into a half nelson and pull him away, Gurgen's face was covered in blood, and he was rolling on the ground in pain.

"Okay, okay." Max shook Doku off and stood with his chest heaving. "Put him on his knees."

Doku hesitated.

Still gasping for breath, Max pointed at Gurgen. "Sultan's death is his fault. He set us up."

Doku and Ruman hauled Gurgen up by the arms and balanced him on his feet before kicking at the backs of his legs to force him to his knees. Tendrils of blood and mucus hung from Gurgen's mouth and one eye was swollen shut. He spit a tooth into the dirt and looked at Max with his one good eye. The corner of his bloody mouth was turned up in a smirk.

Max approached Gurgen wiping his bloody fist on his jeans while addressing Sultan's men. "Take the boy away. Over past the bushes, and out of earshot. This is going to get ugly."

———

When Khassam was far enough away, Max squirted water from a bottle on Gurgen's face. Blood mixed with water glistened on the man's craggy face. His one good eye was defiant.

Max leaned so his face was within inches of the beaten man. "Gurgen, you fuck. You set this whole thing up."

Max slapped him, splashing blood and water to the dusty ground. "Gurgen, can you hear me?"

Gurgen worked his jaw and muttered something unintelligible.

Doku squatted to get a better look of the captive. "I think his jaw is broken."

"Gurgen. I can't hear you. If you want to survive, you need to talk." Max removed the Glock from its holster and racked the slide.

Gurgen's head lolled forward, but he managed a faint mumble. "I can talk."

"Good. That means I don't have to kill you. Yet."

Max handed Doku the Glock and removed a packet of cigarettes from his pocket. They were the same brand as the ones he'd given Gurgen as a gift. He shook one out and put it between the captive's lips and lit the end with his Zippo.

Max knelt on a knee and lit a cigarette for himself. "You wanted to know where I'm from." He showed the captive the lighter. "Recognize this flag?"

Gurgen managed to get his eyes partway open. He looked and nodded.

"Now you know."

Gurgen's voice was raspy. "I knew your father."

Max contemplated that. This information hadn't been in Gurgen's file. "What? How?"

"He tried to recruit me. Like Sultan."

Max let this new information roll around in his head. Did Gurgen know who he was from the beginning? That would explain how he'd set the trap. "And?"

Gurgen tried to smile, but it came off as a hideous grimace. "I played him. Just like I played you."

Max took a drag on his cigarette. "You were a double agent."

Gurgen's laugh came out like a cough, spraying drool and blood from his mouth. The cigarette dangled from the corner of his mouth, stuck to drying blood.

Max took the cigarette from Gurgen's mouth and crushed it in his hand before tossing it to the ground. "That's where the money in your Lebanese bank account came from."

Gurgen nodded.

"You took the KGB's money and fed them false information."

Gurgen nodded again, pride evident in his eyes.

Max flicked away his cigarette butt as he stood and took the pistol back from Doku. "I have two questions, Gurgen, and I need answers fast. I don't have a lot of time. Do you understand?"

Gurgen, held up by two of Sultan's men, swayed on his knees.

Max looked at Doku. "Get a pair of pliers from the back of the Land Cruiser."

Doku pivoted on a foot and walked to the SUV.

Gurgen's one good eye widened at the mention of the tool.

Max stuck the pistol in his waistband. "They say pain is a poor interrogation technique. But they also say a man will do just about anything, say anything, to stop the pain."

Doku returned and slapped a tool into Max's hand. "No pliers, but here's a pair of wire cutters."

"Perfect." Max slapped Gurgen hard. "I believe pain can be pretty effective if the man is weak and untrained for this sort of thing. Are you weak, Gurgen?"

The captive mumbled something too low for Max to hear.

Max grabbed Gurgen's right hand and twisted, forcing

him onto his back. As Sultan's men stepped away, Max placed his boot on Gurgen's wrist and stepped down with all his weight. "Hold him down." Doku pressed down on Gurgen's shoulders with his knee while Ruman held his legs.

Holding tight to Gurgen's hand, Max selected his index finger and fit the wire cutters around the middle joint. "Are you right-handed, Gurgen?"

Gurgen coughed and sputtered. "Wait. I'll tell you. What do you want to know?"

Max heaved, snapping the wire cutters closed around Gurgen's middle finger. The separated digit fell to the blood-soaked dirt while blood ran freely from the fresh wound. Gurgen's screams reverberated around the valley, echoing among the trees and mountain tops.

"That was for Sultan." Max fit the bloody wire cutters around Gurgen's thumb. "You know how hard it is to hold onto a weapon without the thumb of your shooting hand?"

Gurgen's chest heaved with panic. "Okay, okay." Gurgen panted between words. "He's in the next town over. I swear. Just five kilometers to the south."

"What's the name of the town?"

Gurgen sputtered while blood bubbles emerged from between his lips. "Chokhi."

"House?"

"Red house, door painted white."

Max pressed down on the wire cutters, drawing blood from Gurgen's thumb. "How do I know this isn't another setup?"

Gurgen breathed in short raspy gasps. "It's not, I swear."

"How do I know, Gurgen?"

The captive didn't answer, so Max dug the wire cutters deeper into his skin.

Gurgen screamed. When Max let up on the cutters, Gurgen spoke in a rush. "Because Usam's my brother. In the house. There's a picture of me. You will see it. Please. Don't kill me. I want to see Khassam one more time."

Max tossed the wire cutters away and stood back while Doku and Ruman lifted Gurgen to his knees. "Do you think the victims of Usam's bombs got a chance to see their loved ones just one more time? Don't you think the survivors would have done anything to see their wives, husbands, brothers, sisters, parents, one more time before they were brutally killed by your brother?"

Gurgen's head hung while drops of blood fell from his nose into the dirt.

Max raised the Glock and put it to Gurgen's forehead.

Ruman looked away, but Doku set his jaw. "Do it for Sultan."

Max held the gun steady, rage pulsing through his veins, before pulling it away and shoving it in his holster.

"We might need him."

FORTY

Chokhi, Georgia

This time Max went alone. It was after midnight, and the overcast sky was dark, lit only by a few stars peeking through the cloud cover. Max used mud to darken his face and wore a black boonie hat on his head. An AK-47 was strapped to his back, and he carried the Glock in a two-handed grip. He followed a path running along the river, parallel to the road. When he neared the first of the village's buildings, he slowed his pace to a crawl and watched for signs of movement.

A light flared in the darkness, causing him to freeze. Through a stand of beech trees, he saw a shadow in the shape of a man put a match to the end of a cigarette. Max dislodged a rock from the trail and crept along the dirt track until he was behind the sentry. Using the oldest trick in the book, Max heaved the stone high in the air before drawing his knife. When the stone crashed to the ground, the man whirled in the direction of the sound and brought up a rifle.

Max used the distraction to step behind the sentry and swipe the knife across his trachea. Blood spurted from the severed carotid artery, cutting off the man's screams before they escaped his mouth. Max eased the body to the ground before continuing along the path. He dispatched two more guards with the knife before reaching the edge of the village.

He paused to survey the darkened buildings and listen for anything that might indicate a human presence. He heard nothing, although smoke curled from a chimney several houses over while the blue images of a television flashed from a window. At least this town had signs of life.

Before sneaking into the village, Max and Doku had sat on the rear bed of the pickup, waiting for darkness, smoking cigarettes, and telling stories about Sultan. Max learned the former commander had received millions of dollars from Max's father in exchange for information on the Chechen rebels, but he gave it all away to the Chechen families who'd lost men in the two wars with Russia. Doku's brother was killed in the first conflict, and his family received a share. Doku used the money to start a fitness center in Grozny and now the income from the gym supported his parents, grand-parents, and his two children.

Doku had strenuously argued to come with Max so he could get vengeance for Sultan's death, but Max forbade it, telling him that he needed to get back to Grozny alive so he could look after his family. As the last vestiges of light disap-peared over the mountains, Doku departed the valley with the remainder of the fighters and Gurgen tied up in the back of the pickup, leaving Max the Land Cruiser after making him vow to avenge their friend's death. What Doku ended up doing with Gurgen was Doku's business.

A dog barked several streets over, causing Max to freeze

in place. He let several quiet minutes slip by before inching down a narrow road between two wooden structures, hugging the wall of one of the buildings with his gun held straight ahead. He would give anything for a suppressor, since a gunshot would wake the entire town, but he would make do. *Sometimes, my boy, you have to pee in the sink*, his father liked to say.

He threaded his way through the decrepit buildings and spied the red cottage with the white door not too far from the river. The roof was made of scraps of corrugated metal, and the front yard was littered with trash and discarded appliances. A beat-up white pickup sat in the drive. A satellite dish was attached to a pole on the roof of the house. Several windows were covered with plastic, and a metal screen door hung askew from one hinge. He edged up to the truck and put his hand on the hood, finding it cold to the touch.

Max circled around the back of the house, staying close to the river. He saw a well-maintained vegetable garden, a small pen made from split-rail fencing that looked like a home for pigs, a small chicken coop, and a small enclosure made from a green tarpaulin attached to wooden stakes next to the house, it's purpose unknown. A circle of metal chairs sat near the dwelling's back door. He pictured Usam Islamov sitting in one of the chairs, smoking, chatting with other men from the village, or perhaps directing a courier to deliver a message. Max crept across the backyard and crouched by the back door to listen. He heard nothing.

When he tried the door knob, he found it unlocked but hesitated before pushing the door open, mindful of the last explosion. Max moved to the green tarp and used his knife to cut an opening through the material. As he pulled the cloth aside, he saw a set of hatch-styled doors leading into the basement. Using the penlight, he examined the door handles. No lock was evident, and the grips were shiny from use. Holding his breath, he tested the door. It moved without a sound on well-oiled hinges. He stepped into the dark basement and eased the doors shut behind him.

Careful to watch for trip wires and pressure plates, he picked his way around boxes, discarded appliances, and broken furniture. A quick examination revealed no bomb-making equipment or work areas. After inspecting the wooden stairs and finding them free from explosives, he crept up and through an open door into a dark makeshift kitchen. Plastic chairs were scattered around a Formica table, and a wooden plank set on boxes served as a kitchen counter. A wood-burning stove sat in the corner and several sagging cabinets were bolted to the wall. Max smelled the distinct odor of onions and rancid cooking oil and noticed a jumble of pots and pans in a basin.

As he moved into the dank living room, he noticed a different odor, antiseptic and damp, like the smell of someone dying. In the main sitting room, a modern widescreen TV sat on a crate opposite a sunken couch. He crept over to a bookcase along the far wall with a row of pictures in standing picture frames and shined his light on the images. The center frame showed a picture of a much younger Gurgen, squatting in the dirt, wearing an army jacket and holding a rifle.

He stepped into a hallway and saw an open bedroom door. In the murky darkness, he was surprised to see a hospital bed along with an IV stand and a cart holding an EKG monitor. A small table held a jumble of pill bottles. The EKG's monitor was dark and the bed was empty, with its sheets wadded up like someone had left in a hurry. Max

flashed his light around the room and saw nothing more of
interest. He continued down the hall.

He heard the breathing before he saw the man. The
sound was heavy and wet, like he was suffering from croup
or a bad head cold. Max peeked around the corner, heart in
his throat, flashlight held next to his raised Glock, light
beam playing around the room. What he saw stopped
him cold.

———

"Come in, *sadiqi*. Come in."

The man spoke with a slow cadence, and the voice was
raspy with mucus. Despite the overture, and the man's use
of the Arabic word for friend, Max stood rooted to the
ground, unsure whether to heed the invitation or run.

His flashlight came to rest on the figure of a pink-
skinned man with a clean face and shaved head sitting in a
wheelchair. Unlike Wilbur Lynch's posh motorized chair,
this one was hospital standard issue. Its footrests were
folded up and the man's feet, encased in ratty slippers, hung
at an awkward angle. He wore an ankle-length tunic known
as a *thawb* with white gauzy material peeking out from
under the garment. The man held up a quivering arm to
ward off the light.

The man was Usam Islamov.

A plastic garbage can without its lid sat on the floor next
to the wheelchair. Coming out of the can was a cord
attached to a small device the man now clutched in a quivering hand.

Max kept the gun pointed at the man's head, but angled
the flashlight down while he calculated his options.

Islamov coughed violently, sending flecks of phlegm

through the air. He made no attempt to cover his mouth. When the spasm died down, he spoke through a clogged throat. "I know what you are thinking, sadiqi. You're wondering whether you can kill me with a gunshot before I press this trigger. As you know, sometimes muscles spasm and contract during death, especially the smaller ones, like those in fingers." He waggled his trigger hand. "You might be calculating how far you can make it down the hallway before this trash can explodes. I assure you, it's a gamble you don't want to make."

Islamov had indeed nailed Max's train of thought. Although rare, muscle contractions can occur as the heart and tissues die and may conceivably force the trigger to compress. The odds were long, but they were enough to give Max pause. "That's some cold you have, Usam."

That made the bomb maker laugh, which turned into a roaring coughing fit. When it passed, Islamov wiped his mouth with the back of the hand holding the trigger. Max almost fired but held back. Despite the standoff, he wanted information from Islamov.

"Lung cancer." Another round of coughing. "At first, they gave me a couple months, but I've been kicking around now for over a year."

Max remained rooted in place. "Not getting enough fruits and vegetables?"

Another laughing fit, followed by more hacking and wheezing. "Who knows. I doubt it was the five packs-a-day cigarette habit."

Max took a step into the room. The smell of death hanging in the room covered another faint odor that took him a moment to identify. It was ammonia. "Got some HMX in that trash can, Usam?"

"Maybe." Islamov's smile never wavered. "Interesting

partnership you have with British law enforcement. Too bad they'll never find the stuff that connects me to the West Brompton thing. You're going to die with your name pinned to the tragedy. Such a shame." He hawked up a mouthful of mucus and spit it out on the floor at Max's feet.

Max chanced a glance around the room. Other than the wheelchair and the trash can, the room was empty. "Shaved your beard, I see."

A dreamy smile crossed Islamov's face.

Max shuffled several inches in the direction of the trash can. "Shave your pubic hair too? I bet there isn't a strand of hair left on your body. Preparing to enter heaven, are we?"

Islamov waved the trigger.

"I hate to burst your bubble, Usam, but it's all bullshit. The shaving practice of terrorists originated with Pashtun tribesmen of Afghanistan, who shaved their bodies before going into battle to help regulate their body temperature. It's got nothing to do with Paradise. It's got nothing to do with the Koran. Didn't the Four Imams agree that shaving the beard is effeminate?"

Anger flickered through Islamov's eyes.

"Where's the rest of the HMX, Usam?"

Islamov regained his composure. "I hear you met my nephew, Khassam. Such a bright young man. He's got a real future in this business. Sad that he was born with the American diabetes."

"He's dead, Usam. I shot him just before I came over here. One less future terrorist in the world."

Anger again rippled through Islamov's features before it disappeared. "I don't think so, sadiqi. You are a man of principle, a man of values. Western morals dictate guilt must be proven before punishment."

Max took another step into the room. "Oh, he's guilty.

He just didn't know it." Now Max could see into the trash can. On top of a white powder mixture was something that looked like a sausage link Max identified as a Tovex water-gel explosive. The trigger cord was attached to the Tovex. If Islamov had constructed the bomb correctly, the trigger would cause the Tovex to explode, in turn igniting the trash can of HMX, which in turn would vaporize a large portion of the house with both of them in it.

Islamov smiled as he eyed Max examining the bomb. "I don't believe you, but there are plenty more where he came from. Thanks to the selfish behavior of Western governments, mostly the Americans, young idealists will never be in short supply. The Russians will keep killing Chechens. They can't help it. The Americans won't stop invading Muslim countries to protect their oil interests. And so it goes."

"Why'd you do it, Usam? Why did you kill all those innocent people in London?"

Usam's hand holding the trigger dropped to his lap, and his eyes drooped. "Are they truly innocent? 'Soon shall We cast terror into the hearts of the Unbelievers, for that they joined companions with Allah, for which He had sent no authority.'"

Max groaned. "Don't give me that Koran shit. You might have believed that when you were young and fighting for your independence. You might have believed that when you blew up the movie theater in Blagodarny. But something changed, Usam. You became a killer for hire. Why?"

Islamov cleared phlegm from his throat. "'But the Messenger, and those who believe with him, strive and fight with their wealth and their persons: for them are (all) good things: and it is they who will prosper.'"

It clicked in Max's mind. "The first attack you did for

money was in Paris back in 2006, about a year after Khassam was born. That would have been about the time he was diagnosed with diabetes."

Islamov smiled. "You are quite the detective. Your western medicine is expensive."

"Especially if you don't have health insurance." Max took a step to his right. "The second attack in Rotterdam in 2009 was after your mother was diagnosed with breast cancer. According to our file, she's alive and cancer-free in a Jordanian retirement home."

"An expensive one at that."

"But this last one? Why this one?"

Islamov spread his arms. "Money doesn't go as far as it used to, does it, sadiqi?"

Max took another step. "Lung cancer is expensive to treat, isn't it?"

Islamov brandished the trigger. "Come no closer."

Max took a step sideways so Islamov had to turn his head to watch him. "You kill innocent westerners to earn money so you can pay to use Western medicine to keep your family healthy. Doesn't that seem fucked up to you, sadiqi?" He spit out the last word in disgust.

Islamov raised his voice an octave. "'Oh, you who believe! fight those of the unbelievers who are near to you and let them find in your hardness.'"

Max shook his head. "Where is the rest of the HMX?"

Islamov's voice grew stronger. "Somewhere no one will ever find it. Once I'm in Paradise and you are in Jahannam, it won't matter."

Islamov's face became drawn, his eyes glassy. He belted out another phlegm-laced cough before his face softened. His mind was elsewhere, the hand with the trigger now resting in his lap. This time he spoke in a murmur. "'Surely,

God has cursed the disbelievers, and has prepared for them a flaming Fire wherein they will abide forever.'"

Max's finger tightened on the trigger.

Islamov closed his eyes. "Allāhu—"

The tiny room was filled with a tremendous roar.

FORTY-ONE

Washington DC

Kate wondered why it always seemed to rain when two spies met on a park bench. She cinched her mackintosh tighter and tucked her chin down into a cashmere scarf. It was unseasonably chilly for an early September day, the rain coming down in a steady beat on the rocks under her feet. She held an umbrella in her left hand, signaling the meeting was on. If she moved the umbrella to her right hand, Bill was to keep walking.

Despite the umbrella, her shoes were soaked through. West Potomac Park overlooked the Potomac River, and only a few hearty souls braved the rain to enjoy the scenery. She watched a woman jog by while pushing a baby stroller with its precious cargo bundled up against the weather. A man in an olive green raincoat and a black trilby sauntered by, favoring a limp, making good progress without a cane. She saw only three other people in the hour she'd stood there.

Rows of benches facing the river all afforded a view of

the Thomas Jefferson Memorial. The white domed building was enveloped in a hazy mist blurring the structure from her vantage point. She took comfort in the idea that the founding fathers had rebelled against an oppressive monarchy. She thought Thomas Jefferson would approve of her own subversive goals—to take down a corrupt CIA director.

Bill approached, walking through the row of cherry blossoms lining the tidal basin. He was bent against the rain, wrapped in a trench coat, head covered with a fedora-styled hat. She avoided his glance as he stole a look to see which hand she held the umbrella in before taking a seat on a bench overlooking the river. Kate waited a few minutes before joining him.

He took the umbrella from her hand and held it over both their heads. "You get anything from the bug you planted in Montgomery's phone?"

She crossed one leg over the other and adjusted her coat. "Hello to you too."

When he stared at her, she saw dark bags under his eyes, and his face looked like it had filled out, like he'd gained weight. "Sorry."

She leaned closer to him. "You look terrible. Are you okay?"

His attention was across the river, in the direction of the Memorial. When he spoke, his voice was far away. "Have you seen these trees in bloom?"

Something was wrong. Kate studied the park around them and saw no one other than a group of teenagers in hoodies hurrying along the asphalt path next to the river. The man in the green coat was gone. "Yes, once. Many years ago."

His eyes kept staring off in the distance. "It's a beautiful sight. They're over a hundred years old."

Kate uncrossed her leg and twisted to look behind them and saw nothing but rain falling among the cherry trees. "Bill, what the fuck is going on?"

When he turned to her, his eyes were wet. "Nothing. I'm fine. Did you get anything from that bug you planted on Montgomery's phone?"

Alarm thudded in her temples. This wasn't the Bill she had known for a dozen years. The confident and stoic operator who had guided her through the male-dominated world of the CIA was gone. Something was amiss. "Bill, why are we meeting? You insisted we do it in person."

As Bill turned away, she thought she heard a sniffle. "I'm sorry, Kate."

Something snapped in her mind, and it all made sense. The insistence they meet in person. The location at the park. His line of questioning.

"Bill, are you wearing a wire?"

He didn't answer.

As panic rose in her chest, she stood. "I have to go."

When she turned, she almost ran into a man in a dark blue overcoat whose hand shot out and grabbed her arm, the power of his grip crushing her bicep. He wore an earpiece in his left ear attached to a curled wire that disappeared under his collar. She tried to wrench her arm away as another man in a blue coat materialized behind the bench. The whole thing happened too fast for her to react.

The first man addressed her with a baritone voice. "Kate Shaw, come with us, please."

Two more men in blue overcoats appeared. One frisked her and removed the pistol from her jacket pocket.

The other man took Bill's arm and coaxed him from the bench. They walked as a group along a path past the Franklin Delano Roosevelt Memorial to a waiting van parked along West Basin Drive. Once in the van, Kate's hands were bound in front of her with plastic cuffs.

Bill sat next to her, his hands also tied. As the van pulled away from the curb, he muttered, "I'm sorry, I'm sorry," over and over again.

Kate moved her secured hands to his leg and gave him a tiny squeeze.

———

Seven thousand miles from Washington DC, in a wealthy suburb of Dubai in the United Arab Emirates, a vanload of men dressed all in black waited for the signal. Each man wore identical tactical pants, black body armor over black tunics, black riot helmets, and dark goggles. The rest of their faces were covered with black balaclavas. No name tags were attached to the Velcro patch on their breasts, and their backs were devoid of markings. Each man was armed with a Glock 9mm pistol, Austrian designed, and a T91 compact assault rifle, Chinese made. Riot cuffs, extra magazines, and flash-bang grenades hung from each man's tactical belt. The mood in the van was tense but professional. This was the UAE State Security's elite tactical assault team.

Trained in infiltration and close quarters combat, these men were used to snatch and grab operations. Most of their targets were never heard from again. The UAE federal monarchy called it enforcing Sharia law. Behind closed doors, UAE's citizens called it terrorism.

It was 3:00 am, and the neighborhood was quiet. Overhead, a slivered moon offered little light, but rows of street lamps cast pale yellow pools along the tree-lined street. Two blocks away, the fenced estate where their target resided stood in silence, its inhabitants asleep, its rooms dark.

Kahlid Nasar, the squad commander and a career man with the UAE's State Security, sat with a finger to his earpiece and his head bent in concentration. When he got the signal to proceed, Nasar motioned to the man sitting across from him, who tapped the screen of a small handheld tablet. The streetlights winked off, leaving the men in pure darkness.

As the officer with the tablet tapped another icon, the stillness of the morning air was shattered by an explosive pop. The van lurched forward on solid rubber tires, gathering speed as it approached the compound's wrought-iron gates. The driver wrenched the wheel to the left, and the van's reinforced steel bumper hit the metal gate, the lock of which had been weakened by the small charge of C-4 that just detonated. The van roared up the drive and avoided a large fountain before screeching to a halt in front of the home's tall double doors.

Men in black piled out of the van and scattered. Two moved left while two others moved right to secure the perimeter. Two more used a battering ram to pop open the front door. Men poured into the house, assault rifles held at the ready, neither announcing their presence nor uttering commands. In formation, they hustled from room to room, searching for inhabitants or threats. Two men remained in the master bedroom, pointing rifles at the home's terrified patriarch and his wife. Two more secured the daughter's room, ignoring her screams while dodging the random items she threw at them.

Four of the men in black burst into a large plush room on the ground floor that was filled to the brim with computer terminals, monitors, and several desks. The walls were covered in egg carton-styled soundproofing and a set of speakers blared western pop music. A young man with jet-black hair, dark skin, a rose-colored dress shirt, and bright blue tie in a thick Windsor knot glared at the intruders with deep brown hate-filled eyes.

When the squad leader issued a command, the young man's wrists were bound. Another command sent the agents scurrying to gather all the computer equipment in the room. His orders were clear—all computer equipment found in the house was to be confiscated. The squad leader realized there was so much gear that another vehicle was required.

As he scanned the room, his mind became confused. The floor was littered with pieces of plastic, metal, and glass. All the computer monitors were intact, but all the CPUs were in pieces on the floor. Several laptops had been smashed to bits. There wasn't any computer equipment left intact.

One of his men walked up to him and handed him a wooden baseball bat. On the side of the bat, emblazoned in an oval, were the words *Louisville Slugger*. The commander looked at his prisoner and the young man mouthed something at him. The squad leader was familiar with enough English to realize he was mouthing the words *fuck you*.

———

Spencer White turned up the collar on his olive green mackintosh and tugged the brim of his trilby tighter on his head. The thick glasses he wore as part of his disguise were prone to gathering drops of rain water, and he was constantly cleaning the lenses with the tail of the sport coat he wore under his raincoat. He cursed the moisture, he cursed the pain in his hip that got worse in the damp air, and he cursed the CIA, his former employer.

From his location a dozen meters down the bike path and partially hidden behind foliage, he watched four men in blue overcoats converge on the bench where Kate and Bill sat. Fear gripped him as he typed a text message on his mobile phone, but Kate failed to remove her phone from her pocket. Even if she had, it would have been too late. Spencer was powerless to stop it, and with a deep pit of fear in his stomach, he watched as the four men escorted Bill, the CIA's Director of Special Operations, and Kate, the CIA's former Assistant Director of Special Operations, off to a waiting van.

The take down had been so abrupt, so organized, it made Spencer think the whole meet was a setup. Spencer had walked the park for the better part of two hours and had not seen any men loitering in blue overcoats. If he had seen even one, he would have called off the meet. Spencer's fear turned to anger as he realized the only one who could have set her up was Bill.

He shifted his position so he could see the van's location. Removing his phone from his pocket, he held it close to his body as he snapped several pictures of the vehicle's rear, including the DC tags. He slipped the phone into his pocket, pulled the belt tighter on his green mackintosh, and walked in the opposite direction while ignoring the pain in his hip.

As he walked, he glanced at the cold river, barely seeing the thousands of raindrops pelting its surface. He pictured Kate trussed up in a holding cell somewhere in a black-ops site, far away from the mainstream court system, with a team of men using every tactic they knew to pull information out of her. He figured they had less than forty-eight hours before she would break, at which point the bug in Montgomery's phone would become useless and the secure server sites they shared with Max and Goshawk would become compromised. Spencer would be unable to return to the safe house in Alexandria. They were as good as blown.

After he was a sufficient distance away, he stopped and leaned against the cold metal railing protecting him from the Potomac River and glanced over his shoulder. No one was following him. He removed his phone and typed a quick message to Kaamil, included the image of the van, and requested registration details. After that, he typed a message he hoped he would never have to send. He attached the same image and addressed it to the secure emails of Max, Goshawk, and Kaamil. It was a prearranged signal, only to be used if one or more of them were captured by authorities. *Kate was picked up. Our goose is cooked.* After he hit send, he tossed his phone into the river before disappearing from the park.

FORTY-TWO

Tbilisi, Georgia

On the outskirts of the Georgian capital city, Max ditched the Land Cruiser in a shopping mall parking lot and caught a cab into the old town area. He was exhausted, but needed to keep moving. He could sleep on the plane, but first he needed to do a couple things. He was subsisting on cigarettes and coffee, a combination that had served him well through his years in the Red Army and KGB training, and it kept him going now.

Max had spent little time in Tbilisi, but was surprised to see that the city had modernized, and it now had a cosmopolitan feel to it. Students drove by on motor scooters and tourists meandered the cobblestone paths among boutique shops and outdoor cafés. On the hill above the town, Max noticed the monument to the city's founder, King Vakhtang Gorgasali. One of the oldest cities in the world, Tbilisi sat at one of the most important trade routes between Europe and Asia and was at the center of various conflicts for centuries. Over time the area had been under the Roman empire, Persia, the Byzantine empire, and Russian rule, and the city's geography reflected the centuries of turmoil. The buildings were an eclectic mixture of medieval, Middle Eastern, Stalinist, and modernist designs. Red roofs on stone buildings that crawled up the leafy treed hillside of the Narikala fortress dominated the skyline. A river, with the impossible name of Mt'k'vari, most always green in color, meandered through the city center.

The cab dropped him off at an internet café, and Max paid the cabbie with a handful of lari before disappearing into the store. He paid cash for some computer time and found a seat at the back of the room next to a group of what looked like students.

The battery on his Blackphone had died the previous day, so now he used a dongle to plug it into the café's computer, trusting the phone's security algorithms to prevent it from leaving any kind of data signature on the CPU. While the mobile phone charged, he accessed a series of secure email servers using the computer. He froze when he saw the note from Spencer. *Kate was picked up. Our goose is cooked.*

Max typed a reply, asking for more details, and requested that Spencer join him and Julia at the safe cottage outside Barcelona. He rubbed his face, and for a moment, he pictured Kate strapped to a chair in some off-the-books CIA facility, undergoing every form of interrogation technique possible. He felt a heaviness in his heart for his friend, knowing what she must be going through, before he got angry and almost punched the monitor in front of him. He was fighting battles on multiple fronts, and every time he took a step forward, he found himself two steps back instead. He briefly wavered, wondering how much fight he had left in him, but dismissed the thought as weakness brought on by extreme fatigue. When things got tough, his father, who was a man of many quotes, would say, *Son, life is about collecting the scars to prove we showed up.*

Max spent the next few minutes shutting down several secure server sites and email locations that Kate knew about before changing the passwords and encryption of his personal servers that Kate didn't know about. As he went through his accounts, he saw numerous messages from Julia, wondering where he was, growing more worried with each note. He dashed off a message to let her know he was alive, he was en route to Barcelona, and Spencer White would join them.

When he got to the last server, one he rarely used and only served as a backup to his backup systems, he paused. There was a file with an unknown extension and a modified date of yesterday—something that clearly shouldn't be there. His skin prickled with fear, as he was sure he was the only one that knew about this server. The file's name was a random string of characters and numbers that meant nothing with a file extension he didn't recognize. He could either try to open it or execute a command to wipe the server clean and spend hours establishing yet another secure backup server.

Noting his phone was sufficiently charged, he composed a message to Baxter. In the note, he gave the MI6 man the GPS coordinates of the red cottage with the white door in the tiny village of Chokhi, Georgia.

Max returned to his backup server and contemplated the offending file. The file's extension was .mmdf. He opened a Google window, typed in the extension and learned the file was a Multi-Channel Memorandum Distribution Facility mailbox format file. It looked like a message file, so he steeled himself and double-clicked it. Nothing happened for several heartbeats before the computer told him it didn't have the necessary application to open the file, but gave him a list of other choices. He selected Notepad, smiling when he saw the contents of the file.

I'm alive and in the fight. I will have something for you soon. Be safe. -G

One step forward, he thought as he shut the computer down and exited the café into the Tbilisi sunshine.

FORTY-THREE

Chokhi, Georgia

The joint MI6 and Georgian State Security Service task force, with oversight from Georgia's Intelligence Service and support from the Georgian Special Forces Brigade, descended upon the tiny village using eight Mi-24 attack flying tank helicopters. The armored birds, their tiny wings weighted down with air-to-surface missile systems, were forced to land one by one in a tight field surrounded by craggy cliffs on three sides to discharge their cargo.

A squad of Georgian soldiers secured the town's perimeter while another went door to door, herding terrified civilians into a tiny mosque, the village's only public gathering space. Identities were checked, recorded, and cross-checked against databases of known terrorists. Yet another team of soldiers began a slow, careful, and thorough search of every building in the village, oblivious to the damage they were doing to the townspeople's personal effects. Eventually, a team from the Red Cross arrived to tend to the villagers' needs.

By the time Callum Baxter, Cindy Wallace, and John Taylor stepped out of the last helicopter, the townspeople were secured and the search of the town was in full swing. They strode grim faced to the blue house with the white roof and watched from afar while a command post was set up by the State Security Service and a bomb-detection team, complete with two canines and a soldier in an explosive ordnance disposal suit, prepared to search the property.

Despite repeated questioning by John Taylor, Baxter refused to provide information about how he had found the bomber, and the mood was tense between the two men.

Taylor stood with his hip cocked and arms crossed. His suit was rumpled from travel, and he hadn't slept more than a few hours in days. "You can't hold out forever, Callum."

Baxter watched as a small robot motored up to the blue house with the white roof and affixed a small charge to the front doorjamb. When the robot was a safe distance away, a Georgian explosives specialist yelled, "Fire in the hole!" A moment later, a puff of smoke appeared and the door exploded inward. The robot, its head-like camera slowly spinning, disappeared into the interior.

"I'm sorry, John. It's a classified source. You know how it is."

John Taylor harrumphed. "Bullocks. We'll see about that."

"The important thing is we found the bomber."

"Did we?"

Baxter flipped his Blackberry in his hand. In the two days since Asimov sent him the note, both the assassin and Bluefish had been radio silent. "We'll know as soon as we can match the HMX here to the residue found in West Brompton."

"My wager is it won't."

A titter was heard from the team when the robot found the bomb in the spare bedroom along with a decomposing body. From the camera angle on the robot, they couldn't make out the body's identity. Baxter and Taylor were forced to sit at a camp table and drink bad coffee for another two hours before the tactical team pronounced the house free from booby traps and allowed the bomb disposal unit inside. While the two men sat in silence, Cindy busied herself with a small laptop connected to a satellite uplink. It was several hours before the trash can bomb was disarmed and the three were given permission to enter the house.

The first thing that hit Baxter when he stepped into the building was the smell. "Decomp."

Cindy's face paled as she entered, but she held the collar of her sweater over her nose and soldiered on.

They performed a cursory search in the kitchen and main room before stepping carefully down the hall and into the room with the bomb. Here the smell of putrescine was overwhelming. A team of hazmat-suited forensics technicians were at work.

Taylor breathed through his tie while Baxter snapped on latex gloves and knelt in front of the corpse. He used a penlight to examine the body from head to toe before removing a picture from his pocket and holding it near the body's face. "Usam Islamov, sans beard. Do you agree?"

Taylor studied the picture and the man's face. "I do. Must have known he was going to die. Got himself ready for Paradise and everything."

The corpse sat slumped in a wheelchair, it's head lolled back. A single bullet wound was in the center of the forehead with a trickle of dried blood running parallel to his eyebrow. Blood had dripped onto the floor from the wound and now sat in a dark brown coagulated pool. A second bullet hole was in the body's left chest, but very little blood was on the tunic.

Baxter's poke to the corpse's left arm felt firm. "Rigor mortis, but bloat hasn't started yet."

Taylor examined the white powder in the trash can. "By the smell of the decomp, the bloat will start soon."

Baxter nodded. He touched the man's skin, which felt loose to the touch. "Skin is loosening."

"What do you think, about forty-eight hours?"

"About that."

Taylor turned to one of the technicians and pointed at the trash can. "Do you have the tools to test this material?" When the technician shot him a look, Taylor added, "It's urgent."

With a huff, the forensic tech retrieved a kit from his crate of tools and busied himself with a test tube, a beaker, some sulfuric acid, a tiny bit of ethanol, and some thymol.

Taylor watched with rapt attention. "If it turns blue-green, it's HMX. If it turns deep blue, it's RDX."

Baxter watched as Cindy performed a search of the floor on her hands and knees, looking like she was now used to the gut-wrenching smell. When she stood, the color had returned to her face.

"No brass," she said.

Baxter nodded. "He took it with him. That almost tells us more than the shell casing would have."

Baxter did a cursory search of the body, noticing the white gauzy shroud Islamov wore underneath his thawb, before performing a second search of the floor by walking in concentric circles around the body.

"Baxter, look at this." John Taylor's voice was a low growl.

Baxter looked up to see Taylor holding a test tube up to the light. It had the unmistakable color of royal blue. The material in the trash can was RDX, not HMX.

Baxter took the test tube for a closer look, his heart sinking. "Test it again."

While the technician mixed another batch of thymol and sulfuric acid, Baxter walked outside to get some fresh air with Cindy trailing behind him. Soldiers stood in clusters in the yard, smoking and laughing, while Georgian law enforcement officers examined every square inch of the property. Baxter longed for his pipe, but had forgotten it in his haste to get halfway across the world from London. He removed his Blackberry and spun it in his hand while he looked around.

If it weren't for the dead body and the ammonium nitrate bomb in the house behind him, it might be an idyllic spot. A river gurgled by, running low by the rocky bank. Fir and Douglas pines competed for sunlight with thick oak trees, making Baxter think he could string up a hammock and have a peaceful nap. As a sparrow hawk circled lazily above, framed by a blue sky, he strolled in the direction of the river.

To his right was a small fenced area filled with dirt and mud, and next to that was a chicken coop, it's closed door preventing the birds from wandering the yard. The chickens clucked in protest at their captivity and pecked at the ground in search of food. After living in the city all his life, Baxter had little experience with farm animals—he preferred a cognitive state of separation from his food sources. He walked over to the pen, noticing the acrid smell of what he assumed was chicken manure. To his surprise, nestled down in the mud and muck, next to a filthy trough and huddled together for warmth, was a passel of five hogs.

He stared at the pigs for a long moment before retrieving his Blackberry and clicking a few buttons to pull up the message he received from Max Austin forty-eight hours ago.

You'll find the target in Chokhi, Georgia. 42.456818, 44.712159. Deceased. Compare material found at the site to event in question to determine proof.

The note was accompanied by a lengthy memo outlining the events in Chechnya and Asimov's evidence pointing to Islamov. The document was meticulously constructed and detailed in nature, but the evidence was anecdotal without the HMX match.

Baxter was jolted out of his thoughts by a whistle from John Taylor. He turned to see the MI5 man emerge from the house shaking his head before strolling to the folding tables that formed a makeshift command center. Baxter watched him fill a cup with coffee from the urn and put a satellite phone to his ear. Baxter leaned his forearms on the pigpen's wooden fence, his mind spinning. Cindy came up beside him and he caught himself marveling at how she could smell fresh as a daisy after a long day of travel and hours in close confinement with a rotting corpse.

"What's it mean?" Cindy asked.

Baxter grunted. "It means the white powder in the house isn't the same material that made up the Brompton Street bomb."

He let out a long breath. All the evidence pointed to

Usam Islamov as the bomber. The money trail, the involvement of his brother and nephew. They had confirmed Islamov's mother lived in Jordan, and MI6's forensic accountants traced the money trail to the bank in Lebanon. The evidence was piling up, but without a connection to the HMX, they lacked the smoking gun. Still, Baxter refused to believe the assassin got the wrong guy. Something felt off.

Yanking on his goatee, he went over in his mind all the components of the three terrorist bombs built by Islamov. There was the HMX. There were the Torvex blasting sausages. The HMX had to be mixed with the right amount of ammonium nitrate, a common ingredient in fertilizer.

He breathed deep. As he did, the smell of the manure assaulted his nostrils, and it clicked. It was literally right under his nose. Why would a Muslim family, whose beliefs regarded pigs as filthy animals, keep hogs in their back yard?

He gave Cindy a sideways glance. "What here doesn't look right to you?"

She didn't reply immediately. Abruptly, she beamed in comprehension and a wide smile covered her face.

He waggled his bushy eyebrows causing her to hide a giggle behind her hand before turning to yell at Taylor. "John, get over here. And bring a shovel."

FORTY-FOUR

Outside Bad Tölz, Germany

Julia and Max were whisked from the Munich airport in a large black German-made sedan with tinted windows and a glass partition separating them from the two large men in the front. They motored south at a high rate of speed, fought their way around Munich, and continued up the foothills into Bavaria. Thirty minutes later they pulled into a winding drive curling through lush green mountain fields and ending at a whitewashed A-frame Bavarian cottage. The window boxes were filled with red and blue flowers and a wide porch ran along the front. A familiar figure sat on the porch drinking beer from a large stein. Max stepped out of the car, walked up the steps, and gave Spencer White a big hug.

Dinner was subdued, the three of them lost in their own thoughts. Max thought of Kate and the ordeal she must be going through. His relief at having found the true perpe-trator of the West Brompton bombing was replaced by a hollow pit in his gut for the welfare of his friend. He found himself unable to stop thinking about her.

He pushed away his plate with the food untouched. Spencer swirled his salad with a fork, lost in what Max figured was guilt over his failure to protect first Max's family and then Kate. Estranged from his own daughters, Spencer was a man who needed someone to rescue, someone to watch over. Julia checked her watch and glanced at her smartphone every so often. A bottle of Gewurztraminer sat untouched while beads of perspiration dripped onto the wooden table.

After they finished eating and cleaning the kitchen, there was a disturbance at the entrance to the cottage. Max stiffened and reached for the pistol at his back, but Julia put a restraining hand on his arm.

"It's okay. We have a visitor."

The man who walked through the kitchen door was tall and imposing, with skin the color of limestone and a face carved from granite. He wore a well-tailored light gray suit and a solid blue silk tie. His dull, lifeless eyes regarded Max with a stoic stare while he greeted Julia with a silent nod. Through the kitchen window, Max saw two large black SUVs surrounded by a ring of tall fair-haired security men in suits.

Julia introduced the newcomer. "Max, I'd like you to meet my boss, Frederick Wolf. Frederick, meet my son, Mikhail."

In a baritone voice thick with a Germanic accent, Frederick Wolf said, "Mikhail Asimov, it's a distinct pleasure to meet you. I've waited a long time for this moment."

Wolf's hand was dry and cold, his grip crushing, as if his hand was made of stone. Max, unbowed by Wolf's strength, returned the grip and stared into the man's gray eyes. "Pleasure."

Something felt familiar about the man, but Max was sure he'd never seen him before.

Wolf turned and shook Spencer's hand with a faint smile. "The famous Spencer White. I've heard a lot about you, sir. We're in your debt."

Spencer shook Wolf's hand with a quizzical look on his face. Max got the impression that Spencer felt like Max—somehow, he knew this man.

Wolf set a metal briefcase on the counter and shed his suit jacket before accepting a glass of white wine from Julia. They all took a seat around the farmhouse table while Julia set out plates of meats, cheeses, and vegetables.

While she worked, Max studied Frederick Wolf, searching his memory to place him. The tall German gazed back at Max, as if sizing him up.

After Julia refilled their wine glasses, Wolf speared an olive with a toothpick and studied it before popping it in his mouth. "I'm sorry about your friend, Wing Octavia."

Max crossed his arms. "How do you—"

"Ms. Octavia and I were well acquainted. Although I suspect if she were here right now, she would try to take my head off."

Max glanced at Spencer before looking back at the stoic German. "Explain."

Wolf looked at Julia. "Maybe it's better coming from you."

Julia gave Max a wan grin. "For the past three years, Frederick has been deep undercover, attempting to penetrate the consortium."

The statement caused something to nag at the back of his mind. "Undercover where?"

Julia fidgeted with her smart phone and glanced at Wolf before answering. "Wilbur Lynch's personal bodyguard and assistant."

Wolf gave Max a detached stare. "Right up until you killed him. Three years of hard work and sacrifice wasted."

Max shrugged. "All you had to do was tell me."

Julia shook her head. "We couldn't risk blowing Frederick's cover. I did brief him, though. My assessment was that you would succeed in your quest to find the list and kill Lynch."

Wolf speared another olive. "I didn't believe her assessment. I dismissed it as a mother's blind love. I thought the odds were Lynch would take you out. To my own detriment, you accomplished in a few weeks what we couldn't do in five years."

Max stifled a smile. "Recover the list?"

Wolf drained his wine. "Correct. We have some of the names, but not the entire roster. Wilbur Lynch was the consortium's errand boy, and we thought he would lead us to them. He was obsessed with the group, deluded into thinking they would take on a thirteenth member."

"Where were you the night Lynch died?"

Wolf drained his wine glass. "Are you asking if I was there the night you shot him?"

Max watched Wolf's face and tapped his finger on the table. Frederick Wolf looked to be the consummate professional intelligence man, able to prevent all emotions from showing on his face. He wouldn't want to interrogate him.

Wolf glanced at Julia. "I was in Berlin, meeting with our service. Julia warned me to be away that night but wouldn't tell me why."

Max smiled. "Good thing you weren't there."

Spencer stood and refilled Julia's glass before adding some wine to his own. He set the bottle back on the table.

Wolf glanced at Spencer. "Perhaps. But whether we're better off with the list in our possession and Lynch dead is yet to be seen."

Max sat back in his chair. "The list in my possession."

Wolf nodded. "I get that. That's why I'm here. It appears our objectives are aligned." Wolf stood and retrieved the metal case and set it on the kitchen table. Popping the latches, he opened the lid and removed a thick file. The two-inch-thick dossier was marked with red tape and had the German words *Confidential, Top Secret* stamped on the front in big red letters. The file looked like the dossier Julia had given him on Erich Stasko.

Wolf dropped the file on the table, where it landed with a *thump*. The folder itself was made from legal-sized hardback cardboard and the papers within were held together with stout metal binding. Several thick rubber bands were wrapped around the outside to keep the file closed.

Wolf leaned back against the kitchen counter. "I understand Julia has briefed you on the consortium and one of its key objectives."

Max eyed the folder, remembering the story his sister told him about seeing their father in the possession of a file with German markings. "She did. The consortium has more than one objective?"

Wolf crossed his arms and stroked his chin with his fingers. "Control over the global energy market is one of their goals. And with good reason. Every industrialized nation needs to ensure they are invested in oil reserves over the long haul. Petroleum resources are finite, a scary proposition for a world dependent on the stuff. The Americans know this, as do the British. The Chinese certainly know this. The Germans also know this. Some generation after ours will have to live with the rising prices associated with a limited supply of oil. Eventually, the world will need to adapt to its scarcity."

Max thought of young Alex and the life he had ahead of him. He and Arina agreed on one thing: They both wanted Alex to have all the opportunities for a normal life they never had growing up as the children of a master spy. If Alex wanted to become a doctor, a businessman, or a veterinarian, Max wanted to provide him with that opportunity. The prospect of Alex, or Alex's children, living in a world without oil was sobering. "Does Germany have an answer to the consortium?"

Wolf pulled the plate of food toward him and helped himself to a hunk of cheese. "The west is slow on the uptake in some ways. We're burdened by ethics and the rule of law."

Max snorted. "The west is not burdened by ethics and the rule of law. That's imperialist dogma."

Wolf's face remained detached. "We're also burdened by the fact that the Americans are further ahead than any other country. They're increasing their own vast reserves, deploying new technology like fracking, making agreements with countries like Saudi Arabia, and investments in alternative fuels prove they are already on a path."

"Without using illegal collusion to protect control and pricing?"

Wolf rubbed his nose with a long finger. "We believe they're doing that, too."

Max cocked his eyebrow.

"They're up to something, we're just not sure what. As you can see from the news, our Chancellor and the American president aren't exactly on friendly terms."

Spencer helped himself to a cracker with a hunk of cheese and a slice of prosciutto. "I don't think anyone is on friendly terms with the American administration these days."

"Except the Saudis."

Max nodded. "Right. Sounds like the Germans are left out in the cold without a partner to collude with. I'm guessing your objective is to obstruct the consortium's progress through disruption, subterfuge, spycraft, and other clandestine means."

Wolf nodded. "That's the standard blueprint for spies since Sun Tzu penned The Art of War."

"So, what's next?"

Wolf looked at the file on the table.

Max took a stab in the dark. "Is that the file my father was working on?"

Frederick Wolf's face was sober as he glanced at Julia. If there was any communication between them, Max saw no evidence of it. It was as if they came to an agreement through telepathic means.

Wolf looked back at Max and shook his head. "I'm not sure what file you're talking about. This file contains a dossier on Leoniod Petrov, the number five man in the consortium." Wolf took a deep breath. "May I ask your intentions with the list of the consortium members?"

Max shrugged. "They killed my parents. They won't rest until I'm dead. They have a contract out on my sister and nephew, who are both innocent bystanders. They messed with the wrong family. I'm going to hunt down each one and put a bullet in their head. Anyone who gets in my way..."

Wolf nodded. "Do you think killing everyone on the list will guarantee your family's safety?"

Max shrugged. "Until I come up with a better plan."

Wolf grunted. "What if I can offer you one?"

Max didn't like the direction this conversation was heading. Intelligence agencies often believed their objectives superseded all else. It was a common brainwashing tactic among top intelligence agency brass. Agents were expected to subject themselves to the greater cause at all cost, including great personal sacrifice. The Germans were famous for being direct, which made him wonder why Wolf wasn't coming out with whatever he had to say.

Wolf reached for his wine glass, found it empty, and set it on the counter. "Our understanding is that you're currently unemployed. You've deserted from the Belarus KGB. You've been effectively fired from the CIA. We know they tried to kill you and your colleague after you took out Volkov. Now you have two highly motivated and well-funded groups out to kill you. Perhaps you need money, resources—"

Max drummed his fingers on the table. "I have money. I'm resourceful." The last thing he wanted was to be beholden to yet another government agency that only cared about its own agenda.

Julia put a hand on his arm. "Hear him out, Max."

Wolf forced a smile. "What about intel? Your main computer resource, a woman by the most interesting name of Goshawk is, I understand, missing in action. Your other analyst, a loyal Emirati and former CIA analyst, is now restrained in a dark dungeon under the Arabian desert and may never again see the light of day."

Max's eyes flickered and his gut clenched. Kaamil was young and inexperienced, but he was still a member of their team. Max looked at Spencer, whose face was pale.

"I see you didn't know that young Kaamil Marafi was

picked up by the UAE's State Security. It happened about the time Kate Shaw and William Blackstone were picked up by the CIA."

Max pushed his chair back from the table. "Why don't you get to the point."

Wolf glanced at Julia, and this time Max saw her make a curt nod.

"You may think you can just kill every member of the consortium. And with your skills, I have no doubt you'll eventually be successful. But killing each person on that list of twelve will not guarantee the safety of you and your family."

"So people keep saying. Get to the point."

Wolf let out a long breath and glanced at the file on the table. "That's your next target."

Max reached for the file.

Wolf leaned down and put a large hand on top of the folder. "That file, Mr. Asimov, comes with a price."

Max withdrew his hand and crossed his arms. "What kind of price?"

Wolf dipped his hand into the open briefcase and withdrew two thin white 8.5-inch by 11-inch-sized envelopes. He set one in front of Max and slid the other to Spencer.

"What is this?" Max asked.

Spencer picked his envelope up and turned it over. Max could see it was sealed, and the front was bare except for the words *Spencer White* typed in English. His own envelope was similarly adorned with his own name.

Frederick Wolf accepted a refill of wine from Julia. "That, as they say, is an offer you can't refuse."

Max contemplated the envelope while Spencer tossed his back onto the table. He caught Spencer's eye, and an unseen message passed between the two men. Max stood before grasping the envelop in two hands and tearing it into two pieces. He arranged the two pieces on top of each other and ripped them into four pieces. He tore it two more times and tossed the bits of paper on the table.

Ignoring his mother's surprised look, he turned on his heel and left the kitchen with Spencer following in his wake.

FORTY-FIVE

Biasca, Switzerland

The Ehang 184 Autonomous Aerial Vehicle floated through the nighttime sky, propelled by four dual rotors attached at its corners. Max glanced through the clear Plexiglas front quarter panel but could barely make out the ground slipping beneath him through the murky moonless night. No lights were visible on the ground among the pastures and grassy hillocks that rolled beneath him. He returned his gaze to the dashboard-mounted tablet. The panel's left side showed a view of the ground through an optical night-vision sensor attached to the bottom of the craft. The tablet's right side showed the drone's key statistics, including airspeed, elevation, wind speed, wind direction, and remaining battery life. At just over 500 pounds, the drone could fly for an hour on one charge at speeds of up to 100 knots.

The Bird, as he called her, was a heavily customized military spec version of a personal drone not yet available on the retail market. There were several modifications to the military-grade version of the drone that the civilian edition of the Ehang 184 would never see. The first was the bullet-proof Plexiglas and armor plating. Longer and wider rotors, beefier electronic motors, and more robust batteries compensated for the additional weight of the armor and accounted for the craft's top speed. Attached to a swivel on the bottom of the drone was a 20mm rotary cannon that was controllable by the pilot. The most important modification was the installation of rotor dampeners that allowed the drone to fly in stealth mode. It was this last feature that Max hoped worked as advertised, otherwise he would face a barrage of machine gun fire from the castle during his approach.

Victor Dedov's château appeared on the outer edge of the tablet's map. Max banked into a turn, keeping the castle on his right, skirting the edge of the same rocky ridge he hiked over on his previous visit. As the wind speed picked up, he was careful to feel for wind shear, a sudden variation in wind velocity at right angles to the wind's direction that might drive him into the rocks blurring by his left side.

He executed another turn, following an undulating tree line, impressed with The Bird's maneuverability. He took on elevation and applied speed, aiming the drone for a spot where the castle's guard towers were the farthest apart. When he was directly over the compound, hovering sound-lessly in the pitch darkness, he dropped The Bird like a rock into the middle of the grassy ward between the keep and the chapel. He applied enough upward force just as the landing gear brushed the grass to keep the craft hovering off the ground before pushing the joystick forward. He set her down under an overhang along one of the exterior walls, killed the power, and exited the drone, keeping to the shadows of the tall stone wall. Crouching, he paused to listen before creeping alongside the wall and stopped when he came to the keep's main door.

One of the flaws in Victor's security was the emphasis on external protection at the expense of internal security. The castle's exterior was well guarded, but if a threat managed to penetrate the wall's defenses, little internal security existed to put up a fight. Max added the topic to the list of things to discuss with the former KGB director. It took Max only ninety seconds to pick the keep door's lock, and a few minutes later, he stood next to a thick oak door in the servant's quarters area one level below the ground floor.

Victor employed several staff members to help cook, clean, and maintain the huge castle. One of the hired hands was a man named Günther Thomas. Günther was a retired German army mechanic who failed to distinguish himself during his long stint in the military. It was Güther's job to maintain the vehicles used by the security team and the two Range Rovers Victor kept for personal use.

Max drew a Heckler & Koch USP compact 9mm pistol, screwed on a suppressor, and stuck the gun in his belt. After picking the door's ancient lock, he stepped into the bedroom and had the suppressor stuck under Günther's chin before the groggy man could sit up. When the mechanic's eyes sprang open, Max saw fear.

Pandemonium broke out in the castle as its inhabitants awoke to the chilly morning air. At 5:32 am, as the sun attempted to cast a warm light over the keep's main ward, a shout came from a guard who found a mysterious mini-helicopter sitting dark and quiet in the shadows of the main wall. The resulting alarm awakened Victor Dedov, who stumbled out of his bedroom in a robe carrying a tactical shotgun and shoving a comm line in his ear. Victor was followed by a pajama-clad Arina brandishing a Glock .45. She ran down the hall to Alex's bedroom while Victor swept down the stone staircase in the direction of the keep's great room, attempting to make sense of the reports he was hearing. *A drone large enough to carry a human had landed in their yard without being noticed. What were they talking about?*

He stopped dead in his tracks halfway down the stairs as the great room came into view. The room spanning the width of the building was the keep's centerpiece. An enormous oak table sat under wide windows on one end of the room, while the other half was home to leather couches and wing chairs, a stone fireplace with a hearth as wide as the room, and a towering chimney. Arina had done her best to decorate with colorful throw pillows and afghans and had added plush carpets to warm the cold stone floor.

At the head of the table sat a man with his head bowed. A second man stood pointing a silenced pistol at his back. Victor recognized the sitting form as that of Günther, his household mechanic. When Victor saw the identity of the second man, he groaned.

"Max! What the fuck?"

Victor toggled his mic and gave the all-clear as he stomped down the stairs. He set the shotgun and the comm device on the long table and put his hands on his hips. Max's black eyes flashed with anger, while the mechanic sat with his head hung and his arms secured behind his back.

Max pushed the gun's barrel against the mechanic's head. "I'm about one second away from splattering his brains all over your table."

"What's the meaning of this, Max? How did you—"

Max's eyes darted to the table where a tablet computer lay in front of Günther. "Look for yourself."

Victor glared at both men before grabbing the tablet and turning it on. There were two video files on the desktop.

"Start with number one," Max said.

Victor tapped the video file labeled number one. A split screen appeared, with the panel on the left showing a haggard-looking Max Austin from the shoulders up and the panel on the right showing a smiling Alex. With a growing understanding, Victor listened to the recording of Max's video chat with the ten-year-old. He flushed when Max said on the video, "Tell Victor I'm coming to talk with him real soon, okay?"

Victor looked up from the tablet. "What is going on here?"

Max held the gun against Günther's head with a steady hand. "Watch the other one."

Victor tapped on the second video file. A grainy picture appeared resembling a security surveillance feed. It showed a man walking along a corridor wearing a pair of overalls and a cap pulled low, carrying a laptop computer. From the camera's angle, Victor couldn't see the man's face, but he had a good idea who it was. When the image flickered, Alex's bedroom appeared, and Victor saw the man from the perspective of the room's entrance. This camera angle clearly showed Günther Thomas, Victor's trusted mechanic and Alex's sometime friend.

After a brief dialog between Alex and Günther, the mechanic set up the computer and checked his watch. Victor shut the movie down and tossed the tablet on the table. "I've seen enough." He stepped over and grabbed Günther by the chin, moving the mechanic's head so he could look into his eyes. "How much did they pay you, damn it?"

Footsteps sounded on the stairs, and Arina's head appeared, followed by a groggy ten-year-old. Max moved the gun so it was under the table and hidden from Alex's view.

"Uncle Max!" Alex yelled, suddenly wide-eyed and awake. He ran down the stairs followed by the bounding puppy.

Hidden from Alex's view, Max slipped Victor the gun. "Hey, Sport."

Victor made it disappear into his robe. "Go ahead. I'll handle this."

Max ran over and grabbed Alex in a big hug before spinning him away from the scene at the table. After shooting Arina a wink, Max grabbed the ten-year-old's hand and headed for the keep's front doors, Spike nipping at their heels.

"Alex, remember that drone I promised you? I've got something to show you."

EPILOGUE

London, England

Callum Baxter tromped up wooden stairs slick with rainwater and pushed open the door to his mudroom. He slammed the door closed, dropped his umbrella in the can, and stood frozen in indecision while water dripped from his mackintosh, forming puddles on the clean tile floor. If he took his jacket and galoshes off and carried them through the house, he would have to put them back on to cross through the torrential rain to his backyard office. If he walked through the house with them on, Eve would have his hide the next morning when she found a trail of mud through the kitchen. Erring on the side of expediency, he sloshed through the kitchen and popped out the French doors to the wooden deck overlooking the garden.

Rain gushed from the nighttime sky and he was drenched by the time he made it across the sodden grass to his office door. The rose bushes in the garden bounced up and down from the raindrops. Mud ran from the garden into the grass, making Baxter realize he also would have quite the cleanup in the morning to repair his beloved rose gardens. His thoughts were on his poor plants while he fit the key into the lock with cold trembling fingers. He pushed the door open and kicked it closed before shrugging off his mackintosh and tossing it on a coat-tree already filled with jackets and sweaters.

As he flicked on the light and turned to plop into his chair, Baxter stopped short. His stomach dropped into his bowels, his mouth went dry, and it was all he could do to prevent his bladder from opening. Sitting on the worn leather couch, dressed all in black, and clutching an evil-looking pistol fitted with a suppressor, was the assassin.

"Hello, Callum."

The voice was deep, dry, and laced with acid. His icy black eyes stared at Baxter, causing his knees to almost buckle.

Baxter's voice came out in a stutter, the fear and cold causing his teeth to chatter. "M-M-Max."

The assassin pointed his pistol at the office chair. "Sit down, Callum."

Baxter plunked down, grateful to be off his feet, but blanched when he realized he had never told the assassin his first name.

The assassin stood, his towering frame filling the tiny room, and snapped the lights off before sitting back down on the couch. He set the gun on the couch cushion within easy reach. Light from the back porch fixture glinted off the pistol's black surface. "You look tired."

Baxter tried to appear calm. "Been busy wrapping up the West Brompton thing. I never got a chance to thank—"

"I've come to collect."

Baxter froze. "Of course. Anything. What can I do for you?"

The assassin caressed the leather cushion with a gloved hand. "Callum, you're a good man. Your heart is in the right place. You genuinely want the citizens of the great monarchy of Great Britain to be safe. In an era of escalating terrorism, especially on the European continent, that's a commendable quality."

Relief washed through Baxter's mind, and he managed to cross one leg over the other, trying to appear relaxed and confident. "It's actually a unitary parliamentary constitutional monarchy. And it's the United Kingdom, not Great Britain..." His voice trailed off as the assassin reached over and picked up the gun, pointing the barrel at him.

"Unfortunately, Callum, you got in a little over your head."

Baxter swallowed, his tongue dry. He nodded, unable to help himself.

"Lucky for you, it worked out. We got rid of a dangerous terrorist and diverted the world's attention from me. Maybe the United Kingdom's citizens can sleep a little better now."

Lightning flashed, sending a streak of light through the room. In the sudden brightness, Baxter saw rain water dripping from the assassin's shaved head. He found his voice, but it came out in a croak. "We got the autopsy back. Did you know Islamov suffered from lung cancer?"

The assassin leaned over to put his elbows on his knees and the gun barrel wavered. "He told me." The gun moved so it was again pointed at Baxter. "I found your man. Günther, the mechanic."

Baxter felt the blood drain from his face. "What did you do—"

The assassin shrugged. "I didn't do anything. I left him

for Victor. You know what Victor used to do for a living, right?"

Baxter nodded, wondering whether he was going to throw up or pass out.

The assassin stood and stepped to the filing cabinets, the gun falling to his side. "Try to forget about it, Callum. Günther chose his own fate when he chose to betray me."

Baxter's voice refused to work.

The assassin fished something from his pocket that Baxter couldn't see. "At one point, I think you said something about us not being partners."

Baxter waved his hand at the assassin, a gesture he immediately regretted. "I didn't really mean—"

"Well, now we are partners." The assassin holstered his pistol. "Stand up, Callum."

Baxter didn't know whether to scream or feel relieved that the gun was no longer pointed at him. He stood on shaky legs.

"Turn around."

Baxter did as he was told. Strong arms yanked his wrists back and cold metal jolted his skin as handcuffs were fixed around his wrists. He was spun around and a shove to the chest sent him sprawling back into the chair.

The assassin turned and started opening filing cabinet drawers. "Quite a stockpile of information you have here, Callum."

Baxter's heart sank as he realized Max was looking in the cabinet containing the dossiers on the Asimov family.

The assassin yanked out a stack of files and piled the contents on the office floor before moving to the desk and pushing all the papers stacked there onto the pile. To Baxter's horror, the assassin took a can of lighter fluid from the desk and doused the heap of papers until the can was empty. He produced the Zippo with the Belarusian flag etched on the side and squatted next to the stack. Baxter smelled the acrid stench of the propellant as his stomach sank with the realization that his life's work was about to go up in smoke. He panicked. "No, wait—"

The assassin held the lighter's flame to a piece of paper and tossed it on the stack. He stood and grabbed Baxter by the shirtfront and yanked him out the door and into the rain. Lightning cracked and thunder rumbled as the assassin hustled him across the wet grass and forced him to sit on the edge of the deck. They were soaked through by the time Baxter's rear hit the cold wet wood of the deck. He was surprised when the assassin sat next to him and put his arm around him. As they watched the growing glow from the fire in his office, Baxter's mind turned numb as the rain pelted his head.

"Don't worry, Callum. The rain will keep the fire from spreading to the house or your rose bushes."

Baxter nodded, unable to find words.

The assassin gave his shoulder a little squeeze. "I need something. I have a friend who is going to contact you. Her name is unimportant, but she's pretty handy with a computer. You following me, Callum?"

Baxter dipped his head but was unable to pull his eyes away from the fire.

"She's going to help you erase my name from all the electronic files at MI5 and MI6, got it? All you need to do is get her past a few firewalls. She'll do the rest."

Baxter's voice came out in a croak. "We have paper files, too."

The assassin nodded. "I know. We'll get to those too."

"Every news channel has copies of the articles. You'll never get rid of everything."

The assassin gave his shoulder another squeeze. "Don't worry, Callum. You'll be surprised to see what we can do with an internet bot programmed by an expert. Won't take long before it all disappears."

Pressure from the fire's heat caused an office window to burst. As flames escaped the opening and licked the eves, he felt the assassin place something in his hand. It took him a moment to realize it was a tiny handcuff key.

He turned to the assassin, but he was gone, melting into the dark rainstorm like a wraith, and Baxter was alone.

IF YOU LIKED THIS BOOK ...

I would appreciate it if you would leave a review. An honest review means a lot. The constructive reviews help me write better stories, and the positive reviews help others find the books, which ultimately means I can write more stories.

It only takes a few minutes, but it means everything. Thank you in advance.

-Jack

AUTHOR'S NOTE

This is a work of fiction. Any resemblance to persons living or dead, or actual events, is either coincidental or is used for fictive and storytelling purposes. No elements of this story are inspired by true events; all aspects of the story are imaginative events inspired by conjecture.

The Attack was a true labor of love. Like life, the writing process is a journey, one meant to be savored, and to me it's more about the pilgrimage itself than the destination. I learned a ton while writing this book, and I hope it's reflected in the story and the prose. Only you, dear reader, can be the judge of the results.

Drop me a line if you have feedback or just want to say hi.

Jack Arbor
November, 2017
Aspen, Colorado

ACKNOWLEDGMENTS

What can I say except that this novel wouldn't have seen the light of day without my phenomenal, extraordinary, sensational, and precise editor, Martha Hayes. As Aristotle said, "Quality is not an act, it is a habit." Without Martha, this story would be a pile of elephant dung rotting in the sun. Thank you for everything, Martha.

I also want to acknowledge several of the generous and meticulous readers on my Advanced Reader Team (ART). In no particular order, I'd like to lavishly thank Wahak Kontian, Keith Kay, Valerie Church-McHugh, Murielle Arn, Kurt Neubauer, Kathryn R. Pynch, Bob Kaster, John Kunick, Hugo Ernst, Angie George, Connie Cronenwett, Philip Taylor, Denise Thompson, Fred Schrils, Ken Sanford, Rebecca Partington, Holly Smyth, Jen Close, John Rozum, John McNitt, Scott Barcza, James Farmer, Judith DeRycke, and Diane Sanford. Who knew that cement and concrete are not the same thing?

The most rewarding part of writing stories are the people I meet along the way: my readers, editors, beta readers, and fellow authors. I wish I could thank everyone. Instead, I'll try to honor you all with my writing.

Last but not least, I want to thank my patient and beautiful wife Jill, who suffered with me through the many sleepless nights while I wrote Max into and out of jam after jam. I love you, babe.

JOIN MY MAILING LIST

If you'd like to get updates on new releases as well as notifications of deals and discounts, please join my email list.

I only email when I have something meaningful to say and I never send spam. You can unsubscribe at any time.

Click here to subscribe at www.jackarbor.com

ABOUT THE AUTHOR

Jack Arbor is the author of four thrillers featuring the wayward KGB assassin Max Austin. The stories follow Max as he comes to terms with his past and tries to extricate himself from a destiny he wants to avoid.

Jack works as a digital technologist during the day and writes at night and on weekends, with much love and support from his lovely wife, Jill.

Jill and Jack live outside Aspen, Colorado, where they enjoy trail running and hiking through the natural beauty of the Roaring Fork Valley. Jack also likes to taste new bourbons and grill meat, usually at the same time. They both miss the coffee on the East Coast.

You can get free books as well as pre-release specials and sign up for Jack's mailing list at www.jackarbor.com.

Connect with Jack online:
(e) jack@jackarbor.com
(t) twitter.com/jackarbor
(i) instagram.com/jackarbor/
(f) facebook.com/jackarborauthor
(w) www.jackarbor.com

ALSO BY JACK ARBOR

The Russian Assassin, The Russian Assassin Series, Book
One

You can't go home again...

Max, a former KGB assassin, is content with the life
he's created for himself in Paris. When he's called home to
Minsk for a family emergency, Max finds himself suddenly
running for his life, desperate to uncover secrets about his
father's past to save his family.

Max's sister Arina and nephew Alex become pawns in a
game that started a generation ago. As Max races from the
alleyways of Minsk to the posh neighborhoods of Zurich,
and ultimately to the gritty streets of Prague, he must
confront his past and come to terms with his future to
preserve his family name.

The Russian Assassin is a tight, fast-paced adventure,
staring Jack Arbor's stoic hero, the ex-KGB assassin-for-hire,
Max Austin. Book one of the series forces Max to choose
between himself and his family, a choice that will have
consequences for generations to come.

The Pursuit, The Russian Assassin Series, Book Two

The best way to destroy an enemy is to make him a friend...

Former KGB assassin Max Austin is on the run, fighting to keep his family alive while pursuing his parents' killers. As he battles foes both visible and hidden, he uncovers a conspiracy with roots in the darkest cellars of Soviet history. Determined to survive, Max hatches a plan to even the odds by partnering with his mortal enemy. Even as his adversary becomes his confidant, Max is left wondering who he can trust, if anyone...

If you like dynamic, high-voltage, page-turning thrills, you'll love the second installment of The Russian Assassin series starring Jack Arbor's desperate hero, ex-KGB assassin-for-hire, Max Austin.

Cat & Mouse, A Max Austin Novella

Max, a former KGB assassin, is living a comfortable life in Paris. When not plying his trade, he passes his time managing a jazz club in the City of Light. To make ends meet, he freelances by offering his services to help rid the earth of the world's worst criminals.

Max is enjoying his ritual post-job vodka when he meets a stunning woman; a haunting visage of his former fiancé. Suddenly, he finds himself the target of an assassination plot in his beloved city of Paris. Fighting for his life, Max must overcome his own demons to stay alive.